Praise for *The Very Best of Caitlín R. Kiernan*

"Lyrically compelling tales that are nearly impossible to stop reading . . . fans of weird writers like Carmen Maria Machado, Jeff VanderMeer, and China Miéville will be glad to find this volume and thereby discover a writer who inspired them all."
—*Booklist*

"Caitlín Kiernan is a minister of dark magic, and any collection of her work is a must-read."
—Chuck Wendig, author of *Hyperion* and *The Shield*

"Caitlín Kiernan is one of the true visionaries and finest stylists in our field, and very possibly the most lyrical. Her tales enrich the imagination, and represent the literature of the dark at its most gorgeous and disturbing. This book is a treasure house of wonders and terrors, and an essential purchase for anyone who cares about the great tradition of weird fiction."
—Ramsey Campbell, author of *The Parasite* and *Thirteen Days by Sunset Beach*

"Caitlín R. Kiernan is one of the most inventive, seductive, and wickedly intelligent writers working today in any genre, and this treasury puts her powers on full display. Her stories are promiscuous vampires, eager to draw their energy from folklore, space opera, crime fiction, weird tales, and the dreams of the silver screen. Whether their tone is streetwise or scholarly, archaic or futuristic, these tales share Kiernan's signature flavor of a last drink on the edge of the abyss. She is Our Lady of Elation and Melancholy. A sinister, spellbinding collection."
—Sofia Samatar, author of *A Stranger in Olondria* and *Monster Portraits*

"To begin a Caitlín R. Kiernan story is to enter a world so vividly imagined that it's almost unbearable, on a journey as terrifying as it is irresistible."
—Sam J. Miller, author of *Blackfish City*

"Kiernan's stories will submerge you in a strange world filled with the twisted,

radical reflections of Giger and Lovecraft, their aesthetic skins stretched over anger, pain, queerness, and courage."
—Lara Elena Donnelly, author of the Amberlough Dossier series

Praise for Caitlín R. Kiernan

"Caitlín Kiernan is the poet and bard of the wasted and the lost."
—Neil Gaiman

"Caitlín R. Kiernan is an original."
—Clive Barker

"Caitlín R. Kiernan draws her strength from the most honorable of sources, a passion for the act of writing."
—Peter Straub

Praise for *The Drowning Girl*

"Incisive, beautiful and as perfectly crafted as a puzzle-box, *The Drowning Girl* took my breath away."
—Holly Black, *New York Times* bestselling author of *Red Glove*

"Kiernan pins out the traditional memoir on her worktable and metamorphoses it into something wholly different and achingly familiar, more alien, more difficult, more beautiful, and more true."
—Catherynne M. Valente, *New York Times* bestselling author of *Deathless*

"This is a masterpiece. It deserves to be read in and out of genre for a long, long time."
—Elizabeth Bear, author of *Grail*

"A beautifully written, startlingly original novel."
—Elizabeth Hand, author of *Illyria*

"In this novel, Caitlín R. Kiernan turns the ghost story inside out and transforms it. This is a story about how stories are told, about what they reveal and what they hide, but is no less intense or suspenseful because of that."
—Brian Evenson, author of *Last Days*

"*The Drowning Girl* features all those elements of Caitlín R. Kiernan's writing that readers have come to expect—a prose style of wondrous luminosity, an atmosphere of languorous melancholy, and an inexplicable mixture of aching beauty and clutching terror."
—S. T. Joshi, author of *I Am Providence: The Life and Times of H. P. Lovecraft*

Praise for *Daughter of Hounds*

"Inspired by H. P. Lovecraft's tales of legendary monsters running amok under the streets of New England, Kiernan's fifth novel (after *Low Red Moon*) to feature psychic sensitive Deacon Silvey and his supernaturally scarred family and friends is a hell-raising dark fantasy replete with ghouls, changelings and eerie intimations of a macabre otherworld."
—*Publishers Weekly*

"Kiernan's storytelling is stellar, and the misunderstandings and lies of stories within the main story evoke a satisfying tension in the characters."
—*Booklist*

"A pretty explosive and captivating read. Highly recommended."
—*Green Man Review*

Other Books by Caitlín R. Kiernan

Novels
Silk (1998)
Threshold (2001)
The Five of Cups (2003)
Low Red Moon (2003)
Murder of Angels (2004)
Beowulf (2007)
Daughter of Hounds (2007)
The Red Tree (2009)
The Drowning Girl: A Memoir (2012)
Blood Oranges (writing as Kathleen Tierney; 2013)
Red Delicious (writing as Kathleen Tierney; 2014)
Cherry Bomb (writing as Kathleen Tierney; 2015)
Agents of Dreamland (2017)
Black Helicopters (2018)

Collections
Tales of Pain and Wonder (2000)
Wrong Things (with Poppy Z. Brite; 2001)
From Weird and Distant Shores (2002)
To Charles Fort, With Love (2005)
Alabaster (illustrated by Ted Naifeh; 2006)
A Is for Alien (illustrated by Vince Locke; 2009)
The Ammonite Violin & Others (2010)
*Two Worlds and in Between: The Best of Caitlín R. Kiernan
(Volume One)* (2011)
Confessions of a Five-Chambered Heart (2012)
The Ape's Wife and Other Tales (2013)
*Beneath an Oil-Dark Sea: The Best of Caitlín R. Kiernan
(Volume Two)* (2015)
Dear Sweet Filthy World (2017)
Houses Under the Sea: Mythos Tales (2018)
The Dinosaur Tourist (2018)

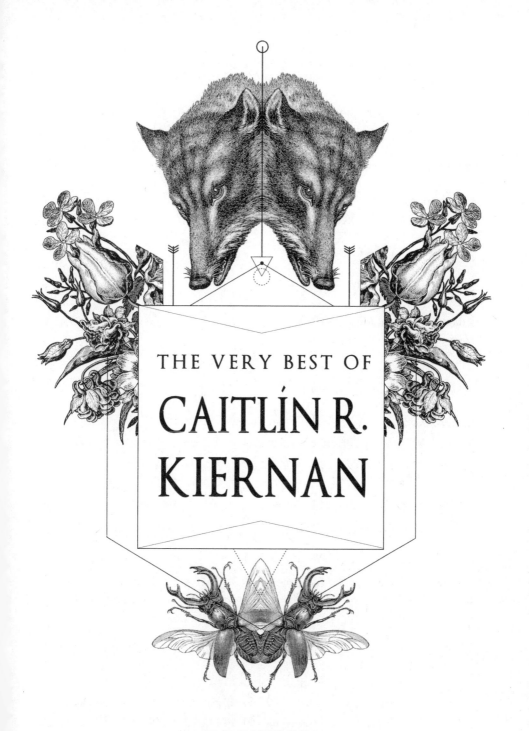

THE VERY BEST OF
CAITLÍN R.
KIERNAN

TACHYON
SAN FRANCISCO

Tachyon Publications LLC
1459 18th Street #139
San Francisco, CA 94107
415.285.5615
www.tachyonpublications.com
tachyon@tachyonpublications.com

Series Editor: Jacob Weisman
Project Editor: Jill Roberts

Print ISBN: 978-1-61696-302-6
Digital ISBN: 978-1-61696-303-3

First Edition: 2019
9 8 7 6 5 4 3 2 1

Printed in the United States by Worzalla.

CONTENTS

INTRODUCTION
Richard Kadrey

CAITLÍN R. KIERNAN isn't a horror writer, though she's often referred to that way. True, there are horrific elements to many of her stories, but none of them are designed to shock, scare, or horrify the reader in the traditional sense of horror writing. Instead, what she gives us is something more subtle and strangely ephemeral. In a way, her best stories are acts of haunting. There's a kind of intoxication to them. They're often nonlinear paths to fantastic destinations, eschewing straightforward plots in favor of mood, mystery, and shadows. If you need to label her, "dark fantasy" is a better description. A "weird tale" writer is another. Not weird as in odd for the sake of oddness, but in the sense that H. P. Lovecraft meant it as "something more than secret murder, bloody bones, or a sheeted form clanking chains." It's weird in the sense of the unknowability of some of the characters, creatures, worlds, and the tales through which they move.

Certain themes and ideas flow through these stories. Gender and gender fluidity are there. So is the natural world, in all its beauty and fearsomeness, which isn't surprising since herpetology and paleontology were some of Kiernan's earliest interests. Water and water-related images abound, both in the text and even the titles themselves, "Houses Under the Sea," "The Mermaid of the Concrete Ocean," "Tidal Forces," and "Galápagos." The liquid tone is set by the opening story, "Andromeda Among the Stones," which begins with a burial by the "relentless Pacific."

Kiernan is also a screenwriter, and some of the stories have a vivid film-like quality to them, as if you're swallowed in the darkness, watching a tale unspooling before your eyes. Film also takes center stage in stories, such as in "The Ape's Wife," and the haunting "The Prayer of Ninety Cats," which contains vivid descriptions of an imaginary film, along with snippets of the screenplay.

There are even touches of the science fictional here. In "Bradbury Weather," we find a Mars populated by women and a mysterious parasite called Fenrir, a name which connects the story from outer space to ancient earthly myths. And you'll find another sort of science fiction in the unsettling "Galápagos," where a woman becomes host to alien organisms.

However, "The Maltese Unicorn" takes you on another unexpected kind of journey. It's told as a noir tale, its name an obvious reference to Dashiell Hammett's *The Maltese Falcon*. But Kiernan's noir takes some very different turns than an ordinary gumshoe tale, as it's the tale of a legendary cursed dildo made of unicorn horn. Kiernan plays with gender roles here too, with a female detective who plays the male role in a traditional noir story, while rejecting strict gender roles out of hand.

What you have in your hands is a book of weirdness in the best sense of the word. Senses, memory, consciousness, even bodies, are unstable and malleable concepts, winding around each other in dreamlike ways, colliding and exploding in a series of darkly alluring surprises. If you're a fan of Kiernan's work, you'll find some of her best work here. If you're new to her stories, get ready. You're traveling to places that might seem familiar at first, but don't get too comfortable. There's something new and wonderful just around the corner, and when it finally reveals itself to you, in all its beauty and strangeness, you won't be able to look away.

ANDROMEDA AMONG
THE STONES

"I cannot think of the deep sea without shuddering . . ."
—H. P. Lovecraft

October 1914

"**A**S SHE REALLY** and truly dead, Father?" the girl asked, and Machen Dandridge, already an old man at fifty-one, looked up at the low buttermilk sky again and closed the black book clutched in his hands. He'd carved the tall headstone himself, the marker for his wife's grave there by the relentless Pacific, black shale obelisk with its hasty death's-head. His daughter stepped gingerly around the raw earth and pressed her fingers against the monument.

"Why did you not give her to the sea?" she asked. "She always wanted to go down to the sea at the end. She often told me so."

"I've given her back to the earth, instead," Machen told her and rubbed at his eyes. The cold sunlight through thin clouds was enough to make his head ache, his daughter's voice like thunder, and he shut his aching eyes for a moment. Just a little comfort in the almost blackness trapped behind his lids, parchment skin too insubstantial to bring the balm of genuine darkness, void to match the shades of his soul, and Machen whispered one of the prayers from the heavy black book and then looked at the grave again.

"Well, that's what she always said," the girl said again, running her fingertips across the rough-hewn stone.

"Things changed at the end, child. The sea wouldn't have taken her. I had to give her back to the earth."

"She said it was a sacrilege, planting people in the ground like wheat, like kernels of corn."

"She did?" He glanced anxiously over his left shoulder, looking back across the waves the wind was making in the high and yellow-brown grass, the narrow trail leading back down to the tall and brooding house that he'd built for his wife twenty-four years ago, back towards the cliffs and the place where the sea and sky blurred seamlessly together.

"Yes, she did. She said only barbarians and heathens stick their dead in the ground like turnips."

"I had no choice," Machen replied, wondering if that was exactly the truth or only something he'd like to believe. "The sea wouldn't take her, and I couldn't bring myself to burn her."

"Only heathens burn their dead," his daughter said disapprovingly and leaned close to the obelisk, setting her ear against the charcoal shale.

"Do you hear anything?"

"No, Father. Of course not. She's dead. You just said so."

"Yes," Machen whispered. "She is." And the wind whipping across the hillside made a hungry, waiting sound that told him it was time for them to head back to the house.

This is where I stand, at the bottom gate, and I hold the key to the abyss . . .

"But it's better that way," the girl said, her ear still pressed tight against the obelisk. "She couldn't stand the pain any longer. It was cutting her up inside."

"She told you that?"

"She didn't have to tell me that. I saw it in her eyes."

The ebony key to the first day and the last, the key to the moment when the stars wink out, one by one, and the sea heaves its rotting belly at the empty, sagging sky.

"You're only a child," he said. "You shouldn't have had to see such things. Not yet."

"It can't very well be helped now," she answered and stepped away from

2

her mother's grave, one hand cupping her ear like maybe it had begun to hurt. "You know that, old man."

"I do," and he almost said her name then, Meredith, his mother's name, but the wind was too close, the listening wind and the salt-and-semen stink of the breakers crashing against the cliffs. "But I can wish it were otherwise."

"If wishes were horses, beggars would ride."

And Machen watched silently as Meredith Dandridge knelt in the grass and placed her handful of wilting wildflowers on the freshly turned soil. If it were spring instead of autumn, he thought, there would be dandelions and poppies. If it were spring instead of autumn, the woman wrapped in a quilt and nailed up inside a pine-board casket would still be breathing. If it were spring, they would not be alone now, him and his daughter at the edge of the world. The wind teased the girl's long yellow hair, and the sun glittered dimly in her warm green eyes.

The key I have accepted full in the knowledge of its weight.

"Remember me," Meredith whispered, either to her dead mother or something else, and he didn't ask which.

"We should be heading back now," he said and glanced over his shoulder again.

"So soon? Is that all you're going to read from the book? Is that all of it?"

"Yes, that's all of it, for now," though there would be more, later, when the harvest moon swelled orange-red and bloated and hung itself in the wide California night. When the women came to dance, then there would be other words to say, to keep his wife in the ground and the gate shut for at least another year.

The weight that is the weight of all salvation, the weight that holds the line against the last, unending night.

"It's better this way," his daughter said again, standing up, brushing the dirt off her stockings, from the hem of her black dress. "There was so little left of her."

"Don't talk of that here," Machen replied, more sternly than he'd intended. But Meredith didn't seem to have noticed or, if she'd noticed, not to have minded the tone of her father's voice.

"I will remember her the way she was before, when she was still beautiful."

"That's what she would want," he said and took his daughter's hand. "That's the way I'll remember her, as well," but he knew that was a lie, as false as any lie any living man ever uttered. He knew that he would always see his wife as the writhing, twisted thing she'd become at the last, the way she was after the gates were almost thrown open, and she placed herself on the threshold.

The frozen weight of the sea, the burning weight of starlight and my final breath. I hold the line. I hold the ebony key against the last day of all.

And Machen Dandridge turned his back on his wife's grave and led his daughter down the dirt and gravel path, back to the house waiting for them like a curse.

November 1914

Meredith Dandridge lay very still in her big bed, her big room with its high ceiling and no pictures hung on the walls, and she listened to the tireless sea slamming itself against the rocks. The sea there to take the entire world apart one gritty speck at a time, the sea that was here first and would be here long after the continents had finally been weathered down to so much slime and sand. She knew this because her father had read to her from his heavy black book, the book that had no name, the book that she couldn't ever read for herself or the demons would come for her in the night. And she knew, too, because of the books he had *given* her, her books—*Atlantis: The Antediluvian World*, *The World Before the Deluge*, and *Atlantis and Lost Lemuria*. Everything above the waves on borrowed time, her father had said again and again, waiting for the day when the sea rose once more and drowned the land beneath its smothering, salty bosom, and the highest mountains and deepest valleys will become a playground for sea serpents and octopuses and schools of herring. Forests to become Poseidon's orchards, her father said, though she knew Poseidon wasn't the true name of the god-thing at the bottom of the ocean, just a name some dead man gave it thousands of years ago.

"Should I read you a story tonight, Merry?" her dead mother asked, sitting right there in the chair beside the bed. She smelled like fish and mud, even though they'd buried her in the dry ground at the top of the hill behind the house. Meredith didn't look at her, because she'd spent so much time already trying to remember her mother's face the way it was *before* and didn't want to see the ruined face the ghost was wearing like a mask. As bad as the face her brother now wore, worse than that, and Meredith shrugged and pushed the blankets back a little.

"If you can't sleep, it might help," her mother said with a voice like kelp stalks swaying slowly in deep water.

"It might," Meredith replied, staring at a place where the wallpaper had begun to peel free of one of the walls, wishing there were a candle in the room or an oil lamp so the ghost would leave her alone. "And it might not."

"I could read to you from Hans Christian Andersen, or one of Grimm's tales," her mother sighed. "'The Little Mermaid' or 'The Fisherman and His Wife'?"

"You could tell me what it's like in Hell," the girl replied.

"Dear, I don't have to tell you that," her ghost mother whispered, her voice gone suddenly regretful and sad. "I know I don't have to ever tell you that."

"There might be different hells," Meredith said. "This one, and the one Father sent you away to, and the one Avery is lost inside. No one ever said there could only be one, did they? Maybe it has many regions. A hell for the dead Prussian soldiers and another for the French, a hell for Christians and another for the Jews. And maybe another for all the pagans."

"Your father didn't send me anywhere, child. I crossed the threshold of my own accord."

"So I would be alone in *this* hell."

The ghost clicked its sharp teeth together, and Meredith could hear the anemone tendrils between its iridescent fish eyes quickly withdrawing into the hollow places in her mother's decaying skull.

"I could read you a poem," her mother said hopefully. "I could sing you a song."

"It isn't all fire and brimstone, is it? Not the region of hell where you are? It's blacker than night and cold as ice, isn't it, Mother?"

"Did he think it would save me to put me in the earth? Does the old fool think it will bring me back across, like Persephone?"

Too many questions, hers and her mother's, and for a moment Meredith Dandridge didn't answer the ghost, kept her eyes on the shadowy wallpaper strips, the pinstripe wall, wishing the sun would rise and pour warm and gold as honey through the drapes.

"I crossed the threshold of my *own* accord," the ghost said again, and Meredith wondered if it thought she didn't hear the first time. Or maybe it was something her mother needed to believe and might stop believing if she stopped repeating it. "Someone had to do it."

"It didn't have to be you."

The wind whistled wild and shrill around the eaves of the house, invisible lips pressed to a vast, invisible instrument, and Meredith shivered and pulled the covers up to her chin again.

"There was no one else. It wouldn't take your brother. The one who wields the key cannot be a man. You know that, Merry. Avery knew that, too."

"There are other women," Meredith said, speaking through gritted teeth, not wanting to start crying but the tears already hot in her eyes. "It could have been someone else. It didn't have to be my mother."

"Some other child's mother, then?" the ghost asked. "Some other mother's daughter?"

"Go back to your hell," Meredith said, still looking at the wall, spitting out the words like poison. "Go back to your hole in the ground and tell your fairy tales to the worms. Tell them 'The Fisherman and His Wife.'"

"You have to be strong now, Merry. You have to listen to your father, and you have to be ready. I wasn't strong enough."

And finally she did turn to face her mother, what was left of her mother's face, the scuttling things nesting in her tangled hair, the silver scales and barnacles, the stinging anemone crown, and Meredith Dandridge didn't flinch or look away.

"One day," she said, "I'll take that damned black book of his, and I'll toss it into the stove. I'll take it, Mother, and toss it into the hearth, and then they can come out of the sea and drag us both away."

Her mother cried out and came apart like a breaking wave against the shingle, water poured from the tin pail that had given it shape, her flesh gone suddenly as clear and shimmering as glass, before she drained away and leaked through the cracks between the floorboards. The girl reached out and dipped her fingers into the shallow pool left behind in the wicker seat of the chair. The water was cold and smelled unclean. And then she lay awake until dawn, listening to the ocean, to all the unthinking noises a house makes in the small hours of a night.

May 1914

Avery Dandridge had his father's eyes, but someone else's soul to peer out through them, and to his sister he was hope that there might be a life somewhere beyond the rambling house beside the sea. Five years her senior, he'd gone away to school in San Francisco for a while, almost a year, because their mother wished him to. But there had been an incident, and he was sent home again, transgressions only spoken of in whispers and nothing anyone ever bothered to explain to Meredith, but that was fine with her. She only cared that he was back, and she was that much less alone.

"Tell me about the earthquake," she said to him, one day not long after he'd returned, the two of them strolling together along the narrow beach below the cliffs, sand the color of coal dust, noisy gulls and driftwood like titan bones washed in by the tide. "Tell me all about the fire."

"The earthquake? Merry, that was eight years ago. You were still just a baby, that was such a long time ago," and then he picked up a shell and turned it over in his hand, brushing away some of the dark sand stuck to it. "People don't like to talk about the earthquake anymore. I never heard them say much about it."

"Oh," she said, not sure what to say next but still full of questions. "Father says it was a sign, a sign from—"

"Maybe you shouldn't believe everything he says, Merry. It was an earthquake." And she felt a thrill then, like a tiny jolt of electricity rising up her spine and spreading out across her scalp, that anyone, much less Avery, would question their father and suggest she do likewise.

"Have you stopped believing in the signs?" she asked, breathless. "Is that what you learned in school?"

"I didn't learn much of anything important in school," he replied and showed her the shell in his palm. Hardly as big around as a nickel, but peaked in the center like a Chinaman's hat, radial lines of chestnut brown. "It's pretty," she said as he placed it in her palm.

"What's it called?"

"It's a limpet," he replied, because Avery knew all about shells and fish and the fossils in the cliffs, things he'd learned from their father's books and not from school. "It's a shield limpet. The jackmackerel carry them into battle when they fight the eels."

Meredith laughed out loud at that last part, and he laughed, too, then sat down on a rock at the edge of a wide tidepool. She stood there beside him, still inspecting the shell in her hand, turning it over and over again. The concave underside of the limpet was smoother than silk and would be white if not for the faintest iridescent hint of blue.

"That's not true," she said. "Everyone knows the jackmackerel and the eels are friends."

"Sure they are," Avery said. "Everyone knows that." But he was staring out to sea now and didn't turn to look at her. In a moment, she slipped the shell into a pocket of her sweater and sat down on the rock next to him.

"Do you see something out there?" she asked, and he nodded his head, but didn't speak. The wind rushed cold and damp across the beach and painted ripples on the surface of the pool at their feet. The wind and the waves seemed louder than usual, and Meredith wondered if that meant a storm was coming.

"Not a storm," Avery said, and that didn't surprise her because he often knew what she was thinking before she said it. "A war's coming, Merry."

"Oh yes, the jackmackerel and the eels." Merry laughed and squinted towards the horizon, trying to see whatever it was that had attracted her brother's attention. "The squid and the mussels."

"Don't be silly. Everyone knows that the squid and the mussels are great friends," and that made her laugh again. But Avery didn't laugh, looked away from the sea and stared down instead at the scuffed toes of his boots dangling a few inches above the water.

"There's never been a war like the one that's coming," he said after a while. "All the nations of the earth at each other's throats, Merry, and when we're done with all the killing, no one will be left to stand against the sea."

She took a very deep breath, the clean, salty air to clear her head, and began to pick at a barnacle on the rock.

"If that were true," she said, "Father would have told us. He would have shown us the signs."

"He doesn't see them. He doesn't dream the way I do."

"But you told him?"

"I tried. But he thinks it's something they put in my head at school. He thinks it's some kind of trick to make him look away."

Merry stopped picking at the barnacle, because it was making her fingers sore and they'd be bleeding soon if she kept it up. She decided it was better to watch the things trapped in the tidepool, the little garden stranded there until the sea came back to claim it. Periwinkle snails and hermit crabs wearing stolen shells, crimson starfish and starfish the shape and color of sunflowers.

"He thinks they're using me to make him look the other way, to catch him off his guard," Avery whispered, his voice almost lost in the rising wind. "He thinks I'm being set against him."

"Avery, I don't believe Father would say that about you."

"He didn't have to say it," and her brother's dark and shining eyes gazed out at the sea and sky again.

"We should be heading back soon, shouldn't we? The tide will be coming in before long," Meredith said, noticing how much higher up the beach the waves were reaching than the last time she'd looked. Another half hour and the insatiable ocean would be battering itself against the rough shale cliffs at their backs.

"'Wave after wave, each mightier than the last,'" Avery whispered, closing his eyes tight, and the words coming from his pale, thin lips sounded like someone else, someone old and tired that Meredith had never loved. "'Till last, a ninth one, gathering half the deep and full of voices, slowly rose and plunged roaring, and all the wave was in a flame—'"

"What's that?" she asked, interrupting because she didn't want to hear anymore. "Is it from Father's book?"

"No, it's not," he replied, sounding more like himself again, more like her brother. He opened his eyes, and a tear rolled slowly down his wind-chapped cheek. "It's just something they taught me at school."

"How can a wave be in flame? Is it supposed to be a riddle?" she asked, and he shook his head.

"No," he said and wiped at his face with his hands. "It's nothing at all, just a silly bit of poetry they made us memorize. School is full of silly poetry."

"Is that why you came home?"

"We ought to start back," he said, glancing quickly over his shoulder at the high cliffs, the steep trail leading back up towards the house. "Can't have the tide catching us with our trousers down, now can we?"

"I don't even wear trousers," Merry said glumly, still busy thinking about that ninth wave, the fire and the water. Avery put an arm around her and held her close to him for a moment while the advancing sea dragged itself eagerly back and forth across the wrack-scabbed rocks.

January 1915

Meredith sat alone on the floor at the end of the hallway, the narrow hall connecting the foyer to the kitchen and a bathroom, and then farther along, leading all the way back to the very rear of the house and this tall door that was always locked. The tarnished brass key always hung on its ring upon her father's belt. She pressed her ear against the wood and strained to hear anything at all. The wood was damp and very cold, and the smell of saltwater and mildew seeped freely through the space between the bottom of the door and the floor, between the door and the jamb. Once-solid redwood that had long since begun to rot from the continual moisture, the ocean's corrosive breath to rust the hinges so the door cried out like a stepped-on cat every time it was opened or closed. Even as a very small child, Meredith had feared this door, even in the days before she'd started to understand what lay in the deep place beneath her father's house.

Outside, the icy winter wind howled, and she shivered and pulled her grey wool shawl tighter about her shoulders; the very last thing her mother had made for her, that shawl. Almost as much hatred in Merry for the wind as for the sea, but at least it smothered the awful thumps and moans that came, day and night, from the attic room where her father had locked Avery away last June.

"There are breaches between the worlds, Merry," Avery had said, a few days before he picked the lock on the hallway door with the sharpened tip-end of a buttonhook and went down to the deep place by himself. "Rifts, fractures, ruptures. If they can't be closed, they have to be guarded against the things on the other side that don't belong here."

"Father says it's a portal," she'd replied, closing the book she'd been reading, a dusty, dog-eared copy of Franz Unger's *Primitive World*.

Her brother had laughed a dry, humourless laugh and shaken his head, nervously watching the fading day through the parlour windows. "Portals are built on purpose, to be used. These things are accidents, at best, casualties of happenstance, tears in space when one world passes much too near another."

"Well, that's not what Father says."

"Read your book, Merry. One day you'll understand. One day soon, when you're not a child anymore, and he loses his hold on you."

And she'd frowned, sighed, and opened her book again, opening it at random to one of the strangely melancholy lithographs—*The Period of the Muschelkalk [Middle Trias]*. A violent seascape, and in the foreground a reef jutted above the waves, crowded with algae-draped driftwood branches and the shells of stranded mollusca and crinoidea. There was something like a crocodile, a beast the author called *Nothosaurus giganteus*, clinging to the reef so it wouldn't be swept back into the storm-tossed depths. Overhead, the night sky was a turbulent mass of clouds with the small, white moon, full or near enough to full, peeking through to illuminate the ancient scene.

"You mean planets?" she'd asked Avery. "You mean moons and stars?"

"No, I mean *worlds*. Now, read your book, and don't ask so many questions."

Meredith thought she heard creaking wood, her father's heavy footsteps, the dry ruffling of cloth rubbing against cloth, and she stood quickly, not wanting to be caught listening at the door again, was still busy straightening her rumpled dress when she realized that he was standing there in the hall behind her, instead. Her mistake, thinking he'd gone to the deep place, when he was somewhere else all along, in his library or the attic room with Avery or outside braving the cold to visit her mother's grave on the hill.

"What are you doing, child?" he asked her gruffly and tugged at his beard. There were streaks of silver-grey that weren't there only a couple of months before, scars from the night they lost her mother, his wife, the night the demons tried to squeeze in through the tear, and Ellen Dandridge had tried to block their way. His face grown years older in the space of weeks, dark crescents beneath his eyes like bruises and deep creases in his forehead. He brushed his daughter's blonde hair from her eyes.

"Would it have been different, if you'd believed Avery from the start?"

For a moment he didn't reply, and his silence, his face set as hard and perfectly unreadable as stone, made her want to strike him, made her wish she could kick open the rotting, sea-damp door and hurl him screaming down the stairs to whatever was waiting for them both in the deep place.

"I don't know, Meredith. But I had to trust the book, and I had to believe the signs in the heavens."

"You were too arrogant, old man. You almost gave away the whole wide world because you couldn't admit you might be wrong."

"You should be thankful that your mother can't hear you, young lady, using that tone of voice with your own father."

Meredith turned and looked at the tall, rotten door again, the symbols drawn on the wood in whitewash and blood.

"She can hear me," Meredith told him. "She talks to me almost every night. She hasn't gone as far away as you think."

"I'm still your father, and you're still a child who can't even begin to understand what's at stake, what's always pushing at the other side of—"

"—the gate?" she asked, interrupting and finishing for him, and she put one hand flat against the door, the upper of its two big panels, and leaned all her weight against it. "What happens next time? Do you know, Father? How much longer do we have left, or haven't the constellations gotten around to telling you that yet?"

"Don't mock me, Meredith."

"Why not?" and she stared back at him over her shoulder, without taking her hand off the door. "Will it damn me faster? Will it cause more men to die in the trenches? Will it cause Avery more pain than he's in now?"

"I was given the book," he growled at her, his stony face flashing to bitter anger, and at least that gave Meredith some mean scrap of satisfaction.

"I was shown the way to this place. They entrusted the gate to me, child. The gods—"

"—must be even bigger fools than you, old man. Now shut up, and leave me alone."

Machen Dandridge raised his right hand to strike her, his big-knuckled hand like a hammer of flesh and bone, iron-meat hammer and anvil to beat her as thin and friable as the veil between Siamese universes.

"You'll need me," she said, not recoiling from the fire in his dark eyes, standing her ground. "You can't take my place. Even if you weren't a coward, you couldn't take my place."

"You've become a willful, wicked child," he said, slowly lowering his hand until it hung useless at his side.

"Yes, Father, I have. I've become a *very* wicked child. You'd best pray that I've become wicked enough."

And he didn't reply, no words left in him, but walked quickly away down the long hall towards the foyer and his library, his footsteps loud as distant gunshots, loud as the beating of her heart, and Meredith removed her hand from the door. It burned very slightly, pain like a healing bee sting, and when she looked at her palm there was something new there, a fat and shiny swelling as black and round and smooth as the soulless eye of a shark.

February 1915

In his dreams, Machen Dandridge stands at the edge of the sea and watches the firelight reflected in the roiling grey clouds above Russia and Austria and East Prussia, smells the coppery stink of Turkish and German blood, the life leaking from the bullet holes left in the Serbian Archduke and his wife. Machen would look away if he knew how, wouldn't see what he can only see too late to make any difference. One small man set adrift and then cast up on the shingle of the cosmos, filled to bursting with knowledge and knowing nothing at all. Cannon fire and thunder, the breakers against the cliff side and the death rattle of soldiers beyond counting.

This is where I stand, at the bottom gate, and I hold the key to the abyss...

"A *world* war, Father," Avery says. "Something without precedent. I can't even find words to describe the things I've seen."

"A world war, without precedent?" Machen replies skeptically and raises one eyebrow, then goes back to reading his star charts. "Napoleon just might disagree with you there, young man, and Alexander, as well."

"No, you don't understand what I'm saying—"

And the fire in the sky grows brighter, coalescing into a whip of red-gold scales and ebony spines, the dragon's tail to lash the damned. *Every one of us is damned*, Machen thinks. *Every one of us, from the bloody start of time.*

"I have the texts, Avery, and the aegis of the seven, and all the old ways. I cannot very well set that all aside because you've been having nightmares, now can I?"

"I know these things, Father. I know them like I know my own heart, like I know the number of steps down to the deep place."

"There is trouble brewing in Coma Berenices," his wife whispers, her eye pressed to the eyepiece of the big telescope in his library. "Something like a shadow."

"She says that later," Avery tells him. "That hasn't happened yet, but it will. But you won't listen to her, either."

And Machen Dandridge turns his back on the sea and the dragon, on the battlefields and the burning cities, looking back towards the house he built twenty-five years ago. The air in the library seems suddenly very close, too warm, too thick. He loosens his paper collar and stares at his son sitting across the wide mahogany desk from him.

"I'm not sure I know what you mean, boy," he says, and Avery sighs loudly and runs his fingers through his brown hair.

"Mother isn't even at the window now. That's still two weeks from now," and it's true that no one's standing at the telescope. Machen rubs his eyes and reaches for his spectacles. "By then, it'll be too late. It may be too late already," Avery says.

"Listen to him, Father," Meredith begs with her mother's voice, and then she lays a small, wilted bouquet of autumn wildflowers on Ellen Dandridge's grave. The smell of the broken earth at the top of the hill is not so different from the smell of the French trenches.

"I did listen to him, Merry."

"You let him talk. You know the difference."

"Did I ever tell you about the lights in the sky the night that you were born?"

"Yes, Father. A hundred times."

"There were no lights at your brother's birth."

Behind him, the sea makes a sound like a giant rolling over in its sleep, and Machen looks away from the house again, stares out across the surging black Pacific. There are the carcasses of whales and sea lions and a billion fish and the bloated carcasses of things even he doesn't know the names for, floating in the surf. Scarlet-eyed night birds swoop down to eat their fill of carrion. The water is so thick with dead things and maggots and blood that soon there will be no water left at all.

"The gate chooses the key," his wife says sternly, sadly, standing at the open door leading down to the deep place beneath the house, the bottomless, phosphorescent pool at the foot of the winding, rickety steps. The short pier and the rock rising up from those depths, the little island with its cave and shackles. "You can't change that part, no matter what the seven have given you."

"It wasn't me sent Avery down there, Ellen."

"It wasn't either one of us. But neither of us listened to him, so maybe it's the same as if we both did."

The sea as thick as buttermilk, buttermilk and blood beneath a rotten moon, and the dragon's tail flicks through the stars.

"Writing the history of the end of the world," Meredith says, standing at the telescope, peering into the eyepiece, turning first this knob, then that one, trying to bring something in the night sky into sharper focus. "That's what he kept saying, anyway. 'I am writing the history of the end of the world. I'm writing the history of the future.' Father, did you know that there's trouble in Coma Berenices?"

"Was that you?" he asks her. "Was that you said that or was that your mother?"

"Is there any difference? And if so, do you know the difference?"

"Are these visions, Merry? Are these terrible visions that I may yet hope to affect?"

"Will you keep him locked in that room forever?" she asks, not answering his questions, not even taking her eye from the telescope.

Before his wife leaves the hallway, before she steps onto the unsteady landing at the top of the stairs, she kisses Meredith on the top of her head and then glares at her husband, her eyes like judgment on the last day of all, the eyes of seraphim and burning swords. The diseased sea slams against the cliffs, dislodging chunks of shale, silt gone to stone when the great reptiles roamed the planet and the gods still had countless revolutions and upheavals to attend to before the beginning of the tragedy of mankind.

"Machen," his wife says. "If you had listened, had you allowed me to listen, everything might have been different. The war, what's been done to Avery, all of it. If you'd but *listened*."

And the dream rolls on and on and on behind his eyes, down the stairs and to the glowing water, his wife alone in the tiny boat, rowing across the pool to the rocky island far beneath the house. The hemorrhaging, pus-colored sea throwing itself furiously against the walls of the cavern, wanting in, and it's always only a matter of time. Meredith standing on the pier behind him, chanting the prayers he's taught her, the prayers to keep the gate from opening before Ellen reaches that other shore.

The yellow-green light beneath the pool below the house wavers, then grows brighter by degrees.

The dragon's tail flicks at the suicidal world.

In his attic, Avery screams with the new mouth the gate gave him before it spit the boy, twisted and insane, back into this place, this time.

The oars dipping again and again into the brilliant, glowing water, the creak of the rusted oarlocks, old nails grown loose in decaying wood; shafts of light from the pool playing across the uneven walls of the cavern.

The dragon opens one blistered eye.

And Ellen Dandridge steps out of the boat onto the island. She doesn't look back at her husband and daughter.

"Something like a shadow," Meredith says, taking her right eye from the telescope and looking across the room at her brother, who isn't sitting in the chair across from Machen.

"It's not a shadow," Avery doesn't tell her, and goes back to the things he has to write down in his journals before there's no time left.

On the island, the gate tears itself open, the dragon's eye, angel eye, and the unspeakable face of the titan sleeper in an unnamed, sunken city, tearing itself wide to see if she's the one it's called down or if it's some other. The summoned or the trespasser. The invited or the interloper. And Machen knows from the way the air has begun to shimmer and sing that the sleeper doesn't like what it sees.

"I stand at the gate and hold the key," she says. "You know my name, and I have come to hold the line. I have come only that you might not pass."

"Don't look, Merry. Close your eyes," and Machen holds his daughter close to him as the air stops singing, as it begins to sizzle and pop and burn.

The waves against the shore.

The dragon's tail across the sky.

The empty boat pulled down into the shimmering pool.

Something glimpsed through a telescope.

The ribsy, omnivorous dogs of war.

And then Machen woke in his bed, a storm lashing fiercely at the windows, the lightning exploding out there like mortar shells, and the distant *thump thump thump* of his lost son from the attic. He didn't close his eyes again, but lay very still, sweating and listening to the rain and the thumping, until the sun rose somewhere behind the clouds to turn the black to cheerless, leaden grey.

August 1889

After his travels, after Baghdad and the ruins of Nineveh and Babylon, after the hidden mosque in Reza'lyah and the peculiar artefacts he'd collected on the southernmost shore of Lake Urmia, Machen Dandridge went west to California. In the summer of 1889, he married Ellen Douglas-Winslow, black-sheep daughter of a fine old Boston family, and together they traveled by train, the smoking iron horses and steel rails that his own father had made his fortune from, riding all the way to the bustling squalor and Nob Hill sanctuaries of San Francisco. For a time they took up residence in a modest house on Russian Hill, while Machen taught his wife the things that he'd learned in the East—archaeology and astrology, Hebrew and Islamic mysticism, the Talmud and Qur'an, the secrets of the terrible black book that had been given to him by a blind and leprous mullah. Ellen had disgraced her family at an early age by claiming the abilities of a medium and then backing up her claims with extravagant séances and spectacular ectoplasmic displays. Machen found in her an eager pupil.

"Why would he have given the book to you?" Ellen asked skeptically, the first time Machen had shown it to her, the first time he'd taken it from its iron and leather case in her presence. "If it's what you say it is, why would he have given it to anyone?"

"Because, my dear, I had a pistol pressed against his rotten skull," Machen had replied, unwrapping the book, slowly peeling back the layers of lambskin it was wrapped in. "That and knowledge he'd been searching for his entire life. Trust me. It was a fair trade."

And just as the book had led him back from Asia to America and on to California, the brittle, parchment compass of its pages had shown him the way north along the coast to the high cliffs north of Anchor Bay. That first trip, he left Ellen behind, traveling with only the company of a Miwok Indian guide who claimed knowledge of "a hole in the world." But when they finally left the shelter of the redwood forest and stood at the edge of a vast and undulating sea of grass stretching away towards the Pacific, the Miwok had refused to go any farther. No amount of money or talk could persuade him to approach the cliffs waiting beyond the grass, and so Machen continued on alone.

Beneath the hot summer sun, the low, rolling hills seemed to go on forever. The gulls and a pair of red-tailed hawks screamed like harpies warning him away, screeching threats or alarum from the endless cornflower sky. But he found it, finally, the "hole in the world," right where the Miwok guide had said that he would, maybe fifty yards from the cliffs.

From what he'd taught himself of geology, Machen guessed it to be the collapsed roof of a cavern, an opening no more than five or six feet across, granting access to an almost vertical chimney eroded through tilted beds of limestone and shale and probably connecting to the sea somewhere in the darkness below. He dropped a large pebble into the hole and listened and counted as it fell, ticking off the seconds until it splashed faintly, confirming his belief that the cavern must be connected to the sea. A musty, briny smell wafted up from the hole, uninviting, sickly, and though there was climbing equipment in his pack, and he was competent with ropes and knots and had, more than once, descended treacherous, crumbling shafts into ancient tombs and wells, Machen Dandridge only stood there at the entrance, dropping stones and listening to the eventual splashes. He stared into the hole and, after a while, could discern a faint but unmistakable light, not the fading sunlight getting in from some cleft in the cliff face, but light like a glass of absinthe, the sort of light he'd imagined abyssal creatures that never saw the sun might make to shine their way through the murk.

It wasn't what he'd expected, from what was written in the black book, no towering gate of horn and ivory, no arch of gold and silver guarded by angels or demons or beings men had never fashioned names for, just this unassuming hole in the ground. He sat in the grass, watching the sunset burning day to night, wondering if the Miwok had deserted him. Wondering if the quest had been a fool's errand from the very start, and he'd wasted so many years of his life, and so much of his inheritance, chasing connections and truths that only existed because he wished to see them. By dark, the light shone up through the hole like some unearthly torch, taunting or reassuring but beckoning him forward. Promising there was more to come.

"What is it you think you will find?" the old priest had asked after he'd handed over the book. "More to the point, what is it you think will find *you?*"

Not a question he could answer then and not one he could answer sitting there with the roar of the surf in his ears and the stars speckling the sky overhead. The question that Ellen had asked him again and again, and always he'd found some way to deflect her asking. But he *knew* the answer, sewn up somewhere deep within his soul, even if he'd never been able to find the words. Proof that the world did not end at his fingertips or with the unreliable data of his eyes and ears or the lies and half-truths men had written down in science and history books, that everything he'd ever seen was merely a tattered curtain waiting to be drawn back so that some more indisputable light might, at last, shine through.

"Is that what you were seeking, Mr. Dandridge?" and Machen had turned quickly, his heart pounding as he reached for the pistol at his hip, only to find the Indian watching him from the tall, rustling grass a few feet away. "Is *this* the end of your journey?" and the guide pointed at the hole.

"I thought you were afraid to come here?" Machen asked, annoyed at the interruption, sitting back down beside the hole, looking again into the unsteady yellow-green light spilling out of the earth.

"I was," the Miwok replied. "But the ghost of my grandfather came to me and told me he was ashamed of me, that I was a coward for allowing you to come to this evil place alone. He has promised to protect me from the demons."

"The ghost of your grandfather?" Machen laughed and shook his head, then dropped another pebble into the hole.

"Yes. He is watching us both now, but he also wishes we would leave soon. I can show you the way back to the trail."

The key I have accepted full in the knowledge of its weight.

"You're a brave man," Machen said. "Or another lunatic."

"All brave men are lunatics," the Indian said and glanced nervously at the hole, the starry indigo sky, the cliff and the invisible ocean, each in its turn. "Sane men do not go looking for their deaths."

"Is that all I've found here? My death?"

There was a long moment of anxious silence from the guide, broken only by the ceaseless interwoven roar of the waves and the wind, and then he took a step back away from the hole, deeper into the sheltering grass.

"I cannot say what you have found in this place, Mr. Dandridge. My grandfather says I should not speak its name."

"Is that so? Well, then," and Machen stood, rubbing his aching eyes, brushed the dust from his pants. "You show me the way back and forget you ever brought me out here. Tell your grandfather's poor ghost that I will not hold you responsible for whatever it is I'm meant to find at the bottom of that pit."

"My grandfather hears you," the Miwok said. "He says you are a brave man and a lunatic, and that I should kill you now, before you do the things you will do in the days to come. Before you set the world against itself."

Machen drew his Colt, cocked the hammer with his thumb, and stood staring into the gloom at the Indian.

"But I will not kill you," the Miwok said. "That is *my* choice, and I have chosen not to take your life. But I will pray it is not a decision I will regret later. We should go now."

"After you," Machen said, smiling through the quaver in his voice that he hoped the guide couldn't hear, his heart racing and cold sweat starting to drip from his face despite the night air. And, without another word, the Indian turned and disappeared into the arms of the whispering grass and the August night.

July 1914

When she was very sure that her father had shut the double doors to his study and that her mother was asleep, when the only sounds were the sea and the wind, the inconstant, shifting noises that all houses make after dark, the mice in the walls, Meredith slipped out of bed and into her flannel dressing gown. The floor was cool against her bare feet, cool but not cold. She lit a candle, and then eased the heavy bedroom door shut behind her and went as quickly and quietly as she could to the cramped stairwell leading from the second story to the attic door. At the top, she sat down on the landing and held her breath, listening, praying that no one had heard her, that neither her father nor mother, nor the both of them together, were already trying to find her.

There were no sounds at all from the other side of the narrow attic door. She set the candlestick down and leaned close to it, pressing her lips against the wood, feeling the rough grain through the varnish against her flesh.

"Avery?" she whispered. "Avery, can you hear me?"

At first there was no reply from the attic, and she took a deep breath and waited a while, waiting for her parents' angry or worried footsteps, waiting for one of them to begin shouting her name from the house below.

But there were no footsteps, and no one called her name.

"*Avery?* Can you hear me? It's *me*, Merry."

That time there was a sudden thumping and a heavy dragging sort of a sound from the other side of the attic door. A body pulling itself roughly, painfully across the pine-board floor towards her, and she closed her eyes and waited for it. Finally, there was a loud thud against the door, and she opened her eyes again. Avery was trying to talk, trying to answer her, but there was nothing familiar or coherent in his ruined voice.

"Hold on," she whispered to him. "I brought a writing pad." She took it out of a pocket of her gown, the pad and a pencil. "Don't try to talk any more. I'll pass this beneath the door to you, and you can write what you want to say. Knock once if you understand what I'm telling you, Avery."

Nothing for almost a full minute and then a single knock so violent that the door shivered on its hinges, so loud she was sure it would bring her parents running to investigate.

"Not so *loud*, Avery," she whispered. "They'll hear us," and now Meredith had begun to notice the odor on the landing, the odor leaking from the attic. Either she'd been much too nervous to notice it at first or her brother had brought it with him when he'd crawled over to the door. Dead fish and boiling cabbage, soured milk and strawberry jam, the time she'd come across the carcass of a grey whale calf, half buried in the sand and decomposing beneath the sun. She swallowed, took another deep breath, and tried not to think about the awful smell.

"I'm going to pass the pencil and a page from the pad to you now. I'm going to slide it under the door to you."

Avery made a wet, strangling sound, and she told him again not to try to talk, just write if he could, write the answers to her questions and anything else that he needed to say.

"Are you in pain? Is there any way I can help?" she asked, and in a moment the tip of the pencil began scritching loudly across the sheet of writing paper. "Not so hard, Avery. If the lead breaks, I'll have to try to find another."

He slid the piece of paper back to her, and it was damp and something dark and sticky was smudged across the bottom. She held it close to her face, never mind the smell so strong it made her gag, made her want to retch, so that she could read what he'd scrawled there. It was nothing like Avery's careful hand, his tight, precise cursive she'd always admired and had tried to imitate, but sweeping, crooked letters, blocky print, and seeing that made her want to cry so badly that she almost forgot about the dead-whale-and-cabbages smell.

HURTSS ME MERY MORE THAN CAN NO

NO HELP NO HELLP ME

She laid down the sheet of paper and tore another from her pad, the pad she used for her afternoon lessons, spelling and arithmetic, and she slid it beneath the door to Avery.

"Avery, you *knew* you couldn't bear the key. You knew it had to be me or mother, *didn't* you? That it had to be a woman?"

Again the scritching, and the paper came back to her even stickier than before.

HAD TO TRY MOTER WOULD NOT LISSEN SO
I HAD TOO TRIE

"Oh, Avery," Meredith said. "I'm sorry," speaking so quietly that she prayed he would not hear, and there were tears in her eyes, hot and bitter. A kind of anger and a kind of sorrow in her heart that she'd never known before, anger and sorrow blooming in her to be fused through some alchemy of the soul, and by that fusion be transformed into a pure and golden hate.

She tore another page from the pad and slipped it through the crack between the floor and the attic door.

"I need to know what to *do*, Avery. I'm reading the newspapers, but I don't understand it all. Everyone seems to think war is coming soon, because of the assassination in Sarajevo, because of the Kaiser, but I don't *understand* it all."

It was a long time before the paper came back to her, smeared with slime and stinking of corruption, maybe five minutes of Avery's scritching and his silent pauses between the scritching. This time the page was covered from top to bottom with his clumsy scrawl.

TO LATE ~~IF~~ TO STOP WAR TOO LATE NOW
WAR IS COMING NOW CANT STP THAT MERRY
ALL SET IN MOTION NINTH WAVE REMEMBER?
BUT MERY YOU CAN DONT LISSEN TO FADER
YOU CAN HOLD ~~NINE~~ THEE LINE STILL TYME
YOU OR MOTHER KIN HOLD THEE LIN STILL
IT DOEZ NOT HALF TO BE THE LADST WAR

When she finished reading and then rereading twice again everything Avery had written, Meredith lay the sheet of paper down on top of the other two and wiped her hand on the floor until it didn't feel quite so slimy anymore. By the yellow-white light of the candle, her hand shimmered as though she'd been carrying around one of the big banana slugs that lived in the forest. She quickly ripped another page from the writing pad and passed it under the door. This time she felt it snatched from her fingers, and the scritching began immediately. It came back to her only a few seconds later and the pencil with it, the tip ground away to nothing.

DUNT <u>EVER</u> COME BAK HERE AGIN MERRY
I LOVE YOU ALWAYTS AND WONT FERGET YOU
<u>PROMISS</u> ME YOU WILL KNOT COME BACK
HOLD THEE LINE HOLD THE LINE

"I can't promise you that, Avery," she replied, sobbing and leaning close to the door, despite the smell so strong that it had begun to burn her nose and the back of her throat. "You're my brother, and I can't ever promise you that."

There was another violent thud against the door then, so hard that her father was sure to have heard, so sudden that it scared her, and Meredith jumped back and reached for the candlestick.

"I remember the ninth wave, Avery. I remember what you said—the ninth wave, greater than the last, all in flame. I *do* remember."

And because she thought that perhaps she heard footsteps from somewhere below, and because she couldn't stand to hear the frantic strangling sounds that Avery had begun making again, Meredith hastily gathered up the sticky, scribbled-on pages from the pad and then crept down the attic stairs and back to her bedroom. She fell asleep just before dawn and dreamt of flames among the breakers, an inferno crashing against the rocks.

March 1915

"This is where it ends, Merry," her mother's ghost said. "But this is where it begins, as well. You need to understand that if you understand nothing else."

Meredith knew that this time she was not dreaming, no matter how much it might *feel* like a dream, this dazzling, tumbling nightmare wide-awake that began when she reached the foot of the rickety spiraling staircase leading her down into the deep place beneath the house. Following her mother's ghost, the dim glow of a spectre to be her Virgil, her Beatrice, her guiding lantern until the light from the pool was so bright it outshone Ellen Dandridge's flickering radiance. Meredith stood on the pier, holding her dead mother's barnacle-and-algae-encrusted hand, and stared in fear and wonder towards the island in the pool.

"The infinite lines of causation," the ghost said. "What has brought you here. That is important, as well."

"I'm here because my father is a fool," Meredith replied, unable to look away from the yellow-green light dancing across the stone, shining up from the depths beneath her bare feet.

"No, dear. He is only a man trying to do the work of gods. That never turns out well."

The black eye set deep into the flesh of Meredith's palm itched painfully and then rolled back to show its dead-white sclera. She knew exactly what it was seeing, because it always told her; she knew how close they were to the veil, how little time was left before the breach tore itself open once and for all.

"Try to forget your father, child. Concentrate on time and space, the aether, on the history that has brought you here. All the strands of the web."

Meredith squeezed the ghost's soft hand, and the dates and names and places spilled through her like the sea spilling across the shore, a flood of obvious and obscure connections, and she gritted her teeth and let them come.

On December 2nd, 1870, Bismarck sends a letter to Wilhelm of Prussia urging him to become Kaiser. In 1874, all Jesuits are ordered to leave Italy, and on January 8th, 1877, Crazy Horse is defeated by the U.S. cavalry at Wolf Mountain in Montana. In June 1881, Austria signs a secret treaty with the Serbs, establishing an economic and political protectorate, and Milan is crowned King of Serbia—

"It hurts," she whispered; her mother frowned and nodded her head as the light from the pool began to pulse and spin, casting counterclockwise glare and shadow across the towering rock walls.

"It will always hurt, dear. It will be pain beyond imagining. You cannot be lied to about that. You cannot be led to bear this weight in ignorance of the pain that comes with the key."

Meredith took another hesitant step towards the end of the short pier, and then another, and the light swelled angrily and spun hurricane fury below and about her.

"They are rising, Merry. They have teeth and claws sharp as steel and will devour you if you don't hurry. You must go to the island now. The breach is opening."

"I am afraid, Mother. I'm so sorry, but I *am* afraid."

"Then the fear will lead you where I can't. Make the fear your shield. Make the fear your lance."

Standing at the very end of the pier, Meredith didn't dare look down into the shining pool, kept her eyes on the tiny island only fifteen or twenty feet away.

"They sunk the boat when you crossed over," she said to her mother's ghost. "How am I supposed to reach the gate when they've taken the boat away?"

"You're a strong swimmer, child. Avery taught you well."

A sound like lightning, and *No*, she thought. *I can't do that. I can do anything except step off this pier into that water with them. I can stand the pain, but—*

"If you know another way, Merry, then take it. But there isn't much time left. The lines are converging."

Merry took a deep breath, gulping the cavern's dank and foetid air, hyperventilating, bracing for the breathless cold to come, all the things that her brother had taught her about swimming in the sea. Together they'd swum out past the breakers, to the kelp forest in the deep water farther offshore, the undulating submarine weald where bat rays and harbor seals raced between the gigantic stalks of kelp, where she'd looked up and seen the lead-pale belly of an immense white shark passing silently overhead.

"Time, Merry. It is all in your hands now. See how you stand alone at the center of the web and the strands stretch away from you? See the intersections and interweaves?"

"I see them," she said. "I see them all," and she stepped off into the icy water.

October 30th, 1883, an Austro-German treaty with Roumania is signed, providing Roumania defence against the Russians. November 17th, 1885, the Serbs are defeated at the Battle of Slivnitza and then ultimately saved only by Austrian intervention. 1887, and the Mahdist War with Abyssinia begins. 1889, and a boy named Silas Desvernine sails up the Hudson River and first sees a mountain where a nameless being of moonlight and thunder is held inside a black stone. August 1889, and her father is led to the edge of the Pacific by a Miwok guide. August 27th, 1891, the Franco-Russian Entente—

The strands of the web, the ticking of a clock, the life and death of stars, each step towards Armageddon checked off in her aching head, and the water is liquid ice threatening to freeze her alive. Suddenly, the tiny island seemed miles and miles away.

August 1895, and Kaiser Wilhelm visits England for Queen Victoria's Golden Jubilee. 1896, Charles E. Callwell of the British Army publishes Small Wars—Their Principles and Practice. *February 4th, 1899, the year Aguinaldo leads a Philippine Insurrection against U.S. forces—*

All of these events, all of these men and their actions. Lies and blood and betrayals, links in the chain leading, finally, to this moment, to that ninth wave, mightier than the last, all in flame. Meredith swallowed a mouthful of sea water and struggled to keep her head above the surface.

"Hurry, child!" her mother's ghost shouted from the pier. "They are rising," and Meredith Dandridge began to pray then that she would fail, would surrender in another moment or two and let the deep have her. Imagined sinking down and down for all eternity, pressure to crush her flat and numb, to crush her so small that nothing and no one would ever have any need to harm her again.

Claws sharp as steel swiped at her right ankle, slicing her skin, and her blood mingled with the sea.

And then she was digging her fingers into the mud and pebbles at the edge of the island. She dragged herself quickly from the pool, from the water and the mire, and looked back the way she'd come. There were no demons in the water, and her mother's ghost wasn't watching from the pier. But her father was, Machen Dandridge and his terrible black book, his eyes upturned and arms outstretched to an indifferent Heaven. She cursed him for the last time ever and ignored the blood oozing from the ugly gash in her ankle.

"This is where I stand," she said, getting to her feet and turning towards the small cave at the center of the island, her legs as weak and unsteady as a newborn foal's. "At the bottom gate, and I hold the key to the abyss."

The yellow-green light was almost blinding, and soon the pool would begin to boil.

"The ebony key to the first day and the last, the key to the moment when the stars wink out one by one and the sea heaves its rotting belly at the empty, sagging sky. The blazing key that even angels fear to keep."

For an instant, there was no cave, and no pool, and no cavern beneath a resentful, wicked house. Only the fire, pouring from the cave that was no longer there, to swallow her whole, only the voices of the void, and Meredith Dandridge made her fear a shield and a lance and held the line.

And in the days and weeks that followed, sometimes Machen Dandridge came down the stairs to stand on the pier and gaze across the pool to the place where the thing that had been his daughter nestled in the shadows, in the hollows between the stones. And every day the sea gave her more of its armour, gilding her frail human skin with the calcareous shells and stinging tentacles that other creatures had spent countless cycles of Creation refining from the rawest matter of life, the needle teeth, the scales and poisonous barbs. Where his wife and son had failed, his daughter crouched triumphant as any martyr. And sometimes, late at night, alone with the sound of the surf pounding against the edge of the continent, he sometimes thought of setting fire to the house and letting it burn down around him.

He read the newspapers.

He watched the stars for signs and portents.

When the moon was bright, the women still came to dance beside the sea, but he'd begun to believe they were only bad memories from some time before, and so he rarely paid them any heed.

When the weather was good, he climbed the hills behind the house and sat at the grave of his dead wife and whispered to her, telling her how proud he was of Meredith, reciting snatches of half-remembered poetry for Ellen, telling her the world would come very close to the brink because of what he'd done. Because of his blind pride. But, in the end, it would survive because of what their daughter had done and would do for ages yet.

On a long, rainy afternoon in May, he opened the attic door and killed what he found there with an axe and his old Colt revolver. He buried it beside his wife, but left nothing to mark Avery's grave.

He wrote long letters to men he'd once known in England and New York and Rio de Janeiro, but there were never any replies.

And time rolled on, neither malign nor beneficent, settling across the universe like the grey caul of dust settling thick upon the relics he'd brought back from India and Iran and the Sudan a quarter of a century before. The birth and death of stars, light reaching his aging eyes after a billion years racing across the near-vacuum of space, and sometimes he spent the days gathering fossils from the cliffs and arranging them in precise geometric patterns in the tall grass around the house. He left lines of salt and drew elaborate runes, the meanings of which he'd long since forgotten.

His daughter spoke to him only in his dreams, or hers, no way to ever be sure which was which, and her voice grew stronger and more terrible as the years rushed past. In the end, she was a maelstrom to swallow his withered soul, to rock him to sleep one last time, to show him the way across.

And the house by the sea, weathered and weary and insane, kept its secrets.

LA PEAU VERTE

1.

IN A DUSTY, antique-littered back room of the loft on St. Mark's Place, a room with walls the color of ripe cranberries, Hannah stands naked in front of the towering mahogany-framed mirror and stares at herself. No—not *her* self any longer, but the new thing that the man and woman have made of her. Three long hours busy with their airbrushes and latex prosthetics, grease paints and powders and spirit gum, their four hands moving as one, roaming excitedly and certainly across her body, hands sure of their purpose. She doesn't remember their names, if, in fact, they ever told their names to her. Maybe they did, but the two glasses of brandy she's had have set the names somewhere just beyond recall. Him tall and thin, her thin but not so very tall, and now they've both gone, leaving Hannah alone. Perhaps their part in this is finished; perhaps the man and woman are being paid, and she'll never see either of them again, and she feels a sudden, unexpected pang at the thought, never one for casual intimacies, and they have been both casual and intimate with her body.

The door opens, and the music from the party grows suddenly louder. Nothing she would ever recognize, probably nothing that has a name, even; wild impromptu of drumming hands and flutes, violins and cellos, an incongruent music that is both primitive and drawing-room practiced. The

30

old woman with the mask of peacock feathers and gown of iridescent satin stands in the doorway, watching Hannah. After a moment, she smiles and nods her head slowly, appreciatively.

"Very pretty," she says. "How does it feel?"

"A little strange," Hannah replies and looks at the mirror again. "I've never done anything like this before."

"Haven't you?" the old woman asks her, and Hannah remembers her name, then—Jackie, Jackie something that sounds like Shady or Sadie, but isn't either. A sculptor from England, someone said. When she was very young, she knew Picasso, and someone said that, too.

"No," Hannah replies. "I haven't. Are they ready for me now?"

"Fifteen more minutes, give or take. I'll be back to bring you in. Relax. Would you like another brandy?"

Would I? Hannah thinks and glances down at the crystal snifter sitting atop an old secretary next to the mirror. It's almost empty now, maybe one last warm amber sip standing between it and empty. She wants another drink, something to burn away the last, lingering dregs of her inhibition and self-doubt, but "No," she tells the woman. "I'm fine."

"Then chill, and I'll see you in fifteen," Jackie Whomever says, smiles again, her disarming, inviting smile of perfect white teeth, and she closes the door, leaving Hannah alone with the green thing watching her from the mirror.

The old Tiffany lamps scattered around the room shed candy puddles of stained-glass light, light as warm as the brandy, warm as the dark-chocolate tones of the intricately carved frame holding the tall mirror. She takes one tentative step nearer the glass, and the green thing takes an equally tentative step nearer her. *I'm in there somewhere*, she thinks. *Aren't I?*

Her skin painted too many competing, complementary shades of green to possibly count, one shade bleeding into the next, an infinity of greens that seem to roil and flow around her bare legs, her flat, hard stomach, her breasts. No patch of skin left uncovered, her flesh become a rain-forest canopy, autumn waves in rough, shallow coves, the shells of beetles and leaves from a thousand gardens, moss and emeralds, jade statues and the brilliant scales of poisonous tropical serpents. Her nails polished a green so deep it might almost be black, instead. The uncomfortable scleral contacts to turn her eyes into the blaze of twin chartreuse stars, and Hannah leans a little closer to the mirror, blinking at those eyes, *with* those eyes, the windows to a soul she doesn't have. A soul of everything vegetable and living, everything growing or not, soul of sage and pond scum, malachite and verdigris. The fragile translucent wings sprouting from her shoulder blades—at least another thousand greens to consider in those wings alone—and all the many places where they've been painstakingly attached to her skin are hidden so expertly she's no longer sure where the wings end and she begins.

The one, and the other.

"I definitely should have asked for another brandy," Hannah says out loud, spilling the words nervously from her ocher, olive, turquoise lips.

Her hair—not *her* hair, but the wig *hiding* her hair—like something parasitic, something growing from the bark of a rotting tree, epiphyte curls across her painted shoulders, spilling down her back between and around the base of the wings. The long tips the man and woman added to her ears so dark that they almost match her nails, and her nipples airbrushed the same lightless, bottomless green, as well. She smiles, and even her teeth have been tinted a matte pea green.

There is a single teardrop of green glass glued firmly between her lichen eyebrows.

I could get lost in here, she thinks, and immediately wishes she'd thought something else instead.

Perhaps I am already.

And then Hannah forces herself to look away from the mirror, reaches for the brandy snifter and the last swallow of her drink. Too much of the night still lies ahead of her to get freaked out over a costume, too much left to do and way too much money for her to risk getting cold feet now. She finishes the brandy, and the new warmth spreading through her belly is reassuring.

Hannah sets the empty glass back down on the secretary and then looks at herself again. And this time it *is* her self, after all, the familiar lines of her face still visible just beneath the make-up. But it's a damn good illusion. *Whoever the hell's paying for this is certainly getting his money's worth,* she thinks.

Beyond the back room, the music seems to be rising, swelling quickly towards crescendo, the strings racing the flutes, the drums hammering along underneath. The old woman named Jackie will be back for her soon. Hannah takes a deep breath, filling her lungs with air that smells and tastes like dust and old furniture, like the paint on her skin, more faintly of the summer rain falling on the roof of the building. She exhales slowly and stares longingly at the empty snifter.

"Better to keep a clear head," she reminds herself.

Is that what I have here? And she laughs, but something about the room or her reflection in the tall mirror turns the sound into little more than a cheerless cough.

And then Hannah stares at the beautiful, impossible green woman staring back at her, and waits.

2.

"Anything forbidden becomes mysterious," Peter says and picks up his remaining bishop, then sets it back down on the board without making a move. "And mysterious things always become attractive to us, sooner or later. Usually sooner."

"What is that? Some sort of unwritten social law?" Hannah asks him, distracted by the Beethoven that he always insists on whenever they play chess. *Die Geschöpfe des Prometheus* at the moment, and she's pretty sure he only does it to break her concentration.

"No, dear. Just a statement of the fucking obvious."

Peter picks up the black bishop again, and this time he almost uses it to capture one of her rooks, then thinks better of it. More than thirty years her senior and the first friend she made after coming to Manhattan, his salt-and-pepper beard and mustache that's mostly salt, his eyes as grey as a winter sky.

"Oh," she says, wishing he'd just take the damn rook and be done with it. Two moves from checkmate, barring an act of divine intervention. But that's another of his games, Delaying the Inevitable. She thinks he probably has a couple of trophies for it stashed away somewhere in his cluttered apartment, chintzy *faux* golden loving cups for his Skill and Excellence in Procrastination.

"Taboo breeds desire. Gluttony breeds disinterest."

"Jesus, I ought to write these things down," she says, and he smirks at her, dangling the bishop teasingly only an inch or so above the chessboard.

"Yes, you really should. My agent could probably sell them to someone or another. *Peter Mulligan's Big Book of Tiresome Truths*. I'm sure it would be more popular than my last novel. It certainly couldn't be *less*—"

"Will you stop it and *move* already? Take the damned rook, and get it over with."

"But it *might* be a mistake," he says and leans back in his chair, mock suspicion on his face, one eyebrow cocked, and he points towards her queen. "It could be a trap. You might be one of those predators that fakes out its quarry by playing dead."

"You have no idea what you're talking about."

"Yes I do. You know what I mean. Those animals, the ones that only *pretend* to be dead. You might be one of those."

"I *might* just get tired of this and go the hell home," she sighs, because he knows that she won't, so she can say whatever she wants.

"Anyway," he says, "it's work, if you want it. It's just a party. Sounds like an easy gig to me."

"I have that thing on Tuesday morning though, and I don't want to be up all night."

"Another shoot with Kellerman?" asks Peter and frowns at her, taking his eyes off the board, tapping at his chin with the bishop's mitre.

"Is there something wrong with that?"

"You hear things, that's all. Well, *I* hear things. I don't think you ever hear anything at all."

"I need the work, Pete. The last time I sold a piece, I think Lincoln was still president. I'll never make as much money painting as I do posing for *other* people's art."

"Poor Hannah," Peter says. He sets the bishop back down beside his king and lights a cigarette. She almost asks him for one, but he thinks she quit three months ago, and it's nice having at least that one thing to lord over him; sometimes it's even useful. "At least you *have* a fallback," he mutters and exhales; the smoke lingers above the board like fog on a battlefield.

"Do you even know who these people are?" she asks and looks impatiently at the clock above his kitchen sink.

"Not firsthand, no. But then they're not exactly my sort. Entirely too, well ..." and Peter pauses, searching for a word that never comes, so he continues without it. "But the Frenchman who owns the place on St. Mark's, Mr. Ordinaire—excuse me, *Monsieur* Ordinaire—I heard he used to be some sort of anthropologist. I think he might have written a book once."

"Maybe Kellerman would reschedule for the afternoon," Hannah says, talking half to herself.

"You've actually never tasted it?" he asks, picking up the bishop again and waving it ominously towards her side of the board.

"No," she replies, too busy now wondering if the photographer will rearrange his Tuesday schedule on her behalf to be annoyed at Peter's cat and mouse with her rook.

"Dreadful stuff," he says and makes a face like a kid tasting Brussels sprouts or Pepto-Bismol for the first time. "Might as well have a big glass of black jelly beans and cheap vodka, if you ask me. *La Fée Verte*, my fat ass."

"Your ass isn't fat, you skinny old queen." Hannah scowls playfully, reaching quickly across the table and snatching the bishop from Peter's hand. He doesn't resist. This isn't the first time she's grown too tired of waiting for him to move to wait any longer. She removes her white rook off the board and sets the black bishop in its place.

"That's suicide, dear," Peter says, shaking his head and frowning. "You're aware of that, yes?"

"You know those animals that *bore* their prey into submission?"

"No, I don't believe I've ever heard of them before."

"Then maybe you should get out more often."

"Maybe I should," he replies, setting the captured rook down with all the other prisoners he's taken. "So, are you going to do the party? It's a quick grand, you ask me."

"That's easy for you to say. You're not the one who'll be getting naked for a bunch of drunken strangers."

"A fact for which we should *all* be forevermore and eternally grateful."

"You have his number?" she asks, giving in, because that's almost a whole month's rent in one night and, after her last gallery show, beggars can't be choosers.

"There's a smart girl," Peter says and takes another drag off his cigarette.

"The number's on my desk somewhere. Remind me again before you leave. Your move."

3.

"How old were you when that happened, when your sister died?" the psychologist asks, Dr. Edith Valloton and her smartly-cut hair so black it always makes Hannah think of fresh tar, or old tar gone deadly soft again beneath a summer sun to lay a trap for unwary, crawling things. Someone she sees when the nightmares get bad, which is whenever the painting isn't going well or the modeling jobs aren't coming in or both. Someone she can tell her secrets to who has to *keep* them secret, someone who listens as long as she pays by the hour, a place to turn when faith runs out and priests are just another bad memory to be confessed.

"Almost twelve," Hannah tells her and watches while Edith Valloton scribbles a note on her yellow legal pad.

"Do you remember if you'd begun menstruating yet?"

"Yeah. My periods started right after my eleventh birthday."

"And these dreams, and the stones. This is something you've never told anyone?"

"I tried to tell my mother once."

"She didn't believe you?"

Hannah coughs into her hand and tries not to smile, that bitter, wry smile to give away things she didn't come here to show.

"She didn't even *hear* me," she says.

"Did you try more than once to tell her about the fairies?"

"I don't think so. Mom was always pretty good at letting us know whenever she didn't want to hear what was being said. You learned not to waste your breath."

"Your sister's death, you've said before that it's something she was never able to come to terms with."

"She never tried. Whenever my father tried, or I tried, she treated us like traitors. Like we were the ones who put Judith in her grave. Or like we were the ones *keeping* her there."

"If she couldn't face it, Hannah, then I'm sure it did seem that way to her."

"So, no," Hannah says, annoyed that she's actually paying someone to sympathize with her mother. "No. I guess I never really told anyone about it."

"But you think you want to tell me now?" the psychologist asks and sips her bottled water, never taking her eyes off Hannah.

"You said to talk about all the nightmares, all the things I think are nightmares. It's the only one that I'm not sure about."

"Not sure if it's a nightmare, or not sure if it's even a dream?"

"Well, I always thought I was awake. For years, it never once occurred to me I might have only been dreaming."

Edith Valloton watches her silently for a moment, her cat-calm, cat-smirk face unreadable, too well-trained to let whatever's behind those dark eyes slip and show. Too detached to be smug, too concerned to be indifferent. Sometimes, Hannah thinks she might be a dyke, but maybe that's only because the friend who recommended her is a lesbian.

"Do you still have the stones?" the psychologist asks, finally, and Hannah shrugs out of habit.

"Somewhere, probably. I never throw anything away. They might be up at Dad's place, for all I know. A bunch of my shit's still up there, stuff from when I was a kid."

"But you haven't tried to find them?"

"I'm not sure I *want* to."

"When is the last time you saw them, the last time you can remember having seen them?"

And Hannah has to stop and think, chews intently at a stubby thumbnail and watches the clock on the psychologist's desk, the second hand traveling round and round and round. Seconds gone for pennies, nickels, dimes.

Hannah, this is the sort of thing you really ought to try to get straight ahead of time, she thinks in a voice that sounds more like Dr. Valloton's than her own thought-voice. *A waste of money, a waste of time. . . .*

"You can't remember?" the psychologist asks and leans a little closer to Hannah.

"I kept them all in an old cigar box. I think my grandfather gave me the box. No, wait. He didn't. He gave it to Judith, and then I took it after the accident. I didn't think she'd mind."

"I'd like to see them someday, if you ever come across them again. Wouldn't that help you to know whether it was a dream or not, if the stones are real?"

"Maybe," Hannah mumbles around her thumb. "And maybe not."

"Why do you say that?"

"A thing like that, words scratched onto a handful of stones, it'd be easy for a kid to fake. I might have made them all myself. Or someone else might have made them, someone playing a trick on me. Anyone could have left them there."

"Did people do that often? Play tricks on you?"

"Not that I can recall. No more than usual."

Edith Valloton writes something else on her yellow pad and then checks the clock.

"You said that there were always stones after the dreams. Never before?"

"No, never before. Always after. They were always there the next day, always in the same place."

"At the old well," the psychologist says, like Hannah might have forgotten and needs reminding.

"Yeah, at the old well. Dad was always talking about doing something about it, before the accident, you know. Something besides a couple sheets of corrugated tin to hide the hole. Afterwards, of course, the county ordered him to have the damned thing filled in."

"Did your mother blame him for the accident, because he never did anything about the well?"

"My mother blamed *everyone*. She blamed him. She blamed me. She blamed whoever had dug that hole in the first goddamn place. She blamed God for putting water underground so people would dig wells to get at it. Believe me, Mom had blame down to an art."

And again, the long pause, the psychologist's measured consideration, quiet moments she plants like seeds to grow ever deeper revelations.

"Hannah, I want you to try to remember the word that was on the first stone you found. Can you do that?"

"That's easy. It was *follow*."

"And do you also know what was written on the last one, the very last one that you found?"

And this time she has to think, but only for a moment.

"*Fall*," she says. "The last one said *fall*."

4.

Half a bottle of Mari Mayans borrowed from an unlikely friend of Peter's, a goth chick who DJs at a club that Hannah's never been to because Hannah doesn't go to clubs. Doesn't dance and has always been more or less indifferent to both music and fashion. The goth chick works days at Trash and Vaudeville on St. Mark's, selling Doc Martens and blue hair dye only a couple of blocks from the address on the card that Peter gave her. The place where the party is being held. *La Fête de la Fée Verte*, according to the small white card, the card with the phone number. She's already made the call, has already agreed to be there, seven o'clock sharp, seven on the dot, and everything that's expected of her has been explained in detail, twice.

Hannah's sitting on the floor beside her bed, a couple of vanilla-scented candles burning because she feels obligated to make at least half a half-hearted effort at atmosphere. Obligatory show of respect for mystique that doesn't interest her, but she's gone to the trouble to borrow the bottle of liqueur; the bottle passed to her in a brown paper bag at the boutique, anything but inconspicuous, and the girl glared out at her, cautious from beneath lids so heavy with shades of black and purple that Hannah was amazed the girl could open her eyes.

"So, you're supposed to be a friend of Peter's?" the girl asked suspiciously.

"Yeah, supposedly," Hannah replied, accepting the package, feeling vaguely, almost pleasurably illicit. "We're chess buddies."

"A painter," the girl said.

"Most of the time."

"Peter's a cool old guy. He made bail for my boyfriend once, couple of years back."

"Really? Yeah, he's wonderful," and Hannah glanced nervously at the customers browsing the racks of leather handbags and corsets, then at the door and the bright daylight outside.

"You don't have to be so jumpy. It's not illegal to have absinthe. It's not even illegal to drink it. It's only illegal to import it, which you didn't do. So don't sweat it."

Hannah nodded, wondering if the girl was telling the truth, if she knew what she was talking about. "What do I owe you?" she asked.

"Oh, nothing," the girl replied. "You're a friend of Peter's, and, besides, I get it cheap from someone over in Jersey. Just bring back whatever you don't drink."

And now Hannah twists the cap off the bottle, and the smell of anise is so strong, so immediate, she can smell it before she even raises the bottle to her nose. *Black jelly beans*, she thinks, just like Peter said, and that's something else she never cared for. As a little girl, she'd set the black ones aside—and the pink ones too—saving them for her sister. Her sister had liked the black ones.

She has a wine glass, one from an incomplete set she bought last Christmas, secondhand, and she has a box of sugar cubes, a decanter filled with filtered tap water, a spoon from her mother's mismatched antique silverware. She pours the absinthe, letting it drip slowly from the bottle until the fluorescent yellow-green liquid has filled the bottom of the glass. Then Hannah balances the spoon over the mouth of the goblet and places one of the sugar cubes in the tarnished bowl of the spoon. She remembers watching Gary Oldman and Winona Ryder doing this in *Dracula*, remembers seeing the movie with a boyfriend who eventually left her for another man, and the memory and all its associations are enough to make her stop and sit staring at the glass for a moment.

"This is so fucking silly," she says, but part of her, the part that feels guilty for taking jobs that pay the bills, but have nothing to do with painting, the part that's always busy rationalizing and justifying the way she spends her time, assures her it's a sort of research. A new experience, horizon-broadening something to expand her mind's eye, and, for all she knows, it might lead her art somewhere it needs to go.

"Bullshit," she whispers, frowning down at the entirely uninviting glass of Spanish absinthe. She's been reading *Absinthe: History in a Bottle* and *Artists and Absinthe*, accounts of van Gogh and Rimbaud, Oscar Wilde and Paul-Marie Verlaine and their various relationships with this foul-smelling liqueur. She's never had much respect for artists who use this or that drug as a crutch and then call it their muse; heroin, cocaine, pot, booze, what-the-hell-ever, all the same shit as far as she's concerned. An excuse, an inability in the artist to hold himself accountable for his *own* art, a lazy cop-out, as useless as the idea of the muse itself. And *this* drug, this drug in particular, so tied up with art and inspiration there's even a Renoir painting decorating the Mari Mayans label, or at least it's something that's supposed to *look* like a Renoir.

But you've gone to all this trouble. Hell, you may as well taste it, at least. Just a taste, to satisfy curiosity, to see what all the fuss is about.

Hannah sets the bottle down and picks up the decanter, pouring water over the spoon, over the sugar cube. The absinthe louches quickly to an opalescent, milky white-green. Then she puts the decanter back on the floor and stirs the half-dissolved sugar into the glass, sets the spoon aside on a china saucer.

"Enjoy the ride," the goth girl said as Hannah walked out of the shop. "She's a blast."

Hannah raises the glass to her lips, sniffs at it, wrinkling her nose, and the first, hesitant sip is even sweeter and more piquant than she expected, sugar-soft fire when she swallows, a seventy-proof flower blooming hot in her belly. But the taste not nearly as disagreeable as she'd thought it would be, the sudden licorice and alcohol sting, a faint bitterness underneath that she guesses might be the wormwood. The second sip is less of a shock, especially since her tongue seems to have gone slightly numb.

She opens *Absinthe: History in a Bottle* again, opening the book at random, and there's a full-page reproduction of Albert Maignan's *The Green Muse*. A blonde woman with marble skin, golden hair, wrapped in diaphanous folds of olive, her feet hovering weightless above bare floorboards, her hands caressing the forehead of an intoxicated poet. The man is gaunt and seems lost in some ecstasy or revelry or simple delirium, his right hand clawing at his face, the other hand open in what might have been meant as a feeble attempt to ward off the attentions of his unearthly companion. *Or,* Hannah thinks, *perhaps he's reaching for something.* There's a shattered green bottle on the floor at his feet, a full glass of absinthe on his writing desk.

Hannah takes another sip and turns the page.

A photograph, Verlaine drinking absinthe in the Café Procope.

Another, bolder swallow, and the taste is becoming familiar now, almost, *almost* pleasant.

Another page. Jean Béraud's *Le Boulevard, La Nuit.*

When the glass is empty, and the buzz in her head, behind her eyes, is so gentle, buzz like a stinging insect wrapped in spider silk and honey, Hannah takes another sugar cube from the box and pours another glass.

5.

"Fairies.

'Fairy crosses.'

Harper's Weekly, 50–715:

That, near the point where the Blue Ridge and the Allegheny Mountains unite, north of Patrick County, Virginia, many little stone crosses have been found.

A race of tiny beings.

They crucified cockroaches.

Exquisite beings—but the cruelty of the exquisite. In their diminutive way they were human beings. They crucified.

The 'fairy crosses,' we are told in *Harper's Weekly*, range in weight from one-quarter of an ounce to an ounce: but it is said, in the *Scientific American*, 79–395, that some of them are no larger than the head of a pin.

They have been found in two other states, but all in Virginia are strictly localized on and along Bull Mountain . . . I suppose they fell there."

Charles Fort, *The Book of the Damned* (1919)

6.

In the dream, which is never the same thing twice, not precisely, Hannah is twelve years old and standing at her bedroom window watching the backyard. It's almost dark, the last rays of twilight, and there are chartreuse fireflies dappling the shadows, already a few stars twinkling in the high indigo sky, the call of a whippoorwill from the woods nearby.

Another whippoorwill answers.

And the grass is moving. The grass grown so tall because her father never bothers to mow it anymore. It could be wind, only there is no wind; the leaves in the trees are all perfectly, silently still, and no limb swaying, no twig, no leaves rustling in even the stingiest breeze. Only the grass.

It's probably just a cat, she thinks. *A cat, or a skunk, or a raccoon.*

The bedroom has grown very dark, and she wants to turn on a lamp, afraid of the restless grass even though she knows it's only some small animal, awake for the night and hunting, taking a short cut across their backyard. She looks over her shoulder, meaning to ask Judith to please turn on a lamp, but there's only the dark room, Judith's empty bunk, and she remembers it all again. It's always like the very first time she heard, the surprise and disbelief and pain always that fresh, the numbness that follows that absolute.

"Have you seen your sister?" her mother asks from the open bedroom door. There's so much night pooled there that she can't make out anything but her mother's softly glowing eyes the soothing color of amber beads, two cat-slit pupils swollen wide against the gloom.

"No, Mom," Hannah tells her, and there's a smell in the room then like burning leaves.

"She shouldn't be out so late on a school night."

"No, Mom, she shouldn't," and the eleven-year-old Hannah is amazed at the thirty-five-year-old's voice coming from her mouth. The thirty-five-year-old Hannah remembers how clear, how unburdened by time and sorrow, the eleven-year-old Hannah's voice could be.

"You should look for her," her mother says.

"I always do. That comes later."

"Hannah, have you seen your sister?"

Outside, the grass has begun to swirl, rippling round and round upon itself, and there's the faintest green glow dancing a few inches above the ground.

The fireflies, she thinks, though she knows it's not the fireflies, the way she knows it's not a cat, or a skunk, or a raccoon making the grass move.

"Your father should have seen to that damned well," her mother mutters, and the burning leaves smell grows a little stronger. "He should have done something about that years ago."

"Yes, Mom, he should have. You should have made him."

"No," her mother replies angrily. "This is not my fault. None of it's my fault."

"No, of course it's not."

"When we bought this place, I told him to see to that well. I *told* him it was dangerous."

"You were right," Hannah says, watching the grass, the softly pulsing cloud of green light hanging above it. The light is still only about as big as a basketball. Later, it'll get a lot bigger. She can hear the music now, pipes and drums and fiddles, like a song from one of her father's albums of folk music.

"Hannah, have you seen your sister?"

Hannah turns and stares defiantly back at her mother's glowing, accusing eyes.

"That makes three, Mom. Now you have to leave. Sorry, but them's the rules," and her mother does leave, that obedient phantom fading slowly away with a sigh, a flicker, a half second when the darkness seems to bend back upon itself, and she takes the burning leaves smell with her.

The light floating above the backyard grows brighter, reflecting dully off the windowpane, off Hannah's skin and the room's white walls. The music rises to meet the light's challenge.

Peter's standing beside her now, and she wants to hold his hand, but doesn't, because she's never quite sure if he's supposed to be in this dream.

"I am the Green Fairy," he says, sounding tired and older than he is, sounding sad. "My robe is the color of despair."

"No," she says. "You're only Peter Mulligan. You write books about places you've never been and people who will never be born."

"You shouldn't keep coming here," he whispers, the light from the backyard shining in his grey eyes, tinting them to moss and ivy.

"Nobody else does. Nobody else ever could."

"That doesn't mean—"

But he stops and stares speechlessly at the backyard.

"I should try to find Judith," Hannah says. "She shouldn't be out so late on a school night."

"That painting you did last winter," Peter mumbles, mumbling like he's drunk or only half awake. "The pigeons on your windowsill, looking in."

"That wasn't me. You're thinking of someone else."

"I hated that damned painting. I was glad when you sold it."

"So was I," Hannah says. "I should try to find her now, Peter. My sister. It's almost time for dinner."

"I am ruin and sorrow," he whispers.

And now the green light is spinning very fast, throwing off gleaming flecks of itself to take up the dance, to swirl about their mother star, little worlds newborn, whole universes, and she could hold them all in the palm of her right hand.

"What I need," Peter says, "is blood, red and hot, the palpitating flesh of my victims."

"Jesus, Peter, that's purple even for you," and Hannah reaches out and lets her fingers brush the glass. It's warm, like the spring evening, like her mother's glowing eyes.

"I didn't write it," he says.

"And I never painted pigeons."

She presses her fingers against the glass and isn't surprised when it shatters, explodes, and the sparkling diamond blast is blown inward, tearing her apart, shredding the dream until it's only unconscious, fitful sleep.

7.

"I wasn't in the mood for this," Hannah says and sets the paper saucer with three greasy, uneaten cubes of orange cheese and a couple of Ritz crackers down on one corner of a convenient table. The table is crowded with fliers about other shows, other openings at other galleries. She glances at Peter and then at the long, white room and the canvases on the walls.

"I thought it would do you good to get out. You never go anywhere anymore."

"I come to see you."

"My point exactly, dear."

Hannah sips at her plastic cup of warm merlot, wishing she had a beer instead.

"And you said that you liked Perrault's work."

"Yeah," she says. "I'm just not sure I'm up for it tonight. I've been feeling pretty morbid lately, all on my own."

"That's generally what happens to people who swear off sex."

"Peter, I didn't *swear off* anything."

And she follows him on their first slow circuit around the room, small talk with people that she hardly knows or doesn't want to know at all, people who know Peter better than they know her, people whose opinions matter and people whom she wishes she'd never met. She smiles and nods her head, sips her wine, and tries not to look too long at any of the huge, dark canvases spaced out like oil and acrylic windows on a train.

"He's trying to bring us down, down to the very core of those old stories," a woman named Rose tells Peter. She owns a gallery somewhere uptown, the sort of place where Hannah's paintings will never hang. "'Little Red Riding Hood,' 'Snow White,' 'Hansel and Gretel,' all those old fairy tales," Rose says. "It's a very post-Freudian approach."

"Indeed," Peter says. *As if he agrees,* Hannah thinks, *as if he even cares,* when she knows damn well he doesn't.

"How's the new novel coming along?" Rose asks him.

"Like a mouthful of salted thumbtacks," he replies, and she laughs.

Hannah turns and looks at the nearest painting, because it's easier than listening to the woman and Peter pretend to enjoy one another's company. A somber storm of blacks and reds and greys, dappled chaos struggling to resolve itself into images, images stalled at the very edge of perception. She thinks she remembers having seen a photo of this canvas in *Artforum.*

A small beige card on the wall to the right of the painting identifies it as *Night in the Forest.* There isn't a price, because none of Perrault's paintings are ever for sale. She's heard rumors that he's turned down millions, tens of millions, but suspects that's all exaggeration and PR. Urban legends for modern artists, and from the other things that she's heard he doesn't need the money, anyway.

Rose says something about the exploration of possibility and fairy tales and children using them to avoid any *real* danger, something that Hannah's pretty sure she's lifted directly from Bruno Bettelheim.

"Me, I was always rooting for the wolf," Peter says, "or the wicked witch or the three bears or whatever. I never much saw the point in rooting for silly girls too thick not to go wandering about alone in the woods."

Hannah laughs softly, laughing to herself, and takes a step back from the painting, squinting at it. A moonless sky pressing cruelly down upon a tangled, writhing forest, a path and something waiting in the shadows, stooped shoulders, ribsy, a calculated smudge of scarlet that could be its eyes. There's no one on the path, but the implication is clear—there will be, soon enough, and the thing crouched beneath the trees is patient.

"Have you seen the stones yet?" Rose asks and no, Peter replies, no we haven't.

"They're a new direction for him," she says. "This is only the second time they've been exhibited."

If I could paint like that, Hannah thinks, *I could tell Dr. Valloton to kiss my ass. If I could paint like that, it would be an exorcism.*

And then Rose leads them both to a poorly lit corner of the gallery, to a series of rusted wire cages, and inside each one is a single stone. Large pebbles or small cobbles, stream-worn slate and granite, and each stone has been crudely engraved with a single word.

The first one reads "follow."

"Peter, I need to go now," Hannah says, unable to look away from the yellow-brown stone, the word tattooed on it, and she doesn't dare let her eyes wander ahead to the next one.

"Are you sick?"

"I need to go, that's all. I need to go *now*."

"If you're not feeling well," the woman named Rose says, trying too hard to be helpful, "there's a restroom in the back."

"No, I'm fine. Really. I just need some air."

And Peter puts an arm protectively around her, reciting his hurried, polite goodbyes to Rose. But Hannah still can't look away from the stone, sitting there behind the wire like a small and vicious animal at the zoo.

"Good luck with the book," Rose says, and smiles, and Hannah's beginning to think she *is* going to be sick, that she will have to make a dash for the toilet, after all. There's a taste like foil in her mouth, and her heart like a mallet on dead and frozen beef, adrenaline, the first eager tug of vertigo.

"It was good to meet you, Hannah," the woman says. Hannah manages to smile, manages to nod her head.

And then Peter leads her quickly back through the crowded gallery, out onto the sidewalk and the warm night spread out along Mercer Street.

———

8.

"Would you like to talk about that day at the well?" Dr. Valloton asks, and Hannah bites at her chapped lower lip.

"No. Not now," she says. "Not again."

"Are you sure?"

"I've already told you everything I can remember."

"If they'd found her body," the psychologist says, "perhaps you and your mother and father would have been able to move on. There could have at least been some sort of closure. There wouldn't have been that lingering hope that maybe someone would find her, that maybe she was alive."

Hannah sighs loudly, looking at the clock for release, but there's still almost half an hour to go.

"Judith fell down the well and drowned," she says.

"But they never found the body."

"No, but they found enough, enough to be sure. She fell down the well. She drowned. It was very deep."

"You said you heard her calling you."

"I'm not sure," Hannah says, interrupting the psychologist before she can say the things she was going to say next, before she can use Hannah's own words against her. "I've never been absolutely sure. I told you that."

"I'm sorry if it seems like I'm pushing," Dr. Valloton says.

"I just don't see any reason to talk about it again."

"Then let's talk about the dreams, Hannah. Let's talk about the day you saw the fairies."

9.

The dreams, or the day from which the dreams would arise and, half-forgotten, seek always to return. The dreams or the day itself, the one or the other, it makes very little difference. The mind exists only in a moment, always, a single flickering moment, remembered or actual, dreaming or awake or something liminal between the two, the precious, treacherous illusion of Present floundering in the crack between Past and Future.

The dream of the day—or the day itself—and the sun is high and small and white, a dazzling July sun coming down in shafts through the tall trees in the woods behind Hannah's house. She's running to catch up with Judith, her sister two years older and her legs grown longer, always leaving Hannah behind. *You can't catch me, slowpoke. You can't even keep up.* Hannah almost trips in a tangle of creeper vines and has to stop long enough to free her left foot.

"Wait up!" she shouts, and Judith doesn't answer. "I want to see. Wait for me!"

The vines try to pull one of Hannah's tennis shoes off and leave bright beads of blood on her ankle. But she's loose again in only a moment, running down the narrow path to catch up, running through the summer sun and the oak-leaf shadows.

"I found something," Judith said to her that morning after breakfast. The two of them sitting on the back porch steps. "Down in the clearing by the old well," she said.

"What? What did you find?"

"Oh, I don't think I should tell you. No, I *definitely* shouldn't tell you. You might go and tell Mom and Dad. You might spoil everything."

"No, I wouldn't. I wouldn't tell them anything. I wouldn't tell anyone."

"Yes, you would, big mouth."

And, finally, she gave Judith half her allowance to tell, half to be shown whatever there was to see. Her sister dug deep down into the pockets of her jeans, and her hand came back up with a shiny black pebble.

"I just gave you a whole dollar to show me a *rock?*"

"No, stupid. *Look* at it," and Judith held out her hand.

The letters scratched deep into the stone—JVDTH—five crooked letters that almost spelled her sister's name, and Hannah didn't have to pretend not to be impressed.

"Wait for me!" she shouts again, angry now, her voice echoing around the trunks of the old trees and dead leaves crunching beneath her shoes. Starting to guess that the whole thing is a trick after all, just one of Judith's stunts, and her sister's probably watching her from a hiding place right this very second, snickering quietly to herself. Hannah stops running and stands in the center of the path, listening to the murmuring forest sounds around her.

And something faint and lilting that might be music.

"That's not all," Judith said. "But you have to *swear* you won't tell Mom and Dad."

"I swear."

"If you do tell, well, I *promise* I'll make you wish you hadn't."

"I won't tell anyone *anything*."

"Give it back," Judith said, and Hannah immediately handed the black stone back to her. "If you *do* tell—"

"I already said I won't. How many times do I have to say I won't tell?"

"Well then," Judith said and led her around to the back of the little tool shed where their father kept his hedge clippers and bags of fertilizer and the old lawnmowers he liked to take apart and try to put back together again.

"This better be *worth* a dollar," Hannah said.

She stands very, very still and listens to the music, growing louder. She thinks it's coming from the clearing up ahead.

"I'm going back home, Judith!" she shouts, not a bluff because suddenly she doesn't care whether or not the thing in the jar was real, and the sun doesn't seem as warm as it did only a moment ago.

And the music keeps getting louder.

And louder.

And Judith took an empty mayonnaise jar out of the empty rabbit hutch behind the tool shed. She held it up to the sun, smiling at whatever was inside.

"Let me see," Hannah said.

"Maybe I should make you give me another dollar first," her sister replied, smirking, not looking away from the jar.

"No way," Hannah said indignantly. "Not a snowball's chance in Hell," and she grabbed for the jar, then, but Judith was faster, and her hand closed around nothing at all.

In the woods, Hannah turns and looks back towards home, then turns back towards the clearing again, waiting for her just beyond the trees.

"Judith! This isn't funny! I'm going home right this second!"

Her heart is almost as loud as the music now. Almost. Not quite, but close enough. Pipes and fiddles, drums and a jingle like tambourines.

Hannah takes another step towards the clearing, because it's nothing at all but her sister trying to scare her. Which is stupid, because it's broad daylight, and Hannah knows these woods like the back of her hand.

Judith unscrewed the lid of the mayonnaise jar and held it out so Hannah could see the small, dry thing curled in a lump at the bottom. Tiny mummy husk of a thing, grey and crumbling in the morning light.

"It's just a damn dead mouse," Hannah said disgustedly. "I gave you a whole dollar to see a rock and a dead mouse in a jar?"

"It's *not* a mouse, stupid. Look closer."

And so she did, bending close enough that she could see the perfect dragonfly wings on its back, transparent, iridescent wings that glimmer faintly in the sun. Hannah squinted and realized that she could see its face, realized that it *had* a face.

"Oh," she said, looking quickly up at her sister, who was grinning triumphantly. "Oh, Judith. Oh my god. What is it?"

"Don't you know?" Judith asked her. "Do I have to tell you everything?"

Hannah picks her way over the deadfall just before the clearing, the place where the path through the woods disappears beneath a jumble of fallen, rotting logs. There was a house back here, her father said, a long, long time ago. Nothing left but a big pile of rocks where the chimney once stood, and also the well covered over with sheets of rusted corrugated tin. There was a fire, her father said, and everyone in the house died.

On the other side of the deadfall, Hannah takes a deep breath and steps out into the daylight, leaving the tree shadows behind, forfeiting her last chance not to see.

"Isn't it cool?" Judith said. "Isn't it the coolest thing you've ever seen?"

Someone's pushed aside the sheets of tin, and the well is so dark that even the sun won't go there. And then Hannah sees the wide ring of mushrooms, the perfect circle of toadstools and red caps and spongy brown morels growing round the well. The heat shimmers off the tin, dancing mirage shimmer as though the air here is turning to water, and the music is very loud now.

"I found it," Judith whispered, screwing the top back onto the jar as tightly as she could. "I found it, and I'm going to keep it. And you'll keep your mouth shut about it, or I'll never, *ever* show you anything else again."

Hannah looks up from the mushrooms, from the open well, and there are a thousand eyes watching her from the edges of the clearing. Eyes like indigo berries and rubies and drops of honey, like gold and silver coins, eyes like fire and ice, eyes like seething dabs of midnight. Eyes filled with hunger beyond imagining, neither good nor evil, neither real nor impossible.

Something the size of a bear, squatting in the shade of a poplar tree, raises its shaggy charcoal head and smiles.

"That's another pretty one," it growls.

And Hannah turns and runs.

10.

"But you *know*, in your soul, what you must have really seen that day," Dr. Valloton says and taps the eraser end of her pencil lightly against her front teeth. There's something almost obscenely earnest in her expression, Hannah thinks, in the steady *tap, tap, tap* of the pencil against her perfectly spaced, perfectly white incisors. "You saw your sister fall into the well, or you realized that she just had. You may have heard her calling out for help."

"Maybe I *pushed* her in," Hannah whispers.

"Is that what you *think* happened?"

"No," Hannah says and rubs at her temples, trying to massage away the first dim throb of an approaching headache. "But, most of the time, I'd rather *believe* that's what happened."

"Because you *think* it would be easier than what you remember."

"Isn't it? Isn't easier to believe she pissed me off that day, and so I shoved her in? That I made up these crazy stories so I'd never have to feel guilty for what I'd done? Maybe that's what the nightmares are, my conscience trying to fucking force me to come clean."

"And what are the stones, then?"

"Maybe I put them all there myself. Maybe I scratched those words on them myself and hid them there for me to find, because I knew that would make it easier for me to believe. If there was something that real, that tangible, something solid to remind me of the story, that the story is supposed to be the truth."

A long moment that's almost silence, just the clock on the desk ticking and the pencil tapping against the psychologist's teeth. Hannah rubs harder at her temples, the real pain almost within sight now, waiting for her just a little ways past this moment or the next, vast and absolute, deep purple shot through with veins of red and black. Finally, Dr. Valloton lays her pencil down and takes a deep breath.

"Is this a confession, Hannah?" she asks, and the obscene earnestness is dissolving into something that may be eager anticipation, or simple clinical curiosity, or only dread. "Did you kill your sister?"

And Hannah shakes her head and shuts her eyes tight.

"Judith fell into the well," she says calmly. "She moved the tin, and got too close to the edge. The sheriff showed my parents where a little bit of the ground had collapsed under her weight. She fell into the well, and she drowned."

"Who are you trying so hard to convince? Me or yourself?"

"Do you really think it matters?" Hannah replies, matching a question with a question, tit for tat.

"Yes," Dr. Valloton says. "Yes, I do. You need to know the truth."

"Which one?" Hannah asks, smiling against the pain swelling behind her eyes, and this time the psychologist doesn't bother answering, lets her sit silently with her eyes shut until the clock decides her hour's up . . .

11.

Peter Mulligan picks up a black pawn and moves it ahead two squares; Hannah removes it from the board with a white knight. He isn't even trying today, and that always annoys her. Peter pretends to be surprised that's he's lost another piece, then pretends to frown and think about his next move while he talks.

"In Russian," he says, "*chernobyl* is the word for wormwood. Did Kellerman give you a hard time?"

"No," Hannah says. "No, he didn't. In fact, he said he'd actually rather do the shoot in the afternoon. So everything's jake, I guess."

"Small miracles," Peter sighs, picking up a rook and setting it back down again. "So you're doing the anthropologist's party?"

"Yeah," she replies. "I'm doing the anthropologist's party."

"*Monsieur* Ordinaire. You think he was born with that name?"

"I think I couldn't give a damn, as long as his check doesn't bounce. A thousand dollars to play dress-up for a few hours. I'd be a fool not to do the damned party."

Peter picks the rook up again and dangles it in the air above the board, teasing her. "Oh, his book," he says. "I remembered the title the other day. But then I forgot it all over again. Anyway, it was something on shamanism and shapeshifters, werewolves and masks, that sort of thing. It sold a lot of copies in '68, then vanished from the face of the earth. You could probably find out something about it online." Peter sets the rook down and starts to take his hand away.

"Don't," she says. "That'll be check mate."

"You could at least let me *lose* on my own, dear," he scowls, pretending to be insulted.

"Yeah, well, I'm not ready to go home yet," Hannah replies, and Peter Mulligan goes back to dithering over the chessboard and talking about Monsieur Ordinaire's forgotten book. In a little while, she gets up to refill both their coffee cups, and there's a single black and grey pigeon perched on the kitchen windowsill, staring in at her with its beady piss-yellow eyes. It almost reminds her of something she doesn't want to be reminded of, and so she raps on the glass with her knuckles and frightens it away.

12.

The old woman named Jackie never comes for her. There's a young boy, instead, fourteen or fifteen, sixteen at the most, his nails polished poppy red to match his rouged lips, and he's dressed in peacock feathers and silk. He opens the door and stands there, very still, watching her, waiting wordlessly. Something like awe on his smooth face, and for the first time Hannah doesn't just feel nude, she feels *naked*.

"Are they ready for me now?" she asks him, trying to sound no more than half as nervous as she is, and then turns her head to steal a last glance at the green fairy in the tall mahogany mirror. But the mirror is empty. There's no one there at all, neither her nor the green woman, nothing but the dusty backroom full of antiques, the pretty hard-candy lamps, the peeling cranberry wallpaper.

"My Lady," the boy says in a voice like broken crystal shards, and then he curtsies. "The Court is waiting to receive you, at your ready." He steps to one side, to let her pass, and the music from the party grows suddenly very loud, changing tempo, the rhythm assuming a furious speed as a thousand notes and drumbeats tumble and boom and chase one another's tails.

"The mirror," Hannah whispers, pointing at it, at the place where her reflection should be, and when she turns back to the boy there's a young girl standing there instead, dressed in his feathers and make-up. She could be his twin.

"It's a small thing, My Lady," she says with the boy's sparkling, shattered tongue.

"What's happening?"

"The Court is assembled," the girl child says. "They are all waiting. Don't be afraid, My Lady. I will show you the way."

The path, the path through the woods to the well. The path down to the well . . .

"Do you have a name?" Hannah asks, surprised at the calm in her voice; all the embarrassment and unease at standing naked before this child, and the one before, the boy twin, the fear at what she didn't see gazing back at her in the looking glass, all of that gone now.

"My name? I'm not such a fool as that, My Lady."

"No, of course not," Hannah replies. "I'm sorry."

"I will show you the way," the child says again. "Never harm, nor spell, nor charm, come our Lady nigh."

"That's very kind of you," Hannah replies. "I was beginning to think that I was lost. But I'm not lost, am I?"

"No, My Lady. You are here."

"Yes. Yes, I *am* here, aren't I?" and the child smiles for her, showing off its sharp crystal teeth. Hannah smiles back, and then she leaves the dusty backroom and the mahogany mirror, following the child down a short hallway; the music has filled in all the vacant corners of her skull, the music and the heavy living-dying smells of wildflowers and fallen leaves, rotting stumps and fresh-turned earth. A riotous hothouse cacophony of odors— spring to fall, summer to winter—and she's never tasted air so violently sweet.

. . . the path down the well, and the still black water at the bottom.

Hannah, can you hear me? Hannah?

It's so cold down here. I can't see . . .

At the end of the hall, just past the stairs leading back down to St. Mark's, there's a green door, and the girl opens it. Green gets you out.

And all the things in the wide, wide room—the unlikely room that stretches so far away in every direction that it could never be contained in any building, not in a thousand buildings—the scampering, hopping, dancing, spinning, flying, skulking things, each and every one of them stops and stares at her. And Hannah knows that she ought to be frightened of them, that she should turn and run from this place. But it's really nothing she hasn't seen before, a long time ago, and she steps past the child (who is a boy again) as the wings on her back begin to thrum like the frantic, iridescent wings of bumblebees and hummingbirds, red wasps and hungry dragonflies. Her mouth tastes of anise and wormwood, sugar and hyssop and melissa. Sticky verdant light spills from her skin and pools in the grass and moss at her bare feet.

Sink or swim, and so easy to imagine the icy black well water closing thickly over her sister's face, filling her mouth, slipping up her nostrils, flooding her belly, as clawed hands dragged her down.

And down.

And down.

And sometimes, Dr. Valloton says, sometimes we spend our entire lives just trying to answer one simple question.

The music is a hurricane, swallowing her.

My Lady. Lady of the Bottle. *Artemisia absinthium,* Chernobyl, *apsinthion,* Lady of Waking Dreaming, Green Lady of Elation and Melancholy.

I am ruin and sorrow.

My robe is the color of despair.

They bow, all of them, and Hannah finally sees the thing waiting for her on its prickling throne of woven branches and birds' nests, the hulking antlered thing with blazing eyes, that wolf-jawed hart, the man and the stag, and she bows, in her turn.

HOUSES UNDER
THE SEA

1.

WHEN I CLOSE MY EYES, I see Jacova Angevine.
I close my eyes, and there she is, standing alone at the end of
the breakwater, standing with the foghorn as the choppy sea
shatters itself to foam against a jumble of grey boulders. The October wind
is making something wild of her hair, and her back's turned to me. The boats
are coming in.

I close my eyes, and she's standing in the surf at Moss Landing, gazing
out into the bay, staring towards the place where the continental shelf
narrows down to a sliver and drops away to the black abyss of Monterey
Canyon. There are gulls, and her hair is tied back in a ponytail.

I close my eyes, and we're walking together down Cannery Row, heading
south towards the aquarium. She's wearing a gingham dress and a battered
pair of Doc Martens that she must have had for fifteen years. I say something
inconsequential, but she doesn't hear me, too busy scowling at the tourists,
at the sterile, cheery absurdities of the Bubba Gump Shrimp Company and
Mackerel Jack's Trading Post.

"That used to be a whorehouse," she says, nodding in the direction of
Mackerel Jack's. "The Lone Star Cafe, but Steinbeck called it the Bear Flag.
Everything burned. Nothing here's the way it used to be."

She says that like she remembers, and I close my eyes.

And she's on television again, out on the old pier at Moss Point, the day they launched the ROV *Tiburón II*.

And she's at the Pierce Street warehouse in Monterey; men and women in white robes are listening to every word she says. They hang on every syllable, her every breath, their many eyes like the bulging eyes of deep-sea fish encountering sunlight for the first time. Dazed, terrified, enraptured, lost.

All of them lost.

I close my eyes, and she's leading them into the bay.

Those creatures jumped the barricades
And have headed for the sea.

All these divided moments, disconnected, or connected so many different ways, that I'll never be able to pull them apart and find a coherent narrative. That's my folly, my conceit, that I can make a mere *story* of what has happened. Even if I could, it's nothing anyone would ever want to read, nothing I could sell. CNN and *Newsweek* and the *New York Times*, *Rolling Stone*, and *Harper's*, everyone already knows what they think about Jacova Angevine. Everybody already knows as much as they want to know. Or as little. In those minds, she's already earned her spot in the death-cult hall of fame, sandwiched firmly in between Jim Jones and Heaven's Gate.

I close my eyes, and "Fire from the sky, fire on the water," she says and smiles; I know that this time she's talking about the fire of September 14, 1924, the day lightning struck one of the 55,000-gallon storage tanks belonging to the Associated Oil Company and a burning river flowed into the sea. Billowing black clouds hide the sun, and the fire has the voice of a hurricane as it bears down on the canneries, a voice of demons, and she stops to tie her shoes.

I sit here in this dark motel room, staring at the screen of my laptop, the clean liquid-crystal light, typing irrelevant words to build meandering sentences, waiting, waiting, waiting, and I don't know what it is that I'm waiting for. Or I'm only afraid to admit that I know exactly what I'm waiting for. She has become my ghost, my private haunting, and haunted things are forever waiting.

"In the mansions of Poseidon, she will prepare halls from coral and glass and the bones of whales," she says, and the crowd in the warehouse breathes in and out as a single, astonished organism, their assembled bodies lesser than the momentary whole they have made. "Down there, you will know nothing but peace, in her mansions, in the endless night of her coils."

"*Tiburón* is Spanish for shark," she says, and I tell her I didn't know that, that I had two years of Spanish in high school, but that was a thousand years ago, and all I remember is *sí* and *por favor*.

What is that noise now? What is the wind doing?

I close my eyes again.

The sea has many voices.

Many gods and many voices.

"November 5, 1936," she says, and *this* is the first night we had sex, the long night we spent together in a seedy Moss Point hotel, the sort of place the fishermen take their hookers, the same place she was still staying when she died. "The Del Mar Canning Company burned to the ground. No one ever tried to blame lightning for that one."

There's moonlight through the drapes, and I imagine for a moment that her skin has become iridescent, mother-of-pearl, the shimmering motley of an oil slick. I reach out and touch her naked thigh, and she lights a cigarette. The smoke hangs thick in the air, like fog or forgetfulness.

My fingertips against her flesh, and she stands and walks to the window.

"Do you see something out there?" I ask, and she shakes her head very slowly.

I close my eyes.

In the moonlight, I can make out the puckered, circular scars on both her shoulder blades and running halfway down her spine. Two dozen or more of them, but I never bothered to count exactly. Some are no larger than a dime, but several are at least two inches across.

"When I'm gone," she says, "when I'm done here, they'll ask you questions about me. What will you tell them?"

"That depends what they ask," I reply and laugh, still thinking it was all one of her strange jokes, the talk of leaving, and I lie down and stare at the shadows on the ceiling.

"They'll ask you everything," she whispers. "Sooner or later, I expect they'll ask you everything."

Which they did.

I close my eyes, and I see her, Jacova Angevine, the lunatic prophet from Salinas, pearls that were her eyes, cockles and mussels, alive, alive-o, and she's kneeling in the sand. The sun is rising behind her and I hear people coming through the dunes.

"I'll tell them you were a good fuck," I say, and she takes another drag off her cigarette and continues staring at the night outside the motel windows.

"Yes," she says. "I expect you will."

2.

The first time that I saw Jacova Angevine—I mean, the first time I saw her in *person*—I'd just come back from Pakistan and had flown up to Monterey to try and clear my head. A photographer friend had an apartment there and he was on assignment in Tokyo, so I figured I could lay low for a couple of weeks, a whole month maybe, stay drunk and decompress. My clothes, my luggage, my skin, everything about me still smelled like Islamabad. I'd spent more than six months overseas, ferreting about for real and imagined connections between Muslim extremists, European middlemen, and Pakistan's leaky nuclear arms program, trying to gauge the damage done by the enterprising Abdul Qadeer Khan, rogue father of the Pakistani bomb, trying to determine exactly what he'd sold and to whom. Everyone already knew—or at least thought they knew—about North Korea, Libya, and Iran, and American officials suspected that al Qaeda and other terrorist groups belonged somewhere on his list of customers as well, despite assurances to the contrary from Major General Shaukat Sultan. I'd come back with a head full of apocalypse and Urdu, anti-India propaganda and Mushaikh poetry, and I was determined to empty my mind of everything except scotch and the smell of the sea.

It was a bright Wednesday afternoon, a warm day for November in Monterey County, and I decided to come up for air. I showered for the first time in a week and had a late lunch at the Sardine Factory on Wave Street—Dungeness crab remoulade, fresh oysters with horseradish, and grilled sanddabs in a lemon sauce that was a little heavy on the thyme—then decided to visit the aquarium and walk it all off. When I was a kid in Brooklyn, I spent a lot of my time at the aquarium on Coney Island, and, three decades later, there were few things a man could do sober that relaxed me as quickly and completely. I put the check on my MasterCard and followed Wave Street south and east to Prescott, then turned back down Cannery Row, the glittering bay on my right, the pale blue autumn sky stretched out overhead like oil on canvas.

I close my eyes, and that afternoon isn't something that happened three years ago, something I'm making sound like a goddamn travelogue. I close my eyes, and it's happening now, for the first time, and there she is, sitting alone on a long bench in front of the kelp forest exhibit, her thin face turned up to the high, swaying canopy behind the glass, the dapple of fish and sea-weed shadows drifting back and forth across her features. I recognize her, and that surprises me, because I've only seen her face on television and in magazine photos and on the dust jacket of the book she wrote before she lost the job at Berkeley. She turns her head and smiles at me, the familiar way you smile at a friend, the way you smile at someone you've known all your life.

"You're in luck," she says. "It's almost time for them to feed the fish." And Jacova Angevine pats the bench next to her, indicating that I should sit down.

"I read your book," I say, taking a seat because I'm still too surprised to do anything else.

"Did you? Did you really?" and now she looks like she doesn't believe me, like I'm only saying that I've read her book to be polite, and from her expression I can tell that she thinks it's a little odd, that anyone would ever bother to try and flatter her.

"Yes," I tell her, trying too hard to sound sincere. "I did really. In fact, I read some of it twice."

"And why would you do a thing like that?"

"Truthfully?"

"Yes, truthfully."

Her eyes are the same color as the water trapped behind the thick panes of aquarium glass, the color of the November sunlight filtered through saltwater and kelp blades. There are fine lines at the corners of her mouth and beneath her eyes that make her look several years older than she is.

"Last summer, I was flying from New York to London, and there was a three-hour layover in Shannon. Your book was all I'd brought to read."

61

"That's terrible," she says, still smiling, and turns to face the big tank again. "Do you want your money back?"

"It was a gift," I reply, which isn't true, and I have no idea why I'm lying to her. "An ex-girlfriend gave it to me for my birthday."

"Is that why you left her?"

"No, I left her because she thought I drank too much and I thought she drank too little."

"Are you an alcoholic?" Jacova Angevine asks, as casually as if she were asking me whether I liked milk in my coffee or if I took it black.

"Well, some people say I'm headed in that direction," I tell her. "But I did enjoy the book, honest. It's hard to believe they fired you for writing it. I mean, that people get fired for writing books." But I know that's a lie, too; I'm not half that naive, and it's not at all difficult to understand how or why *Waking Leviathan* ended Jacova Angevine's career as an academic. A reviewer for *Nature* called it "the most confused and preposterous example of bad history wedding bad science since the Velikovsky affair."

"They didn't fire me for writing it," she says. "They politely asked me to resign because I'd seen fit to publish it."

"Why didn't you fight them?"

Her smile fades a little, and the lines around her mouth seem to grow the slightest bit more pronounced. "I don't come here to talk about the book, or my unfortunate employment history," she says.

I apologize, and she tells me not to worry about it.

A diver enters the tank, matte-black neoprene trailing a rush of silver bubbles, and most of the fish rise expectantly to meet him or her, a riot of kelp bass and sleek leopard sharks, sheephead and rockfish and species I don't recognize. She doesn't say anything else, too busy watching the feeding, and I sit there beside her, at the bottom of a pretend ocean.

I open my eyes. There are only the words on the screen in front of me.

I didn't see her again for the better part of a year. During that time, as my work sent me back to Pakistan, and then to Germany and Israel, I reread her book. I also read some of the articles and reviews, and a brief online interview that she'd given Whitley Strieber's *Unknown Country* website. Then I tracked down an article on Inuit archaeology that she'd written for *Fate* and wondered at what point Jacova Angevine had decided that there was no going back, nothing left to lose and so no reason not to allow herself to become part of the murky, strident world of fringe believers and UFO buffs, conspiracy theorists and paranormal "investigators" that seemed so eager to embrace her as one of its own.

And I wondered, too, if perhaps she might have been one of them from the start.

3.

I woke up this morning from a long dream of storms and drowning and lay in bed, very still, sizing up my hangover and staring at the sagging, water-stained ceiling of my motel room. And I finally admitted to myself that this isn't going to be what the paper has hired me to write. I don't think I'm even trying to write it for them anymore. They want the dirt, of course, and I've never been shy about digging holes. I've spent the last twenty years as a shovel-for-hire. I don't think it matters that I may have loved her, or that a lot of this dirt is mine. I can't pretend that I'm acting out of nobility of soul or loyalty or even some selfish, belated concern for my own dingy reputation. I would write exactly what they want me to write if I could. If I knew how. I need the money. I haven't worked for the last five months, and my savings are almost gone.

But if I'm not writing it for them, if I've abandoned all hope of a paycheck at the other end of this thing, why the hell then am I still sitting here typing? Am I making a confession? Bless me, Father, I can't forget? Do I believe it's something I can puke up like a sour belly full of whiskey, that writing it all down will make the nightmares stop or make it any easier for me to get through the days? I sincerely hope I'm not as big a fool as that. Whatever else I may be, I like to think that I'm not an idiot.

I don't know why I'm writing this, whatever this turns out to be. Maybe it's only a very long-winded suicide note.

Last night, I watched the tape again.

I have all three versions with me: the cut that's still being hawked over the internet, the one that ends right after the ROV was hit, before the lights came back on; the cut that MBARI released to the press and the scientific community in response to the version circulating online; and I have the "raw" footage, the copy I bought from a robotics technician who claimed to have been aboard the R/V *Western Flyer* the day that the incident occurred. I paid him two thousand dollars for it, and the kid swore to both its completeness and authenticity. I knew that I wasn't the first person to whom he'd sold the tape. I'd heard about it from a contact in the chemistry department at UC Irvine. I was never sure exactly how she'd caught wind of it, but I gathered that the tech was turning a handsome little profit peddling his contraband to anyone willing to pony up the cash.

We met at a Motel 6 in El Cajon, and I played it all the way through before I handed him the money. He sat with his back to the television while I watched the tape, rewound and started it over again.

"What the hell are you doing?" he asked, literally wringing his hands and gazing anxiously at the heavy drapes. I'd pulled them shut after hooking up the rented VCR that I'd brought with me, but a bright sliver of afternoon sunlight slipped in between them and divided his face down the middle. "Jesus, man. You think it's not gonna be the exact same thing every time? You think if you keep playing it over and over it's gonna come out any different?"

I've watched the tape more times than I can count, a couple hundred, at least, and I still think that's a good goddamned question.

"So why didn't MBARI release this?" I asked the kid, and he laughed and shook his head.

"Why the fuck do you think?" he replied.

He took my money, reminded me again that we'd never met and that he'd deny everything if I attempted to finger him as my source. Then he got back into his ancient, wheezy VW Microbus and drove off, leaving me sitting there with an hour and a half of unedited color video recorded somewhere along the bottom of the Monterey Canyon. Everything the ROV *Tiburón II*'s starboard camera had seen (the port pan-and-tilt unit was malfunctioning that day), twenty miles out and three kilometers down, and from the start I understood it was the closest I was ever likely to come to an answer, and that it was also only a different and far more terrible sort of question.

Last night I got drunk, more so than usual, a *lot* more so than usual, and watched it for the first time in almost a month. But I turned the sound on the television down all the way and left the lights burning.

Even drunk, I'm still a coward.

The ocean floor starkly illuminated by the ROV's six 480-watt HMI lights, revealing a velvet carpet of grey-brown sediment washed out from Elkhorn Slough and all the other sloughs and rivers emptying into the bay. And even at this depth, there are signs of life: brittle stars and crabs cling to the shit-colored rocks, sponges and sea cucumbers, the sinuous, smooth bodies of big-eyed rattails. Here and there, dark outcroppings jut from the ooze like bone from the decaying flesh of a leper.

My asshole editor would laugh out loud at that last simile, would probably take one look at it and laugh and then say something like, "If I'd wanted fucking purple I'd have bought a goddamn pot of violets." But my asshole editor hasn't seen the tape I bought from the tech.

My asshole editor never met Jacova Angevine, never listened to her talk, never fucked her, never saw the scars on her back or the fear in her eyes.

The ROV comes to a rocky place where the seafloor drops away suddenly, and it hesitates, responding to commands from the control room of the R/V *Western Flyer*. A moment or two later, the steady fall of marine snow becomes so heavy that it's difficult to see much of anything through the light reflecting off the whitish particles of sinking detritus. And sitting there on the floor between the foot of the bed and the television, I almost reached out and touched the screen.

Almost.

"It's a little bit of everything," I heard Jacova say, though she never actually said anything of the sort to me. "Silt, phytoplankton and zooplankton, soot, mucus, diatoms, fecal pellets, dust, grains of sand and clay, radioactive fallout, pollen, sewage. Some of it's even interplanetary dust particles. Some of it fell from the stars."

And *Tiburón II* lurches and glides forward a few feet, then slips cautiously over the precipice, beginning the slow descent into this new and unexpected abyss.

"We'd been over that stretch more than a dozen times, at least," Natalie Billington, chief ROV pilot for *Tiburón II*, told a CNN correspondent after the internet version of the tape first made the news. "But that drop-off wasn't on any of the charts. We'd always missed it somehow. I know that isn't a very satisfying answer, but it's a big place down there. The canyon is over two hundred miles long. You miss things."

For a while—exactly 15.34 seconds—there's only the darkness and marine snow and a few curious or startled fish. According to MBARI, the ROV's vertical speed during this part of the dive is about 35 meters per minute, so by the time it finds the bottom again, depth has increased by some five hundred and twenty-five feet. The seafloor comes into view again, and there's not so much loose sediment here, just a jumble of broken boulders, and it's startling how clean they are, almost completely free of the usual encrustations and muck. There are no sponges or sea cucumbers to be seen, no starfish, and even the omnipresent marine snow has tapered off to only a few stray, drifting flecks. And then the wide, flat rock that is usually referred to as "the Delta stone" comes into view. And this isn't like the face on Mars or von Däniken seeing ancient astronauts on Mayan artifacts. The ∂ carved into the slab is unmistakable. The edges are so sharp, so clean that it might have been done yesterday.

The *Tiburón II* hovers above the Delta stone, spilling light into this lightless place, and I know what's coming next, so I sit very still and count off the seconds in my head. When I've counted to thirty-eight, the view from the ROV's camera pans violently to the right, signaling the portside impact, and an instant later there's only static, white noise, the twelve-second gap in the tape during which the camera was still running, but no longer recording.

I counted to eleven before I switched off the television, and then sat listening to the wind, and the waves breaking against the beach, waiting for my heart to stop racing and the sweat on my face and palms to dry. When I was sure that I wasn't going to be sick, I pressed EJECT and the VCR spat out the tape. I returned it to its navy-blue plastic case and sat smoking and drinking, helpless to think of anything but Jacova.

4.

Jacova Angevine was born and grew up in her father's big Victorian house in Salinas, only a couple of blocks from the birthplace of John Steinbeck. Her mother died when she was eight. Jacova had no siblings, and her closest kin, paternal and maternal, were all back east in New Jersey and Pennsylvania and Maryland. In 1960, her parents relocated to California, just a few months after they were married, and her father took a job teaching high-school English in Castroville. After six months, he quit that job and took another, with only slightly better pay, in the town of Soledad. Though he'd earned a doctorate in comparative literature from Columbia, Theo Angevine seemed to have no particular academic ambitions. He'd written several novels while in college, though none of them had managed to find a publisher. In 1969, his wife five months pregnant with their daughter, he resigned from his position at Soledad High and moved north to Salinas, where he bought the old house on Howard Street with a bank loan and the advance from his first book sale, a mystery novel titled *The Man Who Laughed at Funerals* (Random House, New York).

To date, none of the three books that have been published about Jacova, the Open Door of Night sect, and the mass drownings off Moss Landing State Beach have made more than a passing mention of Theo Angevine's novels. Elenore Ellis-Lincoln, in *Closing the Door: Anatomy of Hysteria* (Simon and Schuster, New York), for example, devotes only a single paragraph to them, though she gives Jacova's childhood an entire chapter. "Mr. Angevine's works received little critical attention, one way or the other, and his income from them was meager," Ellis-Lincoln writes. "Of the seventeen novels he published between 1969 and 1985, only two—*The Man Who Laughed for Funerals* [sic] and *Seven at Sunset*—are still in print. It is notable that the overall tone of the novels becomes significantly darker following his wife's death, but the books themselves never seem to have been more to the author than a sort of hobby. Upon his death, his daughter became the executor of his literary estate, such as it was."

Likewise, in *Lemming Cult* (The Overlook Press, New York), William L. West writes, "Her father's steady output of mystery and suspense potboilers must surely have been a curiosity of Jacova's childhood, but were never once mentioned in her own writings, including the five private journals found in a cardboard box in her bedroom closet. The books themselves were entirely unremarkable, so far as I've been able to ascertain. Almost all are out of print and very difficult to find today. Even the catalog of the Salinas Public Library includes only a single copy each of *The Man Who Laughed at Funerals*, *Pretoria*, and *Seven at Sunset*."

During the two years I knew her, Jacova only mentioned her father's writing once that I can recall, and then only in passing, but she had copies of all his novels, a fact that I've never seen mentioned anywhere in print. I suppose it doesn't seem very significant, if you haven't bothered to read Theo Angevine's books. Since Jacova's death, I've read every one of them. It took me less than a month to track down copies of all seventeen, thanks largely to online booksellers, and even less time to read them. While William West was certainly justified in calling the novels "entirely unremarkable," even a casual examination reveals some distinctly remarkable parallels between the fiction of the father and the reality of the daughter.

I've spent the whole afternoon, the better part of the past five hours, on the preceding four paragraphs, trying to fool myself into believing that I can actually write *about* her as a journalist would write about her. That I can bring any degree of detachment or objectivity to bear. Of course, I'm wasting my time. After seeing the tape again, after almost allowing myself to watch *all* of it again, I think I'm desperate to put distance between myself and the memory of her. I should call New York and tell them that I can't do this, that they should find someone else, but after the mess I made of the Musharraf story, the agency would probably never offer me another assignment. For the moment, that still matters. It might not in another day or two, but it does for now.

Her father wrote books, books that were never very popular, and though they're neither particularly accomplished nor enjoyable, they might hold clues to Jacova's motivation and to her fate. And they might not. It's as simple and contradictory as that. Like everything surrounding the "Lemming Cult"—as the Open Door of Night has come to be known, as it has been labeled by people who find it easier to deal with tragedy and horror if there is an attendant note of the absurd—like everything else about *her*, what seems meaningful one moment will seem irrelevant the next. Or maybe that's only the way it appears to me. Maybe I'm asking too much of the clues.

Excerpt from *Pretoria*, pp. 164–165; Ballantine Books, 1979:

Edward Horton smiled and tapped the ash from his cigar into the large glass ashtray on the table. "I don't like the sea," he said and nodded at the window. "Frankly, I can't even stand the sound of it. Gives me nightmares."

I listened to the breakers, not taking my eyes off the fat man and the thick grey curlicues of smoke arranging and rearranging themselves around his face. I'd always found the sound of waves to have a welcomed, tranquilizing effect upon my nerves and wondered which one of Horton's innumerable secrets was responsible for his loathing of the sea. I knew he'd done a stint in the Navy during Korea, but I was also pretty sure he'd never seen combat.

"How'd you sleep last night?" I asked, and he shook his head.

"For shit," he replied and sucked on his cigar.

"Then maybe you should think about getting a room farther inland."

Horton coughed and jabbed a pudgy finger at the window of the bungalow. "Don't think I wouldn't, if the choice were mine to make. But she wants me *here*. She wants me sitting right here, waiting on her, night and day. She knows I hate the ocean."

"What the hell," I said, reaching for my hat, tired of his company and the stink of his smoldering Macanudo. "You know where to reach me, if you change your mind. Don't let the bad dreams get you down. They ain't nothing but that, bad dreams."

"That's not enough?" he asked, and I could tell from his expression that Horton wished I'd stay a little longer, but I knew he'd never admit it. "Last night, goddamn people marching into the sea, marching over the sand in rows like the goddamn infantry. Must of been a million of them. What you think a dream like that means, anyway?"

"Horton, a dream like that don't mean jack shit," I replied. "Except maybe you need to lay off the spicy food before bedtime."

"You're always gonna be an asshole," he said, and I was forced to agree. He puffed his cigar, and I left the bungalow and stepped out into the salty Santa Barbara night.

Excerpt from *What the Cat Dragged In,* p. 231; Ballantine Books, 1980:

Vicky had never told anyone about the dreams, just like she'd never told any-one about Mr. Barker or the yellow Corvette. The dreams were her secret, whether she wanted them or not. Sometimes they seemed almost wicked, shameful, sinful, like something she'd done that was against God, or at least against the law. She'd almost told Mr. Barker once, a year or so before she left Los Angeles. She'd gone so far as to broach the subject of mermaids, and then he'd snorted and laughed, so she'd thought better of it.

"You got some strange notions in that head of yours," he'd said. "Some-day, you're gonna have to grow out of crap like that, if you want people 'round here to start taking you seriously."

So she kept it all to herself. Whatever the dreams meant or didn't mean, it wasn't anything she would ever be able to explain or confess. Sometimes, nights when she couldn't sleep, she lay in bed staring at the ceiling, thinking about the ruined castles beneath the waves and beautiful, drowned girls with seaweed tangled in their hair.

Excerpt from *The Last Loan Shark of Bodega Bay,* pp. 57–59; Bantam Books, 1982:

"This was way the hell back in the fifties," Foster said and lit another cig-arette. His hands were shaking, and he kept looking over his shoulder. "Fifty-eight, right, or maybe early fifty-nine. I know Eisenhower was still president, though I ain't precisely sure of the year. But I was still stuck in Honolulu, right, still hauling lousy tourists around the islands in the *Saint Chris* so they could fish and snap pictures of goddamn Kīlauea and what have you. The boat was on its last leg, but she'd still get you where you were goin', if you knew how to slap her around."

"What's this got to do with Winkie Anderson and the girl?" I asked, making no effort to hide my impatience.

"Jesus, Frank, I'm getting to it. You want to hear this thing or not? I

70

swear, you come around here asking the big questions, expecting the what's-what, you can at least keep your trap shut and listen."

"I don't have all night, that's all."

"Yeah, well, who the hell does, why don't you tell me that? Anyway, like I was saying, back about fifty-nine, and we was out somewhere off the north shore of Molokai. Old Coop was fishing the thousand fathom line, and Jerry—you remember Jerry O'Neil, right?"

"No," I said, eyeing the clock above the bar.

"Well, whatever. Jerry O'Neil was mouthing off about a twelve-hundred pounder, this big-ass marlin some Mexican businessman from Tijuana had up and hooked just a few weeks before. Fish even made the damn papers, right. Anyway, Jerry said the Mexican was bad news, and we should keep a sharp eye out for him. Said he was a regular Jonah."

"But you just said he caught a twelve-hundred-pound marlin."

"Yeah, sure. He could haul in the fish, this chunt son of a bitch, but he was into some sort of Spanish voodoo shit and had these gold coins he'd toss over the side of the boat every five or ten minutes. Like goddamn clock-work, he'd check his watch and toss out a coin. Gold doubloons or some shit, I don't know what they were. It was driving Coop crazy, 'cause it wasn't enough the Mexican had to do this thing with the coins, he was mumbling some sort of shit nonstop. Coop kept telling him to shut the hell up, people was trying to fish, but this guy, he just keeps mumbling and tossing coins and pulling in the fish. I finally got a look at one of those doubloons, and it had something stamped on one side looked like a damn octopus, and on the other side was this star like a pentagram. You know, those things witches and warlocks use."

"Foster, this is crazy bullshit. I have to be in San Francisco at seven thirty in the morning." I waved to the bartender and put two crumpled fives and a one on the bar in front of me.

"You ever heard of the Momma Hydra, Frank? That's who this chunt said he was praying to."

"Call me when you run out of bullshit," I said. "And I don't have to tell you, Detective Burke won't be half as understanding as I am."

"Jesus, Frank. Hold up a goddamn second. It's just the way I tell stories, right. You know that. I start at the beginning. I don't leave stuff out."

These are only a few examples of what anyone will find, if he or she should take the time to look. There are many more, I assure you. The pages of my copies of Theo Angevine's novels are scarred throughout with yellow high-lighter.

And everything leaves more questions than answers.

You make of it what you will. Or you don't. I suppose that a Freudian might have a proper field day with this stuff. Whatever I knew about Freud I forgot before I was even out of college. It would be comforting, I suppose, if I could dismiss Jacova's fate as the end result of some overwhelming Oedipal hysteria, the ocean cast here as that Great Ur-Mother savior-being who finally opens up to offer release and forgiveness in death and dissolution.

5.

I begin to walk down some particular, perhaps promising, avenue and then, inevitably, I turn and run, tail tucked firmly between my legs. My memories. The MBARI video. Jacova and her father's whodunits. I scratch the surface and then pull my hand back to be sure that I haven't lost a fucking finger. I mix metaphors the way I've been mixing tequila and scotch.

If, as William Burroughs wrote, "Language is a virus from outer space," then what the holy hell were you supposed to be, Jacova?

An epidemic of the collective unconscious. The black plague of belief. A vaccine for cultural amnesia, she might have said. And so we're right back to Velikovsky, who wrote, "Human beings, rising from some catastrophe, bereft of memory of what had happened, regarded themselves as created from the dust of the earth. All knowledge about the ancestors, who they were and in what interstellar space they lived, was wiped away from the memory of the few survivors."

I'm drunk, and I'm not making any sense at all. Or merely much too little sense to matter. Anyway, you'll want to pay attention to this part. It's sort of like the ghost story within the ghost story within the ghost story, the hard nugget at the unreachable heart of my heart's infinitely regressing babooshka, matryoshka, matrioska, matreshka, babushka. It might even be the final straw that breaks the camel of my mind.

Remember, I am wasted, and so that last inexcusable paragraph may be forgiven. Or it may not.

"When I become death, death is the seed from which I grow." Burroughs said that, too. Jacova, you will be an orchard. You will be a swaying kelp forest. There's a log in the hole in the bottom of the sea with your name on it.

Yesterday afternoon, puking sick of looking at these four dingy fucking walls, I drove down to Monterey, to the warehouse on Pierce Street. The last time I was there, the cops still hadn't taken down all the yellow CRIME SCENE—DO NOT CROSS tape. Now there's only a great big for-sale sign and an even bigger no-trespassing sign. I wrote the name and number of the realty company on the back of a book of matches. I want to ask them what they'll be telling prospective buyers about the building's history. Word is the whole block is due to be rezoned next year, and soon those empty buildings will be converted to lofts and condos. Gentrification abhors a void.

I parked in an empty lot down the street from the warehouse, hoping that no one happening by would notice me, hoping, in particular, that any passing police would not notice me. I walked quickly, without running, because running is suspicious and inevitably draws the attention of those who *watch* for suspicious things. I was not so drunk as I might have been, not even so drunk as I *should* have been, and I tried to keep my mind occupied by noting the less significant details of the street, the sky, the weather. The litter caught in the weeds and gravel—cigarette butts, plastic soft-drink bottles (I recall Pepsi, Coke, and Mountain Dew), paper bags and cups from fast-food restaurants (McDonald's, Del Taco, KFC), broken glass, unrecognizable bits of metal, a rusted Oregon license plate. The sky was painfully blue, the blue of nausea, with only very high cirrus clouds to spoil that suffocating pastel heaven. There were no other cars parked along the street and no living things that I noticed. There were a couple of garbage dumpsters, a stop sign, and a great pile of cardboard boxes that had been soaked by rain enough times it was difficult to tell exactly where one ended and another began. There was a hubcap.

When I finally reached the warehouse—the warehouse become a temple to half-remembered gods become a crime scene, now on its way to becoming something else—I ducked down the narrow alley that separates it from the abandoned Monterey Peninsula Shipping and Storage Building (established 1924). There'd been a door around that way with an unreliable lock. If I was lucky, I thought, no one would have noticed, or if they had noticed, wouldn't have bothered fixing it. My heart was racing, and I was dizzy (I tried hard to blame that on the sickening color of the sky) and there was a metallic taste in the back of my mouth, like a freshly filled tooth.

It was colder in the alley than it had been out on Pierce, the sun having already dropped low enough in the west that the alley must have been in shadow for some time. Perhaps it is always in shadow and never truly warm there. I found the side door exactly as I'd hoped to find it, and three or four minutes of jiggling about with the wobbly brass knob was enough to coax it open. Inside, the warehouse was dark and even colder than the alley, and the air stank of mold and dust, bad memories and vacancy. I stood in the doorway a moment or two, thinking of hungry rats and drunken bums, delirious crack addicts wielding lead pipes, the webs of poisonous spiders. Then I took a deep breath and stepped across the threshold, out of the shadows and into a more decided blackness, a more definitive chill, and all those mundane threats dissolved. Everything slipped from my mind except Jacova Angevine, and her followers (if that's what you'd call them), dressed all in white, and the thing I'd seen on the altar the one time I'd come here when this had been a temple of the Open Door of Night.

I asked her about that thing once, a few weeks before the end, the last night that we spent together. I asked where it had come from, who had made it, and she lay very still for a while, listening to the surf or only trying to decide which answer would satisfy me. In the moonlight through the hotel window, I thought she might have been smiling, but I wasn't sure.

"It's very old," she said, eventually. By then I'd almost drifted off to sleep and had to shake myself awake again. "No one alive remembers who *made* it," Jacova continued. "But I don't think that matters, only that it was made."

"It's fucking hideous," I mumbled sleepily. "You know that, don't you?"

"Yeah, but so is the Crucifixion. So are bleeding statues of the Virgin Mary and images of Kali. So are the animal-headed gods of the Egyptians."

"Yeah, well, I don't bow down to any of them, either," I replied, or something to that effect.

"The divine is always abominable," she whispered and rolled over, turning her back to me.

Just a moment ago I was in the warehouse on Pierce Street, wasn't I? And now I'm in bed with the Prophet from Salinas. But I will not despair, for there is no need here to stay focused, to adhere to some restrictive illusion of the linear narrative. It's coming. It's been coming all along. As Job Foster said in Chapter Four of *The Last Loan Shark of Bodega Bay*, "It's just the way I tell stories, right. You know that. I start at the beginning. I don't leave stuff out."

That's horseshit, of course. I suspect luckless Job Foster knew it was horseshit, and I suspect that I know it's horseshit, too. It is not the task of the writer to "tell all," or even to decide what to leave in, but to decide what to leave *out*. Whatever remains, that meager sum of this profane division, that's the bastard chimera we call a "story." I am not building, but cutting away. And all stories, whether advertised as truth or admitted falsehoods, are fictions, cleft from any objective facts by the aforementioned action of cutting away. A pound of flesh. A pile of sawdust. Discarded chips of Carrara marble. And what's left over.

A damned man in an empty warehouse.

I left the door standing open, because I hadn't the nerve to shut myself up in that place. And I'd already taken a few steps inside, my shoes crunching loudly on shards of glass from a broken window, grinding glass to dust, when I remembered the Maglite hidden inside my jacket. But the glare of the flashlight did nothing much to make the darkness any less stifling, nothing much at all but remind me of the blinding white beam of *Tiburón II*'s big HMI rig, shining out across the silt at the bottom of the canyon. *Now*, I thought, *at least I can see anything, if there's anything to see*, and immediately some other, less familiar thought-voice demanded to know why the hell I'd want to. The door had opened into a narrow corridor, mint-green concrete walls and a low concrete ceiling, and I followed it a short distance to its end—no more than thirty feet, thirty feet at the most—past empty rooms that might once have been offices, to an unlocked steel door marked in faded orange letters, EMPLOYEES ONLY.

"It's an empty warehouse," I whispered, breathing the words aloud. "That's all, an empty warehouse." I knew it wasn't the truth, not anymore, not by a long sight, but I thought that maybe a lie could be more comforting than the comfortless illumination of the Maglite in my hand. Joseph Campbell wrote, "Draw a circle around a stone and the stone will become an incarnation of mystery." Something like that. Or it was someone else said it and I'm misremembering. The point is, I knew that Jacova had drawn a circle around that place, just as she'd drawn a circle about herself, just as her father had somehow drawn a circle about her—

Just as she'd drawn a circle around me.

The door wasn't locked, and beyond it lay the vast, deserted belly of the building, a flat plain of cement marked off with steel support beams. There was a little sunlight coming in through the many small windows along the east and west walls, though not as much as I'd expected, and it seemed weakened, diluted by the musty air. I played the Maglite back and forth across the floor at my feet and saw that someone had painted over all the elaborate, colorful designs put there by the Open Door of Night. A thick grey latex wash to cover the intricate interweave of lines, the lines that she believed would form a bridge, a *conduit*—that was the word that she'd used. Everyone's seen photographs of that floor, although I've yet to see any that do it justice. A *yantra*. A labyrinth. A writhing, tangled mass of sea creatures straining for a distant black sun. Hindi and Mayan and Chinook symbols. The precise contour lines of a topographic map of Monterey Canyon. Each of these things and *all* of these things, simultaneously. I've heard that there's an anthropologist at Berkeley who's writing a book about that floor. Perhaps she will publish photographs that manage to communicate its awful magnificence. Perhaps it would be better if she doesn't.

Perhaps someone should put a bullet through her head.

People said the same thing about Jacova Angevine. But assassination is almost always unthinkable to moral, thinking men until *after* a holocaust has come and gone.

I left that door open, as well, and walked slowly towards the center of the empty warehouse, towards the place where the altar had been, the spot where that divine abomination of Jacova's had rested on folds of velvet the color of a massacre. I held the Maglite gripped so tightly that the fingers of my right hand had begun to go numb.

Behind me, there was a scuffling, gritty sort of noise that might have been footsteps, and I spun about, tangling my feet and almost falling on my ass, almost dropping the flashlight. The child was standing maybe ten or fifteen feet away from me, and I could see that the door leading back to the alley had been closed. She couldn't have been more than nine or ten years old, dressed in ragged jeans and a T-shirt smeared with mud, or what looked like mud in the half light of the warehouse. Her short hair might have been blonde, or light brown, it was hard to tell. Most of her face was lost in the shadows.

"You're too late," she said. She sounded tired. Or lost. Or both.

"Jesus *Christ*, kid, you almost scared the holy shit out of me."

"You're too late," she said again.

"Too late for what? Did you follow me in here?"

"The gates are shut now. They won't open again, for you or anyone else."

I looked past her at the door I'd left open, and she looked back that way, too.

"Did you close that door?" I asked her. "Did it ever occur to you that I might have left it open for a reason?"

"I waited as long I dared," she replied, as though that answered my question, and turned to face me again.

I took one step towards her then, or maybe two, and stopped. And at that moment, I experienced the sensation or sensations that mystery and horror writers, from Poe on down to Theo Angevine, have labored to convey—the almost painful prickling as the hairs on the back of my neck and along my arms and legs stood erect, the cold knot in the pit of my stomach, the goose across my grave, a loosening in my bowels and bladder, the tightening of my scrotum. My blood ran cold. Drag out all the fucking clichés, but there's still nothing that comes within a mile of what I felt standing there, looking down at that girl, her looking up at me, the feeble light from the windows glinting off her eyes.

Looking into her face, I felt *dread* as I'd never felt it before. Not in war zones with air-raid sirens blaring, not during interviews conducted with the muzzle of a pistol pressed to my temple or the small of my back. Not waiting for the results of a biopsy after the discovery of a peculiar mole. Not even the day she led them into the sea, and I sat watching it all on fucking CNN from a bar in Brooklyn.

And suddenly I knew that the girl hadn't followed me in from the alley, or closed the door, that she'd been here all along. I also knew that a hundred coats of paint wouldn't be enough to undo Jacova's labyrinth.

"Was you ever bit by a dead bee."

"You shouldn't be here," the girl said, her minotaur's voice lost and faraway and regretful.

"Then where *should* I be?" I asked, and my breath fogged in air gone as frigid as the dead of winter, or the bottom of the sea.

"All the answers were here," she replied. "Everything that you're asking yourself, the things that keep you awake, that are driving you insane. All the questions you're putting into that computer of yours. I offered all of it to you."

And now there was a sound like water breaking against stone, and something heavy and soft and wet, dragging itself across the concrete floor, and I thought of the thing from the altar, Jacova's Mother Hydra, that corrupt and bloated Madonna of the abyss, its tentacles and anemone tendrils and black, bulging squid eyes, the tubeworm proboscis snaking from one of the holes where its face should have been.

Mighty, undying daughter of Typhaôn and serpentine Echidna— Υδρα Λερναια, *Hydra Lernaia, gluttonous whore of all the lightless worlds, bitch-bride and concubine of Father Dagon, Father Kraken.*

I smelled rot and mud, saltwater and dying fish.

"You have to go now," the child said urgently, and she held out a hand as though she meant to show me the way. Even in the gloom, I could see the barnacles and sea lice nestled in the raw flesh of her palm. "You are a splinter in my soul, always. And she would drag you down to finish my own darkness."

And then the girl was gone. She did not vanish, she was simply not *there* anymore. And those other sounds and odors had gone with her. There was nothing left behind but the silence and stink of any abandoned building, and the wind brushing against the windows and around the corners of the warehouse, and the traffic along roads in the world waiting somewhere beyond those walls.

6.

I know *exactly* how all this shit sounds. Don't think that I don't. It's just that I've finally ceased to care.

7.

Yesterday, two days after my trip to the warehouse, I watched the MBARI tape again. This time, when it reached the twelve-second gap, when I'd counted down to eleven, I continued on to twelve, and I didn't switch the television off, and I didn't look away. Surely, I've come too far to allow myself that luxury. I've seen so goddamn much—I've seen so much that there's no reasonable excuse for looking away, because there can't be anything left that's more terrible than what has come before.

And, besides, it was nothing that I hadn't seen already.

Orpheus' mistake wasn't that he turned and looked back towards Eurydice and Hell, but that he ever thought he could *escape.* Same with Lot's wife. Averting our eyes does not change the fact that we are marked.

After the static, the picture comes back, and at first it's just those boulders, same as before, those boulders that ought to be covered with silt and living things—the remains of living things, at least—but aren't. Those strange, clean boulders. And the lines and angles carved deeply into them that cannot be the result of any natural geological or biological process, the lines and angles that can be nothing but what Jacova said they were. I think of fragments of the Parthenon, or some other shattered Greek or Roman temple, the chiseled ornament of an entablature or pediment. I'm seeing something that was *done,* something that was consciously fashioned, not something that simply happened. The *Tiburón II* moves forward very slowly, because the blow before the gap has taken out a couple of the port thrusters. It creeps forward tentatively, floating a few feet above the seafloor, and now the ROV's lights have begun to dim and flicker.

After the gap, I know that there's only 52.2 seconds of video remaining before the starboard camera shuts down for good. Less than a minute, and I sit there on the floor of my motel room, counting—one-one thousand, two-two thousand—and I don't take my eyes off the screen.

The MBARI robotics tech is dead, the nervous man who sold me—and whoever else was buying—his black-market dub of the videotape. The story made the Channel 46 evening news last night and was second page in the *Monterey Herald* this morning. The coroner's office is calling it a suicide. I don't know what else they would call it. He was found hanging from the lowest limb of a sycamore tree, not far from the Moss Landing docks, both his wrists slashed nearly to the bone. He was wearing a necklace of *Loligo* squid strung on baling wire. A family member has told the press that he had a history of depression.

Twenty-three seconds to go.

Almost two miles down, *Tiburón II* is listing badly to starboard, and then the ROV bumps against one of the boulders, and the lights stop flickering and seem to grow a little brighter. The vehicle appears to pause, as though considering its next move. The day he sold me the tape, the MBARI tech said that a part of the toolsled had wedged itself into the rubble. He told me it took the crew of the R/V *Western Flyer* more than two hours to maneuver the sub free. Two hours of total darkness at the bottom of the canyon, after the lights and the cameras died.

Eighteen seconds.

Sixteen.

This time it'll be different, I think, like a child trying to wish away a beating. *This time, I'll see the trick of it, the secret interplay of light and shadow, the hows and whys of a simple optical illusion—*

Twelve.

Ten.

The first time, I thought that I was only seeing something carved into the stone or part of a broken sculpture. The gentle curve of a hip, the tapering line of a leg, the twin swellings of small breasts. A nipple the color of granite.

Eight.

But there's her face—and there's no denying that it's *her* face—Jacova Angevine, her face at the bottom the sea, turned up towards the surface, towards the sky and Heaven beyond the weight of all that black, black water.

Four.

I bite my lip so hard that I taste blood. It doesn't taste so different from the ocean.

Two.

She opens her eyes, and they are *not* her eyes, but the eyes of some marine creature adapted to that perpetual night. The soulless eyes of an anglerfish or gulper eel, eyes like matching pools of ink, and something darts from her parted lips—

And then there's only static, and I sit staring into the salt-and-pepper roar.

All the answers were here. Everything that you're asking yourself . . . I offered all of it to you.

Later—an hour or only five minutes—I pressed EJECT, and the cassette slid obediently from the VCR. I read the label, aloud, in case I'd read it wrong every single time before, in case the timestamp on the video might have been mistaken. But it was the same as always, the day before Jacova waited on the beach at Moss Landing for the supplicants of the Open Door of Night. The day before she led them into the sea. The day before she drowned.

8.

I close my eyes.

And she's here again, as though she never left.

She whispers something dirty in my ear, something profane, and her breath smells like sage and toothpaste.

The protestors are demanding that the Monterey Bay Aquarium Research Institute (MBARI) end its ongoing exploration of the submarine canyon immediately. The twenty-five-mile-long canyon, they claim, is a sacred site that is being desecrated by scientists. Jacova Angevine, former Berkeley professor and leader of the controversial Open Door of Night cult, compares the launching of the new submersible Tiburón II to the ransacking of the Egyptian pyramids by grave robbers. (San Francisco Chronicle)

I tell her that I have to go to New York, that I have to take this assignment, and she replies that maybe it's for the best. I don't ask her what she means; I can't imagine that it's important.

And she kisses me.

Later, when we're done, and I'm too exhausted to sleep, I lie awake, listening to the sea and the small, anxious sounds she makes in her dreams.

The bodies of fifty-three men and women, all of whom may have been part of a religious group known as the Open Door of Night, have been recovered following Wednesday's drownings near Moss Landing, CA. Deputies have described the deaths as a mass suicide. The victims were all reported to be between 22 and 36 years old. Authorities fear that at least two dozen more may have died in the bizarre episode and recovery efforts continue along the coast of Monterey County. (CNN.com)

I close my eyes, and I'm in the old warehouse on Pierce Street again; Jacova's voice thunders from the PA speakers mounted high on the walls around the cavernous room. I'm standing in the shadows all the way at the back, apart from the true believers, apart from the other reporters and photographers and cameramen who have been invited here. Jacova leans into the microphone, angry and ecstatic and beautiful—*terrible*, I think—and that hideous carving is squatting there on its altar beside her. There are candles and smoldering incense and bouquets of dried seaweed, conch shells and dead fish, carefully arranged about the base of the statue.

"We can't remember where it began," she says, "where *we* began," and they all seem to lean into her words like small boats pushing against a violent wind. "We can't remember, of course we can't remember, and they don't want us to even *try*. They're afraid, and in their fear they cling desperately to the darkness of their ignorance. They would have us do the same, and then we would never recall the garden nor the gate, would never look upon the faces of the great fathers and mothers who have returned to the deep."

None of it seems the least bit real, not the ridiculous things that she's saying, or all the people dressed in white, or the television crews. This scene is not even as substantial as a nightmare. It's very hot in the warehouse, and I feel dizzy and sick and wonder if I can reach an exit before I vomit.

I close my eyes, and I'm sitting in a bar in Brooklyn, watching them wade into the sea, and I'm thinking, *Some son of a bitch is standing right there taping this and no one's trying to stop them, no one's lifting a goddamn finger.*

I blink, and I'm sitting in an office in Manhattan, and the people who write my checks are asking me questions I can't answer.

"Good god, you were fucking the woman, for Christ's sake, and you're telling me you had no *idea* whatsoever that she was planning this?"

"Come on. You had to have known *something*."

"They all worshipped some sort of prehistoric fish god, that's what I heard. No one's going to buy that you didn't see this coming—"

"People have a right to know. You still believe that, don't you?"

Answers are scarce in the mass suicide of a California cult, but investigators are finding clues to the deaths by logging onto the Internet and Web sites run by the cult's members. What they're finding is a dark and confusing side of the Internet, a place where bizarre ideas and beliefs are exchanged and gain currency. Police said they have gathered a considerable amount of information on the background of the group, known as the Open Door of Night, but that it may be many weeks before the true nature of the group is finally understood. (CNN.com)

And my clumsy hands move uncertainly across her bare shoulders, my fingertips brushing the puckered chaos of scar tissue there, and she smiles for me.

On my knees in an alley, my head spinning, and the night air stinks of puke and saltwater.

"Okay, so I first heard about this from a woman I interviewed who knew the family," the man in the Radiohead T-shirt says. We're sitting on the patio of a bar in Pacific Grove, and the sun is hot and glimmers white off the bay. His name isn't important, and neither is the name of the bar. He's a student from L.A., writing a book about the Open Door of Night, and he got my e-mail address from someone in New York. He has bad teeth and smiles too much.

"This happened back in '76, the year before Jacova's mother died. Her father, he'd take them down to the beach at Moss Landing two or three times every summer. He got a lot of his writing done out there. Anyway, apparently the kid was a great swimmer, like a duck to water, but her mother never let her go very far out at that beach because there are these bad rip currents. Lots of people drown out there, surfers and shit."

He pauses and takes a couple of swallows of beer, then wipes the sweat from his forehead.

"One day, her mother's not watching, and Jacova swims too far out and gets pulled down. By the time the lifeguards get her back to shore, she's stopped breathing. The kid's turning blue, but they keep up the mouth-to-mouth and CPR, and she finally comes around. They get Jacova to the hospital up in Watsonville, and the doctors say she's fine, but they keep her for a few days anyhow, just for observation."

"She drowned," I say, staring at my own beer. I haven't taken a single sip. Beads of condensation cling to the bottle and sparkle like diamonds.

"Technically, yeah. She wasn't breathing. Her heart had stopped. But *that's* not the fucked-up part. While she's in Watsonville, she keeps telling her mother some crazy story about mermaids and sea monsters and demons, about these things trying to drag her down to the bottom of the sea and drown her, and how it wasn't an undertow at all. She's terrified, convinced that they're still after her, these monsters. Her mother wants to call in a shrink, but her father says no, fuck that, the kid's just had a bad shock, she'll be fine. Then, the second night she's in the hospital, these two nurses turn up dead. A janitor found them in a closet just down the hall from Jacova's room. And here's the thing you're not gonna believe, but I've seen the death certificates and the autopsy reports, and I swear to you this is the God's honest truth."

Whatever's coming next, I don't want to hear it. I know that I don't *need* to hear it. I turn my head and watch a sailboat out on the bay, bobbing about like a toy.

"They'd drowned, both of them. Their lungs were full of saltwater. Five miles from the goddamn ocean, but these two women drowned right there in a *broom closet*."

"And you're going to put this in your book?" I ask him, not taking my eyes off the bay and the little boat.

"Yeah," he replies. "I am. It fucking happened, man, just like I said, and I can prove it."

I close my eyes, shutting out the dazzling, bright day, and wish I'd never agreed to meet with him.

I close my eyes.

"Down there," Jacova whispers, "you will know nothing but peace, in her mansions, in the endless night of her coils."

We would be warm below the storm
In our little hideaway beneath the waves.

I close my eyes. Oh god, I've closed my eyes.

She wraps her strong, suntanned arms tightly around me and takes me down, down, down, like the lifeless body of a child caught in an undertow. And I'd go with her, like a flash I'd go, if this were anything more than a dream, anything more than an infidel's sour regret, anything more than eleven thousand words cast like a handful of sand across the face of the ocean. I would go with her, because, like a stone that has become an incarnation of mystery, she has drawn a circle around me.

BRADBURY WEATHER

STILL HAVE all the old books that Sailor left behind when she finally packed up and went looking for the Fenrir temples. I keep them in a big cargo crate with most of her other things, all that shit I haven't been able to part with. One of the books, a collection of proverbs, was written more than two hundred years ago by a Gyuto monk. It was published after his death in a Chinese prison, the manuscript smuggled out by someone or another, translated into Spanish and English, and then published in America. The monk, who did not wish to be remembered by name, wrote: "No story has a beginning, and no story has an end. Beginnings and endings may be conceived to serve a purpose, to serve a momentary and transient intent, but they are, in their truer nature, arbitrary and exist solely as a construct of the mind of man."

Sometimes, very late at night, or very early in the morning, when I should be sleeping or meditating, I read from Sailor's discarded books, and I've underlined that passage in red. If what I'm about to write down here needs an epigraph, that's probably as good as any I'll ever find, just as this beginning is as arbitrary and suitable as any I could ever choose. She left me. I couldn't have stopped her, not that I ever would have tried. I'm not that sort of woman. It was her decision, and I believed then it would have been wrong for me to interfere. But six months later, after the nightmares began, and I failed a routine mental-health evaluation, I resigned my teaching post and council seat and left to chase rumors and the ghost of her across the Xanthe Terra and Lunae Planum.

In Bhopai, a pornography dealer sold me a peep stick of Sailor dancing in a brothel. And I was told that maybe the stick had been made at Hope VII, a slatternly, backdust agradome that had seen better days and then some. I'd been up there once, on Council business, more than twenty years before; Hope's Heaven, as the locals like to call the place, sits like a boil in the steep basalt hills northwest of Tharsis Tholus. The dome has been breached and patched so many times it looks more like a quilt than a habitat.

I know a woman there. We worked together a few times, but that's ancient fucking history. These days, she runs a whorehouse, though everyone in Hope's Heaven calls her a mechanic, and who the hell am I to argue? Her bulls let me in the front door, despite my bureaucratic pedigree and the Council brands on the backs of my hands. I played the stick for her, played it straight through twice, and Jun'ko Valenzuela shrugged her narrow, tattooed shoulders, shook her head once, and then went back to stuffing the bowl of her pipe with the skunky britch weed she used to buy cheap off the shiks down in New Riyadh.

I waited for her to finish, because I'd spent enough time in the mechanic's company to know that she talked when she was ready and fuck all if that wasn't good enough. If I got impatient, if I got pushy, she'd have one of her girls handing me my hat and hustling me straight back across town to the air station, no ifs, ands, buts, or maybes. So, I sat quietly in my chair and watched while she used an antique ivory tamper to get the weed just the way she wanted it, before lighting the pipe with a match. Jun'ko exhaled, and the smoke was the color of steel, almost the same color as her long dreadlocks.

"I don't do business with the law," she said. "Least ways, not if I have a choice. But you already *knew* that, didn't you, Dorry? You knew that before you came in here."

"I'm not police," I said, starting to feel like I was reading my lines from a script I'd rehearsed until the words had lost their meaning, going through motions designed to waste my time and amuse Jun'ko. "This isn't a criminal investigation," I assured her.

"It's bloody well close enough, *perra*. You're nothing but a bunch of goddamn witches, I say, badges or no badges, the whole lot of you Council rats."

"I don't work for any corporate agency or government corpus, nor do I—"

"Maybe not," she interrupted, "but you do work *with* them," and she squinted at me across the small table, her face wreathed in smoke. "Don't deny it. They say fuck, you ask who. You tell them whatever they need to know, whenever they come around asking questions, especially if there's a percentage for your troubles."

"I already told you, this is a personal matter. I told you that before I ran the stick."

"People tell me lots of things. Most times, turns out they're lying."

"Has it ever occurred to you that just might mean you're running in the wrong circles?" I asked, the question slipping out before I let myself think better of it. There she was trying to pick a fight, looking for any excuse to have me thrown out of her place, and there I was playing along, like I thought I'd ever get a second chance.

"Oh, the thought has crossed my mind," she said calmly around a mouthful of britch smoke, smiled, and the sinuous gold and crimson Chinese dragon tattooed on her left shoulder uncoiled and flashed its gilded eyes. "Why are you *asking* me if I've seen this little share crop of yours?" Jun'ko said, and she motioned at the peep stick with her pipe. "It's obvious that was scratched here, and nothing happens in my place I *don't* know about."

"Was she working for you?"

The dragon on Jun'ko's shoulder showed me teeth like daggers.

"Yeah, Dorry. She worked for me."

"When'd she leave?"

"I didn't say she had."

"But she's not here now—"

"No, she's not," Jun'ko Valenzuela said and stared into the softly glowing bowl of her pipe. "That one, *conchita* cashed out and bought herself a nook on a freighter that came through Heaven a couple months back. One of those big transpolar wagons, hauling ore down from the Acidalia."

"Did this freighter happen to have a name?"

"Oh, no damn doubt about it," she smiled and emptied the bowl of her pipe into an ashtray cut from cobalt-blue glass. "I just don't happen to remember what it was."

"Or where it was headed."

"Lots of places, most likely."

"She's looking for the Fenrir," I said, saying too much, and Jun'ko laughed and tapped her pipe against the edge of the ashtray.

"Jesus, Joseph, and Buddha, you know how to pick 'em, Dorry."

"She never told you that, that she was looking for the temples?"

"Hell, no. She kept to herself, mostly. And if I'd known she was hodging for the wolf, I'd never have put her skinny ass on the menu. *Mierda*. You listen to me. *Sácate el dedo del culo*, and you get yourself right the fuck back to Herschel City. Count yourself slick all this Jane cadged was your heart."

"Is that what you'd do, Jun'ko?"

She looked up at me, her hard brown eyes almost black in the dim light, and the dragon on her shoulder closed its mouth. "I got better sense than to crawl in bed with grey pilgrims," she said. "And you're officially out of time, Dorry. I trust you know the way back down to the street?"

"I think I can figure it out."

"That's 'cause you're such a goddamn smart lady. Of course, maybe you'd like to have a drink and sample the product first," and she nodded towards a couple of girls standing at the bar. "I'll even see you get a little discount, just to show there's no hard feelings."

"Thanks, but—"

"—she took your *huevos* with her when she left."

"I suppose that's one way of putting it," I replied, and she laughed again and began refilling her pipe.

"That's a goddamn shame," Jun'ko said and struck a match. "But you watch yourself out there. Way I hear it told, the Fenrir got more eyes than God. And they say the wolf, he never sleeps."

When I stood up, she pointed at the two girls again. They were both watching me now, and one of them raised her skirt to show me that she had a dick. Jun'ko Valenzuela puffed at her pipe and shook her head. When she talked, smoke leaked from her mouth and from the jaws of the dragon tattoo. "Things ain't always what they seem. You don't forget that, Dorry. Not if you want to find this little *coño* and live to regret it."

The sun was already starting to slip behind Tharsis Tholus by the time I got back to the dingy, dusty sleeper that I'd rented near the eastern locks. The storm that had begun just before dawn still howled down the slopes of the great volcano, extinct two billion years if you trust the geologists, and battered the walls of Hope's Heaven, hammering the thin foil skin of the dome. I've always hated the western highlands, and part of me wanted nothing more than to take the mechanic's advice and go home. I imagined hauling the crate full of Sailor's belongings down the hall to the lift, pictured myself leaving it all piled in the street. It'd be easy, I told myself. It would be the easiest thing I'd ever done.

I ate, and, when the night came, I sat a little while in the darkness—I hadn't paid for electric—gazing out the sleeper's tiny window at the yellow runner lights dotting the avenue below, the street that led back up to Jun'ko's whorehouse or down to the docks, depending whether you turned left or turned right, north or south. When I finally went to bed, the nightmares found me, as they almost always do, and for a while, at least, I wasn't alone.

Just before dawn, I was awakened by a knock at the door, and I lay staring up into the gloom, looking for the ceiling, trying to recall where the hell I was and how I'd gotten myself there. Then I remembered smirking Jun'ko and her kinetitatts, and I remembered Hope VII, and then I remembered everything else. Whoever was out in the corridor knocked again, harder than before. I reached for my pants and vest, lying together on the floor near the foot of the cot.

"Who's there?" I shouted, hoping it was nothing more than someone banging on the wrong door, a drunk or an honest mistake. The only person in town whom I'd had business with was the mechanic, and as far as I was concerned, that business was finished.

"My name is Mikaela," the woman on the other side of the door called back. "I have information about Sailor. I may be able to help you find her. Please, open the door."

I paused, my vest still unfastened, my pants half on, half off. I realized that my mouth had gone dry, and my heart was racing. Maybe I'd pissed old Jun'ko off just a little more than I'd thought. Perhaps, in return, I was about to get the worst beating of my life, or perhaps word had gotten around the dome that the stranger from the east was an easy mark.

"Is that so?" I asked. "Who sent you?" And when she didn't answer, I asked again. "Mikaela, *who* sent you here?"

"This would be easier, Councilor, if you'd open the door. I might have been followed."

"All the more reason for me to keep it shut," I told her, groping about in the dark for anything substantial enough to serve as a weapon, cursing myself for being too cheap to pay the five credits extra for electric.

"I'm one of the mechanic's girls," she said, almost whispering now, "but I swear she didn't send me. Please, there isn't time for this."

My right hand closed around an aluminum juice flask I'd bought in one of Heaven's market plazas the day before. It wasn't much, hardly better than nothing, but it'd have to do. I finished dressing, then crossed the tiny room and stood with my hand on the lockpad.

"I have a gun," I lied, just loud enough I was sure the woman would hear me.

"I don't," she replied. "Open the door. *Please.*"

I gripped the flask a little more tightly, took a deep breath, and punched in the twelve-digit security code. The door slid open immediately, whining on its rusty tracks, and the woman slipped past me while I was still half-blind and blinking at the flickering lamps set into the walls of the corridor.

"Shut the door," she said, and I did, then turned back to the darkened room, to the place where her voice was coming from. Yellow and white splotches drifted to and fro before my eyes, abstract fish in a lightless sea.

"Why is it so dark in here?" she asked, impatiently.

"Same reason I opened the door for you. I'm an idiot."

"Isn't there a window? All these nooks have windows," and I remembered that I'd closed and locked the shutters before going to bed, so the morning sun wouldn't wake me.

"There's a window, but you don't need to see me to explain why you're here," I said, figuring the darkness might at least even the odds if she were lying.

"Christ, you're a nervous nit."

"Why are you *here?*" I asked, trying to sound angry when I was mostly scared and disoriented, and I took a step backwards, setting my shoulders squarely against the door.

"I told you. Sailor and me, we was sheba, until she paid off Jun'ko and headed south."

"South?" I asked. "The freighter was traveling south?"

"That's what she told me. Sailor, I mean. But, look here, Councilor, before I say any more, that quiff left owing me forty creds, and I'm not exactly in a position to play grace and let it slip."

"And what makes you think I'm in a position to pay off her debts, Mikaela? What makes you think I *would?*"

"You're a *titled* woman," she replied, and the tone in her voice made her feelings about the Council perfectly clear. "You've got it. And if you don't, you can get it. And you'll pay me, because nobody comes all the way the hell to Hope's Heaven looking for someone unless they want to find that someone awfully fucking bad. Am I wrong?"

"No," I sighed, because I didn't feel like arguing with her. "You're not wrong. But that doesn't mean you're telling the truth, either."

"About Sailor?"

"About anything."

"She told me about the Fenrir," the woman named Mikaela said. "It's almost all she ever talked about."

"That doesn't prove anything. That's nothing you couldn't have overheard at Jun'ko's yesterday evening."

Mikaela sighed. "I'm going to open the damned window," she said. "I hope you don't mind," and a moment later I heard her struggling with the bolt, heard it turning, and then the shutters spiraled open to reveal the easy, pinkish light of false dawn. Mikaela was prettier than I'd expected, and a little older. Her hair was pulled back in a long braid, and the light through the window revealed tiny wrinkles around her eyes. The face seemed familiar, and then I realized she was one of the women who'd been standing at the bar in Jun'ko's, the one who'd shown me that she had a penis. She sat down on the cot and pointed at the flask in my hand.

"Is *that* your gun?" she asked.

"I need to know whether or not you're telling me the truth," I said. "I don't think that's unreasonable, considering the circumstances."

"I'm a whore. That doesn't necessarily make me a thief and a liar."

"I need something, Mikaela. More than your word."

"I'm actually a pretty good fuck," she said, as though it was exactly what I was waiting for her to say, and lay down on the cot. "You know, I'd wager I'm a skid better fuck than Sailor Li ever was. We could be sheba, you and me, Councilor. I'd go back to Herschel City with you, and you could forget all about her. If she wants to commit suicide, then, hell—"

"Something you couldn't have gotten from Jun'ko," I pressed. She rolled her eyes, which I could see were blue. There aren't many women on Mars with blue eyes.

"Yeah," she said, almost managing to sound disappointed, and clicked her tongue once against the roof of her mouth. "How's this? Sailor was with you for five years, if you count the three months after you started fucking her before you asked her to move into your flat. You lost two teeth in a fight when you were still just a kid, because someone called your birth mother an offworlder bitch, and sometimes the implants ache before a storm. The first time Sailor brought up the Fenrir, you showed her a stick from one of the containment crews and told her if she ever mentioned the temples again, you'd ask her to leave. When she *did* mention them again, you hit her so hard you almost—"

"You've made your point," I said, cutting her off. She smiled, a smug, satisfied smile, and nodded her head.

"I usually do, Dorry." She patted the edge of the cot with her left hand. "Why don't you come back to bed."

"I'm not going to fuck you," I replied and set the aluminum flask down on a shelf near the door. "I'll pay off whatever she owes you. You'll tell me what you know. But that's as far as it goes."

"Sure, if that's the way you want it." Mikaela shut her eyes. "Just thought I'd be polite and offer you a poke."

"You said the freighter was headed south."

"No. I said *Sailor* said it was headed south. And before I say more, I want half what I'm owed."

My eyes were beginning to adjust to the dim light getting in through the window, and I had no trouble locating the hook where I'd left my jacket hanging the night before. I removed my purse from an inside pocket, unfastened the clasp, and took out my credit tab. "How do you want to do this?" I asked, checking my balance, wondering how many more months I could make the dwindling sum last.

"Subdermal," she said. "Nobody out here carries around tabs, especially not whores."

I keyed in the amount, setting the exchange limit at twenty, and handed Mikaela the tab. She pressed it lightly to the inside of her left forearm, and the chip beneath her flesh subtracted twenty credits from my account. Then she handed the tab back to me, and I tried not to notice how warm it was.

"So, she told you the freighter was headed south," I said, anxious to have this over and done with and get this girl out of the sleeper.

"Yeah, that's what she said." Mikaela rolled over onto her right side, and her face was lost in the shadows. "The freighter's a Shimizu-Mochizuki ship, one of the old 500-meter ore buckets. You don't see many of those anymore. This one was hauling ice from a mine in the Chas Boreale to a refinery in Dry Lake, way the hell out on the Solis Planum."

"I know where Dry Lake is," I said, wondering how much of this she was inventing, and I sat down on the floor by the sleeper's door. "You've got an awfully good memory."

"Yes," she replied. "I do, don't I?"

"Do you also remember the freighter's name?"

"The *Oryoku Maru*, as a matter of fact."

"I can check these things out."

"I fully expect you to."

I watched her a minute or more, the angles and curves of her silhouette, wishing I had a pipe full of something strong, though I hadn't smoked in years. The shadows and thin wash of dawn between us seemed thicker than mere light and the absence of light.

"Does she know where she's going?" I asked, wishing I could have kept those words back.

"She *thinks* so. Anyhow, she heard there'd be a Fenrir priest on the freighter. She thought she could get it to talk with her."

"Why did she think that?"

"Sailor can be a very persuasive woman," Mikaela said, and laughed. "Hell, I don't know. Ask her that when you find her."

"She thinks there's a temple somewhere on the Solis?"

"She wouldn't have told me that, and I never bothered to ask. I don't have the mark," and Mikaela held out her left arm for me to see. "She fucked me, and she liked to talk, but she's a pilgrim now, and I'm not."

"Did you try to stop her?"

"Not really. I told her she was fucking gowed, looking for salvation with that bunch of devils, but we're all free out here, Councilor. We choose our own fates."

Down on the street, something big roared and rattled past, its engines sounding just about ready for the scrapyard. Probably a harvester drone on its way to the locks and the fields beyond the dome. The sun was rising, and Hope VII was waking up around us.

"There's something else," Mikaela said, "something she wanted me to show you."

"She knew that I was coming?"

"She *hoped* you were coming. I should have hated her for that, but, like I said—"

"—you're all free out here."

"Bloody straight. Free as the goddamned dust," she replied. There was a little more light coming in the window now, morning starting to clear away the dregs of night, and I could see that Mikaela was smiling despite the bitterness in her voice.

"Did you want to go with her?"

"Are you fucking cocked? I wouldn't have gotten on that freighter with her for a million creds, not if she was right about there being a fucking Fenny priest aboard."

"So, what did she want you to show me?"

"Are you going after her?" Mikaela asked, ignoring my question, offering her own instead, and she sat up and turned her face towards the open window.

"Yes," I told her. "That's why I'm here."

"Then you *must* be cocked. You must be mad as a wind shrake."

"I'm starting to think so. What did she want you to show me, Mikaela?"

"Most people call me Mickie," she said.

And I thought about paying her the other twenty and letting her go back to Jun'ko's or wherever it was she slept. There wasn't much of her street-smart bluster left, and it was easy enough to see that she was scared. It was just as easy to figure out why.

"My mum, she was a good left-footer," Mikaela said. "God, Baby Jesus, the Pope, and St. Teresa, all that tieg crap. And she used to tell me and my sisters that only the *evil* people have any cause to *fear* evil, but what'd she know? She never even left the dome where she was born. She never spent time out on the frontiers, never saw the crazy shit goes off out here. All the evil *she* ever imagined could be chased away with rosary beads and a few Hail Marys."

"Is it something you're afraid to show me, Mickie?" I asked, and she laughed and quickly hid her face in her hands. I didn't say anything else for a while, just sat there with my back to the door of the sleeper, watching the world outside the window grow brighter by slow degrees, waiting until she stopped crying.

I wish I could say that Sailor had lied, or at least exaggerated, when she told Mikaela that I'd beaten her. I wish it with the last, stingy speck of my dignity, the last vestiges of my sense of self-loathing. But if what I'm writing down here is to be the truth, the truth as complete as I might render it, then that's one of the things I have to admit, to myself, to whoever might someday read this. To God, if I'm so unfortunate and the universe so dicked over that she or he or it actually exists.

So, yes, I beat Sailor.

She'd been gone for several days, which wasn't unusual. She would do that sometimes, if we seemed to be wearing on one another. And it was mid-Pisces, deep into the long season of dust storms and endless wind, and we were both on edge. That time of year, just past the summer solstice, all of Herschel seems set on edge, the air ripe with static and raw nerves. I was busy with my duties at the university and, of course, with council business, and I doubt that I even took particular notice of her absence. I've never minded sleeping alone or taking my meals by myself. If I missed her, then I missed the conversation, the sex, the simple contact with another human body.

She showed up just after dark one evening, and I could tell from the way she was dressed that she hadn't been at her mothers' or at the scholars' hostel near the north gate, the two places she usually went when we needed time apart. She was dirty, her hair coppery and stiff with dust, and she was wearing her long coat and heavy boots. So I guessed she'd been traveling outside the dome; maybe she'd taken the tunnel sled up to Gale or all the way down to Molesworth. I was in my study, going over notes for the next day's lectures, and she came in and kissed me. Her lips were chapped and rough, faintly gritty, and I told her she needed a shower.

"Yeah, that'd be nice," she said. "If you stuck me right now, I think I'd bleed fucking dust."

"You were outside?" I asked, turning back to my desk. "That's very adventuresome of you."

"Did you miss me?"

"They've had me so busy, I hardly even noticed you were gone."

She laughed, the way she laughed whenever she wasn't sure that I was joking. Then I heard her unbuckling her boots, and afterwards she was quiet for a bit. Two or three minutes, maybe. When I glanced up, she'd taken off her coat and gloves and rolled her right shirt sleeve up past the elbow.

"Don't be angry," she said. "Please."

"What are you on about now?" I asked, and then I saw the fevery red marks on the soft underside of her forearm. It might have only been a rash, except for the almost perfect octagon formed by the intersection of welts or the three violet pustules at the center of it all. I'd seen the mark before, and I knew exactly what it meant.

"At least hear me out," she said. "I had to know—"

"*What?*" I demanded, getting to my feet, pushing the chair roughly across the floor. "*What* precisely did you have to fucking *know*, Sailor?"

"If it's true. If there's something more—"

"More than what? Jesus fucking Christ. You let them touch you. You let those sick fucks *inside* of you."

"More than *this*," she said, retreating a step or two towards the doorway and the hall, retreating from me. "More than night and goddamn day. More than getting old and dying and no one even giving a shit that I was ever alive."

"How long's it been?" I asked, and she shook her head and flashed me a look like she didn't understand what I meant. "Since contact, Sailor. How long has it been since *contact?*"

"That doesn't matter. I wouldn't take the serum."

"We're not going to fucking argue about this. *Yes*, you're going to take the serum. We're going to the clinic right now, and you're going to start the serum *tonight*. If you're real bloody lucky, it might not be too late—"

"*Stop it!*" she hissed. "This isn't your decision, Dorry. It's my body. It's my goddamn life," and that's when she started crying. And that's when I hit her.

That's when I started hitting her.

There's no point pretending that I remember how many times I struck her. I only stopped when I saw the blood from her broken nose, splattered on the wall of my study. I like to believe that it wouldn't have happened if she hadn't started crying, those tears like a shield, like a weapon she'd fashioned from her weakness. I've always loathed the sight of tears, for no sane reason, and I like to think everything would have played out some other way if she just hadn't started crying. But that's probably bullshit, and even if it isn't, it wouldn't matter, would it? So, whatever I said earlier about not being the sort of woman to interfere in another's decisions, forget that. Remember this, instead.

Sailor left that night, and I haven't seen or heard from her since. I waited for a summons to appear before the quarter magistrate on charges of assault, but the summons never came, and one day I returned home from my morning classes to find that most of her clothes were gone. I never found out if she retrieved them herself or if someone did it for her. A couple of weeks later, I learned that three Fenrir priests had been arrested near Kepler City, and that the district marshals suspected they'd passed near Molesworth and Herschel earlier in Pisces, that they'd been camped outside Mensae sometime back in Capricorn.

And that morning in Hope VII, all those months later, I sat and listened to Jun'ko's billygirl sobbing because she was afraid, and I dug my nails into my palms until the pain was all that mattered.

———————

"I think you must miss her," Mikaela said, looking back over her left shoulder at me, answering a question I hadn't asked. "To have left Herschel and come all the way out here, to go poking around Jun'ko's place. Lady, no one comes to Heaven, not if she can help it."

"I've been here before," I said. "When I was young, about your age."

"Yeah, that's what Jun'ko was telling me," she replied, and I wanted to ask what else the mechanic might have told her, but I didn't. I was following Mikaela down a street so narrow it might as well have been an alleyway, three or four blocks over from the dome's main thoroughfare. Far above us, sensors buried in the framework of the central span were busy calibrating the skylights to match the rising sun outside. But some servo or relay-drive bot responsible for this sector of Hope VII had been down for the last few months, according to Mikaela. So we walked together in the lingering gloom, the patchy frost crunching softly beneath our feet, while the rest of the dome brightened and warmed. Once or twice, I noticed someone watching us through a smudgy window, suspicious eyes set in wary, indistinct faces, but there was no one on the street yet. The lack of traffic added to my unease and the general sense of desolation and decay; this was hardscrabble, even by the standards of Hope's Heaven. That far back from town center, almost everything was adobe brick and pressed sand-tile, mostly a jumble of warehouses, garages, and machine shops, with a shabby handful of old-line modular residential structures stacked about here and there. If Mikaela were leading me into an ambush, she couldn't have chosen a better setting.

"You hang close to me, Councilor," she said. "People around here, they don't care so much for outsiders. It's a bad part of town."

"You mean to say there's a *good* part?" I asked, and she laughed, then stopped and peered down a cross street, rubbing her hands together for warmth. Her breath steamed in the morning air.

"No," she said. "I sure wouldn't go so far as to say that. But there's bad and there's worse." She frowned and looked back the way we'd come.

"Is something wrong?" I asked. She shook her head, then pointed east, towards the cross street.

"It's that way, just a little piece farther," she said, and then she changed the subject. "Is it true you've been offworld? That's what Jun'ko said, that you've been up to Eos Station, that you've seen men. Men from Earth."

I nodded my head, still looking in the direction she'd pointed. "It's true. But that was a long time ago."

"What were they like?" she asked, and I shrugged.

"Different," I replied, "but not half so different as most of us think. Two eyes, two hands, one mouth, a dick," and I jabbed a thumb at her skirt. "More like some of us than others."

It was a crude comment, one I never would have made if I hadn't been so nervous, and I half expected her to get pissed or something. But Mikaela only kicked at a loose paving tile and rubbed her hands together a little harder, a little faster.

"Yeah, well, that was Jun'ko's idea," she said. "She even paid the surgeon. Claimed I wasn't pretty enough, that I needed something special, you know, something exotic, if I was gonna work out of her place. It's not so bad. Like I said, I'm a pretty good fuck. Better than I was before."

"No regrets, then?"

She made a half-amused, snorting noise, wiped her nose on the sleeve of her jacket, and stared at her shoes. "I was born here," she said. "What the hell would I do with a thing like regret?"

"When are you going to tell me what's waiting for me down there, Mickie?" I asked, and she almost smiled.

"Sailor said you'd be like this."

"Like what?"

"She said you weren't a very trusting person. She said you had a nasty habit of stabbing people in the back before they could beat you to it."

I suppose that was payback for the remark about her penis, nothing I didn't have coming, but it made me want to slap her. Before I could think of a reply, she was moving again, walking quickly away from me down the side street. I thought about turning around and heading straight back to the station. It was still three long hours until the next zep, but I could try to get a secure uplink and see what there was to learn about the *Oryoku Maru*. Following the whore seemed like a lazy way to commit suicide.

I followed her, anyway.

A couple of minutes later, we ducked through a low archway into what appeared to be an abandoned repair shop. It was dark inside, almost too dark to see, and even colder than it had been out on the street. The air stank of spent engine oil and hydrosol, dust and mildew and rat shit, and the place was crowded with the disassembled, rusting skeletons of harvesters and harrow rigs. They loomed around us and hung from ceiling hoists, broken, forgotten beasts with sickle teeth.

"Watch your step, Councilor," Mikaela warned, calling back to me after I tripped over some piece of machinery or another and almost stumbled into an open garage pit. I paused long enough to catch my breath, long enough to whisper a thankful prayer and be sure I hadn't broken my ankle.

"We need a fucking torch," I muttered, my voice much louder than I'd expected, magnified and thrown back at me by the darkness pressing in around us.

"Well, I don't have one," she said, "so you'll just have to be more careful."

She took my hand and guided me out of the repair bay, along a pitch-black corridor that turned left, then right, then left again, before finally ending in a dim pool of light spilling in through a number of ragged, fist-sized holes in the roof. I imagined it was sunlight, though it wasn't, of course, imagined it was warm against my upturned face, though it wasn't that, either.

"Down here," she said, and I turned towards her voice, blinking back orange and violet afterimages. We were standing at the top of a stairwell.

"I hid it when Sailor left," Mikaela said. "Jun'ko has our rooms tossed once or twice a month, regular as clockwork, so I couldn't leave it in the house. But I figured it'd be safe here. When I was a kid, my sister and I used to play hide-and-seek in this place."

"You have a sister?" I asked, and she started down the stairs without me, taking them two at a time despite the dark. I hurried to catch up, more afraid of being left alone in this place than wherever she might be leading me.

"Yeah," she called back. "I've got a little sister. She's out there somewhere. Sheba'd up with a guild mason down in Arsia Mons, last I heard. But we don't talk much these days. She got sick on Allah and doesn't approve of whoring anymore."

We reached the bottom of the stairs, and I glanced back up at the patch of imitation daylight we'd left at the top. "How much farther, Mickie?" I asked, trying hard to sound calm, trying to sound confident, trying desperately to bury my anxiety in a pantomime of equipoise. But the darkness was quickly becoming more than I could handle, so much darkness crammed into the gap between the walls and floor and ceiling. It was becoming inconceivable that this place might somehow simultaneously contain so much darkness and ourselves. *I'm a little claustrophobic*, I pretended to have said, so that the mechanic's girl would understand and get this the hell over and done with. Past the bottom of the stairs, the air was damp and smelled of mold and stagnant water, mushrooms and rotting cardboard. I was sweating now, despite the cold.

"She made me promise that I'd keep it safe," Mikaela said, as if she hadn't heard my question or had simply chosen to ignore it. "I'm not really used to people trusting me with things. Not with things that matter to—"

"How much *farther?*" I asked again, more insistent than before. "We need to hurry this up, or I'll miss my flight."

"Here," she said. "Right there, on your left," and when I turned my head that way, there was the faintest chartreuse glow, like some natural fungal phosphorescence, a glow that I could have sworn hadn't been there only a few seconds before. "Just inside the doorway, on the table," Mikaela said.

I took a deep breath of the fetid air and stepped past her through an opening leading into what might once have been a storeroom or maintenance locker. The glow became much brighter than it had been out in the corridor, illuminating the bare concrete walls, an M5 proctor droid that had been stripped raw and left for dead, and the intestine tangle of sagging pipes above my head. The yellow-green light was coming from a five- or six-liter translucent plastic catch cylinder, something that had probably been manufactured as part of a dew-farm's cistern. And I stood staring at the pale thing floating inside the cylinder—not precisely dead because it had probably never been precisely alive—a wad of hair and mottled flesh, bone and the scabby shell of a half-formed exoskeleton.

"She said it was yours, Dorry," Mikaela whispered from somewhere behind me. "She said she didn't know, when she took the mark, didn't know she was pregnant."

I said something. I honestly can't remember what.

It hardly matters.

The thing in the cylinder twitched and opened what I hadn't realized was an eye. It was all pupil, that eye, and blacker than space.

"She lost it before she even got here," the whore said, "when she was working up in Sytinskakya. She couldn't have taken it with her to the temples, and I promised her that I'd keep it safe. She thought you might want to take it back with you."

I turned away from the unborn thing, which might or might not have seen my face, pushing my way roughly past Mikaela and back out into the corridor. The darkness there seemed almost kind after the light from the catch cylinder, and I let it swallow me whole as I ran. I only fell twice or maybe three times, tripping over my own feet and sprawling hard on sand-tile or steel, then right back up in an instant, blindly making my way to the stairwell and the cluttered repair shop above, and, finally, to the perpetually shadowed street. I stopped and looked back then, breathless and faint and sick to my belly, pausing only long enough to see that Jun'ko's girl hadn't followed me. By the time I reached the transfer station at the lower end of Avenue South Eight, the morning was fading towards noon, and what I'd seen below Hope's Heaven seemed hardly as substantial, hardly as thinkable, as any woman's guilty dreams of Hell.

I have Sailor's book of proverbs from the cargo crate open on the table in front of me, the one written by the twentieth-century Tibetan monk. There's a passage here on dreams, one of the passages I've underlined in red, which reads: "The pathway to Nirvana is a road along which the traveler penetrates the countless illusions of his waking mind, his dreams and dreamless sleep. There must be a full and final awakening from all illusion, waking and dreaming. By many forms of meditation a man may at last achieve this necessary process of waking up in his life and in his dreams and nightmares. He may follow Vipassanā in search of lasting, uninterrupted self-awareness, finally catching himself in the very act of losing himself in the cacophonous labyrinth of his thoughts and fantasies and the obscuring tides of emotion and sexual impulse that work to impede awakening."

I like to think that I know what most of that means, but, then again, I'm an arrogant woman, and admitting ignorance galls me. I may not have the faintest clue.

On the long flight from Hope VII, from the ages-dead caldera of Tharsis Tholus towards the greater, but equally spent, craters of Pavonis Mons and Arsia Mons, skirting the sheer, narrow fissures of the Noctis Fossae and the dismal mining operations scattered like old scabs out along the edges of that district, as the zep drifted high above the rust-colored world, I dozed, losing myself in those obscuring tides. It's not the same dream every time. I'm not sure I believe in dreams which recur with such absolute perfection that they're always the same dream. So, then, this is a collective caricature of the dreams that I've had since Sailor left, an approximation of the dream I must have had as the drone of the zep's engines answered my exhaustion and dragged me down to sleep.

I'm standing outside the vast, impenetrable dome of Herschel City, locked safely inside my pressure suit, breathing clean, fresh air untainted by the fine red dust blowing down from Elysium. I can hear the wind through my comms, wild and terrible as any mythological banshee long since exiled here from Earth. In the distance, far across the plain, I can see a procession, a single-file line of robed figures and their cragged assortment of sandrovers and skidwagons. A great cloud of dust rises up behind them and hangs like a caul, despite the wind. *Impervious* to the wind. And I am filled with such complete dread, a fear like none that I have ever known, but I take one step forward. There's music coming through my helmet, flutes and violins and the *thump-thump-thump* of drums. I know that music at once, though I've never heard it before. I know that music instinctively.

"They're not for you, Dorry," Sailor says, and I turn, turning my back on the procession, and she's standing there with her left hand on the shoulder of my suit. She isn't wearing one herself. She isn't wearing much of anything, and the dust has painted her skin muted shades of terra-cotta. She might be another race entirely, another species, something alien or angelic or ghostly that I have fucked and loved thinking she was only a human girl.

"They would never let you follow," she says. "Not as you are now."

I don't wonder how she can breathe, or how her body is enduring the bitter cold or the low pressure or radiation. I only want to hold her, because it's been so long, and I never imagined I would really see her again. But then she pushes me away, frowning, that look she used to get whenever she thought I was being particularly stupid. She licks her red-brown lips, and her tongue is violet.

"No," she says, sounding almost angry, almost hateful. "You *hit* me, Dorry. And I don't need that shit. If I needed that shit, I'd have stayed with fucking Erin Antimisiaris. If I needed to be someone's punch hound, I'd go hunt up my asshole swap-mother and let *her* have another go at me."

She says other, more condemning things, and I say nothing at all in my defense, because I *know* she's telling the truth, laying it all out for me as the sun crawls feebly across the wide china sky. And then, slowly, grain by grain, the wind takes her apart, weathers her away until her face is hardly recognizable, a granite statue that might have stood at this spot a thousand years; her body has begun to crumble, too, reclaimed by the ground beneath our feet. I turn once more towards the procession, but it has passed beyond the range of my vision.

And then we are lying in my bed, and the air smells like fresh cinnamon and clean linen, a musky, faint hint of sweat and sex, and Sailor lights her pipe. I wonder how long I've been sleeping, how long the dream could have lasted, and as I turn to tell her about it all—an act of sharing secrets to rob the nightmare of its claws—the room dissolves around me, and I'm standing alone at the edge of a crater so wide I can see only a little ways across it. I'm facing west, I think, and the sky is a roiling kaleidoscope of clotted, oily grays and blues, blacks and deep purples, no sky that any woman has ever seen on Mars. *That's the color of nausea*, I think. *That's the color of plague and decay.*

I hear the music again, then. The pipes. The bows drawn across taut strings. The drums sounding out loudly across the flat, monotonous floor of the impact crater. A billion years ago, something fell screaming from the sky and buried itself here, broke apart in a storm of fire and vaporized stone, and here it has been waiting. It was here when the progenitors of humankind were mere protoplasmic slime clinging desperately to the sanctuary of abyssal hydrothermal vents. It was waiting when our australopithecine foremothers first looked up and noticed the red star hanging above African skies. It was here when men finally began to send their probes and landers, waiting while the human invasion was planned and executed. But not waiting patiently, because nothing so burned and shattered and hungry can wait patiently, but waiting all the same, because it has been left no choice. It has been cast down, gravity's prisoner, and I look back once, looking back at the wastes stretching out behind me, before I begin the long, painful climb down to the place where the music is coming from.

2.

I was having a bowl of sage tea, the strong stuff the airlines serve, when I first noticed the journalist. She was sitting across the aisle from me, a few rows nearer the front of the passenger cabin, and she made no attempt to hide the fact that she was watching me. Her red hair was tied back in the high, braided topknot that has become so fashionable in the eastern cities, held up with an elaborate array of hematite and onyx pins. She was wearing a stiff brown MBS uniform, and when she saw me looking at her, she nodded and stood up.

"Fuck me," I muttered and then turned to stare out the portal, through thin, hazy clouds at the barren landscape fifteen hundred feet below the zep. We'd already made the stop at the new Keeslar-Nguyen depot near Arsia Mons and, afterwards, the airship had turned east, heading out across the Solis Planum.

"May I sit with you, Councilor?" the journalist asked a few moments later, and when I looked up, she was pointing at the empty seat opposite me. She was smiling, that practiced smile to match the casual tone of her voice, all of it meant to put me at ease and none of it doing anything of the sort.

"Do I really have any say in the matter?"

Her smile almost faded; not quite, but it faltered just enough that I could see she was nervous, her confidence a thin act, and I wondered how long it had been since the net had given this one her implants and press docs and sent her off into the world. I think I was even a little insulted that I didn't rate someone more seasoned.

"You must have known I was coming," she said. "You must have known *someone* would come."

"I know I'm going to die one day, and I'm not so happy about that, either."

"Why don't we skip this part, Councilor?" she asked, sitting down. "I'm just doing my job. I only want to ask you a few questions."

"Even though you know ahead of time that I don't want to answer them." I sipped at my tea, which was growing cold, and looked out the portal again.

"Yes. Something like that," she replied, and I knew that the cameras floating on her corneas, jacked into her forebrain and the MBS satellites, were relaying every word that passed between us, every move I made, to the network's clearcast facilities in Herschel. The footage would be trawled, filtered, and edited as we spoke and then broadcast seconds after our conversation ended.

"Have you ever been out this far?" I asked.

"No," she said, and I allowed myself to be impressed that the question hadn't thrown her. "Before this jaunt, I've never been any farther west than the foundries at Ma'adim Vallis."

"And how are you liking it so far, the frontiers?"

"It's big," she said, and cleared her throat. "Too damned big."

I drank the last of my tea and set the bowl down on the empty seat to my right; one of the attendants would be along soon to take it away.

"You were at that whorehouse in Hope VII," she said, "looking for your lover, Sailor Li."

"Is that so? Tell me, whoever the hell you are, is this what's passing for investigative work at MBS these days?" I asked and laughed. It felt good to laugh, and I tried to remember the last time I'd done it. I couldn't.

"My name is Ariadne," she said and sighed. "Ariadne Vaughn. You know, it might be in your best interest to try not to be such an asshole."

"And why is that, Ariadne?"

She stared at me a long second or two, then rubbed hard at the bridge of her nose like maybe it had started to itch. She sighed again and glanced at the portal. She couldn't have been much older than thirty, thirty-five at the outside, and I realized I wanted to fuck her. I suppose that should have elicited in me some sort of shame or disgust with myself, but it didn't.

"I asked you a simple question, Ariadne. Why might it be in my best interest not to be such an asshole."

107

"Because I might know where Sailor is," she said. "All we want is the story. You're the first council member known to have involvement with the Fenrir. Answer a few questions, and I'll tell you what I know."

My mouth had gone dry, and I wished I had another bowl of the hot, too-strong tea. "Sailor's the pilgrim here," I told the journalist, "not me. If you think otherwise, you're sorely mistaken."

"The way the network sees it, if your lover's chasing the wolf and *you're* chasing your lover, that places you pretty damned close to—"

"I can have you put off at the next port," I said, interrupting her. "I still have that much authority."

"And how's that going to look, Councilor?" she asked, beginning to sound more confident now, and she leaned towards me and lowered her voice. I caught the sour-sweet scent of slake on her breath and realized why she'd been rubbing her nose. "I mean, unless this little walkabout of yours is some sort of suicide slag," she said, almost whispering.

"You're a junkie," I replied, as indifferently, as matter-of-factly, as I could manage. "Does the network buy it for you, the slake? With that much circuitry in your skull, I know *they* must know you're dragging."

Ariadne Vaughn blinked her left eye, shutting down the feed.

"I'm just wondering how it all works out," I continued. "Does the MBS have a special arrangement with the cops to protect junkie remotes from prosecution?"

"They warned me you were a cunt," she said.

"They did their homework. Good for them."

Then she didn't say anything for a minute or two. One of the attendants came by, took my empty bowl, and I ordered another, this time with a shot of brandy.

"Are you lying to me about Sailor?" I asked the journalist, and she narrowed her dark eyes, eyes the color of polished agate, then shook her head and tried to look offended. "Because if you *are*," I said, "after what I've been through and seen the past eight months, you ought to understand that I'd have no problem whatsoever with making a few calls that'll land you in flush so fast you won't even have time for one last fix before they plug you into scrub." I stabbed an index finger at her nostrils, and she flinched.

"That's a fact, little girl. You fuck me on this, and once the plumbers are finished, there won't be enough of you left for the network gats to bother salvaging the hardware. Are we absolutely clear?"

"Yes, Councilor," she said very softly, rubbing at her nose again. "I understand you very well."

I looked down the long aisle towards the zeppelin's small kitchen, wishing the attendant would hurry up with my tea and brandy. "Then ask me your questions, Ariadne Vaughn," and I glanced at my watch. "You have ten minutes."

"Ten *minutes?*" she balked. "No, Councilor, I'm afraid I'll need quite a bit more than that if—"

"Nine minutes and fifty-four seconds," I replied, and she nodded and blinked her agate-colored camera eyes on again.

Sometimes, in the dreams, I actually reach the floor of the crater. And I see it all with such clarity, a clarity that doesn't fade upon waking, a clarity such that I have sometimes been tempted to identify the crater as a real place, existing beyond the limits of my recurring nightmares. I take down a chart or my big globe and put a finger *there*, or *there*, or *there*. It might be Lomonosov, far out and alone on the Vastitas Borealis. Or it might be Kunowsky farther to the south, smaller, but just as desolate. I was once almost certain that it was the vast, weathered scar of Huygens. No one ever goes there, that pockmarked wasteland laid out above the dead inland sea of the Hellas Planitia. Not even the prospectors and dirt mags make it that far west, and if they do, they don't make it back. *Anything* at all might be hiding in a place like that. Anything. But I know that it *isn't* Huygens, and it isn't Lomonosov or Kunowsky, either, and, in the end, I always set the globe back in its place on my shelf and return the charts to their drawers.

Sometimes, I make it all the way down to the bottom.

The music rises and swells around me like a dust storm, like all the dust storms that have ever scrubbed the raw face of this god-forsaken planet. I stand there, wrapped in a suffocating melody that is almost cacophony, melody to drown me, trying to remember where I've heard this music before, knowing only that I have. I gaze back up at the rim of the crater, so sharp against the star-filled night sky, and trace my footprints and the displaced stones and tiny avalanches that mark the zigzag path of my descent.

I know full well that I'm being watched—some vestigial, primitive lobe of my brain pricked by that needling music, pricked by a thousand alien eyes—and I turn and begin the long march into the crater, towards its distant central peak and the place where the music might be coming from. I know that she's out there somewhere—Sailor—not waiting for me. I know that she's already given herself over to the Fenrir, and that means she's something worse than dead now. But I also know that doesn't mean I'm not supposed to find her.

The sky is full of demons.

Blood falls from Heaven.

I was sent to the containment facility just north of Apollinaris Patera only three months after my election to the Council. On all the fedstat grids it's marked as IHF21, a red biohazard symbol at Latitude -9.8, Longitude 174.4E to scar the northern slope of the volcano. But the physicians and epidemiologists, virologists and exobiologists and healers who work and live there call it something else, something I'd rather not write down just now. The patients or detainees or whatever you might choose to call them, if *they* have a name for the place, then I've never learned it. I'd never want to.

That was seventeen years ago, not long after a pharmaceutical multinational working with the Asian umbrella came up with the serum, the toxic antiviral cocktail that either kills you or slows down the Fenrir contagion and sometimes even stops it cold, but never reverses the alterations already made to the genome of the infected individual. So, there was something like hope in IHF21 when I arrived. That is, there was hope among the staff, not the inmates, who were each and every one being administered the serum against their will. The scientists reasoned that if a serum that inhibited the contagion had been found, a genuine cure might not be far behind it. But by the time I left, almost four years later, with no cure in sight and a resistance to the serum manifesting in some of the infected, that hope had been replaced by something a lot more like resignation.

The blood from Heaven is black and hisses when it strikes the hard, dusty ground. I step over and around the accumulated carcasses of creatures

I know no names for, the hulks of other things I'm not even sure were ever alive. Corpses that might have belonged to organisms or machines or some perverse amalgam of the two. With every step, the plain before me seems ever more littered with these bodies, if they are, indeed, dead things. Some of them are so enormous that I step easily between ebony ribs and follow hallways roofed by fossilized vertebrae and scales like the hull plating of starships. The music is growing louder, yet through it I can hear the whisperers, the mumbling phantoms that I've never once glimpsed.

Three days after I arrived at IHF21, a senior physician, an earthborn woman named Zyra McNamara, led me on a tour of the Primary Ward, where the least advanced cases were being tended. The *least* advanced cases. There was hardly anything human left among them. I spent the better part of half an hour in a lavatory, puking up my lunch and breakfast and anything else that would come. Then I sat with Dr. McNamara in a staff lounge, a small room with a view of the mountain, sipping sour, hot coffee and listening to her talk.

"Is it true that they're not dying?" I asked, and she shrugged her shoulders.

"Yes. Strictly speaking, it's true that no one's died of the contagion, so far. But, you have to understand, we're dealing with such fundamental questions of organismal integrity—" and then she paused to stare out the window for a moment. There was a strong wind from the east, and it howled around the low plastic tower that held the lounge, rattled the windowpane, roared around the ancient ash and lava dome of Apollinaris Patera rising more than five kilometers above datum.

"It's now my belief," she said, "that we have to stop thinking of this thing as a disease. If I'm right, it's really much more like a parasite. Or rather, it's a viroid that reduces its victims to obligate parasites." And she was silent for a moment then, as though giving me a chance to reply or ask a question. When I didn't, because I was much too busy trying to calm my stomach for questions, she went on.

"On Earth, there are a number of species of fish that live in the deepest parts of the oceans. They're commonly, collectively, called anglerfish, and in these anglerfish, the males are very much smaller than the females. The males manage to locate the female fish in total darkness by homing in on the light from bioluminescent organs which the females possess."

"We're talking about *fish?*" I asked. "After what you just showed me, those things lying in there, we're sitting here talking about fucking fish?"

Dr. McNamara took a deep breath and let it out slowly. "Yes, Councilor. We're talking about fish. You see, the anglerfish males begin their lives as autonomous organisms, but when they finally locate a female, which must be an almost impossible task given the environmental conditions involved, they attach themselves to her body with their jaws and become parasitic. In time, they completely fuse with the female's body, losing much of their skeletal structure, sharing a common circulatory system, becoming, in essence, no more than reproductive organs. The question is, do the males, in some sense, *die?* They can no longer live free of the host female. They receive all of their nutrients via her bloodstream and—"

"I don't understand what you're saying," I told her, and looked down at the floor between my feet, starting to think I was going to vomit again.

"Don't worry about it, Councilor. We'll talk again later, when you're feeling better. There's no hurry."

There's no hurry.

But in my dreams, as I make my way across that corpse-strewn crater, my head and lungs and soul filled to bursting with the Fenrir's music, I am seized by an urgency beyond anything that I've ever known before. My feet cannot move quickly enough, and, after a while, I realize that it's not even Sailor that I'm looking for, not her that I'm navigating this terrible, impossible graveyard to find.

I have never reached the center.

I have never reached the center yet.

Since I was a child, I've loved the zeps. When I was four or five, my mothers took me to the Carver Street transfer station, and we watched together as one enormous gray airship docked and another departed. There was even a time when I fantasized that I might someday become a pilot, or an engineer. I read books on general aerodynamics and the development of Martian zeps, technical manuals on hybrid tricyclohydrazine/solar fuel cells and prop configuration and the problems of achieving low-speed lift in a thin

CO_2-heavy atmosphere. I built plastic models that my mothers had bought for me in Earthgoods shops. And then, at some point, I moved on to other, less-remarkable things. Puberty. Girls. And my mathematics and low-grade psi aptitude scores that eventually led to my seat on the Council. But I still love the zeps, and I love traveling on them. They are elegant things in a world where we have created very little elegance and much ugliness. They drift regally above Mars like strange helium-filled animals, almost like the gigantic floaters that evolved some three hundred and fifty million miles away in the Jovian atmosphere. I'd been praying that the long flight from Hope VII to the military port at the eastern edge of the Claritas Fossae might be some small relief after the horror that Jun'ko's billygirl had shown me. But first there'd been the nightmare, and now this network *mesuinu* and her camera eyes and questions I'd agreed to hear.

"How do you spell 'anglerfish'?" she asked, scribbling something on a pad she'd pulled from the breast pocket of her brown jacket.

"*What?*"

"Anglerfish. Is it one word or two? I've never heard it before."

"How the hell would I know? What the fuck difference does it make? You're doing this on short delay, right?"

She frowned and wrote something on the pad. It was somehow sickeningly quaint, watching a cyborg with an eight-petabyte recall chip making handwritten notes.

"Do you think you'll forget?" I asked and sipped my second bowl of tea. The brandy was strong and better than I'd expected, the steam from the tea filling my head and making Ariadne Vaughn's questions a little easier to endure.

She laughed and thumped the pad with one end of her stylus. "Oh, that. It's just an old habit. I don't think I'll ever quite get over it."

"I don't know how to spell 'anglerfish,'" I lied.

"Jun'ko Valenzuela told me that you were trailing a freighter, that one of her girls said Sailor Li had booked passage on a freighter named *Oryoku Maru.*"

"How much did you have to pay her to tell you that?" I asked. "Or did you find that threats were more effective with Jun'ko?"

"Are there currently any plans to allow civilian press into the containment facilities?"

"No," I said, watching her over the rim of my bowl. "The Council's public affairs office could have told you that."

"They did," she replied. "But I wanted to hear it from you. Now, there are rumors that you physically abused Sailor Li before she left you. Is that true, Councilor?"

I didn't answer right away. I sipped at my tea, glaring at her through the steam, trying to grasp the logic behind her seemingly random list of questions. The progression from one topic to another escaped me, and I wondered if something in her head was malfunctioning.

"Councilor, did you ever *beat* your lover?" she asked again and chewed at her lower lip.

I thought about lying, and then I said, "I hit her."

"After she took the mark?"

"Yes. I hit her after she took the mark."

"But no charges were ever filed with the magistrate's office in Herschel. Why do you think that is?"

I smiled and set my bowl down on the portal ledge. Vibrations through the wall of the airship sent tiny concentric ripples across the surface of the dark liquid.

"There have been allegations that the Council saw to it that no charges were filed against you," the journalist said. "Are you aware of that?"

"Sailor never brought charges against me because she knew if the case went to trial that I'd confess, and if I were in jail, I couldn't follow her. And, besides, she didn't have time left to waste on trials, Ms. Vaughn. The clock was ticking. She had more pressing matters to attend to."

"You mean the Fenrir?"

"No, Ms. Vaughn, I mean making a fortune as a whore in Hope VII."

She laughed, the comfortable sort of laugh she might have laughed if we were old, close friends and what I'd just said was no more than a joke. Once, not long after I returned to Herschel City from IHF21, one of the members of the Council's Board of Review and Advancement told me that she was deeply disturbed at my cynicism, my propensity for hatred, and that I was so quick to judge and anger. I admitted the fault and promised to meditate twice daily towards freeing myself of these shortcomings. I might as well have promised to raise the dead or make Mars safe for the XY chromo crowd. And now, sitting there on the *Barsoom XI*, facing this woman for whom my life and Sailor's life and the Fenrir contagion were together no more than a chance for early promotion and a fat bonus from the network snigs, I realized that I cherished my ability to hate. I cherished it as surely as I'd cherished Sailor. As surely as I'd once stood in the shadows of docking zeppelins, joyful and dizzy with the bottomless wonder of childhood.

I could have killed the smiling bitch then and there, could have slammed her head against the aluminum-epoxy alloy wall of the zep's cabin until there was nothing left to shatter, and my fingers were slick and sticky with her blood and brains and the yellowish lube and cooling fluids of her ruptured optical and superpalatal implants.

I could have done it in an instant, with no regrets. But there was still Sailor and the Fenrir's music, that beckoning anglerfish bioluminescence shining brightly through absolute blackness and cold, leading me to a different and more unthinkable end than the sanctuary of a prison cell.

"Do you really think you'll find her?" Ariadne Vaughn asked.

"If I live long enough," I replied, turning to the portal again. The sun was beginning to set.

"There are rumors, Councilor, that you've already been infected, that the contagion was passed to you by Sailor."

I slowly, noncommittally, nodded my head for her, for everyone at MBS studios and everyone who would soon be seeing this footage, and watched as the western sky turned the color of bruises. I didn't bother telling her what she already knew, repeating data stored in her pretty patchwork skull, that the viroid can only be contracted directly from specialized delivery glands inside the cloaca of a Fenrir drone. The infected aren't contagious. She knew that.

"That's fifteen," I said instead, glancing from the portal to my watch, even though it had actually been more like twenty minutes since she'd started asking me questions. "Time's all up."

"Well then, we wish you luck," she said, mock cheerfully, ending the rambling interview, "and Godspeed in your return to Herschel City."

"Bullshit," I said quickly, before she had a chance to blink the o-feed down. She frowned and shook her head.

"You know that's going to be edited out," she said, returning the pad and stylus to her breast pocket. "You *know* that, Councilor."

"Yeah, I know that. But it felt good, anyway. Now, Ms. Vaughn, you tell me where you think she is," I said and smiled at the flight attendant as she passed our seats.

"I assume you've had a look at the *Oryoku Maru*'s route db," she said, rubbing at her itching nose again. I wondered how long it would be before the acidic slake necessitated reconstructive rhinoplasty, or, if perhaps, it already had. "So you know its last refueling stop before the south polar crossing is at Lowell Station."

"Yes," I told her. "I know that. But I don't think Sailor will go that far. I think she'll get off before Lowell. I'm guessing Bosporos."

"Then you're guessing wrong, Councilor."

"And just what the hell makes you think that?" I asked. Ariadne Vaughn cocked her head ever so slightly to one side, raised her left eyebrow, and I imagined her rehearsing this moment in front of mirrors and prompts and vidloops, working to get that ah-see-this-is-what-I-know-that-you-*don't* expression just exactly fucking right. I began to suspect there were other cameras planted in the cabin, that we were still being pixed for MBS. "There's nothing in Lowell. There hasn't been since the war."

"We have some reliable contacts in the manifest dep and hangar crews down there," she replied, leaning back in her seat, either putting distance between us or playing out another part of the pantomime. "The last couple of years, Fenrir cultists have been moving in, occupying the old federal complex and some of the adjacent buildings. All the company people stay away from the place, of course, but they've seen some things. Some of them even think it's a temple."

There was an excited prickling at the back of my neck, a dull but hopeful flutter deep in my chest and stomach, but I did my best not to give anything away. The journalist knew too much already. She certainly didn't need me giving her more. "That's interesting" I said. "But the Council has a complete catalog of possible temple locations, as does the MCDC, and there's nothing in either of them about Lowell."

"Which means what, Councilor? That the Council's omniscient now? That it's infallible? That the MCDC never fucks shit up? I think we both know that none of those things are true."

As she talked, I tried to recall what little I knew about Lowell Crater.

It was an old settlement, one of the first, but a couple of fusion warheads dropped from orbit just after the start of the war had all but destroyed it. When the dust settled, after treaties had been signed and the plagues had finally burned themselves out, the Transit Authority had decided what was left at Lowell would make a good last stop before the South Pole. And that's about all that I could recall, and none of it suggested that the Fenrir would choose Lowell as a temple site.

"Assuming you're not just yanking this out of your ass, Ms. Vaughn, why hasn't MBS released this information? Why hasn't the TA already filed disclosure reports with the MCDC and Offworld Control?"

"Ask them," she said, staring up at the ceiling of the cabin now. *Maybe that's where they hid the other cameras*, I thought, not caring how paranoid I'd become. "My guess," she continued, "they're afraid the military's gonna come sweeping in to clear the place out, and they'll lose a base they can't afford to lose, the economy being what it is. It'd cost them a fortune to relocate."

"And what about the network?"

"The network?" she asked, looking at me again. "Well, we just want to be sure of our sources. No sense broadcasting stories that might cause a panic and have severe pecuniary consequences, if there's a chance it's all just something dreamed up by a few bored mechs stuck in some shithole at the bottom of the world. MBS will release the story, when we're ready. Maybe you'll be a part of it, Councilor, before this thing is done."

And then she stood up, thanked me for my time, and walked back to her assigned seat nearer the front of the passenger cabin. I sat alone, silently repeating all the things she'd said, hearing her voice in my head—*But they've seen some things. Some of them even think it's a temple.* Outside the airship's protective womb, night was quickly claiming the high plains of the Sun, and I could just make out the irregular red-orange silhouette of Phobos rising— or so it seemed, that illusion of ascension—above the western horizon.

It took me another two weeks to reach Lowell. The commercial airships don't run that far south, and I deplaned at Holden (noting that Ariadne Vaughn did not) and then spent four days trying to find someone willing to transport me the two-thousand-plus kilometers south and west to Bosporos City. From there, I hoped to buy a nook on the TA line the rest of the way down to Lowell.

Finally, I paid a platinum prospector half of what was left in my accounts to make the trip. She grumbled endlessly about pirates and dust sinks, about the wear and mileage the trip would put on her rusted-out crawler. But it was likely more money than she'd see in the next three or four years cracking rocks and tagging cores, and we only broke down once, when the aft sediment filter clogged and the engine overheated. I had a narrow, filthy bunk behind the Laskar coils, and spent much of the trip asleep or watching the monotonous terrain roll by outside the windows. To the east, there were occasional, brief glimpses of shadowed canyonlands which I knew led down to the wide, empty expanse of the Argyre Planitia laid out almost six klicks below the surrounding plains. I considered the possibility that it might be the corpse-strewn crater from my dreams, this monstrous wound carved deep into the face of Mars almost four thousand million years ago during the incessant bombardments of the Noachian Age, when the solar system was still young and hot and violent.

That thought only made the nightmares worse, of course. I considered asking the prospector to find another route, one not so near the canyons, but I knew she'd only laugh her bitter laugh, start in on dust sinks again, and tell me to go to hell. So I didn't say anything. Instead, I lay listening to the stones being ground to powder beneath the crawler's treads, to the wind battering itself against the hull, to the old-womanish wheeze of the failing Laskar coils, trying not to remember the thing Mikaela had shown me beneath Hope VII or what I might yet find in the ruins of Lowell. I slept, and I dreamed.

And on the final afternoon before we reached Bosporos City, dreaming, I made my way at last to the center of the crater. There was a desperate, lightless crawl through the mummified intestines of some leviathan while the Fenrir's pipes and strings and drums pounded at my senses. My ears and nose were bleeding when I emerged through a gaping tear in the creature's gut and stood, half-blind, blinking up at towering ebony spires and soaring arches and stairways that seemed to reach almost all the way to the stars. The music poured from this black city, gushed from every window and open doorway, and I sank to my knees and cried.

"You weren't ever meant to come here," Sailor said, and I realized she was standing over me. "You weren't invited."

"I can't *do* this shit anymore," I sobbed, for once not caring if she saw my weakness. "I can't."

"You never should have started."

My tears turned to crystal and fell with a sound like wind chimes. My heart turned to cut glass in my chest.

"Is this what you were looking for?" I asked her, gazing up at the spires and arches, hating that cruel, singing architecture, even as my soul begged it to open up and swallow me alive.

"No. This is only a dream, Dorry," she said, speaking to me as she might a child. "*You* made this place. You've been building it all your life."

"No. That's not true," I replied, though I understood perfectly well that it was, that it *must* be. The distance across the corpse-littered crater was only half the diameter of my own damnation, nothing more.

"If I let you see, will go back?" she asked. "Will you go back and forget me?" She was speaking very softly, but I had no trouble hearing her over the wind and the music and the wheezing Laskar coils. I must have answered, must have said yes, because she took my hand in hers, and the black city before us collapsed and dissolved, taking the music with it, and I stood, instead, on a low platform in what I at first mistook for a room. But then I saw the fleshy, pulsing walls, the purple-green interlace of veins and capillaries, the massive supporting ribs or ridges, blacker than the vanished city, dividing that place into seven unequal crescent chambers. I stood somewhere within a living thing, within something that dwarfed even the fallen giants from the crater.

And each of the crescent chambers contained the remains of a single gray pilgrim, their bodies metamorphosed over months or years or decades to serve the needs of this incomplete, demonic biology. They were each no more than appendages now, human beings become coalesced obligate parasites or symbiotes, their glinting, chitinous bodies all but lost in a labyrinth of mucosal membranes, buried by the array of connective tissues and tubes that sprouted from them like cancerous umbilical cords.

Anglerfish. Is it one word or two?

And there, half buried in the chamber walls, was what remained of

119

Sailor, just enough left of her face that I could be sure it was her. Something oily and red and viscous that wasn't blood leaked from the hole that had been her mouth, from the wreck of her lips and teeth, her mouth become only one more point of exit or entry for the restless, palpitating cords connecting her with this enormous organism. Her eyes opened partway, those atrophied slits parting to reveal bright, wet orbs like pools of night, and the fat, segmented tube emerging from the gap of her thighs began to quiver violently.

Can you see me now, Dorry? she whispered, her voice burrowing in behind my eyes, filled with pain and joy and regret beyond all comprehension. *Have you seen enough? Or do you need to see more?*

"No," I told her, waking up, opening my eyes wide and vomiting onto the floor beneath my bunk. The Laskar coils had stopped wheezing, and the crawler was no longer moving. I rolled over and lay very still, cold and sick and sweating, staring up at the dingy, low ceiling until the prospector finally came looking for me.

When I left home back in Aries, I brought the monk's book with me, the book from Sailor's crate of discards. I sit here on my bedroll in one corner of one room inside the concrete and steel husk of a bombed-out federal compound in Lowell. I have come this far, and I am comforted by the knowledge that there's only a little ways left to go. I open the book and read the words aloud again, the words underlined in red ink, that I might understand how not to lose my way in this tale which is almost all that remains of me: "No story has a beginning, and no story has an end. Beginnings and endings may be conceived to serve a purpose, to serve a momentary and transient intent, but they are, in their truer nature, arbitrary and exist solely as a construct of the mind of man."

I think this means I can stop when I'm ready.

I've been in Lowell for almost a full week now, writing all this shit down. Today is Monday, Libra 17th. We are so deep in winter, and I have never been this far south.

There is a silence here, in this dead city, that seems almost as solid as the bare concrete around me. I'm camped far enough in from the transfer station that the hangar noise, the comings and goings of the zeps and spinners, the clockwork opening and closing of the dome, seem little more than a distant, occasional thunder. I'm not sure I've ever known such a profound silence as this. Were I sane, it might drive me mad. There *are* sounds, sounds other than the far-off noise of the station, but they are petty things that only seem to underscore the silence. They're more like the too-often recollected *memory* of sound, an ancient woman deaf since childhood remembering what sound was like before she lost it forever.

Last night, I lay awake, fighting sleep, listening to my heart and all those other petty sounds. I dozed towards dawn, and when I woke there was a woman crouched a few feet from my bedroll. She was reading the monk's book, flipping the pages in the dark, and, at first, I thought I was dreaming again, that this was another dream of Sailor. But then she closed the book and looked at me. Even in the dark, I could tell she wasn't as young as Sailor, and I saw that her head was shaved down to the skin. Her eyes were iridescent and flashed blue-green in the gloom.

"May I switch on the light?" I asked, pointing towards the travel lamp near my pillow.

"If you wish," she replied and set the book back down among my things. "If you need it."

I touched the lamp, and it blinked obediently on, throwing long shadows against the walls and floor and ceiling of the room where I was sleeping. The woman squinted, cursed, and turned her face away. I rubbed at my own eyes and sat up.

"What do you want?" I asked her.

"We saw you, yesterday. You were watching."

The woman was a Fenrir priest. She wore the signs on her skin and ragged clothing. Her feet were bare, and there was a simple onyx ring on each of her toes. I could tell that she'd been very beautiful once.

"Yes," I told her. "I was watching."

"But you didn't come for the mark," she said, not asking because she already knew the answer. "You came to find someone."

"Does that happen very often?"

She turned her face towards me again, shading her eyes with her left hand. "Do you think you will find her, Dorry? Do you think you'll take her back?"

It hadn't been hard to locate the temple. The old federal complex lies near the center of the dome, what the bombs left of it, anyway, and finding it was really no more than a matter of walking. The day that I arrived in Lowell City, one of the Transfer Authority's security agents had detained and questioned me for an hour or so, and I'd assured her that I was there as a scholar, looking for records that might have survived the war. I'd shown her the paper map that I'd purchased at a bookshop in Bosporos and pointed out the black X I'd made about half a mile north of the feddy, near one of the old canals. She'd looked at the map two or three times, asked me a few questions about the journey down from Holden, and then made a call to her senior officer before releasing me.

"You don't want to go down that way," she'd told me, tapping the map with an index finger. "I can't hold you here or deport you, Councilor. But you better trust me on this. You don't want to go down there."

"You've been chasing her such a long time," the woman crouched on the floor before me said, speaking more quietly now and smiling. Her teeth were filed to sharp points, and she licked at them with the tip of her violet tongue. "You must have had a lot of chances to give up. There must have been so much despair."

"Is she dead?" I asked, the words slipping almost nonsensically from my lips.

"No one *dies*. You know that. You've known that since the camp. No one ever dies."

"You know where she is?"

"She's with the wolf," the woman whispered. "Three weeks now, she's with the wolf. You came too late, Dorry. You came to her too late," and she drew a knife from her belt, something crude and heavy fashioned from scrap metal. "She isn't waiting anymore."

I kicked her hard, the toe of my right boot catching her in the chest just below her collar bone, and the priest cried out and fell over backwards. The knife slipped from her fingers and skittered away across the concrete.

"Did the wolf tell *you* that you'd never die?" I demanded, getting to my feet and aiming the pistol at her head. I'd bought that in Bosporos, as well, the same day I'd bought the map, black-market military picked up cheap in the backroom of a britch bar. The blinking green ready light behind the sight assured me that the safety was off, that the trip cells were hot, and there was a live charge in the chamber. The woman coughed and clutched at her chest, then spat something dark onto the floor.

"That's what I want to know, bitch," I said, "what I want you to *tell* me," and I kicked her in the ribs. She grunted and tried to crawl away, so I kicked her again, harder than before, and she stopped moving. "I want you to tell me if that's what it *promised* you, that you'd fucking get to live forever if you brought it whatever it needed. Because I want you to know that it fucking lied."

And she opened her mouth wide, then, and I caught a glimpse of the barbed thing uncoiling from the hollow beneath her tongue, and I squeezed the trigger.

I suspect that one gunshot was the loudest noise anyone's heard here since the day bombs fell on Lowell. It echoed off the thick walls, all that noise trapped in such a little room, and left my ears ringing painfully. The priest was dead, and I sat down on my bedroll again. I'd never imagined that there would be so much blood or that killing someone could be so very simple. No, that's not true. That's a goddamn lie. I've imagined it all along.

I've been sitting here on the roof for the last hour, watching as the domeworks begin to mimic the morning light, shivering while the frost clinging to the old masonry melts away as the solar panels warm the air of Lowell. I brought the monk's book with me and half a bottle of whiskey and the gun. And my notebook, to write the last of it down.

When the bottle is empty, maybe then I'll make a decision. Maybe then I'll know what comes next.

A CHILD'S GUIDE TO THE HOLLOW HILLS

BENEATH THE LOW leaf-litter clouds, under endless dry monsoons of insect pupae, strangling rains of millipede droppings, and noxious fungal spores, in this muddy, thin land pressed between soil and bedrock foundations, the fairie girl awakens in the bed of the Queen of Decay. She opens her violet eyes and sees, again, that it was not only some especially unpleasant dream or nightmare, her wild descent, her pell-mell tumble from light and day and stars and moonshine, down, down, down to this mouldering domain of shadow walls and gnarly taproot obelisks. She is *here*, after all. She is *still* here, and slowly she sits up, pushing away those clammy spider-spun sheets that slip in and tangle themselves about her whenever she dares to sleep. *And what*, she thinks, *is sleep, but admitting to myself this is no dream?* Admitting that she has been snared and likely there will be no escape from out this unhappy, foetid chamber. Always she has been afraid of falling, deathly frightened of great heights and holes and wells and all the very deep places of the world. Always she has watched so carefully where fell her feet, and never was she one to climb trees or walls, not this cautious fairie girl. When her bolder sisters went to bathe where the brook grows slow and wide beneath drooping willow boughs, she would venture no farther in than the depth of her ankles. They laughed and taunted her with impromptu fictions of careless, drowning children and hungry snapping turtle jaws and also an enormous catfish that might swallow up any careless fairie girl in a single lazy gulp of its bristling, barbeled lips. *And you only looked beneath a stone,* the Queen sneers, reminding her that she is never precisely alone here, that her thoughts are never only *her* thoughts. *Your own mother, she told you that your sisters were but wicked liars, and there was no monster catfish or snapping turtles waiting in the brook. But, she said, do not go turning over stones.* And the fairie girl would shut her violet eyes now, but knows too well she'd still hear that voice, which is like unto the splintering of granite by frost, the ceaseless tunneling noises of earthworms and moles, the crack of a goblin's whip in air that has never once seen the sky. *Don't you go looking under stones,* the Queen says again and smiles to show off a hundred rusted-needle teeth. *In particular, said she—your poor, unheeded mother—beware the great flat stones that lie in the oldest groves, scabbed over with lichens and streaked with the glinting trails of slugs, the flat stones that smell of salamanders and moss, for these are sometimes doorways, child.* The Queen laughs, and her laughter is so terrible that the fairie girl cringes and *does* close her eyes. *Disobedient urchin, you knew better.* "I was following the green lizard," she whispers, as though this might be some saving defence or extenuation, as if the Queen of Decay has not already heard it from her countless times before. "The green lizard crawled beneath the stone—"—*which you knew damn well not to lift and look beneath. So, here now. Stop your whimpering. You were warned; you knew better.* "I wanted only to find the lizard again. I never meant to—" *You only came knocking at my door, dear sweet thing. I only answered and showed you in. You'd have done well not to entrust your well-being to a fascination with such lowly, squamous things—serpents and lizards and the dirty, clutching feet of birds.* The fairie girl opens her eyes again, trying not to cry, because she almost always cries, and her tears and sobs so delight the Queen. She sees herself staring back with watery sapphire eyes, reflected in the many mirrors hanging from these filthy walls, mirrors which her captor ordered hung all about the chamber so that the girl might also witness the stages of her gradual dissolution. The fracturing and wearing away of her glamour, even as water etches at the most indurate stone. Her eyes have not yet lost their colour, but they have lost their inner light. In the main, her skin is still the uncorrupted white of fresh milk caught inside a milkmaid's pail, but there are ugly, parchment splotches that have begun to spread across her face and arms and chest. And her hair, once so full and luminous, has grown flat and devoid of lustre, without the sympathetic light of sun or moon, wilting even as her soul wilts. She is drinking me, the girl thinks, and, *Yes*, the Queen replies. *I have poured you into my silver cup, and I am drinking you down, mouthful by mouthful. You have a disagreeable taste upon my tongue, but it is a sacred duty, to consume anything so frail as you. I choke you down, lest your treacle and the radiance of you should spread and spoil the murk.* And all around them the walls, wherever there are not mirrors, twitch and titter, and fat trolls and raw-boned redcaps with phosphorescent skins and hungry, bulging eyes watch the depredations of their queen. This is rare sport, and the Queen is not so miserly or selfish that she will not share the spectacle with her subjects. *See*, she says, *but do not touch. Her flesh is deadly as cold iron to the likes of us. I alone have the strength to lay my hands upon so foul a being and live.* In the mirrors hung on bits of root and bone and the fishhook mandibles of beetles, the fairie girl sits on the black bed far below the forest floor, and the Queen of Decay moves across her like an eclipse of the sun. *Do not go looking under stones, your poor mother said. I have heard from the pillbugs and termites that she is a wise woman. You'd have done well to heed her good advices.* It is hard for the girl to see the Queen, for she is mostly fashioned of some viscous, shapeless substance that is not quite flesh, but always there is the dim impression of leathery wings, as if from some immense bat, and wherever the Queen brushes against the girl, there is the sensation of touching, or being touched by, matted fur and the blasted bark of dying, lightning-struck trees. The day the girl chased the quick green lizard through the forest, she was still whole, her maidenhead unbroken, the task of her deflowering promised—before her birth—to a nobleman, an elfin duke who held his court on the shores of a sparkling lake and was long owed a considerable debt by her father. The marriage would settle that account. Would *have* settled that account, for the Queen took the fairie girl's virginity almost at once. *We'll have none of that here*, she said, slipping a sickle thumb between the girl's pale thighs and pricking at her sex. There was only as much pain as she'd always expected, and hardly any blood, but the certain knowledge, too, that she had been undone, ruined, despoiled, and if ever she found some secret stairway leading up and out of the Queen's thin lands, her escape would only bring shame to her family. *Better a daughter lost and dead and picked clean by the ants and crows*, the Queen of Decay told her, *than one who's given herself to me, who's soiled my bedclothes with her body's juices and played my demimondaine.* "Nothing was given," replied the fairie girl, and how long ago *was* that? A month? A season? Only a single night? There is no time in the land of the Queen of Decay. There is no need of time when despair would serve so well as the past and all possible futures. Mark it all the present and be done. *What next?* the Queen asks, mocking the laws of her own timeless realm. *Have you been lying here, child, asking yourself, what is next in store for me?* "No," says the girl, refusing to admit the truth aloud, even if the Queen could hear it perfectly well unspoken. "I do not dwell on it," the girl lies. "You will do as you will, and neither my fear nor anticipation will stay your hand or teach you mercy." And then the Queen swells and rises up around her like a glistening, alveolate wreath of ink and sealing wax, and the spectators clinging to the walls or looking out from their nooks and corners hold their breath, collectively not breathing as though in that moment they have become a single beast divided into many bodies. *I only followed the lizard*, the fairie girl thinks, trying not to hear the wet and stretching noises leaking from the Queen's distorted form, trying not to think what will happen one second later, or two seconds after that. *It was so pretty in the morning sun. Its scales were a rainbow fashioned all of shades of green, a thousand shades of green*, and she bows her head and strains to recall the living warmth of sunlight on her face. *Show me your eyes, child*, growls the Queen of Decay. *We will not do this thing halfway.* And, reminded now of misplaced details, the girl replies, "Its eyes were like faraway red stars twinkling in its skull. I'd never before seen such a lizard—verdant, iridian, gazing out at me with crimson eyes." The moldy air trapped within the chamber seems to shudder then, and the encircling mesh that the Unseelie queen has made of herself draws tighter about the girl from the bright lands that are ever crushing down upon those who must dwell below. *I have not taken everything*, the Queen says. *Not yet. We've hardly begun*, and the fairie girl remembers that she is not chasing a green lizard with red eyes on a summer's morning, that she has finally fallen into that abyss—the razor jaws of a granddaddy snapping turtle half buried in silt and waterlogged poplar leaves, or the gullet of a catfish that has waited long years in the mud and gloom to make a meal of her. There is always farther to fall. This pool has no bottom. She will sink until she at last forgets herself, and still she will go on sinking. She glances up into the void that the Queen of Decay has not bothered to cover with a mask, and something which has hidden itself under the black bed begins to snicker loudly. *You are mine, Daughter,* says the Queen. *And a daughter of loam and toadstools should not go about so gaudily attired. It is indecent,* and, with that, her claws move swiftly and snip away the girl's beautiful dragonfly wings. They slip off her shoulder, falling from ragged stumps to lie dead upon the spider sheets. "My wings," the girl whispers, unsurprised and yet also disbelieving, this new violation and its attendant hurt seeming hardly more real than the bad dreams she woke from some short time ago (if there *were* time here). "You've taken my wings from me," and she reaches for them, meaning to hide them away beneath a pillow or within the folds of her stained and tattered shift before any greater harm is done to those delicate, papery mosaics. But the Queen, of course, knows the girl's will and is far faster than she; the amputated wings are snatched up by clicking, chitinous appendages which sprout suddenly from this or that dank and fleshy recess, then ferried quickly to the sucking void where a face should be. The Queen of Decay devours the fairie girl's wings in an instant, less than half an instant. And there below the leaf-litter clouds and the rustling, grub-haunted roof of this thin, thin world, the Queen, unsated, draws tight the quivering folds of her honeycomb skin and falls upon the screaming, stolen child . . .

. . . and later, the girl is shat out again—that indigestible, fecal lump of her which the Queen's metabolism has found no use for, whatever *remains* when the glamour and magick have been stripped away by acid and cruel enzymes and a billion diligent intestinal cilia. This dull, undying scat which can now recall only the least tangible fragments of its life before the descent, before the fall, before the millennia spent in twisting, turning passage through the Queen's gut, and it sits at one of the mirrors which its mistress has so kindly, so thoughtfully, provided and watches its own gaunt face. On the bed behind it, there is a small green lizard with ruby eyes, and the lizard blinks and tastes the stale, forest-cellar air with a forked tongue the colour of ripe blackberries. *Perhaps,* thinks the thing that is no longer sprite—or nymph—or pixie, that is only this naked stub of gristle, *perhaps you were once a dragon, and then she swallowed you, as she swallowed me, and all that is left now is a little green lizard with red eyes.* The lizard blinks again, neither confirming nor denying the possibility, and the thing staring back at itself from the mirror considers conspiracy and connivance, the lovely little lizard only bait to lead her astray, that she might wander alone into a grove of ancient oaks and lift a flat, slug-streaked stone and . . . fall. The thing in the mirror is only the wage of its own careless, disobedient delight, and with one skeletal hand, it touches wrinkled fingertips to the cold, unyielding surface of the looking glass, reaching out to that *other* it. There is another green lizard, trapped there inside the mirror, and while the remains of the feast of the Queen of Decay tries to recall what might have come before the grove and the great flat stone and the headlong plunge down the throat of all the world, the tiny lizard slips away, vanishing into the shadows that hang everywhere like murmuring shreds of midnight.

THE AMMONITE VIOLIN
(MURDER BALLAD NO. 4)

F HE WERE EVER to try to write this story, he would not know where to begin. It's that sort of a story, so fraught with unlikely things, so perfectly turned and filled with such wicked artifice and contrivances that readers would look away, unable to suspend their disbelief even for a page. But he will never try to write it, because he is not a poet or a novelist or a man who writes short stories for the newsstand pulp magazines. He is a collector. Or, as he thinks of himself, a Collector. He has never dared to think of himself as *The* Collector, as he is not without an ounce or two of modesty, and there must surely be those out there who are far better than he, shadow men, and maybe shadow women, too, haunting a busy, forgetful world that is only aware of its phantoms when one or another of them slips up and is exposed to flashing cameras and prison cells. Then people will stare, and maybe, for a time, there is horror and fear in their dull, wet eyes, but they soon enough forget again. They are busy people, after all, and they have lives to live, and jobs to show up for five days a week, and bills to pay, and secret nightmares all their own, and in their world there is very little *time* for phantoms.

He lives in a small house in a small town near the sea, for the only time the Collector is ever truly at peace is when he is in the presence of the sea. Even collecting has never brought him to that complete and utter peace, the quiet which finally fills him whenever there is only the crash of waves against a granite jetty and the saltwater mists to breathe in and hold in his lungs like opium fumes. He would love the sea, were she a woman. And sometimes he imagines her so, a wild and beautiful woman clothed all in blue and green, trailing sand and mussels in her wake. Her grey eyes would contain hurricanes, and her voice would be the lonely toll of bell buoys and the cries of gulls and a December wind scraping itself raw against the shore. But, he thinks, were the sea but a woman, and were she his lover, then he would *have* her, as he is a Collector and *must* have all those things he loves, so that no one else might ever have them. He must draw them to him and keep them safe from a blind and busy world that cannot even comprehend its phantoms. And having her, he would lose her, and he would never again know the peace which only she can bring.

He has two specialties, this Collector. There are some who are perfectly content with only one, and he has never thought any less of them for it. But he has two, because, so long as he can recall, there has been this dual fascination, and he never saw the point in forsaking one for the other. Not if he might have them both and yet be a richer man for sharing his devotion between the two. They are his two mistresses, and neither has ever condemned his polyamorous heart. Like the sea, who is *not* his mistress but only his constant savior, they understand who and what and *why* he is, and that he would be somehow diminished, perhaps even undone, were he forced to devote himself wholly to the one or the other. The first of the two is his vast collection of fossilized ammonites, gathered up from the quarries and ocean-side cliffs and the stony, barren places of half the globe's nations. The second are all the young women he has murdered by suffocation, *always* by suffocation, for that is how the sea would kill, how the sea *does* kill, usually, and in taking life he would ever pay tribute and honor to that first mother of the world.

That first Collector.

He has never had to explain his collecting of suffocations, of the deaths of suffocated girls, as it is such a commonplace thing and a secret collection, besides. But he has frequently found it necessary to explain to some acquaintance or another, someone who thinks that she or he *knows* the Collector, about the ammonites. The ammonites are not a secret and, it would seem, neither are they commonplace. It is simple enough to say that they are mollusks, a subdivision of the Cephalopoda, kin to the octopus and cuttlefish and squid, but possessing exquisite shells, not unlike another living cousin, the chambered nautilus. It is less easy to say that they became extinct at the end of the Cretaceous, along with most dinosaurs, or that they first appear in the fossil record in early Devonian times, as this only leads to the need to explain the Cretaceous and Devonian. Often, when asked that question, *What is an ammonite?*, he will change the subject. Or he will sidestep the truth of his collection, talking only of mathematics and the geometry of the ancient Greeks and how one arrives at the Golden Curve. Ammonites, he knows, are one of the sea's many exquisite expressions of that logarithmic spiral, but he does not bother to explain that part, keeping it back for himself. And sometimes he talks about the horns of Ammon, an Egyptian god of the air, or, if he is feeling especially impatient and annoyed by the question, he limits his response to a description of the Ammonites from the *Book of Mormon* and how they embraced the god of the Nephites and so came to know peace. He is not a Mormon, of course, as he has use of only a single deity, who is the sea and who kindly grants him peace when he can no longer bear the clamor in his head or the far more terrible clamor of mankind.

On this hazy winter day, he has returned to his small house from a very long walk along a favorite beach, as there was a great need to clear his head. He has made a steaming cup of Red Zinger tea with a few drops of honey and sits now in the room which has become the gallery for the best of his ammonites, oak shelves and glass display cases filled with their graceful planispiral or heteromorph curves, a thousand fragile aragonite bodies transformed by time and geochemistry into mere silica or pyrite or some other permineralization. He sits at his desk, sipping his tea and glancing occasionally at some beloved specimen or another—*this* one from South Dakota or *that* one from the banks of the Volga River in Russia or one of the *many* that have come from Whitby, England. And then he looks back to the desktop and the violin case lying open in front of him, crimson silk to cradle this newest and perhaps most precious of all the items which he has yet collected in his lifetime, the single miraculous piece which belongs strictly in neither one gallery nor the other. The piece which will at last form a bridge, he believes, allowing his two collections to remain distinct, but also affording a tangible transition between them.

THE AMMONITE VIOLIN (MURDER BALLAD NO. 4)

The keystone, he thinks. *Yes, you will be my keystone.* But he knows, too, that the violin will be something more than that, that he has devised it to serve as something far grander than a token unification of the two halves of his delight. It will be a *tool*, a mediator or go-between in an act which may, he hopes, transcend collecting in its simplest sense. It has only just arrived today, special delivery, from the Belgian luthier to whom the Collector had hesitantly entrusted its birth.

"It must be done *precisely* as I have said," he told the violin-maker, four months ago, when he flew to Hotton to hand-deliver a substantial portion of the materials from which the instrument would be constructed. "You may not deviate in any significant way from these instructions."

"Yes," the luthier replied, "I understand. I understand completely." A man who appreciates discretion, the Belgian violin-maker, so there were no inconvenient questions asked, no prying inquiries as to *why*, and what's more, he'd even known something about ammonites beforehand.

"No substitutions," the Collector said firmly, just in case it needed to be stated one last time.

"No substitutions of any sort," replied the luthier.

"And the back must be carved—"

"I understand," the violin-maker assured him. "I have the sketches, and I will follow them exactly."

"And the pegs—"

"Will be precisely as we have discussed."

And so the Collector paid the luthier half the price of the commission, the other half due upon delivery, and he took a six a.m. flight back across the wide Atlantic to New England and his small house in the small town near the sea. And he has waited, hardly daring to *half*-believe that the violin-maker would, in fact, get it all right. Indeed—for men are ever at war with their hearts and minds and innermost demons—some infinitesimal scrap of the Collector has even *hoped* that there *would* be a mistake, the most trifling portion of his plan ignored or the violin finished and perfect but then lost in transit and so the whole plot ruined. For it is no small thing, what the Collector has set in motion, and having always considered himself a very wise and sober man, he suspects that he understands fully the consequences he would suffer should he be discovered by lesser men who have no regard for the ocean and her needs. Men who cannot see the flesh and blood phantoms walking among them in broad daylight, much less be bothered to pay tithes which are long overdue to a goddess who has cradled them all, each and every one, through the innumerable twists and turns of evolution's crucible, for three and a half thousand million years.

But there has been no mistake, and, if anything, the violin-maker can be faulted only in the complete sublimation of his craft to the will of his customer. In every way, this is the instrument the Collector asked him to make, and the varnish gleams faintly in the light from the display cases. The top is carved from spruce, and four small ammonites have been set into the wood—*Xipheroceras* from Jurassic rocks exposed along the Dorset Coast at Lyme Regis—two inlaid on the upper bout, two on the lower. He found the fossils himself, many years ago, and they are as perfectly preserved an example of their genus as he has yet seen anywhere, for any price. The violin's neck has been fashioned from maple, as is so often the tradition, and, likewise, the fingerboard is the customary ebony. However, the scroll has been formed from a fifth ammonite, and the Collector knows it is a far more perfect logarithmic spiral than any volute that could have ever been hacked out from a block of wood. In his mind, the five ammonites form the points of a pentacle. The luthier used maple for the back and ribs, and when the Collector turns the violin over, he's greeted by the intricate bas-relief he requested, faithfully reproduced from his own drawings—a great octopus, the ravenous devilfish of so many sea legends, and the maze of its eight tentacles makes a looping, tangled interweave.

As for the pegs and bridge, the chinrest and tailpiece, all these have been carved from the bits of bone he provided the luthier. They seem no more than antique ivory, the stolen tusks of an elephant or a walrus or the tooth of a sperm whale, perhaps. The Collector also provided the dried gut for the five strings, and when the violin-maker pointed out that they would not be nearly so durable as good stranded steel, that they would be much more likely to break and harder to keep in tune, the Collector told him that the instrument would be played only once and so these matters were of very little concern. For the bow, the luthier was given strands of hair which the Collector told him had come from the tail of a gelding, a fine grey horse from Kentucky thoroughbred stock. He'd even ordered a special rosin, and so the sap of an Aleppo Pine was supplemented with a vial of oil he'd left in the care of the violin-maker.

And now, four long months later, the Collector is rewarded for all his painstaking designs, rewarded or damned, if indeed there is some distinction between the two, and the instrument he holds is more beautiful than he'd ever dared to imagine it could be.

The Collector finishes his tea, pausing for a moment to lick the commingled flavors of hibiscus and rosehips, honey and lemon grass from his thin, chapped lips. Then he closes the violin case and locks it, before writing a second, final check to the Belgian luthier. He slips it into an envelope bearing the violin-maker's name and the address of the shop on the rue de Centre in Hotton; the check will go out in the morning's mail, along with other checks for the gas, telephone, and electric bills, and a handwritten letter on lilac-scented stationery, addressed to a Brooklyn violinist. When he is done with these chores, the Collector sits there at the desk in his gallery, one hand resting lightly on the violin case, his face marred by an unaccustomed smile and his eyes filling up with the gluttonous wonder of so many precious things brought together in one room, content in the certain knowledge that they belong to him and will never belong to anyone else.

The violinist would never write this story, either. Words have never come easily for her. Sometimes, it seems she does not even think in words, but only in notes of music. When the lilac-scented letter arrives, she reads it several times, then does what it asks of her, because she can't imagine what else she would do. She buys a ticket and the next day she takes the train through Connecticut and Rhode Island and Massachusetts until, finally, she comes to a small town on a rocky spit of land very near the sea. She has never cared for the sea, as it has seemed always to her some awful, insoluble mystery, not so very different from the awful, insoluble mystery of death. Even before the loss of her sister, the violinist avoided the sea when possible. She loathes the taste of fish and lobster and of clams, and the smell of the ocean, too, which reminds her of raw sewage. She has often dreamt of drowning, and of slimy things with bulging black eyes, eyes as empty as night, that have slithered up from abyssal depths to drag her back down with them to light-less plains of silt and diatomaceous ooze or to the ruins of haunted, sunken cities. But those are *only* dreams, and they do her only the bloodless harm that comes from dreams, and she has lived long enough to understand that she has worse things to fear than the sea.

She takes a taxi from the train depot, and it ferries her through the town and over a murky river winding between empty warehouses and rotting docks, a few fishing boats stranded at low tide, and then to a small house painted the color of sunflowers or canary feathers. The address on the mailbox matches the address on the lilac-scented letter, so she pays the driver and he leaves her there. Then she stands in the driveway, watching the yellow house, which has begun to seem a disquieting shade of yellow, or only a shade of yel-low made disquieting because there is so much of it all in one place. It's almost twilight, and she shivers, wishing she'd thought to wear a cardigan under her coat, and then a porch light comes on and there's a man waving to her.

He's the man who wrote the letter, she thinks. *The man who wants me to play for him,* and for some reason she had expected him to be a lot younger and not so fat. He looks a bit like Captain Kangaroo, this man, and he waves and calls her name and smiles. And the violinist wishes that the taxi were still waiting there to take her back to the station, that she didn't need the money the fat man in the yellow house had offered her, that she'd had the good sense to stay in the city where she belongs. *You could still turn and walk away,* she reminds herself. *There's nothing at all stopping you from just turning right around and walking away and never once looking back, and you could still forget about this whole ridiculous affair.*

And maybe that's true, and maybe it isn't, but there's more than a month's rent on the line, and the way work's been lately, a few students and catch-as-catch-can, she can't afford to find out. She nods and waves back at the smiling man on the porch, the man who told her not to bring her own instrument because he'd prefer to hear her play a particular one that he'd just brought back from a trip to Europe.

"Come on inside. You must be freezing out there," he calls from the porch, and the violinist tries not to think about the sea all around her or that shade of yellow, like a pool of melted butter, and goes to meet the man who sent her the lilac-scented letter.

The Collector makes a steaming-hot pot of Red Zinger, which the violinist takes without honey, and they each have a poppy-seed muffin, which he bought fresh that morning at a bakery in the village. They sit across from one another at his desk, surrounded by the display cases and the best of his ammonites, and she sips her tea and picks at her muffin and pretends to be interested while be explains the importance of recognizing sexual dimorphism when distinguishing one species of ammonite from another. The shells of females, he says, are often the larger and so are called macroconchs by paleontologists. The males may have much smaller shells, called microconchs, and one must always be careful not to mistake the microconchs and macroconchs for two distinct species. He also talks about extinction rates and the utility of ammonites as index fossils and *Parapuzosia bradyi*, a giant among ammonites and the largest specimen in his collection, with a shell measuring only slightly under six feet in diameter, a Kraken of the warm Cretaceous seas.

"They're all quite beautiful," she says, and the violinist doesn't tell him how much she hates the sea, and everything that comes from the sea, or that the thought of all the fleshy, tentacled creatures that once lived stuffed inside those pretty spiral shells makes her skin crawl. She sips her tea and smiles and nods her head whenever it seems appropriate to do so, and when he asks if he can call her Ellen, she says yes, of course.

"You won't think me too familiar?"

"Don't be silly," she replies, half-charmed at his manners and wondering if he's gay or just a lonely old man whose grown a bit peculiar because he has nothing but his rocks and the yellow house for company. "That's my name. My name is Ellen."

"I wouldn't want to make you uncomfortable or take liberties that are not mine to take," the Collector says and clears away their china cups and saucers, the crumpled paper napkins and a few uneaten crumbs, and then he asks if she's ready to see the violin.

"If you're ready to show it to me," she tells him.

"It's just that I don't want to rush you," he says. "We could always talk some more, if you'd like."

And so the violinist explains to him that she's never felt comfortable with conversation, or with language in general, and that she's always suspected she was much better suited to speaking through her music. "Sometimes, I think it speaks for me," she tells him and apologizes, because she often apologizes when she's actually done nothing wrong. The Collector grins and laughs softly and taps the side of his nose with his left index finger.

"The way I see it, language is language is language," he says. "Words or music, bird songs or all the fancy, flashing colors made by chemoluminescent squids, what's the difference? I'll take conversation however I can wrangle it." And then he unlocks one of the desk drawers with a tiny brass-colored key and takes out the case containing the Belgian violin.

"If words don't come when you call them, then, by all means, please, talk to me with this," and he flips up the latches on the side of the case and opens it so she can see the instrument cradled inside.

"Oh my," she says, all her awkwardness and unease forgotten at the sight of the ammonite violin. "I've never seen anything like it. Never. It's lovely. No, it's much, *much* more than lovely."

"Then you will play it for me?"

"May I touch it?" she asks, and he laughs again.

"I can't imagine how you'll play it otherwise."

Ellen gently lifts the violin from its case, the way that some people might lift a newborn child or a Minoan vase or a stoppered bottle of nitroglycerine, the way the Collector would lift a particularly fragile ammonite from its bed of excelsior. It's heavier than any violin she's held before, and she guesses that the unexpected weight must be from the fossil shells set into the instrument. She wonders how it will affect the sound, those five ancient stones, how they might warp and alter this violin's voice.

"It's never been played, except by the man who made it, and that hardly seems to count. You, my dear, will be the very first."

And she almost asks him why *her*, because surely, for what he's paying, he could have lured some other, more talented player out here to his little yellow house. Surely someone a bit more celebrated, more accomplished, someone who doesn't have to take in students to make the rent, but would still be flattered and intrigued enough by the offer to come all the way to this squalid little town by the sea and play the fat man's violin for him. But then she thinks it would be rude, and she almost apologizes for a question she hasn't even asked.

And then, as if he might have read her mind, and so maybe she should have apologized after all, the Collector shrugs his shoulders and dabs at the corners of his mouth with a white linen handkerchief he's pulled from a shirt pocket. "The universe is a marvelously complex bit of craftsmanship," he says. "And sometimes one must look very closely to even begin to understand how a given thing connects with another. Your late sister, for instance—"

"My *sister?*" she asks and looks up, surprised and glancing away from the ammonite violin and into the friendly, smiling eyes of the Collector. All at once, there's a cold knot deep in her belly and an unpleasant pricking sensation along her forearms and the back of her neck, goosebumps and histrionic ghost-story clichés, and now the violin feels unclean and dangerous, and she wants to return it to its case. "What do you know about my sister?"

The Collector blushes and peers down at his hands, folded there in front of him on the desk. He begins to speak and stammers, as if, possibly, he's really no better with words than she.

"What do *you* know about my sister?" Ellen asks again. "*How* do you know about her?"

The Collector frowns and licks nervously at his chapped lips. "I'm sorry," he says. "That was terribly tactless of me. I should not have brought it up."

"How do you know about my sister?"

"It's not exactly a secret, is it?" the Collector asks, letting his eyes drift by slow, calculated degrees from his hands and the desktop to her face. "I do read the newspapers. I don't usually watch television, but I imagine it was there, as well. She was murdered—"

"They don't know that. No one knows that for sure. She is *missing*," the violinist says, hissing the last word between clenched teeth.

"Well, then she's been missing for quite some time," the Collector replies, feeling the smallest bit braver now and beginning to suspect he hasn't quite overplayed his hand.

"But they do not know that she's been murdered. They don't *know* that. No one ever found her body," and then Ellen decides that she's said far too much and stares down at the fat man's violin. She can't imagine how she ever thought it a lovely thing, only a moment or two before, this grotesque *parody* of a violin resting in her lap. It's more like a gargoyle, she thinks, or a sideshow freak, or a sick, sick joke, and suddenly she wants very badly to wash her hands.

"Please forgive me," the Collector says, sounding as sincere and contrite as any lonely man in a yellow house by the sea has ever sounded. "I am unaccustomed to company. I forget myself and say things I shouldn't. Please, Ellen. Play it for me. You've come all this way, and I would so love to hear you play. It would be such a pity if I've gone and spoiled it all with a few inconsiderate words. I so admire your work—"

"No one *admires* my work," she replies, wondering how long it would take the taxi to show up and carry her back over the muddy, murky river, past the rows of empty warehouses to the depot, and how long she'd have to wait for the next train to New York. "I still don't even understand how you found me?"

And at this opportunity to redeem himself, the Collector's face brightens, and he leans across the desk towards her. "Then I will tell you, if that will put your mind at ease. I saw you play at an art opening in Manhattan, you and your sister, a year or so back. At a gallery on Mercer Street. It was called . . . damn, it's right on the tip of my tongue—"

"Eyecon," Ellen says, almost whispering. "The name of the gallery is Eyecon."

"Yes, yes, that's it. Thank you. I thought it was such a very silly name for a gallery, but then I've never cared for puns and wordplay. It was at a reception for a French painter, Albert Perrault, and I confess I found him quite completely hideous, and his paintings were dreadful, but I loved listening to the two of you play. I called the gallery, and they were nice enough to tell me how I could contact you."

"I didn't like his paintings, either. That was the last time we played together, my sister and I," Ellen says and presses a thumb to the ammonite shell that forms the violin's scroll.

"I didn't know that. I'm sorry, Ellen. I wasn't trying to dredge up bad memories."

"It's not a *bad* memory," she says, wishing it were all that simple and that were exactly the truth, and then she reaches for the violin's bow, which is still lying in the case lined with silk dyed the color of ripe pomegranates.

"I'm sorry," the Collector says again, certain now that he hasn't frightened her away, that everything is going precisely as planned. "Please, I only want to hear you play again."

"I'll need to tune it," Ellen tells him, because she's come this far, and she needs the money, and there's nothing the fat man has said that doesn't add up.

"Naturally," he replies. "I'll go to the kitchen and make us another pot of tea, and you can call me whenever you're ready."

"I'll need a tuning fork," she says, because she hasn't seen any sign of a piano in the yellow house. "Or if you have a metronome that has a tuner, that would work."

The Collector promptly produces a steel tuning fork from another of the drawers and slides it across the desk to the violinist. She thanks him, and when he's left the room and she's alone with the ammonite violin and all the tall cases filled with fossils and the amber wash of incandescent bulbs, she glances at a window and sees that it's already dark outside. *I will play for him*, she thinks. *I'll play on his violin, and drink his tea, and smile, and then he'll pay me for my time and trouble. I'll go back to the city, and tomorrow or the next day, I'll be glad that I didn't chicken out. Tomorrow or the next day, it'll all seem silly, that I was afraid of a sad old man who lives in an ugly yellow house and collects rocks.*

"I will," she says out loud. "That's exactly how it will go," and then Ellen begins to tune the ammonite violin.

And after he brings her a rickety old music stand, something that looks like it has survived half a century of high-school marching bands, he sits behind his desk, sipping a fresh cup of tea, and she sits in the overlapping pools of light from the display cases. He asked for Paganini; specifically, he asked for Paganini's Violin Concerto No. 3 in E. She would have preferred something contemporary—Górecki, maybe, or Philip Glass, a little something she knows from memory—but he had the sheet music for Paganini, and it's his violin, and he's the one who's writing the check.

"Now?" she asks, and he nods his head.

"Yes, please," he replies and raises his tea cup as if to toast her.

So Ellen lifts the violin, supporting it with her left shoulder, bracing it firmly with her chin, and studies the sheet music a moment or two more before she begins. *Introduzione, allegro marziale*, and she wonders if he expects to hear all three movements, start to finish, or if he'll stop her when he's heard enough. She takes a deep breath and begins to play.

From his seat at the desk, the Collector closes his eyes as the lilting voice of the ammonite violin fills the room. He closes his eyes tightly and remembers another winter night, almost an entire year come and gone since then, but it might only have been yesterday, so clear are his memories. His collection of suffocations may indeed be more commonplace, as he has been led to conclude, but it is also the less frequently indulged of his two passions. He could never name the date and place of each and every ammonite acquisition, but in his brain the Collector carries a faultless accounting of all the suffocations. There have been sixteen, sixteen in twenty-one years, and now it has been almost one year to the night since the most recent. Perhaps, he thinks, he should have waited for the anniversary, but when the package arrived from Belgium, his enthusiasm and impatience got the better of him. When he wrote the violinist his lilac-scented note, he wrote "at your earliest possible convenience" and underlined "earliest" twice.

And here she is, and Paganini flows from out the ammonite violin just as it flowed from his car stereo that freezing night, one year ago, and his heart is beating so fast, so hard, racing itself and all his bright and breathless memories.

Don't let it end, he prays to the sea, whom he has faith can hear the prayers of all her supplicants and will answer those she deems worthy. *Let it go on and on and on. Let it never end.*

He clenches his fists, digging his short nails deep into the skin of his palms, and bites his lip so hard that he tastes blood. And the taste of those few drops of his own life is not so very different from holding the sea inside his mouth.

At last, I have done a perfect thing, he tells himself, himself and the sea and the ammonites and the lingering souls of all his suffocations. *So many years, so much time, so much work and money, but finally I have done this one perfect thing.* And then he opens his eyes again, and also opens the top middle drawer of his desk and takes out the revolver that once belonged to his father, who was a Gloucester fisherman who somehow managed never to collect anything at all.

Her fingers and the bow dance wild across the strings, and in only a few minutes Ellen has lost herself inside the giddy tangle of harmonics and drones and double stops, and if ever she has felt magic—*true* magic—in her art, then she feels it now. She lets her eyes drift from the music stand and the printed pages, because it is all right there behind her eyes and burning on her fingertips. She might well have written these lines herself and then spent half her life playing at nothing else, they rush through her with such ease and confidence. This is ecstasy and this is abandon and this is the tumble and roar of a thousand other emotions she seems never to have felt before this night. The strange violin no longer seems unusually heavy; in fact, it hardly seems to have any weight at all.

Perhaps there is *no violin,* she thinks. *Perhaps there never* was *a violin, only my hands and empty air, and that's all it takes to make music like this.*

Language is language is language, the fat man said, and so these chords have become her words. No, *not* words, but something so much less indirect than the clumsy interplay of her tongue and teeth, larynx and palate. They have become, simply, her *language,* as they ever have been. Her soul speaking to the world, and all the world need do in return is *listen.*

She shuts her eyes, no longer requiring them to grasp the progression from one note to the next, and at first there is only the comfortable darkness there behind her lids, which seems better matched to the music than all the distractions of her eyes.

Don't let it stop, she thinks, not praying, unless this is a prayer to herself, for the violinist has never seen the need for gods. *Please, let it be like this forever. Let this moment never end, and I will never have to stop playing and there will never again be silence or the noise of human thoughts and conversation.*

"It can't be that way, Ellen," her sister whispers, not whispering in her ear but from somewhere within the Paganini concerto or the ammonite violin or both at once. "I wish I could give you that. I would give you that if it were mine to give."

And then Ellen sees, or hears, or simply *understands* in this language which is *her* language, as language is language is language, the fat man's hands about her sister's throat. Her sister dying somewhere cold near the sea, dying all alone except for the company of her murderer, and there is half an instant when she almost stops playing.

No, her sister whispers, and that one word comes like a blazing gash across the concerto's whirl, and Ellen doesn't stop playing, and she doesn't open her eyes, and she watches as her lost sister slowly dies.

The music is a typhoon gale flaying rocky shores to gravel and sand, and the violinist lets it spin and rage, and she watches as the fat man takes four of her sister's fingers and part of a thighbone, strands of her ash-blonde hair, a vial of oil boiled and distilled from the fat of her breasts, a pink-white section of small intestine—all these things and the five fossils from off an English beach to make the instrument he wooed her here to play for him. And now there are tears streaming hot down her cheeks, but still Ellen plays the violin that was her sister and still she doesn't open her eyes.

The single gunshot is very loud in the room, and the display cases rattle and a few of the ammonites slip off their Lucite stands and clatter against wood or glass or other spiraled shells.

And finally the violinist opens her eyes.

And the music ends as the bow slides from her fingers and falls to the floor at her feet.

"No," she says, "please don't let it stop, please," but the echo of the revolver and the memory of the concerto are so loud in her ears that her own words are almost lost to her.

That's all, her sister whispers, louder than any suicide's gun, soft as a midwinter night coming on, gentle as one unnoticed second bleeding into the next. *I've shown you, and now there isn't anymore.*

Across the room, the Collector still sits at his desk, but now he's slumped a bit in his chair and his head is thrown back so that he seems to be staring at something on the ceiling. Blood spills from the black cavern of his open mouth and drips to the floor.

There isn't anymore.

And when she's stopped crying and is quite certain that her sister will not speak to her again, that all the secrets she has any business seeing have been revealed, the violinist retrieves the dropped bow and stands, then walks to the desk and returns the ammonite violin to its case. She will not give it to the police when they arrive, after she has gone to the kitchen to call them, and she will not tell them that it was the fat man who gave it to her. She will take it back to Brooklyn, and they will find other incriminating things in another room in the yellow house and so have no need of the violin and these stolen shreds of her sister. The Collector has kindly written every-thing down in three books bound in red leather, all the names and dates and places, and there are other souvenirs, besides. And she will never try to put this story into words, for words have never come easily to her, and like the violin, the story is hers now and hers alone.

A SEASON OF
BROKEN DOLLS

August 14, 2027

SABIT'S THE ONE with a hard-on for stitchwork, not me. It is not exactly (or at all) my particular realm of expertise, not my cuppa, not my *scene*—as the beatniks used to say, back there in those happy Neolithic times. I mean the plethora of Lower Manhattan flesh-art dives like Guro/Guro or Twist or that pretentious little shitstain way down on Pearl—*Corpus Ex Machina*—the one that gets almost as much space in the police blotters as in the glossy snip-art rags. Me, I'm still laboring alone or nearly so in the Dark Ages, and she never lets me forget it. My unfashionable and unprofitable preoccupation with mere canvas and paint, steel and plaster, all that which has been deemed *démodé, passé,* Post-Relevant, all that which is fit only to fill up musty old museum vaults and public galleries, gathering more dust even than my career. *You still write on a goddamn keyboard, for chris'sakes,* she laughs. *You're the only woman I ever fucked made being a living fossil a goddamn point of pride.* And then Sabit checks for my pulse—two fingers pressed gently to a wrist or the side of my throat— bcause, hey, maybe I'm not a living fossil at all. Maybe I'm that other kind, like Pollock and Mondrian, Henry Moore and poor old Man Ray. *No, no, no, the blood's still flowing sluggishly along,* she smiles and lights a cigarette. *Too bad. Maybe there's hope for you yet, my love.* Sabit likes to talk almost as much as she likes to watch. It's not as though the bitch has a mark on her hide anywhere, not as though she's anything but a tourist with a hard-on, a fetishist who cannot ever get enough of her kink. Prick her for a crimson bead and the results would come back same as mine, 98% the same as any chimpanzee. She knows how much contempt is reserved in those quarters for tourists and trippers, but I think that only makes her more zealous. She exhales, and smoke lingers like an unearned halo about her face. I should have dumped her months ago, but I'm not as young as I used to be, and I'm just as addicted to sex as she is to nicotine and pills and vicarious stitchwork. She calls herself a poet, but she has never let me read a word she's written, if she's ever written a word. I found her a year ago, almost a year ago, found her in a run-down titty bar getting fucked-up on vodka and laudanum and speed and the too-firm silicone breasts of women who might have been the real thing—even if their perfect boobs were not—or might only have been cheap japandroids. She followed me home, fifteen years my junior, and the more things change, the more things stay the way they were day before day before yesterday, day before I met Sabit and her slumberous Arabian eyes. My sloe-eyed stitch-fiend of a girlfriend, and I have her, and she has me, and we're as happy as happy can be, and I pretend it means something more than orgasms and not being alone, something more than me annoying her and her taunting ~~and insulting~~ me. Now she's telling me there's a new line-up down @ *Corpus Ex Machina* (hereafter known simply as *CeM*), and we have to be there tomorrow night. *We have to be there*, she says. *The Trenton Group is showing, and last time the Trenton Group showed, there was almost a riot, so we have to be there.* I have deadlines that have nothing whatsoever to do with that constantly revolving meat-market spectacle, and in a moment I'll finish this entry & then I'll tell her that, and she'll tell me we have to be there, we have to be there, & there will be time to finish my articles later. There always is, & I'm never late. Never late enough to matter. I'll go with her, bcause I do not trust her to go alone—not go alone *and* come back here again—she'll tell me that, and she'll be right as fucking rain. Her smug triumph, well that's a given. Just as my obligatory refusal followed by inevitable, reluctant acquiescence is also a given. We play by the same rules every time. Now she's on about some scandal @ Guro/Guro—chicanery and artifice, prosthetics, and she says, *They're all a bunch of gidding poseurs, the shitheels*

147

run that sorry dump. Someone ought to burn it to the ground for this. You know how to light a match, I reply, & she rolls her dark eyes @ me. No rain today. No rain since . . . June. The sky at noon is the color of rust, and I wish it were winter. Enough for now. Maybe she'll shut up for 10 or 15 if I fuck her.

August 16, 2027

"You're into that whole *scene*, right?" Which only shows to go once again that my editor still has her head rammed so far up her ass that her farts smell like toothpaste. But I said yeah, sure, bcause she wanted someone with cred on the Guro/Guro story, the stitch chicanery, allegations of fraud among the freaks, & what else was I supposed to say? I can't remember the last time I had the nerve to turn down a paying assignment. Must have been years before I met Sabit, at least. So, yeah, I tagged along last night, just like she wanted—both of them wanted—she & she, but @ least I can say it's work, and Berlin picked up the tab. Sabit's out, so I don't have her yammering in my goddamn ear, an hour to myself, perhaps, half an hour, however long it takes her to get back with dinner. I wanted to put something down, something that isn't in the notes and photos I've already filed with the pre-edit gleets. Fuck. I've been popping caps from Sabit's pharmacopoeia all goddamn day long, I don't even know what, the baby-blue ones she gets $300/two dozen from Peru, the ones she says calm her down but they're not calming me down. They haven't even dulled the edge, so far as I can tell. But, anyway, there we were @ *CeM*, in the crowded Pearl St. warehouse passing itself off as a *slaughter*house or a zoo or an exhibition or what the fuck ever, and there's this bird from Tokyo, and I never got her name, but she had eyes all the colors of peacock feathers, iridescent eyes, and she recognized me. Some monied bird with pretty peacock eyes. She'd read the series I wrote in '21 when the city finally gave up and let the sea have the subway. *I read a lot,* she said. *I might have been a journalist myself,* she said. That sort of shit. Thought she was going to ask me to sign a goddamn cocktail napkin. And I'm smiling & nodding yes, bcause that's agency policy, be nice to the readers, don't feed the pigeons, whatever. But I can't take my eyes off the walls. The walls are new. They were just walls last time Sabit dragged me down to one of her snip affairs. Now they're alive, every square inch, mottled shades of pink and gray and whatever you call that shade between pink and gray. Touch them (Sabit must have touched them a hundred times) and they twitch or sprout goose bumps. They sweat, those walls. And the peacock girl was in one ear, and Sabit was in the other, the music so loud I was already getting a headache before my fourth drink, and I was trying to stop looking at those walls. *Pig,* Sabit told me later in the evening. *It's all just pig,* and she sounded disappointed. Most of this is in the notes, though I didn't say how unsettling I found those walls of skin. I save the revulsion for my own dime. Sabit says they're working on adding functional genitalia and . . . fuck. I hear her at the door. Later, then. She has to shut up and go to sleep eventually.

August 16, 2027 (later, 11:47 p.m.)

Sabit came back with a bag full of Indian takeaway, when she'd gone out for sushi. I really couldn't care less, one way or the other, these days food is only fucking food—curry or wasabi, but when I *asked* why she'd changed her mind, she just stared at me, eyes blank as a goddamn dead codfish, & shrugged. Then she was quiet all night long, & the last thing I need just now is Sabit Abbasi going all silent and creepy on me. She's asleep, snoring bcause her sinuses are bad bcause she smokes too much. & I'm losing the momentum I needed to say *anything* more about what happened @ CeM on Sat. night. It's all fading, like a dream. I've been reading one of Sabit's books, *The Breathing Composition* (Welleran Smith, 2025), something from those long-ago days when the avant-garde abomination of stitch & snip was still hardly more than nervous rumor & theory & the wishful thinking of a handful of East Coast art pervs. I don't know what I was looking for, if it was just research for the article, don't know what I thought I might find—or what any of this has to do with Sat. nite. Am I afraid to write it down? That's what Sabit would say. But I won't ask Sabit. What do *you* dream, Sabit, my dear sadistic plaything? Do you *dream* in installations, muscles and tendons, gallery walls of sweating pig flesh, living bone exposed for all to see, vivisection as not-quite still life, portrait of the artist as a young atrocity? Are your sweet dreams the same things keeping me awake, making me afraid to sleep?

There was so goddamn much @ *CeM* to turn my fucking stomach, but just this one thing has me jigged and sleepless and popping your blue Peruvian bonbons. Just this one thing. I'm not the squeamish sort, and everyone knows it. That's one reason the agency tossed the Guro/Guro story at me. Gore & sex and mutilation? Give it to Schuler. She's seen the worst and keeps coming back for more. Wasn't she one of the first into Brooklyn after the bomb? & she did that crazy whick out on the Stuyvesant rat attacks. How many murders and suicides and serial killers does that make for Schuler now? 9? Fourteen? 38? That kid in the Bronx, the Puerto Rican bastard who sliced up his little sister & then fed her through a food processor, that was one of Schuler's, yeah? *Ad infinitum, ad nauseam,* Hail Mary, full of beans. Cause they know I won't be on my knees puking up lunch when I should be making notes & getting the vid or asking questions. But now, *now* Sabit, I'm dancing round this one thing. This one little thing. So, here there's a big ol' chink in these renowned nerves of steel. Maybe I've got a weak spot after fucking all. Rings of flesh, towers of iron—oh yeah, sure—fucking corpses heaped in dumpsters and rats eating fucking babies alive & winos & don't forget the kid with the Cuisinart—sure, fine—but that one labeled #17, oh, now *that's* another goddamn story. She saw something there, & ol' Brass-Balls Schuler was never quite the same again, isn't that the way it goes?

Are you laughing in your dreams, Sabit? Is that why you're smiling next to me in your goddamn sleep? I've dog-eared a page in your book, Sabit, a page with a poem written in a New Jersey loony bin by a woman, & Welleran Smith just calls her Jane Doe so I do not know her name. But Welleran Smith & that mangy bunch of stitch prophets called her a visionary, & I'm writing it down here, while I try to find the nerve to say whatever it is I'd wanted to say about #17:

> *spines and bellies knitted & proud and all open*
> *all watching spines and bellies and the three;*
> *triptych & buckled, ragdoll fusion*
> *3 of you so conjoined, my eyes from yours,*
> *arterial hallways knitted red proud flesh*
> *Healing and straining for cartilage & epidermis*
> *Not taking, we cannot imagine*

So many wet lips, your sky Raggedy alchemy
And all expecting Jerusalem

And Welleran Smith, he proclaims Jane Doe a "hyperlucid transcendent schizo-oracle," a "visionary calling into the maelstrom." & turns out, here in the footnotes, they put the bitch away bcause she'd drugged her lover—she was a lesbian; of course, she had to be a lesbian—she drugged her lover and used surgical thread to sew the woman's lips & nostrils closed, *after* performing a crude tracheotomy so she wouldn't suffocate. Jane Doe sewed her own vagina shut, and she removed her own nipples & then tried grafting them onto her gf's belly. She kept the woman (not named, sorry, lost to anonymity) cuffed to a bed for almost 6 weeks before someone finally came poking around & jesus fucking christ, Sabit, this is the sort of sick bullshit set it all in motion. Jane Doe's still locked away in her padded cell, I'm guessing—*hyperlucid* & worshipped by the snips—& maybe the woman she mutilated is alive somewhere, trying to forget. Maybe the doctors even patched her up (ha, ha fucking ha). Maybe even made her good as new again, but I doubt it. I need to sleep. I need to lie down & close my eyes & not see #17 and sweating walls and Sabit ready to fucking cum bcause she can never, ever get enough. It's half an hour after midnight, & they expect copy from me tomorrow night, eight sharp, when I haven't written a goddamn word about the phony stitchwork @ Guro/Guro. Fuck you, Sabit, and fuck Jane Doe & that jackoff Welleran Smith and the girl with peacock eyes that I should have screwed just to piss you off, Sabit. I should have brought her back here and fucked her in our bed, let her use your toothbrush, & maybe you'd have found some other snip tourist & even now I could be basking in the sanguine cherry glow of happily ever fucking after.

August 18, 2027

I'm off the Guro/Guro story. Missed the *extended* DL tonight, no copy, never even made it down to the gallery. Just my notes and photos from *CeM* for someone else to pick up where I left off. Lucky the agency didn't let me go. Lucky or unlucky. But they can't can me, not for missing a deadline or two. I have rep, I have creds, I have awards & experience & loyal god-damn readers. Hell, I still get a byline on this thing; it's in my contract. Fuck it. Fuck it all.

August 19, 2027

Welleran Smith's "Jane Doe" died about six months ago, back in March. I asked some questions, said it was work for the magazine, tagged some people who know people who could get to the files. It was a suicide—oh, and never you mind that she'd been on suicide watch for years. This one was a certified trouper, a bona-fide martyr in the service of her own undoing. She chewed her tongue in half & choked herself on it. She had a name, too. Don't know if Smith knew it & simply withheld it, or if he never looked that far. Maybe he only prigged the bits he needed to put the snips in orbit & disregarded the rest. "Jane Doe" was Judith Louise Darger, born 1992, Ph.D. in Anthropology from Yale, specialized in urban neomythology, syncretism, etc. & did a book with HarperC back in '21—*Bloody Mary, La Llorona, and the Blue Lady: Feminine Icons in a Fabricated Child's Apocalypse*. Sold for shit, out of print by 2023. But found a battered copy cheap uptown @ Paper Museum. Darger's gf and victim, she's dead, too. Another suicide, not long after they put Darger away. Turns out, she had a history of neurosis and *self*-mutilation going back to high school, & there was all sorts of shit there I'm not going to get into, but she told the courts that what Darger did to her, and to herself, they'd planned the whole thing for months. So, why the fuck did good old Welleran Smith leave *that* part out? It was in the goddamn press, no secret. I have a photograph of Judith Darger, right here on the dj of her book. She could not look less remarkable. Sabit says there's another Trenton Group show this weekend & don't I wanna go? She's hardly said three words to me the last couple of days, but she told me this. Get another look at #17, she said, & I almost fucking hit her. No more pills, Schuler. No more pills. You're frying.

———

August 20, 2027

No sleep last night. Today, I filed for my next assignment, but so far the green bin's still empty. Maybe I'm being punished for blowing the DL on Weds. night, some sort of pass-ag bullshit bcause that's the best those weasels in senior edit can ever seem to manage. Or maybe it's only a sloooowwww week. I am having a hard time caring, either way. No sleep last night. No, I said that already. Time on my hands and that's never a good thing. Insomnia and black coffee and gin, takeaway and durian Pop-Tarts and a faint throb that wants to be a headache (how long since one of those?), me locked in my office last night reading a few chapters of Darger's grand flop, but there's nothing in there—fascinating and I don't know why it wasn't better received, but still leading me nowhere, nowhere at all (where did I *think* it would lead?). This bit re: La Llorona ("Bloody Mary") from Ch. 3—"Some girls with no home feel claws scratching under the skin on their arms. Their hand [sic] looks like red fire." And this one, from a *Miami New Times* article: "When a child says he got the story from the spirit world, as homeless children do, you've hit the ultimate *non sequitur.*" Homeless kids and demons and angels, street gangs, drugs, the socioeconomic calamities of thirty goddamn years ago. News articles from 1997. A journalistic scam. None of this is gonna answer any of my questions, if I truly have questions to be answered. But this is "Jane Doe's" magnum opus, and there is some grim fascination I can't shake—How did she get from *there* to *there*, from phony diy street myths to sewing her gf's mouth shut? Maybe it wasn't such a short goddamn walk. Maybe, one night, she stood before a dark mirror in a darkened room, the mirror coated with dried saltwater—going native or just too fucking curious, whatever—and maybe she *stood* there chanting *Bloody Mary, Bloody Mary,* over and over and over and La Llorona scratched her way out through the looking glass, scarring the anthropologist's soul with her rosary beads. Maybe that's where this began, the snips and stitches, #17. Maybe it all goes back to those homeless kids in Miami, back before the flood, before the W. Antarctic ice sheet melted and Dade County FL sank like a stone, and all along it was the late Dr. J. L. Darger let this djinn out of its gin bottle in ways people like Sabit have not yet begun to suspect and never will. I'm babbling, and if that's the best I can do, I'm going to stop keeping a damned journal. I've agreed to be @ *CeM* tomorrow night with Sabit. I'm a big girl. I can sip my shitty Merlot and nibble greasy orange cheese and stale crackers with the best of them. I can bear the soulless conversation and the sweating porcine walls. I can look at #17 and see nothing there but bad art, fucked-up artless crap, pretentious carnage and willful suffering. Maybe then I can put *all* this shit behind me. Who knows, maybe I can even put Sabit behind me, too.

August 20, 2027 (later, p.m.)

Sabit says the surgeon on #17 will be at the show t'morrow night. I think maybe it's someone Sabit was screwing before she started screwing me. Oh, & this, from *The Breathing Composition*, which I've started reading again & frankly wish I had not. Seems Welleran Smith somehow got his paws on Darger's diary, or one of her diaries, & he quotes it at length (& no doubt there are contextual issues; don't know the fate of the original text):

"We are all alone on a darkling plain, precisely as Matt. Arnold said. We are so very alone here, and we yearn each day for the reunification promised by priests and gurus and by some ancient animal instinct. We are evolution's grand degenerates, locked away forever in the consummate prison cells of our conscious minds, each divided always from the other. I met a man from Spain, and he gave me a note card with the number seventeen written on it seventeen times. He thought that surely I would understand right away, and he was heartbroken when I did not. When I asked, he would not explain. I've kept the card in my files, and sometimes I take it out and stare at it, hoping that I will at last discern its message. But it remains perfectly opaque, bcause my eyes are the eyes of the damned."

& I'm looking thru the program for the Trenton Show on the 15th, last Sun., & only one piece is *numbered*, only 1 piece w/a # for a title—#17. Yes, I know. I'm going in circles here. Chasing my own ass. Toys in the attic. Nutters as the goddamn snips if I don't watch myself. If I don't get some sleep. I haven't seen Sabit all evening, just a call in this afternoon.

———

August 21, 2027 (Saturday, 10:12 a.m.)

Four whole hours sleep last night. & the hangover is not so bad that coffee and aspirin isn't helping. My head feels clearer than it has in days. Sabit came home sometime after I nodded off & I woke with her snoring next to me. When I asked if maybe she wanted breakfast, she smiled, so I made eggs & cut a grapefruit in half. Perhaps I can persuade her to stay home tonight, that we should *both* stay home tonight. There is nothing down there I need to see again.

August 21, 2027 (2:18 p.m.)

No, she says. *We are expected,* she says, & what the fuck is that supposed to mean, anyway? So there was a fight, bcause there always has to be a fight with Sabit, a real 4-alarm screamer this time, & I have no idea where she's run off to but she swore she'd be back by *five* & I better be sober, she said, & I better be dressed & ready for the show. So, yeah, fuck it. I'll go to the damn show with her. I'll rub shoulders with the stitch freaks this one last time. Maybe I'll even have a good long look at #17 (tho' now, I should add, now Sabit says the surgeon won't be there after all). Maybe I'll stand & stare until it's only flesh & wires & hooks & fancy lighting. Sidonie-Gabrielle Colette wrote somewhere, "Look for a long time at what pleases you, and for a longer time at what pains you." Maybe I'll shame them all with my staring. They only feel as much pain as they *want* to feel—isn't that what Sabit is always telling me? The stitchworks, they get all the best painkillers, ever since the Supreme Ct. wigs decided this sick shit constitutes Art—so long as certain lines are not crossed. They bask in glassy-eyed morphine hazes, shocked cold orange on neuroblocks & Fibrodene & Elyzzium, exotic transdermals & maybe all that shit's legal & maybe it ain't, but 2380 no one's asking too many questions as the City of NY has enough on its great collective plate these days w/out stitch-friendly lawyers raising a holy funk about censorship and freedom of expression and 1st Amendment violations. The cops hate the fuckers, but none of the arrests have had jack to do with drugs, just disorderly conduct, riots after shows, shit like that. But yeah, t'morrow night I'll go back to *CeM* with Sabit, my heart's damned desire, my cunt's lazy love, & I will look until they want to fucking charge me extra.

August 21, 2027

So Sabit shows up an hour or so after dark . . . she's gone now, gone again bcause I suppose I have chased her away, again. That's what she would say, I am sure. I have chased her away again. But, as I was saying, she shows up, & I can tell she's been drinking bcause she has that smirk and that swagger she gets when she's been drinking, & I can tell she's still pissed. I'm waiting for the other shoe. I'm waiting, bcause I fucking know whatever's coming next is for my benefit. & I'm thinking, screw it, get it over with, don't let her have the satisfaction of getting in the first blow. I'm thinking, this is where it ends. Tonight. No more of her bullshit. It's been a grandiose act of reciprocal masochism, Sabit, & it's been raw & all, but enough's enough. @ least the sex was good, so let's remember that & move on. & that's when I notice the gauze patch taped to her back, centered between her shoulder blades just so, placed *just so* there between her scapulae, centered on the smooth brown plain of her trapezius (let me write this the way a goddamn snip would write it, cluttered with an anatomist's Latin). & when I ask her what the fuck, she just shrugs, & that swatch of gauze goes up & then down again. But I know. I know whatever it is she's done, whatever comes next, this is it. This is her preemptive volley, so I can just forget all about landing the first punch this time, baby. Sabit knows revenge like a drunk knows an empty bottle, & I should have given up while I was ahead. *I've been wanting some new ink*, she says. *You helped me to finally make up my mind, that's all.* & before she can say anything else, I rip away the bandage. She does not even fucking flinch, even though the tattoo can't be more than a couple hrs old, still seeping & puffy and red, & all I can hear is her laughing. Bcause there on her back is the Roman numeral XVII, & when she asks for the bandage back, I slap her. I *slapped* her. This use of present tense, what's that but keeping the wound open & fresh, keeping the scabs at bay just like some goddamn pathetic stitchwork would do. I *slapped* her. The sound of my hand against her cheek was so loud, crack like a goddamn firecracker, & in the silence afterwards (just as fucking loud) she just smiled & smiled & smiled for me. & then I started yelling—I don't know exactly what—accusations that couldn't possibly have made sense, slurs and insinuation, and truthfully I knew even then none of it was anything but bitterness & disappointment that she'd not only managed to draw first blood (hahaha) this round, she'd finally pushed me far enough to hit her. I'd never hit her before. I had never hit *anyone* before, not since some bullshit high school fights, &, at last, she did not even need to raise her voice. & then she just smiled @ me, & I think I must have finally told her to say something, bcause I was puking sick to death of that smug smile. *I'm glad you approve,* she said. Or maybe she said, *I'm glad you understand.* In this instance, the meanings would be the same somehow. Somehow interchangeable. But I did not apologize. That's the sort of prick I am. I sat down on the kitchen floor & stared @ linoleum Rorschach patterns & when I looked up again she was gone. I don't know if she's *gone,* gone, or if Sabit has merely retreated until she decides it's time for another blitz. Rethinking her maneuvers, the ins & outs of this campaign, logistics and field tactics & what the fuck ever. Cards must be played properly. I know Sabit, & she will never settle for Pyrrhic victory, no wars of attrition, no winner's curse. I sat on the floor until I heard the door shut & so knew I was alone again. I would say at least this gets me out of *CeM* on Sun. night, but I may go alone. Even though I know she'll be there. Clearly, I can hurt some more. Tonight I will get drunk, & that is all.

August 22, 2027 (2:56 a.m.)

Always have I been a sober drunk. I've finished the gin & started on an old bottle of rye whisky—gift from some former lover I won't name here—bcause I didn't feel like walking through the muggy, dusty evening, risking life and limb & lung for another pretty blue bottle of Bombay. A sober & lazy drunk, averse to taking *unnecessary* risks. Sabit has not yet reappeared, likely she will not. I suspect she believes she has won not only the battle, but the war as well. Good for her. May she go haunt some other sad fuck's life. Of course, the apt. is still awash in her junk, her clothes, her stitch lit, the hc zines and discs & her txtbooks filled with diagrams, schematics of skeletons & musculature, neuroanatomy, surgical technique, organic chem and pharmacology, immunology, all that crap. Snip porn. I should dump it all. I should call someone 2830 to cart it all away so I don't have to fucking look at it anymore. The clothes, her lucite ashtrays, the smoky, musky, spicy smell of her, bottles of perfume, cosmetics, music, Sanrio vibrators, jewelry, deodorant, jasmine soap, baby teeth & jesus all the *CRAP* she's left behind to keep me company. I don't know if I'll sleep tonight. I don't want to. I don't want to be awake anymore ever again. Why did she want to rub my nose in #17? Just that she's finally found a flaw, a goddamn weakness, & she has to make the most of it? A talkative, sober drunk. But wait—there is something. There is something else I found in Welleran Smith, & I'm gonna write it down. Something more from the diary/ies of Dr. Judith Darger, unless it's only something Smith concocted to suit his own ends. More & more I consider that likelihood, that Darger is only some lunatic just happened to be where these people needed her to be, but isn't that how it always is with saints and martyrs? Questions of victimhood arise. Who's exploiting who? Who's exploiting whom? Christ I get lost in all these words. I don't *need* words. I'm strangling on words. I need to see Sabit & end this mess & be done with her. According to Welleran Smith, Darger writes (none of the "entries" are dated): "I would not tell a child that it isn't going to hurt. I wouldn't lie. It is going to hurt, and it is going to hurt forever or as long as human consciousness may endure. It is going to hurt until it doesn't hurt anymore. That is what I would tell a child. That is what I tell myself, and what am I but my own child? So, I will not lie to any of you. Yes, there will be pain, and at times the pain will seem unbearable. But the pain will open doorways. The pain *is* a doorway, as is the scalpel and as are the sutures and each and every incision. Pain is to be thrown open wide that all may gaze at the wonders which lie beyond. Why is it assumed this flesh must not be cut? Why is it assumed this is my final corporeal form? What is it we cannot yet see for all our fear of pain and ugliness and disfiguration? I would not tell a child that it isn't going to hurt. I would teach a child to live in pain." Is that what I am learning from you, Sabit? Is that the lesson of #17 and the glassy stare of those six eyes? Would you, all of you, teach me to live with pain?

August 23, 2027

It's almost dawn, that first false dawn & just a bit of hesitant purple where the sky isn't quite night anymore. As much as I have ever seen false dawn in the city, where we try so hard to keep the night away forever. If I had a son, or a daughter, I would tell them a story, how people are @ war with night, & the city—like all cities—is only a fortress built to hold back the night, even though all the world is just a bit of grit floating in a sea of night that might go on almost forever. I'm on the roof. I've never been up here before. Sabit & I never came up here. Maybe another three hours left before it's too hot & bright to sit up here, only 95F now if my watch is telling me the truth. My face & hair are slick with sweat, sweating out the booze & pills, sweating out the sweet & sour memory of Sabit. It feels good to sweat. I went to Pearl St. & the Trenton reveal @ *Corpus ex Machina*, but apparently she did not. Maybe she had something better to do & someone better to be doing it with. I flashed my press tag @ the door, so at least I didn't have to pay the $47 cover. I was not the only pundit in attendance. I saw Kline, who's over @ the Voice these days (that venerable old whore) & I saw Garrison, too. Buzzards w/their beaks sharp, stomachs empty, mouths watering. No, I do not know if birds salivate, but reporters sure fucking do. None of them spoke to me, & I exchanged the favor. The place was *replete*, as the dollymops are wont to say, chock-full, standing room only. I sipped dirty martinis and licorice shides & looked no one in the eye, no one who was not on exhibit. #17 was near the back, not as well lit as some of the others, & I stood there & stared, bcause that is what I'd come for. Sometimes it gazed back @ me, or *they* gazed @ me—I am uncertain of the proper idiom or parlance or phrase. Is *it* One or are *they* 3? I stared & stared & stared, like any good voyeur would do, any dedicated peeper, bcause no clips are allowed, so you stand & drink it all in there the same way the Neanderthals did it or pony up the fat spool of cash for one of the Trenton chips or mnemonic lozenges ("all proceeds for R&D, promo, & ongoing medical expenses," of course). I looked until all I saw was all I was *meant* to see —the sculpted body(ies), living & breathing & con- scious—the perpetually hurting realization of all Darger's nightmares. If I saw beauty there, it was no different from the *beauty* I saw in Brooklyn after

159

the New Konsojaya Trading Co. popped their micro-nuke over on Tillary St. No different from the hundred lingering deaths I've witnessed. Welleran Smith said this was to be "the soul's terrorism against the tyranny of genes & phenotype." I stood there & I saw everything there was to see. Maybe Sabit would have been proud. Maybe she would have been disappointed @ my resolve. It hardly matters, either way. A drop of sweat dissolving on my tongue & I wonder if that's the way the ocean used to taste, when it wasn't suicide to taste the ocean? When I had seen all I had come to see, my communion w/#17, I found an empty stool @ the bar. I thought you might still put in an appearance, Sabit, so I got drunker & waited for a glimpse of you in the crowd. & there was a man sitting next to me, Harvey somebody or another from Chicago, gray-haired with a mustache, & he talked & I listened, as best I could hear him over the music. I think the music was suffocating me. He said, *That's my granddaughter over there, what's left of her,* & he pointed thru the crush of bodies toward a stitchwork hanging from the warehouse ceiling, a dim chandelier of circuitry & bone & muscles flayed & rearranged. I'd looked at the piece on the way in—*The Lighthouse of Francis Bacon*, it was called. The old man told me he'd been following the show for months, but now he was almost broke & would have to head back to Chicago soon. He was only drinking ginger ale. I bought him a ginger ale & listened, leaning close so he didn't have to shout to be heard. The chandelier had once been a student @ the Pritzker School of Medicine, but then, he said, "something happened." I did not ask what. I decided if he wanted me to know, he would tell me. He didn't. Didn't tell me, I mean. He tried to buy me a drink, but I wouldn't let him. The grandfather of *The Lighthouse of Francis Bacon* tried to buy me a drink, & I realized I was thinking like a journalist again, thinking *you dumb fucks—here's your goddamn story—not some bullshit hearsay about chicanery among the snips, no, this old man's your goddamn story, this poor guy probably born way the fuck back before man even walked on the goddamn moon & now he's sitting here at the end of the world, this anonymous old man rubbing his bony shoulders with the tourists and art critics & stitch fiends and freaks because his granddaughter decided she'd rather be a fucking light fixture than a gynecologist.* Oh god, Sabit. If you could have shown him your brand-new tattoo. I left the place before midnight, paid the hack extra to go farther south, to get me as near the ruins as he dared. I needed to see them, that's all. Rings of flesh & towers of iron, right, rust-stained granite and the empty eye sockets where once were windows. The skyscraper stubs of Old Downtown, Wall St. and Battery Park City, all hurricane aftermaths of it inundated by the rising waters there @ the confluence of the Hudson & the E. River. And then I came home, & now I am sitting here on the roof, getting less & less drunk, sweating & listening to traffic & the city waking up around me—the living fossil with her antique keyboard. If you do come back here, Sabit, if that's whatever happens next, you will not find me intimidated by your XVII or by #17, either, but I don't think you ever will. You've moved on. & if you send someone to pack up your shit, I'll probably already be in Bratislava by then. After *CeM*, there were 2 good assigns waiting for me in the green bin, & I'm taking the one that gets me far, far, farthest away from here for 3 weeks in Slovakia. But right now I'm just gonna sit here on the roof & watch the sun come up all swollen & lobster red over this rotten, drowning city, over this rotten fucking world. I think the pigeons are waking up.

IN VIEW OF NOTHING

Oh, pity us here, we angels of lead.
We're dead, we're sick, hanging by thread . . . David Bowie
("Get Real," 1995)

02. The Bed

MY BREASTS ACHE.
I have enough trouble just remembering the name of this city, and I have yet to be convinced that the name remains the same from one day to the next, one night to the next night. Or even that the city itself remains the same. These are the very sorts of details that will be my undoing someday, someday quite soon, if I am anything less than mindful. Today, I believe that I have awakened in Sakyo-ku, in the Kyoto Prefecture, but lying here staring up at the bright banks of fluorescent lights on the ceiling, I might be anywhere. I might well be in Boston or Johannesburg or Sydney, and maybe I've never even been to Japan. Maybe I have lived my entire life without setting foot in Kyoto.

From where I lie, almost everything seems merely various shades of unwelcome conjecture. Almost everything. I think about getting up and going to the window, because from there I might confirm or deny my Kyoto hypothesis. I might spy the Kamo River, flowing down from its source on Mount Sajikigatake, or the withered cherry trees that did not blossom last year and perhaps will not blossom this spring, either. I might see the silver-grey ribbon of the Kamo, running between the neon-scarlet flicker of torii gates at the Kamigamo and Shimogamo shrines. Maybe that window looks eastward, towards the not-so-distant ocean, and I would see Mount Daimonji. Or I might see only the steel and glass wall of a neighboring skyscraper.

I lie where I am and do not go to the window, and I stare up at the low plaster ceiling, the ugly water stains spread out there like bruises or melanoma or concentric geographical features on an ice moon of Saturn or Jupiter or Neptune. This whole goddamn building is rotten; I recall that much clearly enough. The ceiling of my room—if it *is* my room—has more leaks than I can count, and I think it's not even on the top floor. The rain is loud against the window, but the dripping ceiling seems to my ears much louder, as each drop grows finally too heavy and falls to the ceramic tiles. I hear a distinct *plink* for each and every drop that drips down from the motel ceiling, and that *plink* does not quite seem to match what I recall about the sound of water dripping against tile.

The paler-than-oyster sheets are damp, too. As are the mattress and box springs underneath. Why there are not mushrooms, I can't say. There is mold, mold or mildew if there's some difference between the two, because I can smell it, and I can see it. I can taste it.

I lie here on my back and stare up at the leaky ceiling, listening to the rain, letting these vague thoughts ricochet through my incontinent skull. My mind leaks, too, I suspect, and in much the same way that this ceiling leaks. My thoughts and memories have stained the moldering sheets, discrete units of me drifting away in a slow flood of cerebrospinal fluid, my ears for sluice gates—or my eyes—*Liquor cerebrospinalis* draining out a few precious milliliters per day or hour, leaving only vast echoes in emptied subarachnoid cavities.

She looks at me over her left shoulder, her skin as white as snow that never falls, her hair whiter still, her eyes like broken sapphire shards, and she frowns, knitting her white eyebrows. She is talking into the antique black rotary telephone, but looking at me, disapproving of these meandering, senseless thoughts when I have yet to answer her questions to anyone's satis-faction. I turn away—the exact wrong thing to do, and yet I do it, anyway. I wish she would put some clothes on. Her robe is hanging on a hook not far away. I would get it for her, if she would only ask. She lights a cigarette, and that's good, because now the air wrapped all about the bed smells less like the mold and poisonous rainwater.

"We do the best we can," she tells the telephone, whoever's listening on the other end of the line, "given what we have to work with."

Having turned away, I lie on my left side, my face pressed into those damp sheets, shivering and wondering how long now since I have been genuinely warm. Wondering, too, if this season is spring or winter or autumn. I am fairly certain it is not summer. She laughs, but I don't shut my eyes. I imagine that the folds and creases of the sheets are ridges and valleys, and I am the slain giant of some creation myth. My cerebrospinal fluid will form lakes and rivers and seas, and trees will sprout, and grass and ferns and lichen, and all that vegetation shall be imbued with my lost, or merely forfeited, mem-ories. The birds will rise up from fancies that have bled from me.

My breasts ache.

Maybe that has some role to play in this cosmogony, the aching, swollen breasts of the fallen giantess whose mind became the wide white-grey world.

"I need more time, that's all," the naked snow-coloured woman tells the black Bakelite handset. "There were so many more layers than we'd antici-pated."

With an index finger I trace the course of one of the V-shaped sheet val-leys. It gradually widens towards the foot of the bed, towards my *own* feet, and I decide that I shall arbitrarily call that direction *south*, as I arbitrarily think this motel might exist somewhere in Kyoto. Where the sheet valley ends, there is a broad alluvial fan, this silk-cotton blend splaying out into flat deltas where an unseen river at last deposits its burden of mnemonic silt and clay and sand—only the finest particles make it all the way over the faraway edge of the bed to the white-tile sea spread out below. Never mean-ing to, I have made a *flat* white-grey world. Beyond the delta are low hills, smooth ridges in the shadow of my knees. Call it an eclipse, that gloom; *any* shadow in this stark room is Divine.

These thoughts are leading me nowhere, and I think now that they must exist only to erect a defence, this complete absence of direction. She has pried and stabbed and pricked that fragile innermost stratum of the meningeal envelope, the precious pia matter, and so triggered inside me these meandering responses. She thought to find only pliable grey matter waiting underneath, and maybe the answers to her questions—tap in, cross ref, download—but, no, here's this damned firewall, instead. But I did not put it there. I am holding nothing back by choice. I know she won't believe that, though it is the truth.

"Maybe another twelve hours," she tells the handset.

I must be a barren, pitiless goddess, to have placed all those fluorescent tubes for a sun and nothing else. They shed no warmth from out that otherwise starless ivory firmament. Heaven drips to make a filthy sea, and she rings off and places the handset back into its Bakelite cradle. It is all a cradle, I think, this room in this motel in this city I cannot name with any certainty. Perhaps I never even left Manhattan or Atlanta or San Francisco.

"I'm losing patience," she says, and sighs impatiently. "More importantly, they're losing patience with me."

And I apologise again, though I am not actually certain this statement warrants an apology. I turn my head and watch as she leans back against her pillow, lifting the stumps of her legs onto the bed. She once told me how she lost them, and it was not so very long ago when she told me, but I can no longer remember that, either.

She smokes her cigarette, and her blue eyes seem fixed on something beyond the walls of the motel room.

"Maybe I should look at the book again," I suggest.

"Maybe," she agrees. "Or maybe I should put a bullet in your skull and say it was an accident."

"Or that I was trying to escape."

She nods and takes another drag off her cigarette. "If you are a goddess," she asks, "what the fuck does that make me?"

But I have no response for that. No response whatsoever. The smoke from her lips and nostrils hangs above our damp bed like the first clouds spreading out above my flat creation of sheets and fallen giants. Her skin is milk, and my breasts ache.

I close my eyes, and possibly I smell cherry blossoms behind her smoke and the stink of mildew, and I try hard to recollect when I first walked the avenues of Kyoto's Good Luck Meadow—Yoshiwara—the green houses and courtesans, boy whores and tea-shop girls, kabuki and paper dragons.

"You have never left this room," she tells me, and I have no compelling reason either to believe her or to suspect that she's lying.

"We could shut off the lights," I say. "It could be dark for at least a little while."

"There isn't time now," she replies and stubs out her cigarette on the wall beside the bed, then drops the butt to the floor, and I think I hear a very faint hiss when it hits the damp tiles. She's left an ashen smudge on the wall near the plastic headboard, and that, I think, must be how evil enters the world.

04. The Book (1)

This is the very first time that she will show me the scrapbook. I *call* it a scrapbook, because I don't know what else to call it. Her robotic knees whir and click softly as she leans forward and snaps open the leather attaché case. She takes the scrapbook out and sets it on the counter beside the rust-streaked sink. This is an hour or so after the first time we made love, and I'm still in bed, watching her and thinking how much more beautiful she is without the ungainly chromium-plated prosthetics. The skin around the external fix posts and neural ports is pink and inflamed, and I wonder if she even bothers to keep them clean. I wonder how much it must hurt, being hauled about by those contraptions. She closes the lid of the briefcase, her every move deliberate, somehow calculated without seeming stiff, and the ankle joints purr like a tick-tock cat as she turns towards me. She is still naked, and I marvel again at the pallid thatch of her pubic hair. She retrieves the scrapbook from the sink.

"You look at the photographs," she says, "and tell me what you see there. This is what matters now, your impressions. We know the rest already."

"I need a hot shower," I tell her, but she shakes her head, and the robotic legs whir and move her towards the bed on broad tridactyl feet.

"Later," she says. "Later, you can have a hot shower, after we're done here."

And so I take the scrapbook from her when she offers it to me—a thick sheaf of yellowed pages held between two sturdy brown pieces of cardstock, the whole thing bound together with a length of brown string. The string has been laced through perforations in the pages and through small silver grommets set into the cardstock covers, and each end of the string is finished with a black aiglet to keep it from fraying. The string has been tied into a sloppy sort of reef knot. There is nothing printed or written on the cover.

"Open it," she says, and her prosthetics whine and hiss pneumatic laments as she sits down on the bed near me. The box springs creak.

"What am I supposed to see?" I ask her.

"You are not *supposed* to see anything."

I open the scrapbook, and inside each page displays four black-and-white photographs, held in place by black metal photo corners. And at once I see, as it is plainly obvious, that all the photographs in the book are of the same man. Page after page after page, the same man, though not always the same photograph. They look like mug shots. The man is Caucasian, maybe forty-five years old, maybe fifty. His eyes are dark, and always he is staring directly into the camera lens. There are deep creases in his forehead, and his skin is mottled, large pored, acne-scarred, pockmarked. His lips are very thin, and his nose large and hooked. There are bags beneath his eyes.

"Who is he?" I ask.

"That's not your problem," she replies. "Just look at the pictures and tell me what you see."

I turn another page, and another, and another after that, and on every one that haggard face glares back at up me. "They're all the same."

"They are not," she says.

"I mean, they're all of the same man. Who is he?"

"I said that's not your problem. And surely you must know I haven't brought you here to tell me what I can see for myself."

So, I want to ask why she has brought me here, only I cannot recall being brought here. I am not certain I can recall anything before this white dripping room. It seems in this moment to be all I have ever known. I turn more pages, some so brittle they flake at my touch. But there is nothing to see here but the man with the shaved head and the hooked nose.

"Take your time," she says and lights another cigarette. "Just don't take too much of it."

"If this is about the syringes—"

"This isn't about the syringes. But we'll come to that later, trust me. And that Taiwanese chap, too, the lieutenant. What's his name?"

"The war isn't going well, is it?" I ask her, and now I look up from the scrapbook lying open in my lap and watch the darkness filling the doorway to our room. Our room or her room or my room, I cannot say which. That darkness seems as sticky and solid as hot asphalt.

"That depends whose side you're on," she says and smiles and flicks ash onto the floor.

It occurs to me for the first time that someone might be watching from that darkness, getting everything on tape, making notes, waiting and biding their time. I think I might well go mad if I stare too long into that impenetrable black. I look back down at the book, trying to see whatever it is she wants me to see on those pages, whatever it is she needs to know.

03. The Dream

The night after I lost the girl who lost the syringe—if any of that did in fact occur—I awoke in the white room on the not-quite-oyster sheets, gasping and squinting at those bare fluorescent tubes. My mouth so dry, my chest hurting, and the dream already beginning to fade. There was a pencil and a legal pad on the table beside the bed, and I wrote this much down:

This must have been near the end of it all, just before I finally woke. Being on the street of an Asian city, maybe Tokyo, I don't know. Possibly an amalgam of every Asian city I have ever visited. Night. Flickering neon and cosplay girls and noodle shops. The commingled smells of car exhaust and cooking and garbage. And I'm late for an appointment in a building I can see, an immaculate tower of shimmering steel. I can't read any of the street signs, because they're all in Japanese or Mandarin or whatever. I'm lost. Men mutter as they pass me. The cosplay girls laugh and point. There's an immense animatronic Ganesh-like thing directing traffic (and I suppose this is foreshadowing). I finally find someone who doesn't speak English, but she speaks German, and she shows me where to cross the street to reach the steel tower.

There might have been a lobby and an elevator ride, or I may only be filling in a jump cut. But then I was in the examination room of what seemed to be something very like a dentist's office. Only there wasn't that dentist-office smell. There was some other smell that only added to my unease and disorientation. I was asked to take a seat, please, in this thing that wasn't quite a dentist's chair. There was a woman with a British accent asking me questions, checking off items on a form of some sort.

She kept asking about my memory, and if I were comfortable. And then the woman with the British accent placed her thumb beneath my jaw, and I began to feel cold and fevery. She said something like, *We'll be as gentle as we can.* That's when I saw that she was holding my detached jaw in her hands. And I could see my tongue and teeth and gums and lower lip and everything else. The sensation of cold grew more intense, and she told me to please remain calm, that it would all be over soon. Then she pressed something like a dental drill to my forehead, and there was a horrible whine and a burring sort of pain. She set the drill aside and plugged a jack into the roof of my mouth, something attached to an assortment of coaxial cables, and there was a suffocating blackness that seemed to rush up all around me.

I stare for a few moments at what I've written, then return the pencil and the pad to the table. My mouth tastes like onions and curry and aluminum foil, a metallic tang like a freshly filled molar, and I lie back down and shut my eyes tightly, wondering if the throbbing in my chest is the beginning of a heart attack or only indigestion. I'm sick to my stomach and dizzy, and I know that lying down and closing my eyes is the worst thing I could do for either. But I cannot bear the white glare of those bulbs. I will vomit, or it will pass without having vomited, but I won't look up into that cold light. I do not know where I am or how I got here. I cannot recall ever having seen this dingy room before. No, not dingy—squalid. The sound of dripping water is very loud, a leaky ceiling, so at least maybe the damp sheets do not mean that I've pissed myself in my sleep. I lie very still, listening to the dripping water and to my pounding heart and to a restless sound that might be automobiles on the street outside.

05. The White Woman

She leans close, and her lips brush the lobe of my right ear, her tepid breath on my cheek, breath that smells of tobacco and more faintly of Indian cooking (cardamom, tamarind, fenugreek, cloves). She whispers, and her voice is *so* soft, so soft that she might in this moment have become someone else entirely.

"Nothing to be desired anymore," she whispers. "*Nichts gewünscht zu werden.*"

I don't argue. In this place and time, these are somehow words of kindness, words of absolution, and within them seems to rest the vague hope of release. Her body is warm against mine, her flat belly pressed against mine which is not so flat as it once was, her strong thighs laid against my thighs and her small breasts against my breasts. Together, we have formed an improbable binary opposition, lovers drawn from a deck of cards, my skin so pink and raw and hers so chalky and fine.

"*Gelassen gehen Sie,*" she whispers, and I open my eyes and gaze up into hers, those dazzling, broken blue gems. Her beauty is unearthly, and I might almost believe her an exile from another galaxy, a fallen angel, the calculated product of biotech and genetic alchemy. She lifts herself, rising up on those muscular arms, my hips seized firmly and held fast between the stumps of her transfemoral amputations. There was an accident when she was only a child, but that's all I can now recall. *This is how a mouse must feel,* I think, *in the claws of a cat, or a mouse lost in a laboratory maze.* She smiles, and that expression could mean so many different things.

She leans down again and kisses me, her tongue sliding easily between my teeth.

The room is filled with music, which I am almost certain wasn't there only a moment before. The scratchy, brittle tones of a phonograph recording, something to listen to besides the goddamn rain and the leaking ceiling and the creaking bed springs. And then she enters me, and it comes as no surprise that the robotic legs are not the full extent of her prosthetics. She slips her left arm beneath me, pulling me towards her, and I arch my back, finding her rhythm and the more predictable rhythm of the mechanical cock working its way deeper inside me.

In all the universe, there might be nothing but this room. In all the world, there might only be the two of us.

She kisses me again, but this time it is not a gentle act. This time, there is force and a violence only half-repressed, and I think of cats again. I do not want to think of cats, but I do. She will suck my breath, will draw my soul from me through my nostrils and lips to get at whatever it is she needs to know. How many souls would a woman like her have swallowed in her lifetime? She must be filled with ghosts, a gypsum alabaster bottle stoppered with two blue stones—lapis lazuli or chalcedony—cleverly shaped to resemble the eyes of a woman and not a cat and not an alabaster bottle filled with devoured souls.

Our lips part, and if she has taken my soul, it's nothing I ever needed, anyway.

My mouth wanders across the smooth expanse above and between her breasts, and then I find her right nipple, and my tongue traces a mandala three times about her areola. Perhaps I have sorceries all my own.

"No, you don't," she says and thrusts her hips hard against mine.

And maybe I remember something then, so maybe this room is not all there is in all the world. Maybe I recall a train rushing along through long darknesses and brief puddles of mercury-vapour light, barreling forward, floating on old maglev tracks, and all around me are the cement walls of a narrow tunnel carved out deep below a city whose name I *cannot* recollect. But cities might not have names—I presently have no evidence that they do—and so perhaps this is not exactly forgetfulness or amnesia. I turn my head and look out the window as the train races past a ruined and deserted station. I'm gripping a semi-automatic the way some women would hold onto a rosary or a string of tasbih beads. My forefinger slips through the familiar ring of the trigger guard . . .

"You still with me, sister?" the albino woman asks, and I nod as the memory of the train and the gun dissolves and is forgotten once again. I am sweating now, even in this cold, dank room on these sodden not-quite-oyster sheets, I am sweating. I could not say if it is from fear or exertion or from something else entirely.

And she comes then, her head bending back so far I think her neck will snap, the taut V of her clavicles below her delicate throat, and if only I had the teeth to do the job. She comes with a shudder and a gasp and a sudden rush of profanity in some odd, staccato language that I do not speak, have never even heard before, but still I know that those words are profane. I see that she is sweating, too, brilliant drops standing out like nectar on her too-white skin, and I lick away a salty trickle from her chest. So there's another way that she is in me now. Her body shudders again, and she releases me, withdrawing and rolling away to lie on her back. She is breathing heavily and grinning, and it is a perfectly merciless sort of grin, choked with triumph and bitter guile. I envy her that grin and the callous heart in back of it. Then my eyes go to that space between her legs, that fine white thatch of hair, and for a moment I only imagine the instrument of my seduction was not a pros-thesis. For a moment, I watch the writhing, opalescent thing, still glistening and slick with me. Its body bristles with an assortment of fleshy spines, and I cannot help but ponder what venoms or exotic nanorobotic or nubot serums they might contain.

"Only a fleeting trick of the light, my love," she says, still grinning that brutal grin of hers. And I blink, and now there is only a dildo there between her legs, four or five inches of beige silicone molded into an erect phallus. I close my eyes again and listen to the music and the rain tapping against the windowpane.

01. The Train

The girl is sitting across the aisle and only three rows in front of me, and there's almost no one else riding the tube this late, just a very old man reading a paperback novel. But he's seated far away, many rows ahead of us, and only has eyes for his book, which he holds bent double in trembling, liver-spotted hands. The girl is wearing a raincoat made of lavender vinyl, the collar turned up high, so it's hard for me to get a good look at her face. Her hair is long and black and oily, and her hands are hidden inside snug leather gloves that match her raincoat. She's younger than I expected, maybe somewhere in her early twenties, maybe younger still, and a few years ago that might have made what I have to do next a lot harder. But running wet dispatch for the Greeks, you get numb to this sort of shit quick or you get into some other line of work. It doesn't matter how old she is, or that she might still have a mother and a father somewhere who love her, sisters or brothers, or that skimming parcels is the only thing keeping her from a life of whoring or selling herself off bit by bit to the carrion apes. These are most emphatically not my troubles. And soon, they will no longer be hers, either.

I glance back down the aisle towards the geezer, but he's still lost in the pages of his paperback.

The girl in the lavender coat is carrying, concealed somewhere on her person, seven 3/10ths cc syringes, and if I'm real goddamn fortunate, I'll never find out what's in them. It is not my job to know. It is my job to retrieve the package with as little fuss and fanfare and bloodshed as possible and then get it back across the border to the spooks in Alexandroupoli.

She wipes at her nose and then stares out the window at the tube walls hidden in the darkness.

I take a deep breath and glance back towards the old man. He hasn't moved a muscle, unless it's been to flip a page or two.

Mister, I think, *you just stay absolutely goddamn still, and maybe you'll get to find out how it ends.*

Then I check my gun again, to be double fucking sure the safety's off. With any sort of half-assed luck, I won't need the M9 tonight, but you live by better safe than sorry—if you live at all. The girl wipes her nose a second time and sniffles. Then she leans forward, resting her forehead against the back of the seat in front of her.

There's no time left to worry about whether or not the surveillance wasps are still running, taking it all in from their not-so-secret nooks and crannies, taking it all down. Another six minutes and we'll be pulling into the next terminal, and I have no intention of chasing this bitch in her lavender mack all over Ankara.

I stand and move quickly down the aisle towards her, flexing my left wrist to extend the niobium barb implanted beneath my skin. The neurotoxin will stop her heart before she even feels the prick, or so they tell me. Point is, she won't make a sound. It'll look like a heart attack, if anyone bothers with an autopsy, which I suspect they won't. I've been up against the Turks enough times now to know they only recruit the sort no one's ever going to miss.

But then she turns and looks directly at me, and I've never seen eyes so blue. Or I've never seen eyes that *shade* of blue. Eyes that are both so terribly empty and so filled to bursting, and I know that something's gone very, very goddamn wrong. I know someone somewhere's lied to me, and this isn't just some kid plucked from the slums to mule pilfered load. She sits there, staring up at me, and I reach for the 9mm, shit-sure that's exactly the wrong thing to do, knowing that I've panicked even if I can't quite fathom *why* I've panicked. I'm close enough to get her with the barb, though now there might be a struggle, and then I'd have to deal with the old bookworm up front. I've hesitated, allowed myself to be distracted, and there's no way it's not gonna go down messy.

She smiles, a voracious, carnivorous smile.

"Nothing to be desired anymore," she says, and I feel the muscles in my hand and wrist relax, feel the barb retracting. I feel the gun slip from my slack fingers and hear it clatter to the floor.

"Go back to your seat," she tells me, but I've fallen so far into those eyes—those eyes that lead straight down through endless electric blue chasms, and I almost don't understand what she means. She leans over and picks my gun up off the floor of the maglev and hands it back to me.

"Go back to your seat," she says again, and I do. I turn and go back to my seat, returning the M9 to its shoulder holster, and sit staring at my hands or staring out the train window for what seems hours and hours and hours and . . .

06. Marlene Dietrich

I sit alone at the foot of the bed, "south" of that sprawling river delta and the low damp-sheet hills beyond, all rearranged now by the geological upheaval of my movements. I sit there smoking and shivering and watching the dirty rainwater dripping onto the white tiles covering the floor of the room. The phonograph is playing "I May Never Go Home Anymore," and I know all the words, though I cannot remember ever having heard the song before.

"I have always loved her voice," the albino woman says from her place at the window, behind me and to my left.

"It's Marlene Dietrich, isn't it?" I ask, wishing I could say if I have always been afflicted with this patchwork memory. Perhaps this is merely the *nature* of memory, and that's something else I've forgotten.

"That wasn't her birth name," the white woman replies. "But it wasn't a stage name, either. Her parents named her Marie Magdalene—"

"Just like Jesus' whore," I say, interrupting. She ignores me.

"I read somewhere that Dietrich changed it, when she was still a teenager in Schöneberg. Marlene is a contraction of Marie Magdalene. Did you know that? I always thought that was quite clever of her."

I shrug and take a long drag on my cigarette, then glance at the scrapbook lying open on the bed next to me. The black-and-white photographs are all numbered, beginning with .0001, though I'm not at all sure they were the last time I went through it. The voice of the long-dead actress fills the room, making it seem somehow warmer.

Don't ever think about tomorrow.

For tomorrow may never come.

"You should have another good look at the book," the albino woman suggests.

"I don't know what you expect me to see there. I don't understand what it is you want me to *tell* you. I've never *seen* that man before. I don't *remember* ever having seen that man before."

"Of course you don't. But you need to realise, we're running out of time. You're running out of time, love."

Time is nothing as long as I'm living it up this way.

I may never go home anymore.

I turn my head and watch her watching whatever lies on the other side of the windowpane. I still have not had the nerve to look for myself. Some part of me does not want to know, and some part of me still suspects there may be no more to the world than this room. If I look out that window, I might see nothing at all, because nothing may be all there is to see. When I fashioned the flat, rectangular world of the bed, and then this white room which must be the vault of the heavens which surround it, perhaps I stopped at the room's four walls. Plaster painted the same white as the floor tiles and the ceiling and the light shining down from those bare fluorescent stars. Beyond that, there is no more, the edges of my universe, the practical boundaries of my cosmic bubble.

"She really did a number on your skull," the albino says. "I don't know how they expect me to get anything, between the goddamn firewall and what she did."

"What *did* she do?" I ask, not really wanting to know that either, but it doesn't matter, because the albino woman does not answer me. She's still naked, as am I. I still do not know her name. "Are we in Kyoto?" I ask.

"Why the hell would they bother slinging a wog sniper all the way the fuck to Japan?" she wants to know, and I have no answer for that. I seem to have no answers at all.

I've got kisses and kisses galore,
That have never been tasted before.

"Just be a good little girl and look at the book again," she says to me. "Maybe this time you'll see something that you've missed."

I breathe a grey cloud of smoke out through my nostrils, then pick the scrapbook up off the bed. The covers are very slightly damp from lying there on the damp sheets. I don't suppose it matters. I turn the pages and smoke my cigarette. The same careworn, hollow-eyed, middle-aged face looking back at me as before, staring back at whomever took all these pictures. I turn another page, coming to page number nine, the four photos designated .0033 through .0036, and none of it means any more to me than it did the last time through.

"I think that I may remember a good deal about Kyoto," I say. "But I don't remember anything at all about Greece. And I don't look Greek, do I?"

"You don't look Japanese, either."

One last puff, then I drop the butt of my cigarette to the wet tiles, and it sizzles there for half a moment. I run my fingers slowly over the four glossy photographs on the page, as if touching them might make some sort of difference. And, as it happens, I do see a scar on the man's chin I hadn't noticed before. I examine some of the other pages, and the scar is there on every single one of them.

"If I don't find it, whatever it is you want me to find in here—"

"—there are going to be a lot of disappointed people, Sunshine, and you'll be the first."

"Can I have another cigarette?" I ask her.

"Just look at the damned book," she replies, so that's what I do. It's open to page fifteen, .0057–.0060. I try focusing on what the man's wearing instead of his face, but all I can see is the collar of a light-coloured T-shirt, and it's the same in every photograph. My eyes are so tired, and I shut them for a moment. I can almost imagine that the flat illumination from the fluorescent bulbs is draining me somehow, diminishing me, both body and soul. But then I remember that the white woman took my soul when she fucked me, so never mind. I sit there with my eyes shut, listening to the dripping water and listening to Marlene Dietrich and wishing I could at least remember if I've ever had a name.

If you treat me right, this might be the night.
I may never go home, I may never go home.
I may never go home anymore.
I may never go home anymore.

08. The Fire Escape

When I found the umbrella leaning in one corner of the room and opened the window and climbed out onto the fire escape, she didn't try to stop me. She did not even say a word. And there is a world beyond the white room, after all. But it isn't Kyoto. It is no city that I have seen or even dreamt of before. It must *be* a city, because I cannot imagine what else it could possibly be. I'm sitting with the window and the redbrick wall of the motel on my right, my naked ass against the icy steel grating, and the falling rain is very loud on the clear polyvinyl canopy of the umbrella. I think I might never have been this cold in all my life, and I don't know why I didn't take her robe as well. If I have clothes of my own, they are not anywhere to be found in the room.

I peer through the rain-streaked umbrella and try to find words that would do justice to the intricate, towering structures rising up all around

me and the motel (that it is a motel, I will readily admit, is only a working
assumption, and why motel and not hotel?). But I know I don't possess that
sort of vocabulary. Maybe the peculiar staccato language the albino woman
spoke when she came, maybe it contains nouns and verbs equal to these
things I see.

They are both magnificent and terrible, these edifices that might be
buildings and railways, smokestacks and turbines, streets and chimneys and
great glass atriums. They are awful. That word might come the closest, in
all its connotations. I will not say they are beautiful, for there is something
loathsome about these bizarre structures. At least, to me they seem bizarre;
I cannot say with any certainty that they are in an absolute, objective sense.
Possibly, I am the alien here, me and this unremarkable redbrick motel.
Thinking through this amnesiac mist locked up inside my head, there is
no solid point of reference left to me, no external standard by which I may
judge. There is only gut reaction, and my gut reaction is that they are bizarre
and loathsome things.

The air out here smells like rain and ozone, carbon monoxide and chem-
icals I do not know the names for, and yet it still smells very much cleaner
than the white room with its soggy miasma of mold and slow decay.

These spiraling, jointed, ribsy things which might be the skyscrapers
of an unnamed or unnamable city, they are as intricate as the calcareous
or chitinous skeletons of deep-sea creatures. There. I do have a few words,
though they are utterly insufficient. They are mere approximations of what I
see. So, yes, they seem organic, these towers, as though they are the product
not of conscious engineering and construction but of evolution and ontog-
eny. They have grown here, I think—all of them—and I wonder if the men
and women who planted the necessary seeds or embryos, however many
ages ago, are anything like the albino who took my soul away.

And then I hear the noise of vast machineries . . . no, I have been hearing
this noise all along, but only now has my amazement or apprehension or
awe at the sight of this city dimmed enough that I look for the source of
the sounds. And I see, not far away, there is a sort of clearing in this urban,
industrial carapace. And I can see the muddy earth ripped open there, red
as a wound in any living creature. There are great indescribable contraptions
busy making the wound much larger, gouging and drilling out buckets or

mouthfuls of mud and meat to be dumped upon steaming spoilage heaps or fed onto conveyer belts that stretch away into the foggy distance.

And there is something in that hole, something still only partly exposed by the exertions of these machines that might not be machines at all. Something I know (and no, I cannot say how I could ever *know* such a thing) has lain there undisturbed and sleeping for millennia, and now they mean to wake it up.

I look away. I've seen too much already.

Something is creeping slowly along the exterior of one of the strange buildings, and it might be a living tumor—a malignant mass of tissue and corruption and ideas—and, then again, it might be nothing more than an elevator.

I hear knuckles rapping on a windowpane, and when I turn my head back towards the motel, the albino woman is watching me with her bright blue eyes.

07. The Book (II)

Don't ever think about tomorrow.

For tomorrow may never come.

And then the albino woman lifts the phonograph needle from the record and, instantly, the music goes away. I wish she had let it keep on playing, over and over and over, because now the unceasing *drip, drip, drip* from the ceiling to the tiles seems so much louder than when I had the song and Marlene Dietrich's voice to concentrate on. The woman turns my way on her whirring robotic legs and stares at me.

"You never did tell me what happened to your arm," she says and smiles.

"Did you ask?"

"I believe that I did, yes."

I am sitting there at the foot of the bed with the scrapbook lying open on my lap, my shriveled left arm held close to my chest. And it occurs to me that I do not *know* what happened to my arm, and also it occurs to me that I have no recollection whatsoever of there being anything at all wrong with it before she asked how it got this way. And then this *third* observation, which seems only slightly less disconcerting than having forgotten that I'm a cripple (like her), and that I must have been a cripple for a very long time: the book is open to photos .0705–.0708, page 177, and I notice that beside each photo's number are distinct and upraised dimples, like Braille, though I do not know for certain this *is* Braille. I flip back a few pages and see that, yes, the dimples are there on every page.

"That's very thoughtful," I say, so softly that I am almost whispering. "I might have been blind, after all."

"You might be yet," the white woman says.

"If I were," I reply without looking up from the book, "I couldn't even see the damned photographs, much less find whatever it is you *think* I can find in here."

"You don't get off that easily," she laughs, and her noisy mechanical legs carry her from the table with the phonograph to the bed, and she begins the arduous and apparently painful process of detaching herself from the contraptions. I try to focus on the book, trying not to watch the albino or hear the dripping ceiling or smell the dank stench of the room. Trying only to see the photographs. I don't ask why anyone would bother to provide Braille numbers for photographs that a blind person could not see. And this time, she kindly does not answer my unasked question. I return to page 177, then proceed to 178, then on to 179.

"Shit," the albino woman hisses, forcing her curse out through clenched teeth as she disconnects the primary neural lead to her right thigh. There's thick, dark pus and a bead of fresh blood clinging to the plug. More pus leaks from the port and runs down the stump of her leg.

"Is it actually worth all that trouble and discomfort?" I ask. "Wouldn't a wheelchair be—"

"Why don't you try to mind your own goddamn business," she barks at me, and so I do. I go back to the scrapbook, back to photos .0713–.0716 and that face I know I will be seeing for a long time to come, whenever I shut my eyes. I will see him in my sleep, if I am allowed to live long enough to ever sleep again.

The woman sighs a halting, painful sort of sigh and eases herself back onto the sheets, freed now from the prosthetics, which are left standing side by side at the foot of the bed.

"I picked up a patch bug a while back," she says. "Some sort of cross-scripting germ, a quaint little XSSV symbiote. But it's being treated. It's nothing lethal."

And that's when I see it. She's stretched out there next to me talking about viruses and slow-purge reboots, and I notice the puffy reddish rim surrounding photograph number .0715. This *page* is infected, like the albino woman and her robotic legs, and the *site* of the infection is right here beneath .0715.

"I think I've found it," I say and press the pad of my thumb gently to the photograph. It's hot to the touch, and I can feel something moving about beneath the haggard face of the man with the shaved head and the scar on his chin.

She props herself up on her elbows when I hold the scrapbook out so that she can see. "Well, well," she says. "Maybe you have, and maybe you haven't. Either way, Sunshine, it's going to hurt when you pull that scab away."

"Is that what I'm supposed to do?" I ask her, laying the heavy scrapbook back across my lap. Even as I watch, the necrosis has begun to spread across the page towards the other three photographs.

"Do it quickly," she says, and I can hear the eagerness in her voice. "Like pulling off a sticky plaster. Do it fast, and maybe it'll hurt less."

"Is *this* what you wanted me to find? Is this *it?*"

"You're stalling," she says. "Just fucking do it."

And then the black telephone begins to ring again.

09. Exit Music (The Gun)

Sitting beneath the transparent canopy of the borrowed umbrella, sitting naked in the rain on the fire escape, and now she's standing over me, held up by all those shiny chrome struts and gears and pistons. She did not even have to open the window or climb out over the sill, but I cannot ever explain, in words, how it was she exited the room. It only matters that she did. It only matters that she's standing over me holding the Beretta 9mm, aiming it at my head.

"I never made any promises," she tells me, and I nod (because that's true) and lower the umbrella and fold it shut. I support my useless left arm with my right and stare directly up into the cold rain, wishing there were anything falling from that leaden sky clean enough to wash away the weight of all these things I cannot remember or will never be permitted to remember.

"The war isn't going well," she says. "We've lost Hsinchu and Changhua. I think we all know that Taipei can't be far behind. Too many feedback loops. Way too many scratch hits."

"Nothing to be desired anymore," I say and taste the bitter, toxic raindrops on my tongue.

"Nothing at all," she tells me, setting the muzzle of the M9 to my right temple. I am already so chilled I do not feel the cold steel, only the pressure of the gun against my skin. The rain stings my eyes, and I blink. I take a deep breath and try not to shiver.

"Whatever they're digging up over there," and I nod towards the excavations, "they should stop. You should tell them that soon, before they wake it up."

"You think they'd listen . . . to someone like me?" she asks. "Is that what you think?"

"I don't know what I think anymore."

Above me and all around me this lifeless, living husk that might be a city or only the mummified innards of some immense biomechanoid crustacean goes on about its clockwork day-to-day affairs, all its secret metabolisms, its ancient habits. It does not see me—or seeing me, it shows even less regard for me than I might show a single mite nestled deep within a single eyelash follicle. I gaze up at that inscrutable tangle of spires and flying buttresses, rotundas and acroterion flourishes and all the thousands of solemn gushing rainspouts.

"Do not feel unloved," she says, and I shut my eyes and sense all the world move beneath me.

THE APE'S WIFE

NEITHER YET AWAKE nor quite asleep, she pauses in her dreaming to listen to the distant sounds of the jungle approaching twilight. They are each balanced now between one world and another—she between sleep and waking, and the jungle between day and night. Dreaming, she is once again the woman she was before she came to the island, the starving woman on that *other* island, that faraway island that was not warm and green, but had come to seem to her always cold and grey, stinking of dirty snow and the exhaust of automobiles and buses. She stands outside a lunch room on Mulberry Street, her empty belly rumbling as she watches other people eat. The evening begins to fill up with the raucous screams of nocturnal birds and flying reptiles and a gentle tropical wind rustling through the leaves of banana and banyan trees, through cycads and ferns grown as tall or taller than the brick and steel and concrete canyon that surrounds her.

She leans forward, and her breath fogs the lunch room's plate-glass window, but none of those faces turn to stare back at her. They are all too occupied with their meals, these swells with their forks and knives and china platters buried under mounds of scrambled eggs or roast beef on toast or mashed potatoes and gravy. They raise china cups of hot black coffee to their lips and pretend she isn't there. This winter night is too filled with starving, tattered women on the bum. There is not time to notice them all, so better to notice none of them, better not to allow the sight of real hunger to spoil your appetite. A little farther down the street there is a Greek who sells apples and oranges and pears from a little sidewalk stand, and she wonders how long before he catches her stealing, him or someone else. She has never been a particularly lucky girl.

Somewhere close by, a parrot shrieks and another parrot answers it, and finally she turns away from the people and the tiled walls of the lunch room and opens her eyes; the Manhattan street vanishes in a slushy, disorienting flurry and takes the cold with it. She is still hungry, but for a while she is content to lie in her carefully woven nest of rattan, bamboo, and ebony branches, blinking away the last shreds of sleep and gazing deeply into the rising mists and gathering dusk. She has made her home high atop a weathered promontory, this charcoal peak of lava rock and tephra a vestige of the island's fiery origins. It is for this summit's unusual shape—not so unlike a human skull—that white men named the place. And it is here that she last saw the giant ape, before it left her to pursue the moving-picture man and Captain Englehorn, the first mate and the rest of the crew of the *Venture*, left her alone to get itself killed and hauled away in the rusty hold of that evil-smelling ship.

At least, that is one version of the story she tells herself to explain why the beast never returned for her. It may not be the truth. Perhaps the ape died somewhere in the swampy jungle spread out below the mountain, somewhere along the meandering river leading down to the sea. She has learned that there is no end of ways to die on the island, and that nothing alive is so fierce or so cunning as to be entirely immune to those countless perils. The ape's hide was riddled with bullets, and it might simply have succumbed to its wounds and bled to death. Time and again, she has imagined this, the ape only halfway back to the wall but growing suddenly too weak to continue the chase, and perhaps it stopped, surrendering to pain and exhaustion, and sat down in a glade somewhere below the cliffs, resting against the bole of an enormous tree. Maybe it sat there, peering through a break in the perpetual mist and the forest canopy, gazing forlornly back up at the skull-shaped mountain. It would have been a terrible, lonely death, but not so terrible an end as the beast might have met had it managed to gain the ancient aboriginal gates and the sandy peninsula beyond.

She has, on occasion, imagined another outcome, one in which the enraged god-thing overtook the men from the steamer, either in the jungle or somewhere out beyond the wall, in the village or on the beachhead. And though the ape was killed by their gunshots and gas bombs (for surely he would have returned, otherwise), first they died screaming, every last mother's son of them. She has taken some grim satisfaction in this fantasy, on days when she has had need of grim satisfaction. But she knows it isn't true, if only because she watched with her own eyes the *Venture* sailing away from the place where it had anchored out past the reefs, the smoke from its single stack drawing an ashen smudge across the blue morning sky. They escaped, at least enough of them to pilot the ship, and left her for dead or good as dead.

She stretches and sits up in her nest, watching the sun as it sinks slowly into the shimmering, flat monotony of the Indian Ocean, the dying day setting the western horizon on fire. She stands, and the red-orange light paints her naked skin the color of clay. Her stomach growls again, and she thinks of her small hoard of fruit and nuts, dried fish and a couple of turtle eggs she found the day before, all wrapped up safe in banana leaves and hidden in amongst the stones and brambles. Here, she need only fear nightmares of hunger and never hunger itself. There is the faint, rotten smell of sulfur emanating from the cavern that forms the skull's left eye socket, as the mountain's malodorous breath wafts up from bubbling hot springs deep within the grotto. She has long since grown accustomed to the stench and has found that the treacherous maze of bubbling lakes and mud helps to protect her from many of the island's predators. For this reason, more than any other, more even than the sentimentality that she no longer denies, she chose these steep volcanic cliffs for her eyrie.

Stepping from her bed, the stones warm against the thickly calloused soles of her feet, she remembers a bit of melody, a ghostly snatch of lyrics that has followed her up from the dream of the city and the woman she will never be again. She closes her eyes, shutting out the jungle noises for just a moment, and listens to the faint crackle of a half-forgotten radio broadcast.

Once I built a tower up to the sun,

Brick and rivet and lime.
Once I built a tower,
Now it's done.
Brother, can you spare a dime?

And when she opens her eyes again, the sun is almost gone, just a blazing sliver remaining now above the sea. She sighs and reminds herself that there is no percentage in recalling the clutter and racket of that lost world. Not now. Not here. Night is coming on, sweeping in fast and mean on leathery pterodactyl wings and the wings of flying foxes and the wings of ur-birds, and like so many of the island's inhabitants, she puts all else from her mind and rises to meet it. The island has made of her a night thing, has stripped her of old diurnal ways. Better to sleep through the stifling equatorial days than to lie awake through the equally stifling nights; better the company of the sun for her uneasy dreams than the moon's cool, seductive glow and her terror of what might be watching hungrily from the cover of darkness.

When she has eaten, she sits awhile near the cliff's edge, contemplating what month this might be, what month in which year. It is a futile, but harmless, pastime. At first, she scratched marks on stone to keep track of the passing time, but after only a few hundred marks she forgot one day, and then another, and when she finally remembered again, she found she was uncertain how many days had come and gone during her forgetfulness. It was then that she came to understand the futility of counting days in this place—indeed, the futility of the very concept of time. She has thought often that the island must be time's primordial orphan, a castaway, not unlike herself, stranded in some nether region, this sweltering antediluvian limbo where there is only the rising and setting of the sun, the phases of the moon, the long rainy season which is hardly less hot or less brutal than the longer dry. Maybe the men who built the wall long ago were a race of sorcerers, and in their arrogance they committed a grave transgression against time, some unspeakable contravention of the sanctity of months and hours. And so Chronos cast this place back down into the gulf of Chaos, and now it is damned to exist forever apart from the tick-tock, calendar-page blessings of Aion.

Sure, she still recalls a few hazy scraps of Greek mythology, and Roman, too, this farmer's only daughter who always got good marks and waited until school was done before leaving the cornfields of Indiana to go east to seek her fortune in New York and New Jersey. All her girlhood dreams of the stage, the silver screen, and her name on theater marquees, but by the time she reached Fort Lee, most of the studios were relocating west to California, following the promise of a more hospitable, more profitable climate. Black Tuesday had left its stain upon the country, and she never found more than extra work at the few remaining studios, happy just to play anonymous faces in crowd scenes and the like, but finally she could not even find that. Finally, she was fit only for the squalor of bread lines and mission soup kitchens and flop houses, until the night she met a man who promised to make her a star, who, chasing dreams of his own, dragged her halfway round the world and then abandoned her here in this serpent-haunted and time-forsaken wilderness. The irony is not lost on her. Seeking fame and adoration, she has found, instead, what might well be the ultimate obscurity.

Below her, some creature suddenly cries out in pain from the forest tangle clinging to the slopes of the mountain, and she squints into the darkness. She knows that hers are only one of a hundred—or a thousand—pairs of eyes that have stopped to see, to try and catch a glimpse of whatever bloody panoply is being played out among the vines and undergrowth, and that this is only one of the innumerable slaughters to come before sunrise. Something screams and so all eyes turn to see, for every thing that creeps or crawls, flits or slithers upon the island will fall prey, one day or another. And she is no exception.

One day, perhaps, the island itself will fall, not so unlike the dissatisfied angels in Milton or in Blake.

Ann Darrow opens her eyes, having nodded off again, and she is once more only a civilized woman not yet grown old, but no longer young. One who has been taken away from the world and touched, then returned and set adrift in the sooty gulches and avenues and asphalt ravines of this modern, electric city. But that was such a long time ago, before the war that proved the Great War was not so very great after all, that it was not the war to end all wars. Japan has been burned with the fire of two tiny manufactured suns. Europe lies in ruins, and already the fighting has begun again and young men are dying in Korea. History is a steamroller. History is a litany of war.

She sits alone in the Natural History Museum off Central Park West, a bench all to herself in the alcove where the giant ape's broken skeleton was mounted for public exhibition after the creature tumbled from the top of the Empire State, plummeting more than twelve hundred feet to the frozen streets below. There is an informative placard (white letters on black) declaring it *Brontopithecus singularis* Osborn (1934), the only known specimen, now believed extinct. *So there*, she thinks. Denham and his men dragged it from the not-quite-impenetrable sanctuary of its jungle and hauled it back to Broadway; they chained it and murdered it and, in that final act of desecration, they *named* it. The enigma was dissected and quantified, given its rightful place in the grand analytic scheme, in the Latinized order of things, and that's one less blank spot to cause the mapmakers and zoologists to scratch their heads. Now, Carl Denham's monster is no threat at all, only another harmless, impressive heap of bones shellacked and wired together in this stately, static mausoleum. And hardly anyone remembers or comes to look upon these bleached remains. The world is a steamroller. The Eighth Wonder of the World was old news twenty years ago, and now it is only a chapter in some dusty textbook devoted to anthropological curiosities.

He was the king and the god of the world he knew, but now he comes to civilization, merely a captive, a show to gratify your curiosity. Curiosity killed the cat, and it slew the ape, as well, and that December night hundreds died for the price of a theater ticket, the fatal price of *their* curiosity and Carl Denham's hubris. By dawn, the passion play was done, and the king and god and son of Skull Island lay crucified by biplanes, by the pilots and trigger-happy Navy men borne aloft in Curtis Helldivers armed with .50 caliber machine guns. A tiered Golgotha skyscraper, one hundred and two stories of steel and glass and concrete, a dizzying Art-Deco Calvary, and no chance of resurrection save what the museum's anatomists and taxidermists might in time effect.

Ann Darrow closes her eyes, because she can only ever bear to look at the bones for just so long and no longer. Henry Fairfield Osborn, the museum's former president, had wanted to name it after her, in her *honour*—*Brontopithecus darrowii*, "Darrow's thunder ape"—but, for his trouble, she'd threatened a lawsuit against him *and* his museum, and so he'd christened the species *singularis*, instead. She'd played her Judas role, delivering the jungle god to Manhattan's Roman holiday, and wasn't that enough?

Must she also have her name forever nailed up there with the poor beast's corpse? Maybe she deserved as much or far worse, but Osborn's "honour" was poetic justice she managed to evade.

There are voices now, a mother and her little girl, so Ann knows that she's no longer alone in the alcove. She keeps her eyes tightly shut, wishing she could shut her ears as well and not hear the things that are being said.

"Why did they kill him?" asks the little girl.

"It was a very dangerous animal," her mother replies sensibly. "It got loose and hurt people. I was just a child then, about your age."

"They could have put him in a zoo," the girl protests. "They didn't have to kill him."

"I don't think a zoo would ever have been safe. It broke free and hurt a lot of innocent people."

"But there aren't any more monkeys like him."

"There are still plenty of gorillas in Africa," the mother replies.

"Not that big," says the little girl. "Not as big as an elephant."

"No," the mother agrees. "Not as big as an elephant. But then we hardly need gorillas as big as elephants, now do we?"

Ann clenches her jaws, grinding her teeth together, biting her tongue (so to speak), and gripping the edge of the bench with nails chewed down to the quick.

They'll leave soon, she reminds herself. *They always do, get bored and move along after only a minute or so. It won't be much longer.*

"What does *that* part say?" the child asks, so her mother reads to her from the text printed on the placard.

"Well, it says, 'Kong was not a true gorilla, but a close cousin, and belongs in the Superfamily Hominoidea with gorillas, chimpanzees, orang-utans, gibbons, and human beings. His exceptional size might have evolved in response to his island isolation.'"

"What's a *super* family?"

"I don't really know, dear."

"What's a gibbon?"

"Another sort of monkey, I suppose."

"But we don't believe in evolution, do we?"

"No, we don't."

"So God made Kong, just like he made us?"

"Yes, honey. God made Kong, but not like he made us. He gave us a soul. Kong was an animal."

And then there's a pause, and Ann holds her breath, wishing she were still dozing, still lost in her terrible dreams, because this waking world is so much more terrible.

"I want to see the *Tyrannosaurus* again," says the little girl, "and the *Brontosaurus* and *Triceratops*, too." Her mother says okay, there's just enough time to see the dinosaurs again before we have to meet your daddy, and Ann sits still and listens to their footsteps on the polished marble floor, growing fainter and fainter until silence has at last been restored to the alcove. But now the sterile, drab museum smells are gone, supplanted by the various rank odors of the apartment Jack rented for the both of them before he shipped out on a merchant steamer, the *Polyphemus*, bound for the Azores and then Lisbon and the Mediterranean. He never made it much farther than São Miguel, because the steamer was torpedoed by a Nazi U-boat and went down with all hands onboard. Ann opens her eyes, and the strange dream of the museum and the ape's skeleton has already begun to fade. It isn't morning yet, and the lamp beside the bed washes the tiny room with yellow-white light that makes her eyes ache.

She sits up, pushing the sheets away, exposing the ratty grey mattress underneath. The bedclothes are damp with her sweat and with radiator steam, and she reaches for the half-empty gin bottle there beside the lamp. The booze used to keep the dreams at bay, but these last few months, since she got the telegram informing her that Jack Driscoll was drowned and given up for dead and she would never be seeing him again, the nightmares have seemed hardly the least bit intimidated by alcohol. She squints at the clock, way over on the chifforobe, and sees that it's not yet even four a.m. Still hours until sunrise, hours until the bitter comfort of winter sunlight through the bedroom curtains. She tips the bottle to her lips, and the liquor tastes like turpentine and regret and everything she's lost in the last three years. Better she would have never been anything more than a starving woman stealing apples and oranges and bread to try to stay alive, better she would have never stepped foot on the *Venture*. Better she would have died in the green hell of that uncharted island. She can easily imagine a thousand ways it might have gone better, all grim, but better than *this* drunken half-life. She does not torture herself with fairy-tale fantasies of happy endings that never were and never will be. There's enough pain in the world without that luxury.

She takes another swallow from the bottle, then reminds herself that it has to last until morning and sets it back down on the table. But morning seems at least as far away as that night on the island, as far away as the carcass of the sailor she married. Often, she dreams of him, mangled by shrapnel and gnawed by the barbed teeth of deep-sea fish, burned alive and rotted beyond recognition, tangled in the wreckage and ropes and cables of a ship somewhere at the bottom of the Atlantic Ocean. He peers out at her with eyes that are no longer eyes at all, but only empty sockets where hagfish and spiny albino crabs nestle. She usually wakes screaming from those dreams, wakes to the bastard next door pounding on the wall with the heel of a shoe or just his bare fist and shouting how he's gonna call the cops if she can't keep it down. He has a job and has to sleep, and he can't have some goddamn rummy broad half the bay over or gone crazy with the DTs keeping him awake. The old Italian cunt who runs this dump, she says she's tired of hearing the complaints, and either the hollering stops or Ann will have to find another place to flop. She tries not to think about how she'll have to leave soon, anyway. She had a little money stashed in the lining of her coat, from all the interviews she gave the papers and magazines and the newsreel people, but now it's almost gone. Soon, she'll be back out on the bum, sleeping in mission beds or worse places, whoring for the sauce and as few bites of food as she can possibly get by on. She has another month before that, at most, and isn't that what they mean by coming full circle?

She lies down again, trying not to smell herself or the pillowcase or the sheets, thinking about bright July sun falling warm between green leaves. And soon, she drifts off once more, listening to the rumble of a garbage truck down on Canal Street, the rattle of its engine and the squeal of its breaks not so very different from the primeval grunts and cries that filled the torrid air of the ape's profane cathedral.

And perhaps now she is lying safe and drunk in a squalid Bowery tenement and only dreaming away the sorry dregs of her life, and it's not the freezing morning when Jack led her from the skyscraper's spire down to the bedlam of Fifth Avenue. Maybe these are nothing more than an alcoholic's fevered recollections, and she is not being bundled in wool blankets and shielded from reporters and photographers and the sight of the ape's shattered body.

"It's over," says Jack, and she wants to believe that's true, by all the saints in Heaven and all the sinners in Hell, wherever and whenever she is, she wants to believe that it is finally and irrevocably over. There is not one moment to be relived, not ever again, because it has *ended*, and she is rescued, like Beauty somehow delivered from the clutching paws of the Beast. But there is so much commotion, the chatter of confused and frightened bystanders, the triumphant, confident cheers and shouting of soldiers and policemen, and she's begging Jack to get her out of it, away from it. It *must* be real, all of it, real and here and now, because she has never been so horribly cold in her dreams. She shivers and stares up at the narrow slice of sky visible between the buildings. The summit of that tallest of all tall towers is already washed with dawn, but down here on the street, it may as well still be midnight.

> *Life is just a bowl of cherries.*
> *Don't take it serious; it's too mysterious.*
> *At eight each morning I have got a date,*
> *To take my plunge 'round the Empire State.*
> *You'll admit it's not the berries,*
> *In a building that's so tall . . .*

"It's over," Jack assures her for the tenth or twentieth or fiftieth time. "They got him. The airplanes got him, Ann. He can't hurt you, not anymore."

And she's trying to remember through the clamor of voices and machines and the popping of flash bulbs—*Did he hurt me? Is that what happened?*—when the crowd divides like the holy winds of Jehovah parting the waters for Moses, and for the first time she can see what's left of the ape. She screams, and they all *think* she's screaming in terror at the sight of a monster. They do not know the truth, and maybe she does not yet know herself, and it will be weeks or months before she fully comprehends why she is standing there screaming, unable to look away from the impossible, immense mound of black fur and jutting white bone and the dark rivulets of blood leaking sluggishly from the dead and vanquished thing.

"Don't," Jack says, and he covers her eyes. "It's nothing you need to see."

So she does *not* see, shutting her bright blue eyes and all the eyes of her soul, the eyes without and those other eyes within. Shutting *herself*, slamming closed doors and windows of perception, and how could she have known that morning that she was locking in more than she was locking out. *Don't look at it*, he said, much too late, and these images are burned forever into her lidless, unsleeping mind's eye.

A sable hill from which red torrents flow.

Ann kneels in clay and mud the color of a slaughterhouse floor, all the shades of shit and blood and gore, and dips her fingertips into the stream. She has performed this simple act of prostration times beyond counting, and it no longer holds for her any revulsion. She comes here from her nest high in the smoldering ruins of Manhattan and places her hand inside the wound, like St. Thomas fondling the pierced side of Christ. She comes down to remember, because there is an unpardonable sin in forgetting such a forfeiture. In this deep canyon molded not by geologic upheaval and erosion but by the tireless, automatic industry of man, she bows her head before the black hill. God sleeps there below the hill, and one day he will awaken from his slumber, for all those in the city are not faithless. Some still remember and follow the buckled blacktop paths, weaving their determined pilgrims' way along decaying thoroughfares and between twisted girders and the tumbledown heaps of burnt-out rubble. The city was cast down when God fell from his throne (or was pushed, as some have dared to whisper), and his fall broke apart the ribs of the world and sundered even the progression of one day unto the next so that time must now spill backwards to fill in the chasm. Ann leans forward, sinking her hand in up to the wrist, and the steaming crimson stream begins to clot and scab where it touches her skin.

Above her, the black hill seems to shudder, to shift almost imperceptibly in its sleep.

She has thought repeatedly of drowning herself in the stream, has wondered what it would be like to submerge in those veins and be carried along through silent veils of silt and ruby-tinted light. She might dissolve and be no more than another bit of flotsam, unburdened by bitter memory and self-knowledge and these rituals to keep a comatose god alive. She would open her mouth wide, and as the air rushed from her lungs and across her mouth, she would fill herself with His blood. She has even entertained the notion that such a sacrifice would be enough to wake the black sleeper, and as the waters that are not waters carried her away, the god beast might stir. As she melted, He would open His eyes and shake Himself free of the holdfasts of that tarmac and cement and sewer-pipe grave. It *could* be that simple. In her waking dreams, she has learned there is incalculable magic in sacrifice.

Ann withdraws her hand from the stream, and blood drips from her fingers, rejoining the whole as it flows away north and east towards the noxious lake that has formed where once lay the carefully landscaped and sculpted conceits of Mr. Olmsted and Mr. Vaux's Central Park. She will not wipe her hand clean as would some infidel, but rather permit the blood to dry to a claret crust upon her skin, for she has already committed blasphemy enough for three lifetimes. The shuddering black hill is still again, and a vinegar wind blows through the tall grass on either side of the stream.

And then Ann realizes that she's being watched from the gaping brick maw that was a jeweler's window long ago. The frame is still rimmed round about with jagged crystal teeth waiting to snap shut on unwary dreamers, waiting to shred and pierce, starved for diamonds and sapphires and emeralds, but more than ready to accept mere meat. In dusty shafts of sunlight, Ann can see the form of a young girl gazing out at her.

"What do you want?" Ann calls to her, and a moment or two later, the girl replies.

"You have become a goddess," she says, moving a little nearer the broken shop window so that Ann might have a better look at her. "But even a goddess cannot dream forever. I have come a long way and through many perils to speak with you, Golden Mother, and I did not expect to find you sleeping and hiding in the lies told by dreams."

"I'm not hiding," Ann replies very softly, so softly she thinks surely the girl will not have heard.

"Forgive me, Golden Mother, but you are. You are seeking refuge in guilt that is not your guilt."

"I am not your mother," Ann tells her. "I have never been anyone's mother."

A branch whips around and catches her in the face, a leaf's razor edge to draw a nasty cut across her forehead. But the pain slices cleanly through exhaustion and shock and brings her suddenly back to herself, back to *this* night and *this* moment, hers and Jack's mad, headlong dash from the river to the gate. The Cyclopean wall rises up before them, towering above the tree tops. There cannot now be more than a hundred yards remaining between them and the safety of the gate, but the ape is so very close behind. A fire-eyed demon who refuses to be so easily cheated of his prize by mere mortal men. The jungle cringes around them, flinching at the cacophony of Kong's approach, and even the air seems to draw back from that typhoon of muscle and fury, his angry roars and thunderous footfalls to divide all creation. Her right hand is gripped tightly in Jack's left, and he's all but dragging her forward. Ann can no longer feel her bare feet, which have been bruised and gouged and torn, and it is a miracle she can still run at all. Now, she can make out the dim silhouettes of men standing atop the wall, white men with guns and guttering torches, and, for a moment, she allows herself to hope.

"You are needed, Golden Mother," the girl says, and then she steps through the open mouth of the shop window. The blistering sun shimmers off her smooth, dark skin. "You are needed *here* and *now*," she says. "That night and every way that it might have gone, but did not, are passed forever beyond your reach."

"You don't see what I can see," Ann tells the girl, hearing the desperation and resentment in her own voice.

And what she sees is the wall and that last barrier of banyan figs and tree ferns. What she sees is the open gate and the way out of this nightmare, she sees the road home.

"Only dreams," the girl says, not unkindly, and she takes a step nearer the red stream. "Only the phantoms of things that have never happened and never will."

"No," says Ann, and she shakes her head. "We *made* it to the gate. Jack and I both, together. We ran and we ran and we ran, and the ape was right there on top of us all the way, so close that I could smell his rancid breath. But we didn't look back, not even once. We *ran*, and, in the end, we made it to the gate."

"No, Golden Mother. It did not happen that way."

One of the sailors on the wall is shouting a warning now, and at first, Ann believes it's only because he can see Kong behind them. But then something huge lunges from the underbrush, all scales and knobby scutes, scrabbling talons and the blue-green iridescent flash of eyes fashioned for night hunting. The high, sharp quills sprouting from the creature's backbone clatter one against the other like bony castanets, and it snatches Jack Driscoll in its saurian jaws and drags him screaming into the reedy shadows. On the wall, someone shouts, and she hears the staccato report of rifle fire.

The brown girl stands on the far side of the stream flowing along Fifth Avenue, the tall grass murmuring about her knees. "You have become lost in All-At-Once time, and you must find your way back from the Everywhen. I can help, if you'll let me."

"I do not *need* your help," Ann snarls. "You keep away from me, you goddamn, filthy heathen."

Beneath the vast, star-specked Indonesian sky, Ann Darrow stands alone. Jack is gone, taken by some unnamable abomination, and in another second the ape will be upon her. This is when she realizes that she's bleeding, a dark bloom unfolding from her right breast, staining the gossamer rags that are all that remain of her dress and underclothes. She doesn't yet feel the sting of the bullet, a single shot gone wild, intended for Jack's reptilian attacker, but finding her, instead. *I do not blame you*, she thinks, slowly collapsing, going down onto her knees in the thick carpet of moss and bracken. *It was an accident, and I do not blame anyone.*

"That is a lie," the girl says from the other side of the red stream. "You *do* blame them, Golden Mother, and you blame yourself, most of all."

Ann stares up at the dilapidated skyline of a city as lost in time as she, and the Vault of Heaven turns above them like a dime-store kaleidoscope.

Once I built a railroad, I made it run, made it race against time. Once I built a railroad; now it's done. Brother, can you spare a dime? Once I built a tower, up to the sun, brick, and rivet, and lime. Once I built a tower, now it's done. Brother, can you spare a dime?

"When does this end?" she asks, asking the girl or herself or no one at all. "*Where* does it end?"

"Take my hand," the girl replies and reaches out to Ann, a bridge spanning the rill and time and spanning all these endless possibilities. "Take my hand and come back over. Just step across and stand with me."

"No," Ann hears herself say, though it isn't at all what she *wanted* to say or what she *meant* to say. "No, I can't do that. I'm sorry."

And the air around her reeks of hay and sawdust, human filth and beer and cigarette smoke, and the sideshow barker is howling his line of ballyhoo to all the rubes who've paid their two-bits to get a seat under the tent. All the yokels and hayseeds who have come to point and whisper and laugh and gawk at the figure cowering inside the cage.

"Them bars there, they are solid carbon *steel*, mind you," the barker informs them. "Manufactured special for us by the same Pittsburgh firm that supplies prison bars to Alcatraz. Ain't nothing else known to man strong enough to contain *her*, and if not for them iron bars, well . . . rest assured, my good people, we have not in the *least* exaggerated the threat she poses to life and limb, in the absence of such precautions."

Inside the cage, Ann squats in a corner, staring out at all the faces staring in. Only she has not been Ann Darrow in years—just ask the barker or the garish canvas flaps rattling in the chilly breeze of an Indiana autumn evening. She is the Ape Woman of Sumatra, captured at great personal risk by intrepid explorers and hauled out into the incandescent light of the Twentieth Century. She is naked, except for the moth-eaten scraps of buffalo and bear pelts they have given her to wear. Every inch of exposed skin is smeared with dirt and offal and whatever other filth has accumulated in her cage since it was last mucked out. Her snarled and matted hair hangs in her face, and there's nothing the least bit human in the guttural serenade of growls and hoots and yaps that escapes her lips.

The barker slams his walking cane against the iron bars, and she throws her head back and howls. A woman in the front row faints and has to be carried outside.

"She was the queen and the goddess of the strange world she knew," bellows the barker, "but now she comes to civilization, merely a captive, a show to gratify your curiosity. Learned men at colleges—forsaking the words of the Good Book—proclaim that we are *all* descended from monkeys. And, I'll tell you, seeing this wretched bitch, I am *almost* tempted to believe them, and also to suspect that in dark and far-flung corners of the globe there exist to this day beings *still* more simian than human, lower even than your ordinary niggers, hottentots, negritos, and lowly African pygmies."

Ann Darrow stands on the muddy bank of the red stream, and the girl from the ruined and vine-draped jewelry shop holds out her hand, the brown-skinned girl who has somehow found her way into the most secret, tortured recesses of Ann's consciousness.

"The world is still here," the girl says, "only waiting for you to return."

"I have heard tell another tale of her origin," the barker confides. "But I must *warn* you, it is not fit for the faint of heart or the ears of decent Christian women."

There is a long pause, while two or three of the women rise from their folding chairs and hurriedly leave the tent. The barker tugs at his pink suspenders and grins an enormous, satisfied grin, then glances into the cage.

"As I was saying," he continues, "there is *another* story. The Chinaman who sold me this pitiful oddity of human *devolution* said that its mother was born of French aristocracy, the lone survivor of a calamitous shipwreck, cast ashore on black volcanic sands. There, in the hideous misery and perdition of that tropical wilderness, the poor woman was *defiled* by some lustful species of jungle imp, though whether it were chimp or baboon I cannot say."

There is a collective gasp from the men and women inside the tent, and the barker rattles the bars again, eliciting another irate howl from its occupant.

"And here before you is the foul *spawn* of that unnatural union of anthropoid and womankind. The aged Celestial confided to me that the mother expired shortly after giving birth, God rest her immortal soul. Her death was a mercy, I should think, as she would have lived always in shame and horror at having borne into the world this shameful, misbegotten progeny."

"Take my hand," the girl says, reaching into the iron cage. "You do not have to stay here. Take my hand, Golden Mother, and I will help you find the path."

There below the hairy black tumulus, the great slumbering titan belching forth the headwaters of all the earth's rivers, Ann Darrow takes a single hesitant step into the red stream. *This is the most perilous part of the journey,* she thinks, reaching to accept the girl's outstretched hand. *It wants me, this torrent, and if I am not careful, it will pull me down and drown me for my trespasses.*

"It's only a little ways more," the girl tells her and smiles. "Just step across to me."

The barker raps his silver-handled walking cane sharply against the bars of the cage, so that Ann remembers where she is and when, and doing so, forgets herself again. For the benefit of all those licentious, ogling eyes, all those slack jaws that have paid precious quarters to be shocked and titillated, she bites the head off a live hen, and when she has eaten her fill of the bird, she spreads her thighs and masturbates with filthy, bloodstained fingers for the delight of her audience.

Elsewhen, she takes another step towards the girl, and the softly gurgling stream wraps itself greedily about her calves. Her feet sink deeply into the slimy bottom, and the sinuous, clammy bodies of conger eels and salamanders wriggle between her ankles and twine themselves about her legs. She cannot reach the girl, and the opposite bank may as well be a thousand miles away.

I'm only going over Jordan . . .

In a smoke-filled screening room, Ann Darrow sits beside Carl Denham while the footage he shot on the island almost a year ago flickers across the screen at twenty-four frames per second. They are not alone, the room half-filled with low-level studio men from RKO and Paramount and Universal and a couple of would-be financiers lured here by the Hollywood rumor mill. Ann watches the images revealed in grainy shades of grey, in overexposed whites and underexposed smudges of black.

"What exactly are we supposed to be looking at?" someone asks, impatiently.

"We shot this from the top of the wall, once Englehorn's men had managed to frighten away all the goddamn tar babies. Just wait. It's coming."

"Denham, we've already been sitting here half an hour. This shit's pretty underwhelming, you ask me. You're better off sticking to the safari pictures."

"It's *coming*," Denham insists, and chomps anxiously at the stem of his pipe.

And Ann knows he's right, that it's coming, because this is not the first time she's seen the footage. Up there on the screen, the eye of the camera looks out over the jungle canopy, and it always reminds her of Gustave Doré's visions of Eden from her mother's copy of *Paradise Lost*, or the illustrations of lush Pre-Adamite landscapes from a geology book she once perused while seeking shelter in the New York Public Library.

"Honestly, Mr. Denham," the man from RKO sighs. "I've got a meeting in twenty minutes."

"*There*," Denham says, pointing at the screen. "There it is. Right fucking *there*. Do you see it?"

And the studio men and the would-be financiers fall silent as the beast's head and shoulders emerge from the tangle of vines and orchid-encrusted branches and wide palm fronds. It stops and turns its mammoth head towards the camera, glaring hatefully up at the wall and directly into the smoke-filled room, across a million years and nine thousand miles. There is a dreadful, unexpected intelligence in those dark eyes as the creature tries to comprehend the purpose of the weird, pale men and their hand-crank contraption perched there on the wall above it. The ape's lips fold back, baring gigantic canines, eyeteeth longer than a grown man's hand, and there is a low, rumbling sound, then a screeching sort of yell, before the thing the natives called *Kong* turns and vanishes back into the forest.

"Great god," the Universal man whispers.

"Yes, gentlemen," says Denham, sounding very pleased with himself and no longer the least bit anxious, certain that he has them all right where he wants them. "That's just *exactly* what those tar babies think. They worship it and offer up human sacrifices. Why, they wanted Ann here. Offered us six of their women so she could become the *bride* of Kong. And *there's* our story, gentlemen."

"Great god," the Universal man says again, louder than before.

"But an expedition like this costs money," Denham tells them, getting down to brass tacks as the reel ends and the lights come up. "I mean to make a picture the whole damn *world's* gonna pay to see, and I can't do that without committed backers."

"Excuse me," Ann says, rising from her seat, feeling sick and dizzy and wanting to be away from these men and all their talk of profit and spectacle, wanting to drive the sight of the ape from her mind, once and for all.

"I'm fine, really," she tells them. "I just need some fresh air."

On the far side of the stream, the brown girl urges her forward; no more than twenty feet left to go, and Ann will have reached the other side.

"You're waking up," the girl says. "You're almost there. Give me your hand."

I'm only going over Jordan
I'm only going over home . . .

And the moments flash and glimmer as the dream breaks apart around her, and the barker rattles the iron bars of a stinking cage, and her empty stomach rumbles as she watches men and women bending over their plates in a lunchroom, and she sits on a bench in an alcove on the third floor of the American Museum of Natural History. Crossing the red stream, Ann Darrow hemorrhages time and possibility, all these seconds and hours and days vomited forth like a bellyful of tainted meals. She shuts her eyes and takes another step, sinking even deeper in the mud, the blood risen now as high as her waist. Here is the morning they brought her down from the Empire State Building, and the morning she wakes in her nest on Skull Mountain, and the night she watched Jack Driscoll devoured well within sight of the archaic gates. Here's the Bowery tenement, and here the screening room, and here a fallen Manhattan, crumbling and lost in the storm-tossed gulf of eons, set adrift no differently than she has set herself adrift. Every moment, all at once, each as real as every other; never mind the contradictions; each moment damned and equally inevitable, all following from a stolen apple and the man who paid the Greek a dollar to look the other way.

The world is a steamroller.

Once I built a railroad; now it's done.

She stands alone in the seaward lee of the great wall and knows that its gates have been forever shut against her *and* all the daughters of men yet to come. This hallowed, living wall of human bone and sinew erected to protect what scrap of Paradise lies inside, not the dissolute, iniquitous world of men sprawling beyond its borders. Winged Cherubim stand guard on either side, and in their leonine forepaws they grasp flaming swords forged in unknown furnaces before the coming of the World, fiery brands that reach all the way to the sky and about which spin the hearts of newborn hurricanes. The molten eyes of the Cherubim watch her every move, and their indifferent minds know her every secret thought, these dispassionate servants of the vengeful god of her father and her mother. Neither tears nor all her words will ever wring mercy from these sentinels, for they know precisely what she is, and they know her crimes.

I am she who cries out,

and I am cast forth upon the face of the earth.

The starving, ragged woman who stole an apple. Starving in body and in mind, starving in spirit, if so base a thing as she can be said to possess a soul. Starving and ragged in all ways.

I am the members of my mother.

I am the barren one

and many are her sons.

I am she whose wedding is great,

and I have not taken a husband.

And as is the way of all exiles, she cannot kill hope that her exile will one day end. Even the withering gaze of the Cherubim cannot kill that hope, and so hope is the cruelest reward.

Brother, can you spare a dime?

"Take my hand," the girl says, and Ann Darrow feels herself grown weightless and buoyed from that foul brook, hauled free of the morass of her own nightmares and regret onto a clean shore of verdant mosses and zoysia-grass, bamboo and reeds, and the girl leans down and kisses her gently on the forehead. The girl smells like sweat and nutmeg and the pungent yellow pigment dabbed across her cheeks. The girl is salvation.

"You have come *home* to us, Golden Mother," she says, and there are tears in her eyes.

"You don't see," Ann whispers, the words slipping out across her tongue and teeth and lips like her own ghost's death rattle. If the jungle air were not so still and heavy, not so turgid with the smells of living and dying, decay and birth and conception, she's sure it would lift her as easily as it might a stray feather and carry her away. She lies very still, her head cradled in the girl's lap, and the stream flowing past them is only water and the random detritus of any forest stream.

"The world blinds those who cannot close their eyes," the girl tells her. "You were not always a god and have come here from some outer, fallen world, so it may be you were never taught how to travel that path and not become lost in All-At-Once time."

Ann Darrow digs her fingers into the soft, damp earth, driving them into the loam of the jungle floor, holding on and still expecting this scene to shift, to unfurl, to send her tumbling pell-mell and head over heels into some other *now*, some other *where*.

And sometime later, when she's strong enough to stand again, and the sickening vertiginous sensation of fluidity has at last begun to ebb, the girl helps Ann to her feet, and together they follow the narrow dirt trail leading back up this long ravine to the temple. Like Ann, the girl is naked save a leather breechcloth tied about her waist. They walk together beneath the sagging boughs of trees that must have been old before Ann's great-great grandmothers were born, and here and there is ample evidence of the civilization that ruled the island in some murky, immemorial past—glimpses of great stone idols worn away by time and rain and the humid air, disintegrating walls and archways leaning at such precarious angles Ann cannot fathom why they have not yet succumbed to gravity. Crumbling bas-reliefs depicting the loathsome gods and demons and the bizarre reptilian denizens of this place. As they draw nearer to the temple, the ruins are somewhat more intact, though even here the splayed roots of the trees are slowly forcing the masonry apart. The roots put Ann in mind of the tentacles of gargantuan octopuses or cuttlefish, and that is how she envisions the spirit of the jungles and marshes fanning out around this ridge—grey tentacles advancing inch by inch, year by year, inexorably reclaiming what has been theirs all along.

As she and the girl begin to climb the steep, crooked steps leading up from the deep ravine—stones smoothed by untold generations of footsteps—Ann stops to catch her breath and asks the brown girl how she knew where to look, how it was she found her at the stream. But the girl only stares at her, confused and uncomprehending, and then she frowns and shakes her head and says something in the native tongue. In Ann's long years on the island, since the *Venture* deserted her and sailed away with what remained of the dead ape, she has never learned more than a few words of that language, and she has never tried to teach this girl, nor any of her people, English. The girl looks back the way they've come; she presses the fingers of her left hand against her breast, above her heart, then uses the same hand to motion towards Ann.

Life is just a bowl of cherries.

Don't take it serious; it's too mysterious.

By sunset, Ann has taken her place on the rough-hewn throne carved from beds of coral limestone thrust up from the seafloor in the throes of the island's cataclysmic genesis. As night begins to gather once again, torches are lit, and the people come bearing sweet-smelling baskets of flowers and fruit, fish and the roasted flesh of gulls and rats and crocodiles. They lay multicolored garlands and strings of pearls at her feet, a necklace of ankylosaur teeth, rodent claws, and monkey vertebrae, and she is only the Golden Mother once again. They bow and genuflect, and the tropical night rings out with joyous songs she cannot understand. The men and women decorate their bodies with yellow paint in an effort to emulate Ann's blonde hair, and a sort of pantomime is acted out for her benefit, as it is once every month, on the night of the new moon. She does not *need* to understand their words to grasp its meaning—the coming of the *Venture* from somewhere far away, Ann offered up as the bride of a god, her marriage and the death of Kong, and the obligatory ascent of the Golden Mother from a hellish underworld to preside in his stead. She who steals a god's heart must herself become a god.

The end of one myth and the beginning of another, the turning of a page. *I am not lost,* Ann thinks. *I am right here, right now—here and now where, surely, I must belong,* and she watches the glowing bonfire embers rising up to meet the dark sky. She knows she will see that terrible black hill again, the hill that is not a hill and its fetid crimson river, but she knows, too, that there will always be a road back from her dreams, from that All-At-Once tapestry of possibility and penitence. In her dreams, she will be lost and wander those treacherous, deceitful paths of Might-Have-Been, and always she will wake and find herself once more.

THE STEAM DANCER (1896)

1.

MISSOURI BANKS lives in the great smoky city at the edge of the mountains, here where the endless yellow prairie laps gently with grassy waves and locust tides at the exposed bones of the world jutting suddenly up towards the western sky. She was not born here, but came to the city long ago, when she was still only a small child and her father traveled from town to town in one of Edison's electric wagons selling his herbs and medicinals, his stinking poultices and elixirs. This is the city where her mother grew suddenly ill with miner's fever and where all her father's liniments and ministrations could not restore his wife's failing health or spare her life. In his grief, he drank a vial of either antimony or arsenic a few days after the funeral, leaving his only daughter and only child to fend for herself. And so, she grew up here, an orphan, one of a thousand or so dispossessed urchins with sooty bare feet and sooty faces, filching coal with sooty hands to stay warm in winter, clothed in rags, and eating what could be found in trash barrels and what could be begged or stolen.

But these things are only her past, and she has a bit of paper torn from a lending-library book of old plays which reads *What's past is prologue*, which she tacked up on the wall near her dressing mirror in the room she shares with the mechanic. Whenever the weight of Missouri's past begins to press

in upon her, she reads those words aloud to herself, once or twice or however many times is required, and usually it makes her feel at least a little
better. It has been years since she was alone and on the streets. She has the
mechanic, and he loves her, and most of the time she believes that she loves
him, as well.

He found her when she was nineteen, living in a shanty on the edge of
the colliers' slum, hiding away in amongst the spoil piles and the rusting
ruin of junked steam shovels and hydraulic pumps and bent bore-drill
heads. He was out looking for salvage, and salvage is what he found, finding
her when he lifted a broad sheet of corrugated tin, uncovering the squalid
burrow where she lay slowly dying on a filthy mattress. She'd been badly
bitten during a swarm of red-bellied bloatflies, and now the hungry white
maggots were doing their work. It was not an uncommon fate for the likes
of Missouri Banks, those caught out in the open during the spring swarms,
those without safe houses to hide inside until the voracious flies had come
and gone, moving on to bedevil other towns and cities and farms. By the
time the mechanic chanced upon her, Missouri's left leg, her right hand, and
forearm, were gangrenous, seething with the larvae. Her left eye was a pulpy,
painful boil, and he carried her to the charity hospital on Arapahoe where
he paid the surgeons who meticulously picked out the parasites and sliced
away the rotten flesh and finally performed the necessary amputations.
Afterwards, the mechanic nursed her back to health, and when she was well
enough, he fashioned for her a new leg and a new arm. The eye was entirely
beyond his expertise, but he knew a Chinaman in San Francisco who did
nothing but eyes and ears, and it happened that the Chinaman owed the
mechanic a favour. And in this way was Missouri Banks made whole again,
after a fashion, and the mechanic took her as his lover and then as his wife,
and they found a better, roomier room in an upscale boarding house near the
Seventh Avenue irrigation works.

And today, which is the seventh day of July, she settles onto the little
bench in front of the dressing-table mirror and reads aloud to herself the
shred of paper.

"What's past is prologue," she says, and then sits looking at her face and
the artificial eye and listening to the oppressive drone of cicadas outside the
open window. The mechanic has promised that someday he will read her *The*

Tempest by William Shakespeare, which he says is where the line was taken from. She can read it herself, she's told him, because she isn't illiterate. But the truth is she'd much prefer to hear him read, breathing out the words in his rough, soothing voice, and often he does read to her in the evenings.

She thinks that she has grown to be a very beautiful woman, and sometimes she believes the parts she wasn't born with have only served to make her that much more so and not any the less. Missouri smiles and gazes back at her reflection, admiring the high cheekbones and full lips (which were her mother's before her), the glistening beads of sweat on her chin and forehead and upper lip, the way her left eye pulses with a soft turquoise radiance. Afternoon light glints off the galvanized plating of her mechanical arm, the sculpted steel rods and struts, the well-oiled wheels and cogs, all the rivets and welds and perfectly fitted joints. For now, it hangs heavy and limp at her side, because she hasn't yet cranked its tiny double-acting Trevithick engine. There's only the noise of the cicadas and the traffic down on the street and the faint, familiar, comforting chug of her leg.

Other women are only whole, she thinks. Other women are only born, not made. I have been crafted.

With her living left hand, Missouri wipes some of the sweat from her face and then turns towards the small electric fan perched on the chifforobe. It hardly does more than stir the muggy summer air about, and she thinks how good it would be to go back to bed. How good to spend the whole damned day lying naked on cool sheets, dozing and dreaming and waiting for the mechanic to come home from the foundry. But she dances at Madam Ling's place four days a week, and today is one of those days, so soon she'll have to get dressed and start her arm, then make her way to the trolley and on down to the Asian Quarter. The mechanic didn't want her to work, but she told him she owed him a great debt and it would be far kinder of him to allow her to repay it. And, being kind, he knew she was telling the truth. Sometimes, he even comes down to see, to sit among the Coolies and the pungent clouds of opium smoke and watch her on the stage.

———————

2.

The shrewd old woman known in the city only as Madam Ling made the long crossing to America sometime in 1861, shortly after the end of the Second Opium War. Missouri has heard that she garnered a tidy fortune from smuggling and piracy, and maybe a bit of murder, too, but that she found Hong Kong considerably less amenable to her business ventures after the treaty that ended the war and legalized the import of opium to China. She came ashore in San Francisco and followed the railroads and airships east across the Rockies, and when she reached the city at the edge of the prairie, she went no farther. She opened a saloon and whorehouse, the Nine Dragons, on a muddy, unnamed thoroughfare, and the mechanic has explained to Missouri that in China nine is considered a very lucky number. The Nine Dragons is wedged in between a hotel and a gambling house, and no matter the time of day or night seems always just as busy. Madam Ling never wants for trade.

Missouri always undresses behind the curtain, before she takes the stage, and so presents herself to the sleepy-eyed men wearing only a fringed shawl of vermilion silk, her corset and sheer muslin shift, her white linen pantalettes. The shawl was a gift from Madam Ling, who told her in broken English that it came all the way from Beijing. Madam Ling of the Nine Dragons is not renowned for her generosity towards white women, or much of anyone else, and Missouri knows the gift was a reward for attracting a certain clientele, the men who come here just to watch her. She does not have many belongings, but she treasures the shawl as one of her most prized possessions and keeps it safe in a cedar chest at the foot of the bed she shares with the mechanic, and it always smells of the camphor-soaked cotton balls she uses to keep the moths at bay.

There is no applause, but she knows that most eyes have turned her way now. She stands sweating in the flickering gaslight glow, the open flames that ring the small stage, and listens to the men muttering in Mandarin amongst themselves and laying down mahjong tiles and sucking at their pipes. And then her music begins, the negro piano player and the woman who plucks so proficiently at a guzheng's twenty-five strings, the thin man at his xiao flute, and the burly Irishman who keeps the beat on a goatskin bodhrán and always takes his pay in celestial whores. The smoky air fills with a peculiar, jangling rendition of the final aria of Verdi's *La traviata*, because Madam Ling is a great admirer of Italian opera. The four musicians huddle together, occupying the space that has been set aside especially for them, crammed between the bar and the stage, and Missouri breathes in deeply, taking her cues as much from the reliable metronome rhythms of the engines that drive her metal leg and arm as from the music.

This is her time, her moment as truly as any moment will ever belong to Missouri Banks.

And her dance is not what men might see in the white saloons and dance halls and brothels strung out along Broadway and Lawrence, not the schottisches and waltzes of the ladies of the line, the uptown sporting women in their fine ruffled skirts made in New York and Chicago. No one has ever taught Missouri how to dance, and these are only the moves that come naturally to her, that she finds for herself. This is the interplay and synthesis of her body and the mechanic's handiwork, of the music and her own secret dreams. Her clothes fall away in gentle, inevitable drifts, like the first snows of October. Steel toe to flesh-and-bone heel, the graceful arch of an iron calf and the clockwork motion of porcelain and nickel fingers across her sweaty belly and thighs. She spins and sways and dips, as lissome and sure of herself as anything that was ever only born of Nature. And there is such joy in the dance that she might almost offer prayers of thanks to her suicide father and the bloatfly maggots that took her leg and arm and eye. There is such joy in the dancing, it might almost match the delight and peace she's found in the arms of the mechanic. There is such joy, and she thinks this is why some men and women turn to drink and laudanum, tinctures of morphine and Madam Ling's black tar, because they cannot dance.

The music rises and falls, like the seas of grass rustling to themselves out beyond the edges of the city, and the delicate mechanisms of her prosthetics clank and hum and whine. And Missouri weaves herself through this landscape of sound with the easy dexterity of pronghorn antelope and deer fleeing the jaws of wolves or the hunters' rifles, the long haunches and fleet paws of jackrabbits running out before a wildfire. For this moment, she is lost, and, for this moment, she wishes never to be found again. Soon, the air has begun to smell of the steam leaking from the exhaust ports in her leg and arm, an oily, hot sort of aroma that is as sweet to Missouri Banks as rosewater or honeysuckle blossoms. She closes her eyes—the one she was born with and the one from San Francisco—and feels no shame whatsoever at the lazy stares of the opium smokers. The piston rods in her left leg pump something more alive than blood, and the flywheels turn on their axles. She is muscle and skin, steel and artifice. She is the woman who was once a filthy, ragged guttersnipe, and she is Madam Ling's special attraction, a wondrous child of Terpsichore and Industry. Once she overheard the piano player whispering to the Irishman, and he said, "You'd think she emerged outta her momma's womb like that," and then there was a joke about screwing automata and the offspring that would ensue. But, however it might have been meant, she took it as praise and confirmation.

Too soon the music ends, leaving her gasping and breathless, dripping sweat and an iridescent sheen of lubricant onto the boards, and she must sit in her room backstage and wait out another hour before her next dance.

3.

And after the mechanic has washed away the day's share of grime and they're finished with their modest supper of apple pie and beans with thick slices of bacon, after his evening cigar and her cup of strong black Indian tea, after all the little habits and rituals of their nights together are done, he follows her to bed. The mechanic sits down and the springs squeak like stepped-on mice; he leans back against the tarnished brass headboard, smiling his easy, disarming smile while she undresses. When she slips the stocking off her right leg, he sees the gauze bandage wrapped about her knee, and his smile fades to concern.

"Here," he says. "What's that? What happened there?" and he points at her leg.

"It's nothing," she tells him. "It's nothing much."

"That seems an awful lot of dressing for nothing much. Did you fall?"

"I didn't fall," she replies. "I never fall."

"Of course not," he says. "Only us mere mortal folk fall. Of course you didn't fall. So what is it? It ain't the latest goddamn fashion."

Missouri drapes her stocking across the footboard, which is also brass, and turns her head to frown at him over her shoulder.

"A burn," she says, "that's all. One of Madam Ling's girls patched it for me. It's nothing to worry over."

"How bad a burn?"

"I said it's nothing, didn't I?"

"You did," says the mechanic and nods his head, looking not the least bit convinced. "But that secondary sliding valve's leaking again, and that's what did it. Am I right?"

Missouri turns back to her bandaged knee, wishing that there'd been some way to hide it from him, because she doesn't feel like him fussing over her tonight. "It doesn't hurt much at all. Madam Ling had a salve—"

"Haven't I been telling you that seal needs to be replaced?"

"I know you have."

"Well, you just stay in tomorrow, and I'll take that leg with me to the shop, get it fixed up tip-top again. Have it back before you know it."

"It's *fine*. I already patched it. It'll hold."

"Until the *next* time," he says, and she knows well enough from the tone of his voice that he doesn't want to argue with her about this, that he's losing patience. "You go and let that valve blow out, and you'll be needing a good deal more doctoring than a chink whore can provide. There's a lot of pressure builds up inside those pistons. You know that, Missouri."

"Yeah, I know that," she says.

"Sometimes you don't *act* like you know it."

"I can't stay in tomorrow. But I'll let you take it the next day, I swear. I'll stay in Thursday, and you can take my leg then."

"Thursday," the mechanic grumbles. "And so I just gotta keep my fingers crossed until then?"

"It'll be fine," she tells him again, trying to sound reassuring and reasonable, trying not to let the bright rind of panic in her head show in her voice. "I won't push so hard. I'll stick to the slow dances."

And then a long and disagreeable sort of silence settles over the room, and for a time she sits there at the edge of the bed, staring at both her legs, at injured meat and treacherous, unreliable metal. *Machines break down*, she thinks, *and the flesh is weak. Ain't nothing yet conjured by God nor man won't go and turn against you, sooner or later.* Missouri sighs and lightly presses a porcelain thumb to the artificial leg's green release switch; there's a series of dull clicks and pops as it comes free of the bolts set directly into her pelvic bones.

"I'll stay in tomorrow," she says and sets her left leg into its stand near the foot of their bed. "I'll send word to Madam Ling. She'll understand."

When the mechanic doesn't tell her that it's really for the best, when he doesn't say anything at all, she looks and sees he's dozed off sitting up, still wearing his trousers and suspenders and undershirt. "You," she says quietly, then reaches for the release switch on her right arm.

4.

When she feels his hands on her, Missouri thinks at first that this is only some new direction her dream has taken, the rambling dream of her father's medicine wagon and of buffalo, of rutted roads and a flaxen Nebraska sky filled with flocks of automatic birds chirping arias from *La traviata*. But there's something substantial about the pale light of the waxing moon falling though the open window and the way the curtains move in the midnight breeze that convinces her she's awake. Then he kisses her, and one hand wanders down across her breasts and stomach and lingers in the unruly thatch of hair between her legs.

"Unless maybe you got something better to be doing," he mutters in her ear.

"Well, now that you mention it, I *was* dreaming," she tells him, "before you woke me up," and the mechanic laughs.

"Then maybe I should let you get back to it." But when he starts to move his hand away from her privy parts, she takes hold of it and rubs his fingertips across her labia.

"So, what exactly were you dreaming about that's got you in such a cooperative mood, Miss Missouri Banks?" he asks and kisses her again, the dark stubble on his cheeks scratching at her face.

"Wouldn't you like to know," she says.

"I figure that's likely why I inquired."

His face is washed in the soft blue-green glow of her San Francisco eye, which switched on as soon as she awoke, and times like this it's hard not to imagine all the ways her life might have gone but didn't, how very unlikely that it went this way, instead. And she starts to tell him the truth, her dream of being a little girl and all the manufactured birds, the shaggy herds of bison, and how her father kept insisting he should give up peddling his herbs and remedies and settle down somewhere. But at the last, and for no particular reason, she changes her mind, and Missouri tells him another dream, just something she makes up off the top of her sleep-blurred head.

"You might not like it," she says.

"Might not," he agrees. "Then again, you never know," and the first joint of an index finger slips inside her.

"Then again," she whispers, and so she tells him a dream she's never dreamt. How there was a terrible fire and before it was over and done with, the flames had claimed half the city, there where the grass ends and the mountains start. And at first, she tells him, it was an awful, awful dream, because she was trapped in the boarding house when it burned, and she could see him down on the street, calling for her, but, try as they may, neither could reach the other.

"Why you want to go and have a dream like that for?" he asks.

"You wanted to hear it. Now shut up and listen."

So he does as he's bidden, and she describes to him seeing an enormous airship hovering above the flames, spewing its load of water and sand into the ravenous inferno.

"There might have been a dragon," she says. "Or it might have only been started by lightning."

"A dragon," he replies, working his finger in a little deeper. "Yes, I think it must definitely have been a dragon. They're so ill-tempered this time of year."

"Shut up. This is my dream," she tells him, even though it isn't. "I almost died, so much of me got burned away, and they had me scattered about in pieces in the Charity Hospital. But you went right to work, putting me back together again. You worked night and day at the shop, making me a pretty metal face and a tin heart, and you built my breasts—"

"—from sterling silver," he says. "And your nipples I fashioned from out of pure gold."

"And just how the sam hell did you know *that?*" she grins. Then Missouri reaches down and moves his hand, slowly pulling his finger out of her. Before he can protest, she's laid his palm over the four bare bolts where her leg fits on. He smiles and licks at her nipples, then grips one of the bolts and gives it a very slight tug.

"Well, while you were sleeping," he says, "I made a small window in your skull, only just large enough that I can see inside. So, no more secrets. But don't you fret. I expect your hair will hide it quite completely. Madam Ling will never even notice, and nary a Chinaman will steal a glimpse of your sweet, darling brain."

"Why, I never even felt a thing."

"I was very careful not to wake you."

"Until you did."

And then the talk is done, without either of them acknowledging that the time has come, and there's no more of her fiery, undreamt dreams or his glib comebacks. There's only the mechanic's busy, eager hands upon her, only her belly pressed against his, the grind of their hips after he has entered her, his fingertips lingering at the sensitive bolts where her prosthetics attach. She likes that best of all, that faint electric tingle, and she knows *he* knows, though she has never had to tell him so. Outside and far away, she thinks she hears an owl, but there are no owls in the city.

5.

And when she wakes again, the boarding-house room is filled with the dusty light of a summer morning. The mechanic is gone, and he's taken her leg with him. Her crutches are leaned against the wall near her side of the bed. She stares at them for a while, wondering how long it has been since the last time she had to use them, then deciding it doesn't really matter, because however long it's been, it hasn't been long enough. There's a note, too, on her night-stand, and the mechanic says not to worry about Madam Ling, that he'll send one of the boys from the foundry down to the Asian Quarter with the news. Take it easy, he says. Let that burn heal. Burns can be bad. Burns can scar, if you don't look after them.

When the clanging steeple bells of St. Margaret of Castello's have rung nine o'clock, she shuts her eyes and thinks about going back to sleep. St. Margaret, she recalls, is a patron saint of the crippled, an Italian woman who was born blind and hunchbacked, lame and malformed. Missouri envies the men and women who take comfort in those bells, who find in their tolling more than the time of day. She has never believed in the Catholic god or any other sort, unless perhaps it was some capricious heathen deity assigned to watch over starving, maggot-ridden guttersnipes. She imagines what form that god might assume, and it is a far more fearsome thing than any hunchbacked crone. A wolf, she thinks. Yes, an enormous black wolf—or coyote, perhaps—all ribs and mange and a distended, empty belly, crooked ivory fangs, and burning eyes like smoldering embers glimpsed through a cast-iron grate. *That* would be her god, if ever she'd been blessed with such a thing. Her mother had come from Presbyterian stock somewhere back in Virginia, but her father believed in nothing more powerful than the hand and intellect of man, and he was not about to have his child's head filled up with Protestant superstition and nonsense, not in a Modern age of science and enlightenment.

Missouri opens her eyes again, her green eye—all cornea and iris, aqueous and vitreous humours—and the ersatz one designed for her in San Francisco. The crutches are still right there, near enough that she could reach out and touch them. They have good sheepskin padding and the vulcanized rubber tips have pivots and are filled with some shock-absorbing gelatinous substance, the name of which she has been told and cannot recall. The mechanic ordered them for her special from a company in some faraway Prussian city, and she knows they cost more than he could rightly afford, but she hates them anyway. And lying on the sweat-damp sheets, smelling the hazy morning air rustling the gingham curtains, she wonders if she built a little shrine to the wolf god of all collier guttersnipes, if maybe he would come in the night and take the crutches away so she would never have to see them again.

"It's not that simple, Missouri," she says aloud, and she thinks that those could have been her father's words, if the theosophists are right and the dead might ever speak through the mouths of the living.

"Leave me alone, old man" she says and sits up. "Go back to the grave you yearned for, and leave me be."

Her arm is waiting for her at the foot of the bed, right where she left it the night before, reclining in its cradle, next to the empty space her leg *ought* to occupy. And the hot breeze through the window, the street- and coal-smoke-scented breeze, causes the scrap of paper tacked up by her vanity mirror to flutter against the wall. Her proverb, her precious stolen scrap of Shakespeare. *What's past is prologue.*

Missouri Banks considers how she can keep herself busy until the mechanic comes back to her—a torn shirt sleeve that needs mending, and she's no slouch with a needle and thread. Her good stockings could use a rinsing. The dressing on her leg should be changed, and Madam Ling saw to it she had a small tin of the pungent salve to reapply when Missouri changed the bandages. Easily half a dozen such mundane tasks, any woman's work, any woman who is not a dancer, and nothing that won't wait until the bells of St. Margaret's ring ten or eleven. And so she watches the window, the sunlight and flapping gingham, and it isn't difficult to call up with almost perfect clarity the piano and the guzheng and the Irishman thumping his bodhrán, the exotic, festive trill of the xiao. And with the music swelling loudly inside her skull, she can then recall the dance. And she is not a cripple in need of patron saints or a guttersnipe praying to black wolf gods, but Madam Ling's specialty, the steam- and blood-powered gem of the Nine Dragons. She moves across the boards, and men watch her with dark and drowsy eyes as she pirouettes and prances through grey opium clouds.

GALÁPAGOS

March 17, 2037 (Wednesday)

WHENEVER I WAKE up screaming, the nurses kindly come in and give me the shiny yellow pills and the white pills flecked with grey; they prick my skin with hollow needles until I grow quiet and calm again. They speak in exquisitely gentle voices, reminding me that I'm home, that I've been home for many, many months. They remind me that if I open the blinds and look out the hospital window, I will see a parking lot, and cars, and a carefully tended lawn. I will only see California. I will see only Earth. If I look up, and it happens to be day, I'll see the sky, too, sprawled blue above me and peppered with dirty-white clouds and contrails. If it happens to be night, instead, I'll see the comforting pale orange skyglow that mercifully hides the stars from view. I'm home, not strapped into *Yastreb-4*'s taxi module. I can't crane my neck for a glance at the monitor screen displaying a tableau of dusty volcanic wastelands as I speed by the Tharsis plateau, more than four hundred kilometers below me. I can't turn my head and gaze through the tiny docking windows at *Pilgrimage*'s glittering alabaster hull, quickly growing larger as I rush towards the aft docking port. These are merely memories, inaccurate and untrustworthy, and may only do me the harm that memories are capable of doing.

Then the nurses go away. They leave the light above my bed burning and tell me if I need anything at all to press the intercom button. They're just down the hall, and they always come when I call. They're never anything except prompt and do not fail to arrive bearing the chemical solace of pharmaceuticals, only half of which I know by name. I am not neglected. My needs are met as well as anyone alive can meet them. I'm too precious a commodity not to coddle. I'm the woman who was invited to the strangest, most terrible rendezvous in the history of space exploration. The one they dragged all the way to Mars after *Pilgrimage* abruptly, inexplicably diverged from its mission parameters, when the crew went silent and the AI stopped responding. I'm the woman who stepped through an airlock hatch and into that alien Eden; I'm the one who spoke with a goddess. I'm the woman who was the goddess' lover, when she was still human and had a name and a consciousness that could be comprehended.

"Are you sleeping better?" the psychiatrist asks, and I tell him that I sleep just fine, thank you, seven to eight hours every night now. He nods and patiently smiles, but I know I haven't answered his question. He's actually asking me if I'm still having the nightmares about my time aboard *Pilgrimage*, if they've decreased in their frequency and/or severity. He doesn't want to know *if* I sleep, or how *long* I sleep, but if my sleep is still haunted. Though he'd never use that particular word, *haunted*.

He's a thin, balding man with perfectly manicured nails and an unremarkable mid-Atlantic accent. He dutifully makes the commute down from Berkeley once a week, because those are his orders, and I'm too great a puzzle for his inquisitive mind to ignore. All in all, I find the psychiatrist far less helpful than the nurses and their dependable drugs. Whereas they've been assigned the task of watching over me, of soothing and steadying me and keeping me from harming myself, he's been given the unenviable responsibility of discovering what happened during the comms blackout, those seventeen interminable minutes after I boarded the derelict ship and promptly lost radio contact with *Yastreb-4* and Earth. Despite countless debriefings and interviews, NASA still thinks I'm holding out on them. And maybe I am. Honestly, it's hard for me to say. It's hard for me to keep it all straight anymore: what happened and what didn't, what I've said to them and what I've only thought about saying, what I genuinely remember and what I may have fabricated wholesale as a means of self-preservation.

The psychiatrist says it's to be expected, this sort of confusion from someone who's survived very traumatic events. *He* calls the events very traumatic, by the way. I don't; I'm not yet sure if I think of them that way. Regardless, he's diagnosed me as suffering from Survivor Syndrome, which he also calls K-Z Syndrome. There's a jack in my hospital room with filtered and monitored web access, but I was able to look up "K-Z Syndrome." It was named for a Nazi concentration camp survivor, an Israeli author named Yehiel De-Nur. De-Nur published under the pseudonym Ka-Tzetnik 135633. That was his number at Auschwitz, and K-Z Syndrome is named after him. In 1956, he published *House of Dolls*, describing the Nazi "Joy Division, the Freudenabteilung," a system that utilized Jewish women as sex slaves.

The psychiatrist is the one who asked if I would at least try to write it down, what happened, what I saw and heard (and smelled and felt) when I entered the *Pilgrimage* a year and a half ago. He knows, of course, that there have already been numerous written and vidded depositions and affidavits for NASA and the CSS/NSA, the WHO, the CDC, and the CIA and, to tell the truth, I don't *know* who requested and read and then filed away all those reports. He knows about them, though, and that, by my own admission, they barely scratched the surface of whatever happened out there. He knows, but I reminded him, anyway.

"This will be different," he said. "This will be more subjective." And the psychiatrist explained that he wasn't looking for a blow-by-blow linear narrative of my experiences aboard *Pilgrimage*, and I told him that was good, because I seem to have forgotten how to think or relate events in a linear fashion, without a lot of switchbacks and digressions and meandering.

"Just write," he said. "Write what you can remember, and write until you don't want to write anymore."

"That would be now," I said, and he silently stared at me for a while. He didn't laugh, even though I'd thought it was pretty funny.

"I understand that the medication makes this sort of thing more difficult for you," he said, sometime later. "But the medication helps you reach back to those things you don't want to remember, those things you're trying to forget." I almost told him that he was starting to sound like a character in a Lewis Carroll story—riddling and contradicting—but I didn't. Our hour was almost over, anyway.

So, after three days of stalling, I'm trying to write something that will make you happy, Dr. Ostrowski. I know you're trying to do your job, and I know a lot of people must be peering over your shoulder, expecting the sort of results they've failed to get themselves. I don't want to show up for our next session empty-handed.

The taxi module was on autopilot during the approach. See, I'm not an astronaut or mission specialist or engineer or anything like that. I'm an anthropologist, and I mostly study the Middle Paleolithic of Europe and Asia Minor. I have a keen interest in tool use and manufacture by the Neanderthals. Or at least that's who I used to be. Right now, I'm a madwoman in a psych ward at a military hospital in San Jose, California. I'm a case number, and an eyewitness who has proven less than satisfactory. But, what I'm *trying* to say, Doctor, the module *was* on autopilot, and there was nothing for me to do but wait there inside my encounter suit and sweat and watch the round screen divided by a Y-shaped reticle as I approached the derelict's docking port, the taxi barreling forward at 0.06 meters per second. The ship grew so huge so quickly, looming up in the blackness, and that only made the whole thing seem that much more unreal.

I tried hard to focus, to breathe slowly, and follow the words being spoken between the painful, bright bursts of static in my ears, the babble of sound trapped inside the helmet with me. *Module approaching 50-meter threshold. On target and configuring KU-band from radar to comms mode. Slowing now to 0.045 meters per second. Decelerating for angular alignment, extending docking ring,* nine meters, three meters, a whole lot of noise and nonsense about latches and hooks and seals, capture and final position, and then it seemed like I wasn't moving anymore. Like the taxi wasn't moving anymore. We were, of course, the little module and I, only now we were riding piggyback on *Pilgrimage,* locked into geosynchronous orbit, with nothing but the instrument panel to remind me I wasn't sitting still in space. Then the mission commander was telling me I'd done a great job, congratulations, they were all proud of me, even though I hadn't done anything except sit and wait.

But all this is right there in the mission dossiers, Doctor. You don't need me to tell you these things. You already know that *Pilgrimage's* AI would allow no one but me to dock and that MS Lowry's repeated attempts to hack the firewall failed. You know about the nurses and their pills, and

Yehiel De-Nur and *House of Dolls.* You know about the affair I had with the Korean payload specialist during the long flight to Mars. You're probably skimming this part, hoping it gets better a little farther along.

So, I'll try to tell you something you don't know. Just one thing, for now.

Hanging there in my tiny, life-sustaining capsule, suspended two hundred and fifty miles above extinct Martian volcanoes and surrounded by near vacuum, I had two recurring thoughts, the only ones that I can now clearly recall having had. First, the grim hope that, when the hatch finally opened—*if* the hatch opened—they'd all be dead. All of them. Every single one of the men and women aboard *Pilgrimage*, and most especially her. And, secondly, I closed my eyes as tightly as I could and wished that I would soon discover there'd been some perfectly mundane accident or malfunction, and the bizarre, garbled transmissions that had sent us all the way to Mars to try and save the day meant nothing at all. But I only hoped and wished, mind you. I haven't prayed since I was fourteen years old.

March 19, 2037 (Friday)

Last night was worse than usual. The dreams, I mean. The nurses and my physicians don't exactly approve of what I've begun writing for you, Dr. Ostrowski. Of what you've asked me to do. I suspect they would say there's a conflict of interest at work. They're supposed to keep me sane and healthy, but here you are, the latest episode in the inquisition that's landed me in their ward. When I asked for the keypad this afternoon, they didn't want to give it to me. Maybe tomorrow, they said. Maybe the day *after* tomorrow. Right now, you need your rest. And sure, I know they're right. What you want, it's only making matters worse, for them *and* for me, but when I'd finally had enough and threatened to report the hospital staff for attempting to obstruct a federal investigation, they relented. But, just so you know, they've got me doped to the gills with an especially potent cocktail of tranquilizers and antipsychotics, so I'll be lucky if I can manage more than gibberish. Already, it's taken me half an hour to write (and repeatedly rewrite) this one paragraph, so who gets the final laugh?

Last night, I dreamed of the cloud again.

I dreamed I was back in Germany, in Darmstadt, only this time, I wasn't sitting in that dingy hotel room near the Luisenplatz. This time it wasn't a phone call that brought me the news, or a courier. And I didn't look up to find *her* standing there in the room with me, which, you know, is how this one usually goes. I'll be sitting on the bed, or I'll walk out of the bathroom, or turn away from the window, and there she'll be. Even though *Pilgrimage* and its crew is all those hundreds of millions of kilometers away, finishing up their experiments at Ganymede and preparing to begin the long journey home, she's standing there in the room with me. Only not this time. Not last night.

The way it played out last night, I'd been cleared for access to the ESOC central control room. I have no idea why. But I was there, standing near one wall with a young French woman, younger than me by at least a decade. She was blonde, with green eyes, and she was pretty; her English was better than my French. I watched all those men and women, too occupied with their computer terminals to notice me. The pretty French woman (sorry, but I never learned her name) was pointing out different people, explaining their various roles and responsibilities: the ground operations manager, the director of flight operations, a visiting astrodynamics consultant, the software coordinator, and so forth. The lights in the room were almost painfully bright, and when I looked up at the ceiling, I saw it wasn't a ceiling at all, but the night sky, blazing with countless fluorescent stars.

And then that last transmission from *Pilgrimage* came in. We didn't realize it would be the last, but everything stopped, and everyone listened. Afterwards, no one panicked, as if they'd expected something of this sort all along. I understood that it had taken the message the better part of an hour to reach Earth, and that any reply would take just as long, but the French woman was explaining the communications delay, anyway.

"We can't know what that means," somebody said. "We can't *possibly* know, can we?"

"Run through the telemetry data again," someone else said, and I think it was the man the French woman had told me was the director of flight operations.

But it might have been someone else. I was still looking at the ceiling composed of starlight and planets, and the emptiness between starlight and planets, and I knew exactly what the transmission meant. It was a suicide note, of sorts, streamed across space at three hundred kilometers per second. I knew, because I plainly saw the mile-long silhouette of the ship sailing by overhead, only a silvery speck against the roiling backdrop of Jupiter. I saw that cloud, too, saw *Pilgrimage* enter it and exit a minute or so later (and I think I even paused to calculate the width of the cloud, based on the vessel's speed).

You know as well as I what was said that day, Dr. Ostrowski, the contents in that final broadcast. You've probably even committed it to memory, just as I have. I imagine you've listened to the tape more times than you could ever recollect, right? Well, what was said in my dream last night was almost verbatim what Commander Yun said in the actual transmission. There was only one difference. The part right at the end, when the commander quotes from Chapter 13 of the *Book of Revelation*, that didn't happen. Instead, he said:

"Lead us from the unreal to real,

Lead us from darkness to light,

Lead us from death to immortality,

Om Shanti, Shanti, Shanti."

I admit I had to look that up online. It's from the Hindu *Bṛhadāraṇyaka Upanishad*. I haven't studied Vedic literature since a seminar in grad school, and that was mostly an excuse to visit Bangalore. But the unconscious doesn't lose much, does it, Doctor? And you never know what it's going to cough up, or when.

In my dream, I stood staring at the ceiling that was really no ceiling at all. If anyone else could see what I was seeing, they didn't act like it. The strange cloud near Ganymede made me think of an oil slick floating on water, and when *Pilgrimage* came out the far side, it was like those dying sea birds that wash up on beaches after tanker spills. That's exactly how it seemed to me, in the dream last night. I looked away, finally, looked down at the floor, and I was trying to explain what I'd seen to the French woman. I described the ruined plumage of ducks and gulls and cormorants, but I couldn't make her understand. And then I woke up. I woke up screaming, but you'll have guessed that part.

I need to stop now. The meds have made going on almost impossible, and I should read back over everything I've written, do what I can to make myself clearer. I feel like I ought to say more about the cloud, because I've never seen it so clearly in any of the other dreams. It never before reminded me of an oil slick. I'll try to come back to this. Maybe later. Maybe not.

March 20, 2037 (Saturday)

I don't have to scream for the nurses to know that I'm awake, of course. I don't have to scream, and I don't have to use the call button, either. They get everything relayed in real-time, directly from my cerebral cortex and hippocampus to their wrist tops, via the depth electrodes and subdural strips that were implanted in my head a few weeks after the crew of *Yastreb-4* was released from suborbital quarantine. The nurses see it all, spelled out in the spikes and waves of electrocorticography, which is how I know *they* know that I'm awake right now, when I should be asleep. Tomorrow morning, I imagine there will be some sort of confab about adjusting the levels of my benzo and nonbenzo hypnotics to ensure the insomnia doesn't return.

I'm not sure why I'm awake, really. There wasn't a nightmare, at least none I can recall. I woke up and simply couldn't get back to sleep. After ten or fifteen minutes, I reached for the keypad. I find the soft cobalt-blue glow from the screen is oddly soothing, and it's nice to find comfort that isn't injected, comfort that I don't have to swallow or get from a jet spray or IV drip. And I want to have something more substantial to show the psychiatrist come Tuesday than dreams about Darmstadt, oil slicks, and pretty French women.

I keep expecting the vidcom beside my bed to buzz and wink to life, and there will be one of the nurses looking concerned and wanting to know if I'm all right, if I'd like a little extra coby to help me get back to sleep. But the box has been quiet and blank so far, which leaves me equal parts surprised and relieved.

"There are things you've yet to tell anyone," the psychiatrist said. "Those are the things I'm trying to help you talk about. If they've been repressed, they're the memories I'm trying to help you access." That is, they're what he's going to want to see when I give him my report on Tuesday morning.

And if at first I don't succeed . . .

So, where was I?

The handoff.

I'm sitting alone in the taxi, waiting, and below me, Mars is a sullen, rusty cadaver of a planet. I have the distinct impression that it's watching as I'm handed off from one ship to the other. I imagine those countless craters and calderas have become eyes, and all those eyes are filled with jealousy and spite. The module's capture ring has successfully snagged *Pilgrimage*'s aft PMA, and it only takes a few seconds for the ring to achieve proper alignment. The module deploys twenty or so hooks, establishing an impermeable seal, and, a few seconds later, the taxi's hatch spirals open, and I enter the airlock. I feel dizzy, slightly nauseous, and I almost stumble, almost fall. I see a red light above the hatch go blue, and realize that the chamber has pressurized, which means I'm subject to the centripetal force that generates the ship's artificial gravity. I've been living in near zero g for more than eleven months, and nothing they told me in training or aboard the *Yastreb-4* could have prepared me for the return of any degree of gravity. The EVA suit's exoskeleton begins to compensate. It keeps me on my feet, keeps my atrophied muscles moving, keeps me breathing.

"You're doing great," Commander Yun assures me from the bridge of *Yastreb-4*, and that's when my comms cut out. I panic and try to return to the taxi module, but the hatchway has already sealed itself shut again. I have a go at the control panel, my gloved fingers fumbling clumsily at the unfamiliar switches, but can't get it to respond. The display on the inside of my visor tells me that my heart rate's jumped to 186 BPM, my blood pressure's in the red, and oxygen consumption has doubled. I'm hyperventilating, which has my CO_2 down and is beginning to affect blood oxygen levels. The medic on my left wrist responds by secreting a relatively mild anxiolytic compound directly into the radial artery. Milder, I might add, than the shit they give me here.

And yes, Dr. Ostrowski, I know that you've read all this before. I know that I'm trying your patience, and you're probably disappointed. I'm doing this the only way I know how. I was never any good at jumping into the deep end of the pool.

But we're almost there, I promise.

It took me a year and a half to find the words to describe what happened next, or to find the courage to say it aloud, or the resignation necessary to let it out into the world. Whichever. They've been *my* secrets, and almost mine alone. And soon, now, they won't be anymore.

The soup from the medic hits me, and I begin to relax. I give up on the airlock and shut my eyes a moment, leaning forward, my helmet resting against the closed hatch. I'm almost certain my eyes are still shut when the *Pilgrimage*'s AI first speaks to me. And here, Doctor, right *here*, pay attention, because this is where I'm going to come clean and tell you something I've never told another living soul. It's not a repressed memory that's suddenly found its way to the surface. It hasn't been coaxed from me by all those potent psychotropics. It's just something I've managed to keep to myself until now:

"Hello," the computer says. Only, I'd heard recordings of the mainframe's NLP, and this isn't the voice it was given. This is, unmistakably, *her* voice, only slightly distorted by the audio interface. My eyes are shut, and I don't open them right away. I just stand there, my head against the hatch, listening to that voice and to my heart. The sound of my breath is very loud inside the helmet.

"We were not certain our message had been received, or, if it had been, that it had been properly understood. We did not expect you would come so far."

"Then why did you call?" I ask and open my eyes.

"We were lonely," the voice replies. "We have not seen you in a very long time now."

I don't turn around. I keep my faceplate pressed to the airlock, some desperate, insensible part of me willing it to reopen and admit me once more to the sanctuary of the taxi. Whatever I should say next, of all the things I might say, what I *do* say is, simply, "Amery, I'm frightened."

There's a pause before her response, five or six or seven seconds, I don't know, and my fingers move futilely across the control pad again. I hear the inner hatch open behind me, though I'm fairly certain I'm not the one who opened it.

"We see that," she says. "But it wasn't our intent to make you afraid, Merrick. It was never our intent to frighten you."

"Amery, what's happened here?" I ask, speaking hardly above a whisper, but my voice is amplified and made clearer by the vocal modulator in my EVA helmet. "What happened to the ship, back at Jupiter? To the rest of the crew? What's happened to you?"

I expect another pause, but there isn't one.

"The most remarkable thing," she replies. And there's a sort of elation in her voice, audible even through the tinny flatness of the NLP relay. "You will hardly believe it."

"Are they dead, the others?" I ask her, and my eyes wander to the external atmo readout inside my visor. Argon's showing a little high, a few tenths of a percent off Earth normal, but not enough to act as an asphyxiant. Water vapor's twice what I'd have expected, anywhere but the ship's hydroponics lab. Pressure's steady at 14.2 psi. Whatever happened aboard *Pilgrimage*, life support is still up and running. All the numbers are in the green.

"That's not a simple question to answer," she says, Amery or the AI or whatever it is I'm having this conversation with. "None of it is simple, Merrick. And yet, it is so elegant."

"Are they *dead?*" I ask again, resisting the urge to flip the release toggle beneath my chin and raise the visor. It stinks inside the suit, like sweat and plastic, urine and stale, recycled air.

"Yes," she says. "It couldn't be helped."

I lick my lips, Dr. Ostrowski, and my mouth has gone very, very dry. "Did you kill them, Amery?"

"You're asking the wrong questions," she says, and I stare down at my feet, at the shiny white toes of the EVA's overshoes.

"They're the questions we've come all the way out here to have answered," I tell *her*, or I tell *it*. "What questions would you have me ask instead?"

"It may be, there is no longer any need for questions. It may be, Merrick, that you've been called to see, and seeing will be enough. The force that through the green fuse drives the flower, drives my green age; that blasts the roots of trees, is my destroyer."

"I've been summoned to Mars to listen to you quote Dylan Thomas?"

"You're not listening, Merrick. That's the thing. And that's why it will be so much easier if we show you what's happened. What's begun."

"And I am dumb to tell the lover's tomb," I say as softly as I can, but the suit adjusts the volume so it's just as loud as everything else I've said.

"We have not died," she replies. "You will find no tomb here," and, possibly, this voice that wants me to believe it is only Amery Domico has become defensive, and impatient, and somehow this seems the strangest thing so far. I imagine Amery speaking through clenched teeth. I imagine her rubbing her forehead like a headache's coming on, and it's my fault. "I am very much alive," she says, "and I need you to pay attention. You cannot stay here very long. It's not safe, and I will see no harm comes to you."

"Why?" I ask her, only half expecting a response. "Why isn't it safe for me to be here?"

"Turn around, Merrick," she says. "You've come so far, and there is so little time." I do as she says. I turn towards the voice, towards the airlock's open inner hatch.

It's almost morning. I mean, the sun will be rising soon. Here in California. Still no interruption from the nurses. But I can't keep this up. I can't do this all at once. The rest will have to wait.

March 21, 2037 (Sunday)

Dr. Bernardyn Ostrowski is no longer handling my case. One of my physicians delivered the news this morning, bright and early. It came with no explanation attached. And I thought better of asking for one. That is, I thought better of wasting my breath asking for one. When I signed on for the *Yastreb-4* intercept, the waivers and NDAs and whatnot were all very, very clear about things like the principle of least privilege and mandatory access control. I'm told what they decide I need to know, which isn't much. I *did* ask if I should continue with the account of the mission that Dr. O asked me to write, and the physician (a hematologist named Prideaux) said he'd gotten no word to the contrary, and if there would be a change in the direction of my psychotherapy regimen, I'd find out about it when I meet with the new shrink Tuesday morning. Her name is Teasdale, by the way. Eleanor Teasdale.

I thanked Dr. Prideaux for bringing me the news, and he only shrugged and scribbled something on my chart. I suppose that's fair, as it was hardly a sincere show of gratitude on my part. At any rate, I have no idea what to expect from this Teasdale woman, and I appear to have lost the stingy drab of momentum pushing me recklessly towards full disclosure. That in and of itself is enough to set me wondering what my keepers are up to now, if the shrink switch is some fresh skullduggery. It seems counterintuitive, given they were finally getting the results they've been asking for (and I'm not so naïve as to assume that this pad isn't outfitted with a direct patch to some agency goon or another). But then an awful lot of what they've done seems counterintuitive to me. And counterproductive.

Simply put, I don't know what to say next. No, strike that. I don't know what I'm *willing* to say next.

I've already mentioned my indiscretion with the South Korean payload specialist on the outbound half of the trip. Actually, *indiscretion* is hardly accurate, since Amery explicitly gave me her permission to take other lovers while she was gone, because, after all, there was a damned decent chance she wouldn't make it back alive. Or make it back at all. So, *indiscretion* is just my guilt talking. Anyway, her name was Bae Jin-ah—the *Yastreb-4* PS, I mean—though everyone called her Sam, which she seemed to prefer. She was born in Incheon, and was still a kid when the war started. A relative in the States helped her parents get Bae on one of the last transports out of Seoul before the bombs started raining down. But we didn't have many conversations about the past, mine or hers. She was a biochemist obsessed with the structure-function relationships of peptides, and she liked to talk shop after we fucked. It was pretty dry stuff—the talk, not the sex—and I admit I only half listened and didn't understand all that much of what I heard. But I don't think that mattered to Sam. I have a feeling she was just grateful that I bothered to cover my mouth whenever I yawned.

She only asked about Amery once.

We were both crammed into the warm cocoon of her sleeping bag, or into mine; I can't recall which. Probably hers, since the micrograv restraints in my bunk kept popping loose. I was on the edge of dozing off, and Sam asked me how we met. I made up some half-assed romance about an academic conference in Manhattan, and a party, a formal affair at the American Museum of Natural History. It was love at first sight, I said (or something equally ridiculous), right there in the Roosevelt Rotunda, beneath the rearing *Barosaurus* skeleton. Sam thought it was sweet as hell, though, and I figured lies were fine, if they gave us a moment's respite from the crowded day-to-day monotony of the ship, or from our (usually) unspoken dread of all that nothingness surrounding us and the uncertainty we were hurdling towards. I don't even know if she believed me, but it made her smile.

"You've read the docs on the cloud?" she asked, and I told her yeah, I had, or at least the ones I was given clearance to read. And then Sam watched me for a while without saying anything. I could feel her silently weighing options and consequences, duty and need and repercussion.

"So, you *know* it's some pretty hinky shit out there," she said, finally, and went back to watching me, as if waiting for a particular reaction. And, here, I lied to her again.

"Relax, Sam," I whispered, then kissed her on the forehead. "I've read most of the spectroscopy and astrochem profiles. Discussing it with me, you're not in danger of compromising protocol or mission security or anything."

She nodded once and looked slightly relieved.

"I've never given much credence to the exogenesis crowd," she said, "but, Jesus, Mary, and Joseph . . . glycine, DHA, adenine, cytosine, etcetera and fucking etcetera. When—or, rather, *if* this gets out—the panspermia guys are going to go monkey shit. And rightly so. No one saw this coming, Merrick. No one you'd ever take seriously."

I must have managed a fairly convincing job of acting like I knew what she was talking about, because she kept it up for the next ten or fifteen minutes. Her voice assumed that same sort of jittery, excited edge Amery's used to get whenever she'd start in on the role of Io in the Jovian magnetosphere or any number of other astronomical phenomena I didn't quite understand, and how much the *Pilgrimage* experiments were going to change this or that model or theory. Only, unlike Amery's, Sam's excitement was tinged with fear.

"The inherent risks," she said, and then trailed off and wiped at her forehead before starting again. "When they first showed me the back-contamination safeguards for this run, I figured no way, right. No way are NASA and the ESA going to pony up the budget for that sort of overkill. But this was *before* I read Murchison's reports on the cloud's composition and behavior. And afterwards, the thought of intentionally sending a human crew anywhere near that thing, or, shit, anything that had been *exposed* to it? I couldn't believe they were serious. It's fucking crazy. No, it's whatever comes *after* fucking crazy. They should have cut their losses . . ." and then she trailed off again and went back to staring at me.

"You shouldn't have come," she said.

"I had to," I told her. "If there's any chance at all that Amery's still alive, I had to come."

"Of course. Yeah, of course you did," Sam said, looking away.

"When they asked, I couldn't very well say no."

"But do you honestly believe we're going to find any of them alive, that we'll be docking with anything but a ghost ship?"

"You're really not into pulling punches, are you?"

"You read the reports on the cloud."

"I had to come," I told her a third time.

Then we both let the subject drop and neither of us ever brought it up again. Indeed, I think I probably would have forgotten most of it, especially after what I saw when I stepped through the airlock and into *Pilgrimage*. That whole conversation might have dissolved into the tedious grey blur of outbound and been forgotten, if Bae Jin-ah hadn't killed herself on the return trip, just five days before we made Earth orbit.

March 23, 2037 (Tuesday)

Tuesday night now, and the meds are making me sleepy and stupid, but I wanted to put some of this down, even if it isn't what they want me to be writing. I see how it's all connected, even if they never will, or, if seeing, they simply do not care. *They*, whoever, precisely, they may be.

This morning I had my first session with you, Dr. Eleanor Teasdale. I never much liked that bastard Ostrowski, but at least I was moderately certain he was who and what he claimed to be. Between you and me, Eleanor, I think you're an asset, sent in because someone somewhere is getting nervous. Nervous enough to swap an actual psychiatrist for a bug dressed up to pass for a psychiatrist. Fine. I'm flexible. If these are the new rules, I can play along. But it does leave me pondering what Dr. O was telling his superiors (whom I'll assume are also your superiors, Dr. T). It couldn't have been anything so simple as labeling me a suicide risk; they've known that since I stepped off *Pilgrimage*, probably before I even stepped on.

And yes, I've noticed that you bear more than a passing resemblance to Amery. That was a bold and wicked move, and I applaud these ruthless shock tactics. I do, sincerely. This merciless Blitzkrieg waltz we're dancing, coupled with the drugs, it shows you're in this game to win, and if you *can't* win, you'll settle for the pyrrhic victory of having driven the enemy to resort to a scorched-earth retreat. Yeah, the pills and injections, they don't mesh so well with extended metaphor and simile, so I'll drop it. But I can't have you thinking all the theater has been wasted on an inattentive audience. That's all. You wear that rough facsimile of her face, Dr. T. And that annoying habit you have of tap-tap-tapping the business end of a stylus against your lower incisors, that's hers, too. And half a dozen carefully planted turns of phrase. The smile that isn't quite a smile. The self-conscious laugh. You hardly missed a trick, you and the agency handlers who sculpted you and slotted you and packed you off to play havoc with a lunatic's fading will.

My mouth is so dry.

Eleanor Teasdale watches me from the other side of her desk, and behind her, through the wide window twelve stories up, I can see the blue-brown sky, and, between the steel and glass and concrete towers, I can just make out the scrubby hills of the Diablo Range through the smog. She glances over her shoulder, following my gaze.

"Quite a view, isn't it?" she asks, and maybe I nod, and maybe I agree, and maybe I say nothing at all.

"When I was a little girl," she tells me, "my father used to take me on long hikes through the mountains. And we'd visit Lick Observatory, on the top of Mount Hamilton."

"I'm not from around here," I reply. But, then, I'd be willing to bet neither is she.

Eleanor Teasdale turns back towards me, silhouetted against the murky light through that window, framed like a misplaced Catholic saint. She stares straight at me, and I do not detect even a trace of guile when she speaks.

"We all want you to get better, Miss Merrick. You know that, don't you?"

I look away, preferring the oatmeal-colored carpet to that mask she wears.

"It's easier if we don't play games," I say.

"Yes. Yes, it is. Obviously."

"What I saw. What it meant. What she said to me. What I think it means."

"Yes, and talking about those things, bringing them out into the open, it's an important part of you *getting* better, Miss Merrick. Don't you think that's true?"

"I think . . ." and I pause, choosing my words as carefully as I still am able. "I think you're afraid, all of you, of never knowing. None of this is about my getting better. I've understood that almost from the start." And my voice is calm, and there is no hint of bitterness for her to hear; my voice does not betray me.

Eleanor Teasdale's smile wavers, but only a little, and for only an instant or two.

"Naturally, yes, these matters are interwoven," she replies. "Quite intricately so. Almost inextricably, and I don't believe anyone has ever tried to lie to you about that. What you witnessed out there, what you seem unable, or unwilling, to share with anyone else—"

I laugh, and she sits, watching me with Amery's pale blue eyes, tapping the stylus against her teeth. Her teeth are much whiter and more even than Amery's were, and I draw some dim comfort from that incongruity.

"Share," I say, very softly, and there are other things I *want* to say to her, but I keep them to myself.

"I want you to think about that, Miss Merrick. Between now and our next session, I need you to consider, seriously, the price of your selfishness, both to your own well being and to the rest of humanity."

"Fine," I say, because I don't feel like arguing. Besides, manipulative or not, she isn't entirely wrong. "And what I was writing for Dr. Ostrowski, do I keep that up?"

"Yes, please," she replies, and glances at the clock on the wall, as if she expects me to believe she'll be seeing anyone else today, that she even has other patients. "It's a sound approach, and, reviewing what you've written so far, it feels to me like you're close to a breakthrough."

I nod my head, and I also look at the clock.

"Our time's almost up," I say, and she agrees with me, then looks over her shoulder again at the green-brown hills beyond San Jose.

"I have a question," I say.

233

"That's why I'm here," Dr. Eleanor Teasdale tells me, imbuing the words with all the false veracity of her craft. Having affected the role of the good patient, I pretend that she isn't lying, hoping the pretense lends weight to my question.

"Have they sent a retrieval team yet? To Mars, to the caverns on Arsia Mons?"

"I wouldn't know that," she says. "I'm not privileged to such information. However, if you'd like, I can file an inquiry on your behalf. Someone with the agency might get back to you."

"No," I reply. "I was just curious if you knew," and I almost ask her another question, about Darwin's finches, and the tortoises and mocking-birds and iguanas that once populated the Galápagos Islands. But then the black minute hand on the clock ticks forward, deleting another sixty seconds from the future, converting it to the past, and I decide we've both had enough for one morning.

Don't fret, Dr. T. You've done your bit for the cause, swept me off my feet, and now we're dancing. If you were here, in the hospital room with me, I'd even let you lead. I really don't care if the nurses mind or not. I'd turn up the jack, find just the right tune, and dance with the ghost you've let them make of you. I can never be too haunted, after all. Hush, hush. It's just, they give me these drugs, you see, so I need to sleep for a while, and then the waltz can continue. Your answers are coming.

March 24, 2037 (Wednesday)

It's raining. I asked one of the nurses to please raise the blinds in my room so I can watch the storm hammering the windowpane, pelting the glass, smudging my view of the diffident sky. I count off the moments between occasional flashes of lightning and the thunderclaps that follow. Storms number among the very few things remaining in all the world that can actually soothe my nerves. They certainly beat the synthetic opiates I'm given, beat them all the way to hell and back. I haven't ever bothered to tell any of my doctors or the nurses this. I don't know why; it simply hasn't occurred to me to do so. I doubt they'd care, anyway.

I've asked to please not be disturbed for a couple of hours, and I've been promised my request will be honored. That should give me the time I need to finish this.

Dr. Teasdale, I will readily confess that one of the reasons it's taken me so long to reach this point is the fact that words fail. It's an awful cliché, I know, but also a point I cannot stress strongly enough. There are sights and experiences to which the blunt and finite tool of human language is not equal. I know this, though I'm no poet. But I want that caveat understood. This is not what happened aboard *Pilgrimage*; this is the sky seen through a window blurred by driving rain. It's the best I can manage, and it's the best you'll ever get. I've said all along, if the technology existed to plug in and extract the memories from my brain, I wouldn't deign to call it rape. Most of the people who've spent so much time and energy and money trying to prise from me the truth about the fate of *Pilgrimage* and its crew, they're only scientists, after all. They have no other aphrodisiac *but* curiosity. As for the rest, the spooks and politicians, the bureaucrats and corporate shills, those guys are only along for the ride, and I figure most of them know they're in over their heads.

I could make of it a fairy tale. It might begin:

Once upon a time, there was a woman who lived in New York. She was an anthropologist and shared a tiny apartment in downtown Brooklyn with her lover. And her lover was a woman named Amery Domico, who happened to be a molecular geneticist, exobiologist, and also an astronaut. They had a cat and a tank of tropical fish. They always wanted a dog, but the apartment was too small. They could probably have afforded a better, larger place to live, a loft in midtown Manhattan, perhaps, north and east of the flood zone, but the anthropologist was happy enough with Brooklyn, and her lover was usually on the road, anyway. Besides, walking a dog would have been a lot of trouble.

No. That's not working. I've never been much good with irony. And I'm better served by the immediacy of present tense. So, instead:

"Turn around, Merrick," she says. "You've come so far, and there is so little time."

And I do as she tells me. I turn towards the voice, towards the airlock's open inner hatch. There's no sign of Amery, or anyone else, for that matter.

The first thing I notice, stepping from the brightly lit airlock, is that the narrow heptagonal corridor beyond is mostly dark. The second thing I notice is the mist. I know at once that it *is* mist, not smoke. It fills the hallway from deck to ceiling, and, even with the blue in-floor path lighting, it's hard to see more than a few feet ahead. The mist swirls thickly around me, like Halloween phantoms, and I'm about to ask Amery where it's coming from, what it's doing here, when I notice the walls.

Or, rather, when I notice what's growing *on* the walls. I'm fairly confident I've never seen anything with precisely that texture before. It half reminds me (but only half) of the rubbery blades and stipes of kelp. It's almost the same color as kelp, too, some shade that's not quite brown, nor green, nor a very dark purple. It also reminds me of tripe. It glimmers wetly, as though it's sweating, or secreting, mucus. I stop and stare, simultaneously alarmed and amazed and revolted. It *is* revolting, extremely so, this clinging material covering over and obscuring almost everything. I look up and see that it's also growing on the ceiling. In places, long tendrils of it hang down like dripping vines. Dr. Teasdale, I *want* so badly to describe these things, this waking nightmare, in much greater detail. I want to describe it perfectly. But, as I've said, words fail. For that matter, memory fades. And there's so much more to come.

A few thick drops of the almost colorless mucus drip from the ceiling onto my visor, and I gag reflexively. The sensors in my EVA suit respond by administering a dose of a potent antiemetic. The nausea passes quickly, and I use my left hand to wipe the slime away as best I can.

I follow the corridor, going very slowly because the mist is only getting denser and, as I move farther away from the airlock, I discover that the stuff growing on the walls and ceiling is also sprouting from the deck plates. It's slippery and squelches beneath my boots. Worse, most of the path lighting is now buried beneath it, and I switch on the magspots built into either side of my helmet. The beams reach only a short distance into the gloom.

"You're almost there," Amery says, Amery or the AI speaking with her stolen voice. "Ten yards ahead, the corridor forks. Take the right fork. It leads directly to the transhab module."

"You want to tell me what's waiting in there?" I ask, neither expecting, nor actually desiring, an answer.

"Nothing is waiting," Amery replies. "But there are many things we would have you see. There's not much time. You should hurry."

And I do try to walk faster, but, despite the suit's stabilizing exoskeleton and gyros, almost lose my footing on the slick deck. Where the corridor forks, I go right, as instructed. The habitation module is open, the hatch fully dilated, as though I'm expected. Or maybe it's been left open for days or months or years. I linger a moment on the threshold. It's so very dark in there. I call out for Amery. I call out for anyone at all, but this time there's no answer. I try my comms again, and there's not even static. I fully comprehend that in all my life I have never been so alone as I am at this moment, and, likely, I never will be again. I know, too, with a sudden and unwavering certainty, that Amery Domico is gone from me forever, and that I'm the only human being aboard *Pilgrimage*.

I take three or four steps into the transhab, but stop when something pale and big around as my forearm slithers lazily across the floor directly in front of me. If there was a head, I didn't see it. Watching as it slides past, I think of pythons, boas, anacondas, though, in truth, it bears only a passing similarity to a snake of any sort.

"You will not be harmed, Merrick," Amery says from a speaker somewhere in the darkness. The voice is almost reassuring. "You must trust that you will not be harmed, so long as you do as we say."

"What was that?" I ask. "On the floor just now. What was that?"

"Soon now, you will see," the voice replies. "We have ten million children. Soon, we will have ten million more. We are pleased that you have come to say goodbye."

"They want to know what's happened," I say, breathing too hard, much too fast, gasping despite the suit's ministrations. "At Jupiter, what happened to the ship? Where's the crew? Why is *Pilgrimage* in orbit around Mars?"

I turn my head to the left, and where there were once bunks, I can only make out a great swelling or clot of the kelp-like growth. Its surface swarms with what I briefly mistake for maggots.

"I didn't *come* to say goodbye," I whisper. "This is a retrieval mission, Amery. We've come to take you . . ." and I trail off, unable to complete the sentence, too keenly aware of its irrelevance.

"Merrick, are you beginning to see?"

I look away from the not-kelp and the wriggling things that aren't maggots and take another step into the habitation module.

"No, Amery. I'm not. Help me to see. Please."

"Close your eyes," she says, and I do. And when I open them again, I'm lying in bed with her. There's still an hour or so left before dawn, and we're lying in bed, naked together beneath the blankets, staring up through the apartment's skylight. It's snowing. This is the last night before Amery leaves for Cape Canaveral, the last time I see her, because I've refused to be present at the launch or even watch it online. She has her arms around me, and one of the big, ungainly hovers is passing low above our building. I do my best to pretend that its complex array of landing beacons are actually stars.

Amery kisses my right cheek, and then her lips brush lightly against my ear. "We could not understand, Merrick, because we were too far and could not remember," she says, quoting Joseph Conrad. The words roll from her tongue and palate like the spiraling snowflakes tumbling down from that tangerine sky. "We were traveling in the night of first ages, of those ages that are gone, leaving hardly a sign, and no memories."

Once, Dr. Teasdale, when Amery was sick with the flu, I read her most of *Heart of Darkness*. She always liked when I read to her. When I came to that passage, she had me press highlight, so that she could return to it later.

"The earth seemed unearthly," she says, and I blink, dismissing the illusion. I'm standing near the center of the transhab now, and in the stark white light from my helmet I see what I've been brought here to see. Around me, the walls leak, and every inch of the module seems alive with organisms too alien for any earthborn vernacular. I've spent my adult life describing artifacts and fossil bones, but I will not even attempt to describe the myriad of forms that crawled and skittered and rolled through the ruins of *Pilgrimage*. I would fail if I did, and I would fail utterly.

"We want you to know we had a choice," Amery says. "We want you to know that, Merrick. And what is about to happen, when you leave this ship, we want you to know that is also of our choosing."

I see her, then, all that's left of her, or all that she's become. The rough outline of her body, squatting near one of the lower bunks. Her damp skin shimmers, all but indistinguishable from the rubbery substance growing throughout the vessel. Only, no, her skin is not so smooth as that, but pocked with countless oozing pores or lesions. Though the finer features of her face have been obliterated—there is no mouth remaining, no eyes, only a faint ridge that was her nose—I recognize her beyond any shadow of a doubt. She is rooted to that spot, her legs below the knees, her arms below the elbow, simply vanishing into the deck. There is constant, eager movement from inside her distended breasts and belly. And where the cleft of her sex once was . . . I don't have the language to describe what I saw there. But she bleeds life from that impossible wound, and I know that she has become a daughter of the oily black cloud that *Pilgrimage* encountered near Ganymede, just as she is mother and father to every living thing trapped within the crucible of that ship, every living thing but me.

"There isn't any time left," the voice from the AI says calmly, calmly but sternly. "You must leave now, Merrick. All available resources on this craft have been depleted, and we must seek sanctuary or perish."

I nod and turn away from her, because I understand as much as I'm ever going to understand, and I've seen more than I can bear to remember. I move as fast as I dare across the transhab and along the corridor leading back to the airlock. In less than five minutes, I'm safely strapped into my seat on the taxi again, decoupling and falling back towards *Yastreb-4*. A few hours later, while I'm waiting out my time in decon, Commander Yun tells me that *Pilgrimage* has fired its main engines and broken orbit. In a few moments, it will enter the thin Martian atmosphere and begin to burn. Our AI has plotted a best-guess trajectory, placing the point of impact within the Tharsis Montes, along the flanks of Arsia Mons. He tells me that the exact coordinates, -5.636° N, 241.259° E, correspond to one of the collapsed cavern roofs dotting the flanks of the ancient volcano. The pit named Jeanne, discovered way back in 2007.

"There's not much chance of anything surviving the descent," he says. I don't reply, and I never tell him, nor anyone else aboard the *Yastreb-4*, what I saw during my seventeen minutes on *Pilgrimage*.

And there's no need, Dr. Teasdale, for me to tell you what you already know. Or what your handlers know. Which means, I think, that we've reached the end of this confession. Here's the feather in your cap. May you choke on it.

Outside my hospital window, the rain has stopped. I press the call button and wait on the nurses with their shiny yellow pills and the white pills flecked with grey, their jet sprays and hollow needles filled with nightmares and, sometimes, when I'm very lucky, dreamless sleep.

FISH BRIDE (1970)

W
E LIE HERE together, naked on her sheets which are always damp, no matter the weather, and she's still sleeping. I've lain next to her, watching the long, cold sunrise, the walls of this dingy room in this dingy house turning so slowly from charcoal to a hundred successively lighter shades of grey. The weak November morning has a hard time at the window, because the glass was knocked out years ago and she chose as a substitute a sheet of tattered and not-quite-clear plastic she found washed up on the shore, now held in place with mismatched nails and a few thumbtacks. But it deters the worst of the wind and rain and snow, and she says there's nothing out there she wants to see, anyway. I've offered to replace the broken glass, a couple of times I've said that, but it's just another of the hundred or so things that I've promised I would do for her and haven't yet gotten around to doing; she doesn't seem to mind. That's not why she keeps letting me come here. Whatever she wants from me, it isn't handouts and pity and someone to fix her broken windows and leaky ceiling. Which is fortunate, as I've never fixed anything in my whole life. I can't even change a flat tire. I've only ever been the sort of man who does harm and leaves it for someone else to put right again or simply sweep beneath a rug where no one will have to notice the damage I've done. So, why should she be any different? And yet, to my knowledge, I've done her no harm so far.

I come down the hill from the village on those interminable nights and afternoons when I can't write and don't feel like getting drunk alone. I leave that other world, that safe and smothering kingdom of clean sheets and typescript, electric lights and indoor plumbing and radio and window frames with windowpanes, and I follow the sandy path through gale-stunted trees and stolen, burned-out automobiles, smoldering trash-barrel fires and suspicious, underlit glances.

They all know I don't belong here with them, all the other men and women who share her squalid existence at the edge of the sea, the ones who have come down and never gone back up the hill again. When I call them her apostles, she gets sullen and angry.

"No," she says, "it's not like that. They're nothing of the sort."

But I understand well enough that's exactly what they are, even if she doesn't want to admit it, either to herself or to me. And so they hold me in contempt, because she's taken me into her bed—me, an interloper who comes and goes, who has some choice in the matter, who has that option because the world beyond these dunes and shanty walls still imagines it has some use for me. One of these nights, I think, her apostles will do murder against me. One of them alone, or all of them together. It may be stones or sticks or an old filleting knife. It may even be a gun. I wouldn't put it past them. They are resourceful, and there's a lot on the line. They'll bury me in the dog roses, or sink me in some deep place among the tide-worn rocks, or carve me up like a fat sow and have themselves a feast. She'll likely join them, if they are bold enough and offer her a few scraps of my charred, anonymous flesh to complete the sacrifice. And later, much, much later, she'll remember and miss me, in her sloppy, indifferent way, and wonder whatever became of the man who brought her beer and whiskey, candles and chocolate bars, the man who said he'd fix the window, but never did. She might recall my name, but I wouldn't hold it against her if she doesn't.

"This used to be someplace," she's told me time and time again. "Oh, sure, you'd never know it now. But when my mother was a girl, this used to be a town. When I was little, it was still a town. There were dress shops, and a diner, and a jail. There was a public park with a bandshell and a hundred-year-old oak tree. In the summer, there was music in the park, and picnics. There were even churches, *two* of them, one Catholic and one Presbyterian. But then the storm came and took it all away."

FISH BRIDE (1970)

And it's true, most of what she says. There was a town here once. A decade's neglect hasn't quite erased all signs of it. She's shown me some of what there's left to see—the stump of a brick chimney, a few broken pilings where the waterfront once stood—and I've asked questions around the village. But people up there don't like to speak openly about this place, or even allow their thoughts to linger on it very long. Every now and then, usually after a burglary or before an election, there's talk of cleaning it up, pulling down these listing, clapboard shacks and chasing away the vagrants and squatters and winos. So far, the talk has come to nothing.

A sudden gust of wind blows in from off the beach, and the sheet of plastic stretched across the window flaps and rustles, and she opens her eyes.

"You're still here," she says, not sounding surprised, merely telling me what I already know. "I was dreaming that you'd gone away and would never come back to me again. I dreamed there was a boat called the *Silver Star*, and it took you away."

"I get seasick," I tell her. "I don't like boats. I haven't been on a boat since I was fifteen."

"Well, you got on this one," she insists, and the dim light filling up the room catches in the facets of her sleepy grey eyes. "You said that you were going to seek your fortune on the Ivory Coast. You had your typewriter, and a suitcase, and you were wearing a brand-new suit of worsted wool. I was standing on the dock, watching as the *Silver Star* got smaller and smaller."

"I'm not even sure I know where the Ivory Coast is supposed to be," I say.

"Africa," she replies.

"Well, I know that much, sure. But I don't know where in Africa. And it's an awfully big place."

"In the dream, you knew," she assures me, and I don't press the point farther. It's her dream, not mine, even if it's not a dream she's actually ever had, even if it's only something she's making up as she goes along. "In the dream," she continues, undaunted, "you had a travel brochure that the ticket agent had given you. It was printed all in color. There was a sort of tree called a bombax tree, with bright red flowers. There were elephants and a parrot. There were pretty women with skin the color of roasted coffee beans."

"That's quite a brochure," I say, and for a moment I watch the plastic tacked over the window as it rustles in the wind off the bay. "I wish I could have a look at it right now."

"I thought what a warm place it must be, the Ivory Coast," and I glance down at her, at those drowsy eyes watching me. She lifts her right hand from the damp sheets, and patches of iridescent skin shimmer ever so faintly in the morning light. The sun shows through the thin, translucent webbing stretched between her long fingers. Her sharp nails brush gently across my unshaven cheek, and she smiles. Even I don't like to look at those teeth for very long, and I let my eyes wander back to the flapping plastic. The wind is picking up, and I think maybe this might be the day when I finally have to find a hammer, a few ten-penny nails, and enough discarded pine slats to board up the hole in the wall.

"Not much longer before the snow comes," she says, as if she doesn't need to hear me speak to know my thoughts.

"Probably not for a couple of weeks yet," I counter, and she blinks and turns her head towards the window.

In the village, I have a tiny room in a boardinghouse on Darling Street, and I keep a spiral-bound notebook hidden between my mattress and box spring. I've written a lot of things in that book that I shouldn't like any other human being to ever read—secret desires, things I've heard, and read; things she's told me, and things I've come to suspect all on my own. Sometimes, I think it would be wise to keep the notebook better hidden. But it's true that the old woman who owns the place, and who does all the housekeeping herself, is afraid of me, and she never goes into my room. She leaves the clean linen and towels in a stack outside my door. Months ago, I stopped taking my meals with the other lodgers, because the strained silence and fleeting, leery glimpses that attended those breakfasts and dinners only served to give me indigestion. I expect the widow O'Dwyer would ask me to find a room elsewhere, if she weren't so intimidated by me. Or, rather, if she weren't so intimidated by the company I keep.

Outside the shanty, the wind howls like the son of Poseidon, and, for the moment, there's no more talk of the Ivory Coast or dreams or sailing gaily away into the sunset aboard the *Silver Star*.

Much of what I've secretly scribbled there in my notebook concerns that terrible storm that she claims rose up from the sea to steal away the little park and the bandshell, the diner and the jail and the dress shops, the two churches, one Presbyterian and the other Catholic. From what she's said, it must have happened sometime in September of '57 or '58, but I've spent long afternoons in the small public library, carefully poring over old newspapers and magazines. I can find no evidence of such a tempest making landfall in the autumn of either of those years. What I can verify is that the village once extended down the hill, past the marshes and dunes to the bay, and there was a lively, prosperous waterfront. There was trade with Gloucester and Boston, Nantucket and Newport, and the bay was renowned for its lobsters, fat black sea bass, and teeming shoals of haddock. Then, abruptly, the waterfront was all but abandoned sometime before 1960. In print, I've found hardly more than scant and unsubstantiated speculations to account for it, that exodus, that strange desertion. Talk of overfishing, for instance, and passing comparisons with Cannery Row in faraway California and the collapse of the Monterey Bay sardine canning industry back in the 1950s. I write down everything I find, no matter how unconvincing, but I permit myself to believe only a very little of it.

"A penny for your thoughts," she says, then shuts her eyes again.

"You haven't got a penny," I reply, trying to ignore the raw, hungry sound of the wind and the constant noise at the window.

"I most certainly do," she tells me and pretends to scowl and look of-fended. "I have a few dollars, tucked away. I'm not an indigent."

"Fine, then. I was thinking of Africa," I lie. "I was thinking of palm trees and parrots."

"I don't remember any palm trees in the travel brochure," she says. "But I expect there must be quite a lot of them, regardless."

"Undoubtedly," I agree. I don't say anything else, though, because I think I hear voices coming from somewhere outside her shack—urgent, muttering voices that reach me despite the wind and the flapping plastic. I can't make out the words, no matter how hard I try. It ought to scare me more than it does. Like I said, one of these nights, they'll do murder against me. One of them alone, or all of them together. Maybe they won't even wait for the conspiring cover of nightfall. Maybe they'll come for me in broad daylight. I begin to suspect my murder would not even be deemed a crime by the people who live in those brightly painted houses up the hill, back beyond the dunes.

On the contrary, they might consider it a necessary sacrifice, something to placate the flotsam and jetsam huddling in the ruins along the shore, an oblation of blood and flesh to buy them time.

Seems more likely than not.

"They shouldn't come so near," she says, acknowledging that she too hears the whispering voices. "I'll have a word with them later. They ought to know better."

"They've more business being here than I do," I reply, and she silently watches me for a moment or two. Her grey eyes have gone almost entirely black, and I can no longer distinguish the irises from the pupils.

"They ought to know better," she says again, and this time her tone leaves me no room for argument.

There are tales that I've heard, and bits of dreams I sometimes think I've borrowed—from her or one of her apostles—that I find somewhat more convincing than either newspaper accounts of depleted fish stocks or rumors of a cataclysmic hurricane. There are the spook stories I've overheard, passed between children. There are yarns traded by the half dozen or so grizzled old men who sit outside the filling station near the widow's boardinghouse, who seem possessed of no greater ambition than checkers and hand-rolled cigarettes, cheap gin and gossip. I have begun to believe the truth is not something that was entrusted to the press, but, instead, an ignominy the town has struggled, purposefully, to forget, and which is now recalled dimly or not at all. There is remaining no consensus to be had, but there *are* common threads from which I have woven rough speculation.

Late one night, very near the end of summer or towards the beginning of fall, there was an unusually high tide. It quickly swallowed the granite jetty and the shingle, then broke across the seawall and flooded the streets of the harbor. There was a full moon that night, hanging low and ripe on the eastern horizon, and by its wicked reddish glow men and women saw the things that came slithering and creeping and lurching out of those angry waves. The invaders cast no shadow, or the moonlight shone straight through them, but was somehow oddly distorted. Or, perhaps, what came out of the sea that night glimmered faintly with an eerie phosphorescence of its own.

I know that I'm choosing lurid, loaded words here—*wicked, lurching, angry, eerie*—hoping, I suppose, to discredit all the cock and bull I've heard, trying to neuter those schoolyard demons. But, in my defense, the children and the old men whom I've overheard were quite a bit less discreet. They have little use, and even less concern, for the sensibilities of people who aren't going to believe them, anyway. In some respects, they're almost as removed as she, as distant and disconnected as the other shanty dwellers here in the rubble at the edge of the bay.

"I would be sorry," she says, "if you were to sail away to Africa."

"I'm not going anywhere. There isn't anywhere I want to go. There isn't anywhere I'd rather be."

She smiles again, and this time I don't allow myself to look away. She has teeth like those of a very small shark, and they glint wet and dark in healthy pink gums. I have often wondered how she manages not to cut her lips or tongue on those teeth, why there are not always trickles of drying blood at the corners of her thin lips. She's bitten into me enough times now. I have ugly crescent scars across my shoulders and chest and upper arms to prove that we are lovers, stigmata to make her apostles hate me that much more.

"It's silly of you to waste good money on a room," she says, changing the course of our conversation. "You could stay here with me. I hate the nights when you're in the village, and I'm alone."

"Or you could go back with me," I reply. It's a familiar sort of futility, this exchange, and we both know our lines by heart, just as we both know the outcome.

"No," she says, her shark's smile fading. "You know that I can't. You know they'd never have me up there," and she nods in the general direction of the town.

And yes, I do know that, but I've never yet told her that I do.

The tide rose up beneath a low red moon and washed across the waterfront. The sturdy wharf was shattered like matchsticks, and boats of various shapes and sizes—dories and jiggers, trollers and Bermuda-rigged schooners—were torn free of their moorings and tossed onto the shivered docks. But there was no storm, no wind, no lashing rain. No thunder and lightning and white spray off the breakers. The air was hot and still that night, and the cloudless sky blazed with the countless pinprick stars that shine brazenly through the punctured dome of Heaven.

"They say the witch what brought the trouble came from someplace up Amesbury way," I heard one of the old men tell the others, months and months ago. None of his companions replied, neither nodding their heads in agreement, nor voicing dissent. "I heard she made offerings every month, on the night of the new moon, and I heard she had herself a daughter, though I never learned the girl's name. Don't guess it matters, though. And the name of her father, well, ain't nothing I'll ever say aloud."

That night, the cobbled streets and alleyways were fully submerged for long hours. Buildings and houses were lifted clear of their foundations and dashed one against the other. What with no warning of the freakish tide, only a handful of the waterfront's inhabitants managed to escape the deluge and gain the safety of higher ground. More than two hundred souls perished, and for weeks afterwards the corpses of the drowned continued to wash ashore. Many of the bodies were so badly mangled that they could never be placed with a name or a face and went unclaimed, to be buried in unmarked graves in the village beyond the dunes.

I can no longer hear the whisperers through the thin walls of her shack, so I'll assume that they've gone, or have simply had their say and subsequently fallen silent. Possibly, they're leaning now with their ears pressed close to the corrugated aluminum and rotting clapboard, listening in, hanging on her every syllable, even as my own voice fills them with loathing and jealous spite.

"I'll have a word with them," she tells me for the third time. "You should feel as welcome here as any of us."

The sea swept across the land, and, by the light of that swollen, sanguine moon, grim approximations of humanity moved freely, unimpeded, through the flooded thoroughfares. Sometimes they swam, and sometimes they went about deftly on all fours, and sometimes they shambled clumsily along, as though walking were new to them and not entirely comfortable.

"They weren't men," I overheard a boy explaining to his friends. The boy had ginger-colored hair, and he was nine, maybe ten years old at the most. The children were sitting together at the edge of the weedy vacant lot where a traveling carnival sets up three or four times a year.

"Then were they women?" one of the others asked him.

The boy frowned and gravely shook his head. "No. You're not listening.

They weren't women, neither. They weren't anything human. But, what I heard said, if you were to take all the stuff gets pulled up in trawler nets— all the hauls of cod and flounder and eel, the dogfish and the skates, the squids and jellyfish and crabs, all of it and whatever else you can conjure—if you took those things, still alive and wriggling, and could mush them up together into the shapes of men and women, *that's* exactly what walked out of the bay that night."

"That's not true," a girl said indignantly, and the others stared at her. "That's not true at all. God wouldn't let things like that run loose."

The ginger-haired boy shook his head again. "They got different gods than us, gods no one even knows the names for, and that's who the Amesbury witch was worshipping. Those gods from the bottom of the ocean."

"Well, I think you're a liar," the girl told him. "I think you're a blasphemer *and* a liar, and, also, I think you're just making this up to scare us." And then she stood and stalked away across the weedy lot, leaving the others behind. They all watched her go, and then the ginger-haired boy resumed his tale.

"It gets worse," he said.

A cold rain has started to fall, and the drops hitting the tin roof sound almost exactly like bacon frying in a skillet. She's moved away from me, and is sitting naked at the edge of the bed, her long legs dangling over the side, her right shoulder braced against the rusted iron headboard. I'm still lying on the damp sheets, staring up at the leaky ceiling, waiting for the water tumbling from the sky to find its way inside. She'll set jars and cooking pots beneath the worst of the leaks, but there are far too many to bother with them all.

"I can't stay here forever," she says. It's not the first time, but, I admit, those words always take me by surprise. "It's getting harder being here. Every day, it gets harder on me. I'm so awfully tired, all the time."

I look away from the ceiling, at her throat and the peculiar welts just below the line of her chin. The swellings first appeared a few weeks back, and the skin there has turned dry and scaly, and has taken on a sickly greyish-yellow hue. Sometimes, there are boils or seeping blisters. When she goes out among the others, she wears the silk scarf I gave her, tied about her neck so that they won't have to see. So they won't ask questions she doesn't want to answer.

"I don't have to go alone," she says, but doesn't turn her head to look at me. "I don't want to leave you here."

"I can't," I say.

"I know," she replies.

And this is how it almost always is. I come down from the village, and we make love, and she tells me her dreams, here in this ramshackle cabin out past the dunes and dog roses and the gale-stunted trees. In her dreams, I am always leaving her behind, buying tickets on tramp steamers or signing on with freighters, sailing away to the Ivory Coast or Portugal or Singapore. I can't begin to recall all the faraway places she's dreamt me leaving her for. Her nightmares have sent me round and round the globe. But the truth is, *she's* the one who's leaving, and soon, before the first snows come.

I know it (though I play her games of transference), and all her apostles know it, too. The ones who have come down from the village and never gone back up the hill again. The vagrants and squatters and winos, the lunatics and true believers, who have turned their backs on the world, but only after it turned its back on them. Destitute and cast away, they found the daughter of the sea, each of them, and the shanty town is dotted with their tawdry, makeshift altars and shrines. She knows precisely what she is to them, even if she won't admit it. She knows that these lost souls have been blinded by the trials and tribulations of their various, sordid lives, and *she* is the soothing darkness they've found. She is the only genuine balm they've ever known against the cruel glare of the sun and the moon, which are the unblinking eyes of the gods of all mankind.

She sits there, at the edge of the bed. She is always alone, no matter how near we are, no matter how many apostles crowd around and eavesdrop and plot my demise. She stares at the flapping sheet of plastic tacked up where the windowpane used to be, and I go back to watching the ceiling. A single drop of rainwater gets through the layers of tin and tarpaper shingles and lands on my exposed belly.

She laughs softly. She doesn't laugh very often anymore, and I shut my eyes and listen to the rain.

"You can really have no notion how delightful it will be, when they take us up and throw us, with the lobsters, out to sea," she whispers, and then laughs again.

I take the bait, because I almost always take the bait.

"But the snail replied 'Too far, too far!' and gave a look askance," I say, quoting Lewis Carroll, and she doesn't laugh. She starts to scratch at the welts below her chin, then stops herself.

"In the halls of my mother," she says, "there is such silence, such absolute and immemorial peace. In that hallowed place, the mind can be still. There is serenity, finally, and an end to all sickness and fear." She pauses and looks at the floor, at the careless scatter of empty tin cans and empty bottles and bones picked clean. "But," she continues, "it will be lonely down there, without you. It will be something even worse than lonely."

I don't reply, and in a moment, she gets to her feet and goes to stand by the door.

THE MERMAID OF THE CONCRETE OCEAN

THE BUILDING'S ELEVATOR is busted, and so I've had to drag my ass up twelve flights of stairs. Her apartment is smaller and more tawdry than I expected, but I'm not entirely sure I could say what I thought I'd find at the top of all those stairs. I don't know this part of Manhattan very well, this ugly wedge of buildings one block over from South Street and Roosevelt Drive and the ferry terminal. She keeps reminding me that if I look out the window (there's only one), I can see the Brooklyn Bridge. It seems a great source of pride, that she has a view of the bridge and the East River. The apartment is too hot, filled with soggy heat pouring off the radiators, and there are so many unpleasant odors competing for my attention that I'd be hard pressed to assign any one of them priority over the rest. Mildew. Dust. Stale cigarette smoke. Better I say the apartment smells shut away, and leave it at that. The place is crammed wall to wall with threadbare, dust-skimmed antiques, the tattered refuse of Victorian and Edwardian bygones. I have trouble imagining how she navigates the clutter in her wheelchair, which is something of an antique itself. I compliment the Tiffany lamps, all of which appear not to be reproductions and are in considerably better shape than most of the other furnishings. She smiles, revealing dentures stained by nicotine and neglect. At least, I assume they're dentures. She switches on one of the table lamps, its shade a circlet of stained-glass dragonflies, and tells me it was a Christmas gift from a playwright. He's dead now, she says. She tells me his name, but it's no one I've ever heard of, and I admit this to her. Her yellow-brown smile doesn't waver.

"Nobody remembers him. He was *very* avant-garde," she says. "No one understood what he was trying to say. But obscurity was precious to him. It pained him terribly, that so few ever understood that about his work."

I nod, once or twice or three times, I don't know, and it hardly matters. Her thin fingers glide across the lampshade, leaving furrows in the accumulated dust, and now I can see that the dragonflies have wings the color of amber, and their abdomens and thoraces are a deep cobalt blue. They all have eyes like poisonous crimson berries. She asks me to please have a seat and apologizes for not having offered one sooner. She motions to an armchair near the lamp, and also to a chaise lounge a few feet farther away. Both are upholstered with the same faded floral brocade. I choose the armchair and am hardly surprised to discover that all the springs are shot. I sink several inches into the chair, and my knees jut upwards, towards the water-stained plaster ceiling.

"Will you mind if I tape our conversation?" I ask, opening my briefcase, and she stares at me for a moment, as though she hasn't quite understood the question. By way of explanation, I remove the tiny Olympus digital recorder and hold it up for her to see. "Well, it doesn't actually use audio tapes," I add.

"I don't mind," she tells me. "It must be much simpler than having to write down everything you hear, everything someone says. Probably, you do not even know shorthand."

"Much simpler," I say and switch the recorder on. "We can shut it off anytime you like, of course. Just say the word." I lay the recorder on the table, near the base of the dragonfly lamp.

"That's very considerate," she says. "That's very kind of you."

And it occurs to me how much she, like the apartment, differs from whatever I might have expected to find. This isn't *Sunset Boulevard*, Norma Desmond, and her shuffling cadre of "waxwork" acquaintances. There's nothing of the grotesque or Gothic—even that Hollywood Gothic—about her. Despite the advance and ravages of ninety-four years, her green eyes are bright and clear. Neither her voice nor hands tremble, and only the old wheelchair stands as any indication of infirmity. She sits up very straight and whenever she speaks, tends to move her hands about, as though possessed of more energy and excitement than words alone can convey. She's wearing only a little makeup, some pale lipstick and a hint of rouge on her high cheekbones, and her long grey hair is pulled back in a single braid. There's an easy grace about her. Watching by the light of the dragonfly lamp and the light coming in through the single window, it occurs to me that she is showing me *her* face and not some mask of counterfeit youth. Only the stained teeth (or dentures) betray any hint of the decay I'd anticipated and steeled myself against. Indeed, if not for the rank smell of the apartment, and the oppressive heat, there would be nothing particularly unpleasant about being here with her.

I retrieve a stenographer's pad from my briefcase, then close it and set it on the floor near my feet. I tell her that I haven't written out a lot of questions, that I prefer to allow interviews to unfold more organically, like conversations, and this seems to please her.

"I don't go in for the usual brand of interrogation," I say. "Too forced. Too weighted by the journalist's own agenda."

"So, you think of yourself as a journalist?" she asks, and I tell her yes, usually.

"Well, I haven't done this in such a very long time," she replies, straightening her skirt. "I hope you'll understand if I'm a little rusty. I don't often talk about those days, or the pictures. It was all so very long ago."

"Still," I say, "you must have fond memories."

"Must I now?" she asks, and before I can think of an answer, she says, "They're only memories, young man, and, yes, most of them are not so bad, and some are even rather agreeable. But there are many things I've tried to forget. Every life must be like that, wouldn't you say?"

"To some extent," I reply.

She sighs, as if I haven't understood at all, and her eyes wander up to a painting on the wall behind me. I hardly noticed it when I sat down, but now I turn my head for a better view.

When I ask, "Is that one of the originals?" she nods, her smile widening by almost imperceptible degrees, and she points at the painting of a mermaid.

"Yes," she says. "The only one I have. Oh, I've got a few lithographs. I have prints or photographs of them all, but this is the only one of the genuine paintings I own."

"It's beautiful," I say, and that isn't idle flattery. The mermaid paintings are the reason that I've come to New York City and tracked her to the tawdry little hovel by the river. This isn't the first time I've seen an original up close, but it is the first time outside a museum gallery. There's one hanging in Newport, at the National Museum of American Illustration. I've seen it, and also the one at the Art Institute of Chicago, and one other, the mermaid in the permanent collection of the Society of Illustrators here in Manhattan. But there are more than thirty documented, and most of them I've only seen reproduced in books and folios. Frankly, I wonder if this painting's existence is very widely known, and how long it's been since anyone but the model, sitting here in her wheelchair, has admired it. I've read all the artist's surviving journals and correspondence (including the letters to his model), and I know that there are at least ten mermaid paintings that remain unaccounted for. I assume this must be one of them.

"Wow," I gasp, unable to look away from the painting. "I mean, it's amazing."

"It's the very last one he did, you know," she says. "He wanted me to have it. If someone offered me a million dollars, I still wouldn't part with it."

I glance at her, then back to the painting. "More likely, they'd offer you ten million," I tell her, and she laughs. It might easily be mistaken for the laugh of a much younger woman.

"Wouldn't make any difference if they did," she says. "He gave it to me, and I'll never part with it. Not ever. He named this one *Regarding the Shore from Whale Rock*, and that was my idea, the title. He often asked me to name them. At least half their titles, I thought up for him." And I already know this; it's in his letters.

The painting occupies a large, narrow canvas, easily four feet tall by two feet wide—somewhat too large for this wall, really—held inside an ornately carved frame. The frame has been stained dark as mahogany, though I'm sure it's made from something far less costly; here and there, where the varnish has been scratched or chipped, I can see the blond wood showing through. But I don't doubt that the painting is authentic, despite numerous compositional deviations, all of which are immediately apparent to anyone familiar with the mermaid series. For instance, in contravention to his usual approach, the siren has been placed in the foreground, and also somewhat to the right. And, more importantly, she's facing away from the viewer. Buoyed by rough waves, she holds her arms outstretched to either side, as if to say, "Let me enfold you," while her long hair flows around her like a dense tangle of kelp, and the mermaid gazes towards land and a whitewashed lighthouse perched on a granite promontory. The rocky coastline is familiar, some wild place he'd found in Massachusetts or Maine or Rhode Island. The viewer might be fooled into thinking this is only a painting of a woman swimming in the sea, as so little of her is showing above the waterline. She might be mistaken for a suicide, taking a final glimpse of the rugged strand before slipping below the surface. But, if one looks only a little closer, the patches of red-orange scales flecking her arms are unmistakable, and there are living creatures caught up in the snarls of her black hair: tiny crabs and brittle stars, the twisting shapes of strange oceanic worms and a gasping, wide-eyed fish of some sort, suffocating in the air.

"That was the last one he did," she says again.

It's hard to take my eyes off the painting, and I'm already wondering if she will permit me to get a few shots of it before I leave.

"It's not in any of the catalogs," I say. "It's not mentioned anywhere in his papers or the literature."

"No, it wouldn't be. It was our secret," she replies. "After all those years working together, he wanted to give me something special, and so he did this last one and then never showed it to anyone else. I had it framed when I came back from Europe in forty-six, after the war. For years, it was rolled up in a cardboard tube, rolled up and swaddled in muslin, kept on the top shelf of a friend's closet. A mutual friend, actually, who admired him greatly, though I never showed her this painting."

I finally manage to look away from the canvas, turning back towards the woman sitting up straight in her wheelchair. She looks very pleased at my surprise, and I ask her the first question that comes to mind.

"Has *anyone* else ever seen it? Besides that friend, and besides me?"

"Certainly," she says. "It's been hanging right there for the past twenty years, and I *do* occasionally have visitors, every now and then. I'm not a complete recluse. Not quite yet."

"I'm sorry. I didn't mean to imply that you were."

And she's still staring up at the painting, and the impression I have is that she hasn't paused to look at it closely for a long time. It's as though she's suddenly *noticing* it and probably couldn't recall the last time that she did. Sure, it's a fact of her everyday landscape, another component of the crowded reliquary of her apartment. But, like the Tiffany dragonfly lamp given her by that forgotten playwright, I suspect she rarely ever pauses to consider it.

Watching her as she peers so intently at the painting looming up behind me and the threadbare brocade chair where I sit, I'm struck once more by those green eyes of hers. They're the same green eyes the artist gave to every incarnation of his mermaid, and they seem to me even brighter than they did before and not the least bit dimmed by age. They are like some subtle marriage of emerald and jade and shallow saltwater, brought to life by unknown alchemies. They give me a greater appreciation of the painter, that he so perfectly conveyed her eyes, deftly communicating the complexities of iris and sclera, cornea and retina and pupil. That anyone could have the talent required to transfer these precise and complex hues into mere oils and acrylics.

"How did it begin?" I ask, predictably enough. Of course, the artist wrote repeatedly of the mermaids' genesis. I even found a 1967 dissertation on the subject hidden away in the stacks at Harvard. But I'm pretty sure no one has ever bothered to ask the model. Gradually, and, I think, reluctantly, her green eyes drift away from the canvas and back to me.

"It's not as if that's a secret," she says. "I believe he even told a couple of the magazine reporters about the dreams. One in Paris, and maybe one here in New York, too. He often spoke with me about his dreams. They were always so vivid, and he wrote them down. He painted them, whenever he could. Just as he painted the mermaids."

I glance over at the recorder lying on the table and wish that I'd waited until later on to ask that particular question. It should have been placed somewhere towards the end, not right at the front. I'm definitely off my game today, and it's not only the heat from the radiators making me sweat. I've been disarmed, unbalanced, first by *Regarding the Shore from Whale Rock*, and then by having looked so deeply into her eyes. I clear my throat, and she asks if I'd like a glass of water or maybe a cold A & W cream soda. I thank her, but shake my head no.

"I'm fine," I say, "but thank you."

"It can get awfully stuffy in here," she says and glances down at the dingy Persian rug that covers almost the entire floor. This is the first time since she let me through the door that I've seen her frown.

"Honestly, it's not so bad," I insist, failing to sound the least bit honest.

"Why, there are days," she says, "it's like being in a sauna. Or a damned tropical jungle, Tahiti or Brazil or someplace like that, and it's a wonder I don't start hearing parrots and monkeys. But it helps with the pain, usually more than the pills do."

And here's the one thing she was adamant that we not discuss, the childhood injury that left her crippled. She's told me how she has always loathed writers and critics who tried to draw a parallel between the mermaids and her paralysis. "Don't even bring it up," she warned on the phone, almost a week ago, and I assured her that I wouldn't. Only, now *she's* brought it up. I sit very still in the broken-down armchair, there beneath the last painting, waiting to see what she'll say next. I try hard to clear my head and focus, and to decide what question on the short list scribbled in my steno pad might steer the interview back on course.

"There *was* more than his dreams," she admits, almost a full minute later. The statement has the slightly abashed quality of a confession. And I have no idea how to respond, so I don't. She blinks and looks up at me again, the pale ghost of that previous smile returning to her lips. "Would it bother you if I smoke?" she asks.

"No," I reply. "Not at all. Please, whatever makes you comfortable."

"These days, well, it bothers so many people. As though the Pope had added smoking to the list of venial sins. I get the most awful glares, sometimes, so I thought I'd best ask first."

"It's your home," I tell her, and she nods and reaches into a pocket of her skirt, retrieving a pack of Marlboro Reds and a disposable lighter.

"To some, that doesn't seem to matter," she says. "There's a woman comes around twice a week to attend to the dusting and trash and whatnot, a Cuban woman, and if I smoke when she's here, she always complains and tries to open the window, even though I've told her time and time again it's been painted shut for ages. It's not like I don't pay her."

Considering the thick and plainly undisturbed strata of dust, and the odors, I wonder if she's making this up, or if perhaps the Cuban woman might have stopped coming around a long time ago.

"I promised him, when he told me, I would never tell anyone else this," she says, and here she pauses to light her cigarette, then return the rest of the pack and her lighter to their place in her skirt pocket. She blows a grey cloud of smoke away from me. "Not another living soul. It was a sort of pact between us, you understand. But, lately, it's been weighing on me. I wake up in the night, sometimes, and it's like a stone around my neck. I don't think it's something I want to take with me to the grave. He told me the day we started work on the second painting."

"That would have been in May 1939, yes?"

And here she laughs again and shakes her head. "Hell if I know. Maybe you have it written down somewhere in that pad of yours, but I don't remember the date. Not anymore. But . . . I *do* know it was the same year the World's Fair opened here in New York, and I know it was after Amelia Earhart disappeared. He knew her, Amelia Earhart. He knew so many interesting people. But I'm rambling, aren't I?"

"I'm in no hurry," I answer. "Take your time." But she frowns again and stares at the smoldering tip of her cigarette for a moment.

"I like to think, sir, that I am a practical woman," she says, looking directly at me and raising her chin an inch or so. "I have always wanted to be able to consider myself a practical woman. And now I'm very old. Very, very old, yes, and a practical woman must acknowledge the fact that women who *are* this old will not live much longer. I know I'll die soon, and the truth about the mermaids, it isn't something I want to take with me to my grave. So, I'll tell you, and betray his confidence. If you'll listen, of course."

"Certainly," I reply, struggling not let my excitement show through, but feeling like a vulture, anyway. "If you'd prefer, I can shut off the recorder," I offer.

"No, no . . . I want you to put this in your article. I want them to print it in that magazine you write for, because it seems to me that people ought to know. If they're still so infatuated with the mermaids after all this time, it doesn't seem fitting that they *don't* know. It seems almost indecent."

I don't remind her that I'm a freelance and the article's being done on spec, so there's no guarantee anyone's going to buy it, or that it will ever be printed and read. And that information feels indecent, too, but I keep my mouth shut and listen while she talks. I can always nurse my guilty conscience later on.

"The summer before I met him, before we started working together," she begins, and then pauses to take another drag on her cigarette. Her eyes return to the painting behind me. "I suppose that would have been the summer of 1937. The Depression was still on, but his family, out on Long Island, they'd come through it better than most. He had money. Sometimes he'd take commissions from magazines, if the pay was decent. *The New Yorker*, that was one he did some work for, and *Harper's Bazaar*, and *Collier's*, but I guess you know this sort of thing, having done so much research on his life."

The ash on her Marlboro is growing perilously long, though she seems not to have noticed. I glance about and spot an ashtray, heavy lead glass, perched on the edge of a nearby coffee table. It doesn't look as though it's been emptied in days or weeks, another argument against the reality of the Cuban maid. My armchair squeaks and pops angrily when I lean forward to retrieve it. I offer it to her, and she takes her eyes off the painting just long enough to accept it and to thank me.

"Anyway," she continues, "mostly he was able to paint what he wanted. That was a freedom that he never took for granted. He was staying in Atlantic City that summer, because he said he liked watching the people on the boardwalk. Sometimes, he'd sit and sketch them for hours, in charcoal and pastels. He showed quite a lot of the boardwalk sketches to me, and I think he always meant to do paintings from them, but, to my knowledge, he never did.

"That summer, he was staying at the Traymore, which I never saw, but he said was wonderful. Many of his friends and acquaintances would go to Atlantic City in the summer, so he never lacked for company if he wanted it. There were the most wonderful parties, he told me. Sometimes, in the evenings, he'd go down onto the beach alone, onto the sand, I mean, because he said the waves and the gulls and the smell of the sea comforted him. In his studio, the one he kept on the Upper West Side, there was a quart mayonnaise jar filled with seashells and sand dollars and the like. He'd picked them all up at Atlantic City over the years. Some of them we used as props in the paintings, and he also had a cabinet with shells from Florida and Nassau and the Cape and I don't know where else. He showed me conchs and starfish from the Mediterranean and Japan, I remember. Seashells from all over the world, easily. He loved them, and driftwood, too."

She taps her cigarette against the rim of the ashtray and stares at the painting of the mermaid and the lighthouse, and I have the distinct feeling that she's drawing some sort of courage from it, the requisite courage needed to break a promise she's kept for seventy years. A promise she made three decades before my own birth. And I know now how to sum up the smell of her apartment. It smells like time.

"It was late July, and the sun was setting," she says, speaking very slowly now, as though every word is being chosen with great and deliberate care. "And he told me that he was in a foul temper that evening, having fared poorly at a poker game the night before. He played cards. He said it was one of his only weaknesses.

"At any rate, he went down onto the sand, and he was barefoot, he said. I remember that, him telling me he wasn't wearing shoes." And it occurs to me then that possibly none of what I'm hearing is the truth, that she's spinning a fanciful yarn so I won't be disappointed, lying for my benefit, or because her days are so filled with monotony and she is determined this unusual guest will be entertained. I push the thoughts away. There's no evidence of deceit in her voice. Art journalism hasn't made me rich or well known, but I have gotten pretty good at knowing a lie when I hear one.

"He said to me, 'The sand was so cool beneath my feet.' He walked for a while, and then, just before dark, came across a group of young boys, eight or nine years old, and they were crowded around something that had washed up on the beach. The tide was going out, and what the boys had found, it had been stranded by the retreating tide. He recalled thinking it odd that they were all out so late, the boys, that they were not at dinner with their families. The lights were coming on along the boardwalk."

Now she suddenly averts her eyes from the painting on the wall of her apartment, *Regarding the Shore from Whale Rock*, as though she's taken what she needs and it has nothing left to offer. She crushes her cigarette out in the ashtray and doesn't look at me. She chews at her lower lip, chewing away some of the lipstick. The old woman in the wheelchair does not appear sad nor wistful. I think it's anger, that expression, and I want to ask her *why* she's angry. Instead, I ask what it was the boys found on the beach, what the artist saw that evening. She doesn't answer right away, but closes her eyes and takes a deep breath, exhaling slowly, raggedly.

"I'm sorry," I say. "I didn't mean to press you. If you want to stop—"

"I do not want to stop," she says, opening her eyes again. "I have not come this far, and said this much, only to stop. It was a woman, a very young woman. He said that she couldn't have been much more than nineteen or twenty. One of the children was poking at her with a stick, and he *took* the stick and shooed them all away."

"She was drowned?" I ask.

"Maybe. Maybe she drowned first. But she was bitten in half. There was nothing much left of her below the ribcage. Just bone and meat and a big hollowed-out place where all her organs had been, her stomach and lungs and everything. Still, there was no blood anywhere. It was like she'd never had a single drop of blood in her. He told me, 'I never saw anything else even half that horrible.' And, you know, that wasn't so long after he'd come back to the States from the war in Spain, fighting against the fascists, the Francoists. He was at the Siege of Madrid and saw awful, awful things there. He said to me, 'I saw *atrocities*, but this was worse . . .'"

And then she trails off and glares down at the ashtray in her lap, at a curl of smoke rising lazily from her cigarette butt.

"You don't have to go on," I say, almost whispering. "I'll understand—"

"Oh hell," she says and shrugs her frail shoulders. "There isn't that much left to tell. He figured that a shark did it, maybe one big shark or several smaller ones. He took her by the arms, and he hauled what was left of her up onto the dry sand, up towards the boardwalk, so she wouldn't be swept back out to sea. He sat down beside the body, because at first he didn't know what to do, and he said he didn't want to leave her alone. She was dead, but he didn't want to leave her alone. I don't know how long he sat there, but he said it was dark when he finally went to find a policeman.

"The body was still there when they got back. No one had disturbed it. The little boys had not returned. But he said the whole affair was hushed up, because the chamber of commerce was afraid that a shark scare would frighten away the tourists and ruin the rest of the season. It had happened before. He said he went straight back to the Traymore and packed his bags, got a ticket on the next train to Manhattan. And he never visited Atlantic City ever again, but he started painting the mermaids, the very next year, right after he found me. Sometimes," she says, "I think maybe I should have taken it as an insult. But I didn't, and I still don't."

And then she falls silent, the way a storyteller falls silent when a tale is done. She takes another deep breath, rolls her wheelchair back about a foot or so, until it bumps hard against one end of the chaise lounge. She laughs nervously and lights another cigarette. And I ask her other questions, but they have nothing whatsoever to do with Atlantic City or the dead woman. We talk about other painters she's known, and jazz musicians, and writers, and she talks about how much New York's changed, how much the whole world has changed around her. As she speaks, I have the peculiar, disquieting sensation that, somehow, she's passed the weight of that seventy-year-old secret on to me, and I think even if the article sells (and now I don't doubt that it will) and a million people read it, a hundred million people, the weight will not be diminished.

This is what it's like to be haunted, I think, and then I try to dismiss the thought as melodramatic, or absurd, or childish. But her jade-and-surf-green eyes, the mermaids' eyes, are there to assure me otherwise.

It's almost dusk before we're done. She asks me to stay for dinner, but I make excuses about needing to be back in Boston. I promise to mail her a copy of the article when I've finished, and she tells me she'll watch for it. She tells me how she doesn't get much mail anymore, a few bills and ads, but nothing she ever wants to read.

"I am so very pleased that you contacted me," she says, as I slip the recorder and my steno pad back into the briefcase and snap it shut.

"It was gracious of you to talk so candidly with me," I reply, and she smiles.

I only glance at the painting once more, just before I leave. Earlier, I thought I might call someone I know, an ex who owns a gallery in the East Village. I owe him a favor, and the tip would surely square us. But standing there, looking at the pale, scale-dappled form of a woman bobbing in the frothing waves, her wet black hair tangled with wriggling crabs and fish, and nothing at all but a hint of shadow visible beneath the wreath of her floating hair, *seeing* it as I've never before seen any of the mermaids, I know I won't make the call. Maybe I'll mention the painting in the article I write, and maybe I won't.

She follows me to the door, and we each say our goodbyes. I kiss her hand when she offers it to me. I don't believe I've ever kissed a woman's hand, not until this moment. She locks the door behind me, two deadbolts and a chain, and then I stand in the hallway. It's much cooler here than it was in her apartment, in the shadows that have gathered despite the windows at either end of the corridor. There are people arguing loudly somewhere in the building below me, and a dog barking. By the time I descend the stairs and reach the sidewalk, the streetlamps are winking on.

HYDRARGUROS

THE VERY FIRST TIME I see silver, it's five minutes past noon on a Monday and I'm crammed into a seat on the Bridge Line, racing over the slate-grey Delaware River. Philly is crouched at my back, and a one o'clock with the Czech and a couple of his meatheads is waiting for me on the Jersey side of the Ben Franklin. I've been popping since I woke up half an hour late, the lucky greens Eli scores from his chemist somewhere in Devil's Pocket, so my head's buzzing almost bright and cold as the sun pouring down through the late January clouds. My gums are tingling, and my fucking fingertips, too, and I'm sitting here, wishing I was just about anywhere else but on my way to Camden, payday at journey's end or no payday at journey's end. I'm trying to look at nothing that isn't *out there*, on the opposite side of the window, because faces always make me jumpy when I'm using the stuff Eli assures me is mostly only methylphenidate with a little Phenotropil by way of his chemist's Russian connections. I'm in my seat, trying to concentrate on the shadow of the span and the Speedline on the water below, on the silhouettes of buildings to the south, on a goddamn flock of birds, anything out there to keep me focused, keep me awake. But then my ears pop, and there's a second or two of dizziness before I smell ozone and ammonia and something with the carbon stink of burning sugar.

We're almost across the bridge by then, and I tell myself not to look, not to dare fucking look, just mind my own business and watch the window, my sickly, pale reflection *in* the window, and the dingy winter scene the window's holding at bay. But I look anyhow.

There's a very pretty woman sitting across the aisle from me, her skin as dark as freshly ground coffee, her hair dreadlocked and pulled back away from her face. Her eyes are a brilliant, bottomless green. For a seemingly elastic moment, I am unable to look away from those eyes. They manage to be both merciful and fierce, like the painted eyes of Catholic saints rendered in plaster of Paris. And I'm thinking it's no big, and I'll be able to look back out the window; who gives a shit what that smell might have been. It's already starting to fade. But then the pretty woman turns her head to the left, towards the front of the car, and quicksilver trickles from her left nostril and spatters her jeans. If she felt it—if she's in any way aware of this strange excrescence—she shows no sign that she felt it. She doesn't wipe her nose or look down at her pants. If anyone else saw what I saw, they're busy pretending like they didn't. I call it quicksilver, though I know that's not what I'm seeing. Even this first time, I know it's only something that *looks* like mercury, because I have no frame of reference to think of it any other way.

The woman turns back towards me, and she smiles. It's a nervous, slightly embarrassed sort of smile, and I suppose I must have been sitting there gawking at her. I want to apologize. Instead, I force myself to go back to the window, and curse that Irish cunt who's been selling Eli fuck knows what. I curse myself for being such a lazy asshole and popping whatever's at hand when I have access to good clean junk. And then the train is across that filthy, poisoned river and rolling past Campbell Field and Pearl Street. My heart's going a mile a minute, and I'm sweating like it's August. I grip the handle of the shiny aluminum briefcase I'm supposed to hand over to the Czech, assuming he has the cash, and do my best to push back everything but my trepidation of things I know I'm not imagining. You don't go into a face-to-face with one of El Diamante's bastards with a shake on, not if you want to keep the red stuff on the inside where it fucking belongs.

I don't look at the pretty black woman again.

02.

The very first thing you learn about the Czech is that he's not from the Czech Republic or the dear departed Czech Socialist Republic or, for that matter, Slovakia. He's not even European. He's just some Canuck motherfucker who used to haunt Montreal, selling cloned phones and heroin and whores. A genuine Renaissance crook, the Czech. I have no idea where or when or why he picked up the nickname, but it stuck like shit on the wall of a gorilla's cage. The second thing you learn about the Czech is not to ask about the scars. If you're lucky, you've learned both these things before you have the misfortune of making his acquaintance up close and personal.

Anyway, he has a car waiting for me when the train dumps me out at Broadway Station, but I make the driver wait while I pay too much for bottled water at Starbucks. The lucky greens have me in such a fizz I'm almost seeing double, and there are rare occasions when a little H_2O seems to help bring me down again. I don't actually expect *this* will be one of those times, but I'm still a bit weirded out by what I think I saw on the Speedline, and I'm a lot pissed that the Czech's dragged me all the way over to Jersey at this indecent hour on a Monday. So, let the driver idle for five while I buy a lukewarm bottle of Dasani that I know is just twelve ounces of Philly tap water with a fancy blue label slapped on it.

"Czech, he don't like to be kept waiting," says the skinny Mexican kid behind the wheel when I climb into the backseat. I show him my middle finger, and he shrugs and pulls away from the curb. I set the briefcase on the seat beside me, just wanting to be free of the package and on my way back to Eli and our cozy dump of an apartment in Chinatown. As the jet-black Lincoln MKS turns off Broadway onto Mickle Boulevard, heading west, carrying me back towards the river, I think how I'm going to have a chat with Eli about finding a better pusher. My gums feel like I've been chewing foil, and there are wasps darting about behind my eyes. At least the wasps are keeping their stingers to themselves.

"Just how late are we?" I ask the driver.

"Ten minutes," he replies.

"Blame the train."

"You blame the train, Mister. I don't talk to the Czech unless he talks to me, and he never talks to me."

"Fortunate you," I say, and take another swallow of Dasani. It tastes more like the polyethylene terephthalate bottle than water, and I try not to think about toxicity and esters of phthalic acid, endocrine disruption, and antimony trioxide, because that just puts me right back on the Bridge Line watching a pretty woman's silver nosebleed.

We stop at a red light, then turn left onto South Third Street, paralleling the waterfront, and I realize the drop's going to be the warehouse on Spruce. I want to close my eyes, but all those lucky green wasps won't let me. The sun is so bright it seems to be flashing off even the most nonreflective of surfaces. Vast seas of asphalt might as well be goddamn mirrors. I drum my fingers on the lid of the aluminum briefcase, wishing the driver had the radio on or a DVD playing, anything to distract me from the buzz in my skull and the noise the tires make against the pavement. Another three or four long minutes and we're bumping off the road into a parking lot that might have last been paved when Obama was in the White House. And the Mexican kid pulls up at the loading bay, and I open the door and step out into the cold, sunny day. The Lincoln has stirred up a shroud of red-grey dust, but all that sunlight doesn't give a shit. It shines straight on through the haze and almost lays me open, head to fucking toe. I cough a few times on my way from the car to the bald-headed gook in Ray-Bans waiting to usher me to my rendezvous with the Czech. However, the wasps do not take my cough as an opportunity to vacate my cranium, so maybe they're here to stay. The gook pats me down, and then double checks with a security wand. When he's sure I'm not packing anything more menacing than my phone, he leads me out of the flaying day and into merciful shadows and muted pools of halogen.

"You're late," the Czech says, just in case I haven't noticed, and he points at a clock on the wall. "You're almost twelve minutes late."

I glance over my shoulder at the clock, because it seems rude not to look after he's gone to the trouble to point. Actually, I'm almost eleven minutes late.

"You got some more important place to be, Czech?" I ask, deciding it's as good a day as any to push my luck a few extra inches.

"Maybe I do at that, you sick homo fuck. Maybe your ass is sitting at the very bottom of my to-do list this fine day. So, how about you zip it, and let's get this over with."

I turn away from the clock and back to the fold-out card table where the Czech's sitting in a fold-out chair. He's smoking a Parliament, and in front of him there's a half-eaten corned-beef sandwich cradled in white butcher's paper. I try not to stare at the scars, but you might as well try to make your heart stop beating for a minute or two. Way I heard it, the stupid son of a bitch got drunk and went bear-hunting in some Alaskan national park or another, only he tried to make do with a bottle of vodka and a .22 caliber pocket pistol, instead of a rifle. No, that's probably not the truth of it, but his face does look like something a grizzly's been gnawing at.

"You got the goods?" he asks, and I have the impression I'm watching Quasimodo quoting old Jimmy Cagney gangster films. I hold up the briefcase, and he nods and puffs his cigarette.

"But I am curious as hell why you went and switched the drop date," I say, wondering if it's really me talking this trash to the Czech, or if maybe the lucky greens have hijacked the speech centers of my brain and are determined to get me shot in the face. "I might have had plans, you know. And El Diamante usually sticks to the script."

"What El Diamante does, that ain't none of your business, and that ain't my business, neither. Now, didn't I say zip it?" And then he jabs a thumb at a second folding metal chair, a few feet in front of the card table, and he tells me to give him the case and sit the fuck down. Which is what I do. Maybe the greens have decided to give me a break, after all. Or maybe they just want to draw this out as long as possible. The Czech dials the three-digit combination and opens the aluminum briefcase. He has a long look inside. Then he grunts and shuts it again. And that's when I notice something shimmering on the toe of his left shoe. It looks a lot like a few drops of spilled mercury. This is the second time I see silver.

03.

This is hours later, and I'm back in Philly, trying to forget all about the woman on the train and about the Czech's shoes and whatever might have been in the briefcase I delivered. The sun's been down for hours. The city is dark and cold, and there's supposed to be snow before the sun comes up again. I'm lying in the bed I share with Eli, just lying there on my right side watching him read. There are things I want to tell him, but I know full fucking well that I won't. I won't because some of those things might get him killed if a deal ever goes wrong somewhere down the line (and it's only a matter of time) or if I should fall from grace with Her Majesty Madam Adrianne and all the powers that be and keep the axles upon which the world spins greased up and relatively friction-free. And other things I will not tell him because maybe it was only the pills, or maybe it's stress, or maybe I'm losing my god-damn mind, and if it's the latter, I'd rather keep that morsel to myself as long as possible, pretty please and thank you.

Eli turns a page and shifts slightly, to better take advantage of the reading lamp on the little table beside the bed. I scan the spine of the hardback, the words printed on the dust jacket, like I don't already know it by heart. Eli reads books, and I read their dust jackets. Catch me in just the right mood, I might read the flap copy.

"I thought you were asleep," Eli says without bothering to look at me.

"Maybe later, *chica*," I reply, and Eli nods the way he does when he's far more interested in whatever he's reading than in talking to me. So, I read the spine again, aloud this time, purposefully mispronouncing the Korean author's name. Which is enough to get Eli to glance my way. Eli's eyes are emeralds, crossed with some less precious stone. Agate maybe. Eli's eyes are emerald and agate, cut and polished to precision, flawed in ways that only make them more perfect.

"Go to sleep," he tells me, pretending to frown. "You look exhausted."

"Yeah, sure, but I got this fucking hard-on like you wouldn't believe."

"Last time I checked, you also had two good hands and a more than adequate knowledge of how they work."

"That's cold," I say. "That is some cold shit to say to someone who had to go spend the day in Jersey."

Eli snorts, and his emerald and agate eyes, which might pass for only hazel-green if you haven't lived with them as long as I have lived with them, they drift back to the printed page.

"The lube warms up just fine," he says, "you hold it a minute or so first."

He doesn't laugh, but I do, and then I roll over to stare at the wall instead of watching Eli read. The wall is flat and dull, and sometimes it makes me sleepy. I'd take something, but after the lucky greens, it's probably best if I forego the cocktail of pot and prescription benzodiazepines I usually rely on to beat my insomnia into submission. I don't masturbate because, boner from hell or not, I'm not in the right frame of mind to give myself an hj. So, I lie and stare at the wall and listen to the soft sounds of Eli reading his biography of South Korean astronaut Yi So-yeon, who I do recall, and without having to read the book, was the first Korean in space. She might also have been the second Asian woman to slip the surly fucking bonds of Earth and dance the skies or what the hell ever.

"Why don't you take something if you can't sleep," Eli says after maybe half an hour of me lying there.

"I don't think so, *chica*. My brain's still rocking and rolling from the breath mints you been buying off that mick cocksucker you call a dealer. Me, I think he's using drain cleaner again."

"No way," Eli says, and I can tell from the tone of his voice he's only half interested, at best, in whether or not the mad chemist holed up in Devil's Pocket is using Drano to cut his shit. "Donncha's merchandise is clean."

"Maybe *Mr.* Clean," I reply, and Eli smacks me lightly on the back of the head with his book. He tells me to jack off and go to sleep. I tell him to blow me. We spar with the age-old poetry of true love's tin-eared wit. Then he goes back to reading, and I go back to staring at the bedroom wall.

Eli is the only guy I've ever been with more than a month, and here we are going on two years. I found him waiting tables in a noodle and sushi joint over on Race Street. Most of the waiters in the place were either drag queens or trannies, dressed up like geisha whores from some sort of post-apocalyptic Yakuza flick. He was wearing so much makeup, and I was so drunk on Sapporo Black Label and saki, I didn't even realize he was every bit *gai-ko* as me. That first night, back at Eli's old apartment not far from the noodle shop, we screwed like goddamn bunnies on crank. I must have walked funny for a week.

I started eating in that place every night, and almost every one of those nights, we'd wind up in bed together, and that's probably the happiest I've ever been or ever will be. Sure, the sex was absolute supremo, standout—

state of the fucking *art* of fucking—but it never would have been enough to keep things going after a few weeks. I don't care how sweet the cock, sooner or later, if that's all there is interest wanes and I start to drift. I used to think maybe my libido had ADD or something, or I'd convinced myself that commitment meant I might miss out on something better. What matters, though, there was more, and four months later Eli packed up his shit and moved in with me. He never asked what I do to pay the rent, and I've never felt compelled to volunteer that piece of intel.

"You're still awake," Eli says, and I hear him toss his book onto the table beside the bed. I hear him reach for a pill bottle.

"Yeah, I'm still awake."

"Good, 'cause there's something I meant to tell you earlier, and I almost forgot."

"And what is that, pray tell?" I ask, listening as he rattles a few milligrams of this or that out into his palm.

"This woman in the restaurant. It was the weirdest thing. I mean, I'd think maybe I was hallucinating or imagining crap, only Jules saw it, too. Think it scared her, to tell you the truth."

Jules is the noodle shop's post-op hostess, who sometimes comes over to play, when Eli and I find ourselves inclined for takeout of that particular variety. It happens. But, point here is, Eli says these words, words that ought to be nothing more than a passing fleck of conversation peering in on the edge of my not getting to sleep, and I get goddamn goose bumps and my stomach does some sort of roll like it just discovered the pommel horse. Because I know what he's going to say. Not exactly, no, but close enough that I want to tell him to please shut the fuck up and turn off the light and never mind what it is he *thinks* he saw.

But I don't, and he says, "This woman came in alone and so Jules sat her at the bar, right? Total dyke, but she had this whole butch-glam demeanor working for her, like Nicole Kidman with a buzz cut."

"You're right," I mutter at the wall, as if it's not too late for intervention. "That's pretty goddamn weird."

"No, you ass. That's not the weird part. The weird part was when I brought her order out, and I noticed there was this shiny silver stuff dripping out of her left ear. At first, I thought it was only a tragus piercing or something, and I just wasn't seeing it right. But then . . . well, I looked again, and it had run down her neck and was soaking into the collar of her blouse. Jules saw it, too. Freaky, yeah?"

"Yeah," I say, but I don't say much more, and a few minutes later, Eli finally switches off the lamp, and I can stare at the wall without actually having to see it.

04.

It's two days later, as the crow flies, and I'm waiting on a call from one of Her Majesty's lieutenants. I'm holed up in the backroom of a meat market in Bella Vista, on a side street just off Washington, me and Joey the Kike. We're bored and second-guessing our daily marching orders from the pampered, privileged pit bulls those of us so much nearer the bottom of this miscreant food chain refer to as Carrion Dispatch. Not very clever, sure, but all too fucking often, it hits the nail on the proverbial head. I might not like having to ride the Speedline out to Camden for a handoff with the Czech, but it beats waiting, and it sure as hell beats scraping up someone else's road kill and seeing to its discreet and final disposition. Which is where I have a feeling today is bound. Joey keeps trying to lure me into a game of whiskey poker, even though he knows I don't play cards or dice or dominoes or anything else that might lighten my wallet. You work for Madam Adrianne, you already got enough debt stacked up without gambling, even if it's only penny-ante foolishness to make the time go faster.

Joey the Kike isn't the absolute last person I'd pick to spend a morning with, but he's just next door. Back in the Ohs, when he was still just a kid, Joey did a stint in Afghanistan and lost three fingers off his left hand and more than a few of his marbles. He still checks his shoes for scorpions. And most of us, we trust that whatever you hear coming out of his mouth is pure and unadulterated baloney. It's not that he lies, or even exaggerates to make something more interesting. It's more like he's a bottomless well of bullshit, and every conversation with Joey is another tour through the highways and byways of his shattered psyche. For years, we've been waiting for the bastard to get yanked off the street and sent away to his own padded rumpus room at Norristown, where he can while away the days trading his crapola with other guys stuck on that same ever-tilting mental plane of existence. Still, I'll be the first to admit he's ace on the job, and nobody ever has to clean up after Joey the Kike.

He lights a cigarette and takes off his left shoe, and his sock, too, because you never can tell where a scorpion might turn up.

"You didn't open the case?" he asks, banging the heel of his shoe against the edge of a shipping crate.

"Hell no, I didn't open the case. You think we'd be having this delightful conversation today if I'd delivered a violated parcel to the Czech? Or anybody else, for that matter. For pity's sake, Joey."

"You ain't sleeping," he says, not a question, just a statement of the obvious.

"I'm getting very good at lying awake," I reply. "Anyway, what's that got to do with anything?"

"Sleep deprivation makes people paranoid," he says, and bangs his loafer against the crate two or three more times. But if he manages to dislodge any scorpions, they're of the invisible brand. "Makes you prone to erratic behavior."

"Joey, please put your damn shoe back on."

"Hey, dude, you want to hear about the Trenton drop or not?" he asks, turning his sock wrong-side out for the second time. Ash falls from the cigarette dangling at the corner of his mouth.

I don't answer the question. Instead, I pick up my phone and stare at the screen, like I can will the thing to ring. All I really want right now is to get on with whatever inconvenience and unpleasantness the day holds in store, because Joey's a lot easier to take when confined spaces and the odor of raw pork fat aren't involved.

"Do you or don't you?" he prods.

Not that he needs my permission to keep going. Not that my saying no, I *don't* want to hear about the Trenton drop, is going to put an end to it.

"Well," he says, lowering his voice like he's about to spill a state secret, "what we saw when Tony Palamara opened that briefcase—and keep in mind, it was me *and* Jack on that job, so I've got corroboration if you need that sort of thing—what we saw was five or six of these silver vials. I'm not sure Tony realized we got a look inside or not, and, actually, it wasn't much more than a peek. It's not like either of us was *trying* to see inside. But, yeah, that's what we saw, these silver vials lined up neat as houses, each one maybe sixty or seventy milliliters, and they all had a piece of yellow tape or a yellow sticker on them. Jack, he thinks it was some sort of high-tech, next-gen explosive, maybe something you have to mix with something else to get the big bangola, right?"

And I stare at him for a few seconds, and he stares back at me, that one green-and-black argyle sock drooping from his hand like some giant's idea of a novelty prophylactic. Whatever he sees in my face, it can't be good, not if his expression is any indication. He takes the cigarette out of his mouth and balances it on the edge of the shipping crate.

"Joey, were the vials silver, or was the silver what was inside of the vials?"

And I can tell right away it hasn't occurred to him to wonder which. Why the hell would it? He asks me what difference it makes, sounding confused and suspicious and wary all at the same time.

"So you couldn't tell?"

"Like I said, it wasn't much more than a peek. Then Tony Palamara shut the case again. But if I had to speculate, if this was a wager, and there was money on the line? Was that the situation, I'd probably say the silver stuff was inside the vials."

"If you had to speculate?" I ask him, and Joey the Kike bobs his head and turns his sock right-side out again.

"What difference does it make?" he wants to know. "I haven't even gotten around to the interesting part of the story yet."

And then, before I can ask him what the interesting part might be, my phone rings, and it's dispatch, and I stand there and listen while the dog barks. Straightforward janitorial work, because some asshole decided to use a shotgun when a 9mm would have sufficed. Nothing I haven't had to deal with a dozen times or more. I tell the dog we're on our way, and then I tell Joey it's his balls on the cutting board if we're late because he can't keep his shoes and socks on his goddamn feet.

———

05.

Some nights, mostly in the summer, Eli and me, we climb the rickety fire escape onto the roof to try to see the stars. There are a couple of injection-molded plastic lawn chairs up there, left behind by a former tenant, someone who moved out years before I moved into the building. We sit in those chairs that have come all the way from some East Asian factory shithole in Hong Kong or Taiwan, and we drink beer and smoke weed and stare up at the night spread out above Philly, trying to see anything at all. Mostly, it's a white-orange sky-glow haze, the opaque murk of photopollution, and I suspect we imagine far more stars than we actually see. I tell him that some night or another we'll drive way the hell out to the middle of nowhere, someplace where the sky is still mostly dark. He humors me, but Eli is a city kid, born and bred, and I think his idea of a pastoral landscape is Marconi Plaza. We might sit there and wax poetic about planets and nebulas and shit, but I have a feeling that if he ever found himself standing beneath the real deal, with all those twinkling pinpricks scattered overhead and maybe a full moon to boot, it'd probably freak him right the fuck on out.

One night he said to me, "Maybe this is preferable," and I had to ask what he meant.

"I just mean, maybe it's better this way, not being able to see the sky. Maybe, all this light, it's sort of like camouflage."

I squinted back at Eli through a cloud of fresh ganja smoke, and when he reached for the pipe I passed it to him.

"I have no idea what you're talking about," I told him, and Eli shrugged and took a big hit of the 990 Master Kush I get from a grower who's well aware how much time I've spent in Amsterdam, so she knows better than to sell me dirt grass. Eli exhaled and passed the pipe back to me.

"Maybe I don't mean anything at all," he said and gave me half a smile. "Maybe I'm just stoned and tired and talking out my ass."

I think that was the same night we might have seen a falling star, though Eli was of the opinion it wasn't anything but a pile of space junk burning up as it tumbled back to earth.

06.

I've been handling the consequences of other people's half-assed *mokroye delo* since I was sixteen going on forty-five. So, yeah, takes an awfully bad scene to get me to so much as flinch, which is not to say I *enjoy* the shit. Truth of it, nothing pisses me off worse or quicker than some bastard spinning off the rails, running around with that first-person shooter mentality that, more often than not, turns a simple, straight-up hit into a bloodbath. And that is precisely the brand of unnecessary *sangre* pageantry that me and Joey the Kike have just spent the last three hours mopping up. What's left of the recently deceased, along with a bin of crimson rags and sponges and the latex gloves and coveralls we wore, is stowed snugly in the trunk of the car. Another ten minutes, it won't be our problem anymore, soon as we make the scheduled meet and greet with one of Madam Adrianne's garbage men.

So, it's hardly business as usual that Joey's behind the wheel because my hands won't stop shaking enough that I can drive. They won't stop shaking long enough for me to even light a cigarette.

"You really aren't gonna tell me what it was happened back there?" he asks for, I don't know, the hundredth time in the last thirty or forty minutes. I glance at my watch, then the speedometer, making sure we're not late and he's not speeding. At least I have that much presence of mind left to me.

"Never yet known you to be the squeamish type with wet work," he says and stops for a red light.

Most of the snow from Tuesday night has melted, but there are still plenty of off-white scabs hiding in the shadows, and there's also the filthy mix of ice and sand and anonymous schmutz heaped at either side of the street. There are people out there shivering at a bus stop, people rushing along the icy sidewalk, a homeless guy huddled in the doorway of an abandoned office building. Every last bit of that tableau is as ordinary as it gets, the humdrum day to day of the ineptly named City of Brotherly Love, and that ought to help, but it doesn't. All of it comes across as window dressing, meticulously crafted misdirection meant to keep me from getting a good look at what's really going down.

"Dude, seriously, you're starting to give me the heebie-jeebies," Joey says.

"Why don't you just concentrate on getting us where we're going," I tell him. "See if you can do that, all right? 'Cause it's about the only thing in the world you have to worry about right now."

"We're not gonna be late," says Joey the Kike. "At this rate, we might be fucking early, but we sure as hell ain't gonna be late."

I keep my mouth shut. Out there, a thin woman with a purse Doberman on a pink rhinestone leash walks past. She's wearing galoshes and a pink wool coat that only comes down to her knees. At the bus stop, tucked safe inside that translucent half-shell, a man lays down a newspaper and answers his phone. The homeless guy scratches at his beard and talks to himself. Then the traffic light turns green, and we're moving again.

This is the day that I saw silver for the third time. But no way in hell I'm going to tell Joey that.

Just like the first time, sitting on the train as it barreled towards Camden and my tryst with the Czech, I felt my ears pop, and then there was the same brief dizziness, followed by the commingled reek of ammonia, ozone, and burnt sugar. Me and Joey, we'd just found the room with the body, some poor son of a bitch who'd taken both barrels of a Remington in the face. Who knows what he'd done, or if he'd done anything at all. Could been over money or dope or maybe someone just wanted him out of the way. I don't let myself think too much about that sort of thing. Better not to even think of the body as *someone*. Better to treat it the way a stock boy handles a messy cleanup on aisle five after someone's shopping cart has careened into a towering display of spaghetti sauce.

"Sometimes," said Joey, "I wish I'd gone to college. What about you, man? Ever long for another line of work? Something that *don't* involve scraping brains off the linoleum after a throw-down."

But me, I was too busy simply trying to breathe to remind him that I *had* gone to college, too busy trying not to gag to partake in witty repartee. The dizziness had come and gone, but that acrid stench was forcing its way past my nostrils, scalding my sinuses and the back of my throat. And I knew that Joey didn't smell it, not so much as a whiff, and that his ears hadn't popped, and that he'd not shared that fleeting moment of vertigo. He stood there, glaring at me, his expression equal parts confusion and annoyance. Finally, he shook his head and stepped over the dead guy's legs.

"Jesus and Mary, we've both seen way worse than this," he said, and right then, that's when I caught the dull sparkle on the floor. The lower jaw was still in one piece, mostly, so for half a second or so I pretended I was only seeing the glint of fluorescent lighting off a filling or a crown. But then the silvery puddle, no larger than a dime, moved. It stood out very starkly against all that blood, against the soup of brain and muscle tissue punctuated by countless shards of human skull. It flowed a few inches before encountering a jellied lump of cerebellum, and then I watched as it slowly extended . . . what? What the fuck would you call what I saw? A *pseudopod*? Yeah, sure. Let's go for broke. I watched as it extended a pseudopod and began crawling *over* the obstacle in its path. That's when I turned away, and when I looked back, it wasn't there anymore.

Joey curses and honks the horn. I don't know why. I don't ask him. I don't care. I'm still staring out the passenger side window at this brilliant winter day that wants or needs me to believe it's all nothing more or less than another round of the same old same old. I'm thinking about the woman on the Speedline and about the scuffed toe of the Czech's shoe, about whatever Eli saw at the noodle shop and the silver vials Joey and Jack got a peep at when Tony Palamara opened the case they'd delivered to him. I'm drawing lines and making correlations, parsing best I can, dot-to-fucking-dot, right? Nothing it takes a genius to see, even if I've no idea whatsoever what it all adds up to in the end. I blink, and the sun sparks brutally off distant blue-black towers of mirrored glass. Joey hits the horn again, broadcasting his displeasure for all Girard Avenue to hear, and I shut my eyes.

07.

And it's a night or two later that I have the dream. That I have the dream for the first time.

I've never given much thought to nightmares. Sure, I rack up more than my fair share. I wake up sweating and the sheets soaked, Eli awake, too, and asking if I'm okay. But what would you fucking expect? That's how it goes when your life is a never-ending game of Stepin Fetchit and "Mistress may I have another," when you exist in the everlasting umbrage of Madam Adrianne's Grand Guignol of vice and crime and profit. No one lives this life and expects to sleep well—leastways, no one with walking-around sense. That's why white-coated bastards in pharmaceutical labs had to go and invent Zolpidem and so many other merciful soporifics, so the bad guys could get a little more shut-eye every now and again.

This is not my recollection of that first time. Hell, this is not my recollection of *any* single instance of the dream. It has a hundred subtle and not-so-subtle permutations, but always it stays the same. It wears a hundred gaudy masks to half conceal an immutable underlying face. So, take this as the amalgam or composite that it is. Take this as a rough approximation. Be smart, and take this with a goddamn grain of salt.

Let's say it starts with me and Eli in our plastic lawn chairs, sitting on the roof, gazing heavenward, like either one of us has half a snowball's chance at salvation. Sure. This is as good a place to begin as any other. There we sit, holding hands, scrounging mean comfort in one another's company—only, this time, some human agency or force of nature has intervened and swept back all that orange sky-glow. The stars are spread out overhead like an astronomer's banquet, and neither of us can look away. You see pictures like that online, sure, but you don't look up and expect to behold the dazzling entrails of the Milky Way draped above your head, fit to make the ghost of Neil deGrasse Tyson come. You don't live your whole life in the over-illuminated filth of cities and ever expect to glimpse all those stars arching pretty as you please across the celestial hemisphere.

We sit there, content and amazed, and I want to tell Eli those aren't stars. It's only fireworks on the Fourth of July or the moment the clock strikes the New Year. But he's too busy naming constellations to hear me. How Eli would know a constellation from throbbing gristle is beyond me. But there he sits, reciting them for my edification.

"That's Sagittarius," he says. "Right there, between Ophiuchus and Capricornus. The centaur, between the serpent in the west and the goat in the east." And he tells me that more extrasolar planets have been discovered in Sagittarius than in any other constellation. "*That's* why we should keep a close watch on it."

And I realize then, whiz-bang, presto, abracadabra, that the stars are wheeling overhead, exchanging positions in some crazy cosmic square dance, and Eli, *he* sees it, too, and he laughs. I've never heard Eli laugh like this before, not while I was awake. It's the laughter of a child. It's a laughter filled with delight. There's innocence in a laugh like this.

And maybe, after that, I'm not on the roof anymore. Maybe, after that, I'm sitting in a crowded bar down on Locust Street. I know the place, but I can never remember its name, not in the dream. Nothing to write home about, one way or the other. Neither classy enough nor sleazy enough to be especially memorable. Just fags and dykes wall to fucking wall and lousy, ancient disco blaring through unseen speakers. There's a pint bottle of Wild Turkey sitting on the bar in front of me, and an empty shot glass. Someone's holding a gun to the back of my head. And, yeah, I know the feeling of having a gun to my head, because it happened this one time on a run to Atlantic City that went almost bad as bad can be. I also know that it's Joey the Kike holding the pistol, seeing as how there's a dead scorpion the color of pus lying right there on the bar beside the bottle of bourbon.

"This ain't the way it ought to be," he says, and I'm surprised I can hear his voice over the shitty music and all those queers trying to talk over the shitty music.

"Then how about we find some other way to work it out," I say, sounding lame as any asshole ever tried to talk his way out of a slug to the brain. "How about you sit down here next to me and we have a drink and make sure there are no more creepy-crawlies in your shoes."

"I shouldn't be seen in a place like this," he says, and I hear him pull the hammer back. "People talk, they see you hanging round a place like this."

"People do fucking talk," I agree. With my left index finger, I flick the dead scorpion off the bar. No one seems to notice. For that matter, no one seems to notice he's got a gun to my head. I say, "Maybe you should bounce before some hard-nosed bastard takes a notion to make you his bitch, yeah? You ever taken it up the ass, Joey?"

"You're such a smart guy," Joey replies, "you're still gonna be passing woof tickets when you're six feet under, ain't you? Expect you'll manage to smack-talk your way out of Hell, given half a chance."

"Well, you know me, Joey. Never let 'em see you sweat. *Veni, vidi, vici* and all that *hùnzhàng*."

And I'm sitting there waiting to die, when the music stops, and all eyes turn towards the rear of the bar. I look, too, though Joey's still got his 9mm parked on my scalp. A baby spot with a green gel is playing across a tiny stage, and there's Eli with a microphone. I'd think he was actual, factual fish if I didn't know better, that's how good Eli looks in a black evening gown and pumps and a wig that makes me think of Isabella Rossellini playing Dorothy Vallens in *Blue Velvet*. The din of voices is only a murmur now, only a gentle whisper of expectation as we all wait to see which way the wind's about to blow.

"Damn, she's hot," Joey says.

"Fuckin' A, she's hot," I tell him. "You should be so goddamn lucky to get a piece of ass like that one day."

He tells me to keep quiet, zip it and toss the key, that he wants to hear, but it's not *me* he wants to hear. So I make like a good boy and oblige. After all, I want to hear this nightingale, too. And then Eli begins to sing, a cappella and in Spanish, and everyone goes hushed as midnight after Judgment Day. His voice is his voice, not some dream impersonation, and I wonder why I never knew Eli could sing.

Bueno, ahora, pagar la atención
Sólo en caso de que no había oído . . .

And I'm still right there in the bar, but I'm somewhere else, as well. I'm walking in a desert somewhere, like something out of an old Wild and Woolly West flick, and the sun beats down on me from a sky so blue it's almost white. There are mountains far, far away, a hazy jagged line against the horizon, and I wonder if that's where I'm trying to get to. If there's something in the mountains that I need to see. The playa stretches out all around me, a lifeless plain of alkali flats and desiccation cracks. Maybe this was a lake or inland sea, long, long ago. Maybe the water still comes back, from time to time. Sweat runs into my eyes, and I squint against the sting.

On the little stage, Eli sings in Spanish, and I sit on my bar stool with the barrel of Joey's gun prodding my skull. I wish the shot glass weren't empty, 'cause the baking desert sun has me thirsty as a motherfucker. I keep my eyes on Eli, and I hear the parching salt wind whipping across the flats, and I hear that song in a language that I can only half understand.

Basta con mirar hacia el cielo
Y gracias al Gobierno por la nieve
Y cantar la baja hacia abajo . . .

"What's she sayin'?" Joey the Kike wants to know, and I ask him which part of me looks Mexican.

In the desert, I stop walking and peer up at the sun. High above me, there are contrails. And I know that's what Eli's singing about—those vaporous wakes—even if I have no idea why.

"It's a dream," I tell Joey the Kike, growing impatient with the gun. "Specifically, it's *my* dream. I come here all the time, and I don't remember ever inviting you."

The playa crunches loudly beneath my feet.

Tony Palamara opens a briefcase, and I see half a dozen silver vials marked with yellow tape.

A woman on a train wipes at her nose, and my ears pop.

Eli is no longer singing in Spanish, though I don't recall the transition to English. No one says a word. They're all much too busy watching him make love to the resonant phallus of his microphone.

Trying to make it rain.
So when you're out there in that blizzard,
Shivering in the cold,
Just look up to the sky . . .

I kneel on that plain and dig my fingers into the scorched saline crust. I crush the sandy dirt in my hand, and the wind sweeps it away. And that's when I notice what looks like a kid's spinning top—only big around as a tractor-trailer's wheel—lying on the ground maybe twenty yards ahead of me. A tattered drogue parachute is attached to the enormous top by a tangled skein of nylon kernmantle cord. The wind ruffles wildly through the chute, and I notice the skid marks leading from the spinning top that isn't a spinning top, trailing away into the distance.

And sing the low-down experimental cloud-seeding
Who-needs-'em-baby? Silver-iodide blues.

I stand, and look back the way I've come. In the dream, I guess I've come from the south, walking north. So, looking south, the desert seems to run on forever, with no unobtainable mountainous El Dorado to upset the monotony. There's only the sky above, crisscrossed with contrails, and the yellow-brown playa below, the line drawn between them sharp as a paper cut. There's not even the mirage shimmer of heat I'd have expected, but, of course, this desert is only required to obey the dictates of my unconscious mind, not any laws of physical science. I stand staring at the horizon for a moment, and then resume my northwards march. I know now I'm not trying to reach the mountains. No one reaches those mountains, not no way, not no how, right? I'm only trying to go as far as the kid's top that's not a top and its rippling nylon parachute. I understand that now, and I tell Joey to either pull the trigger or put his piece away. I don't have time for reindeer games tonight. And if I did, I still wouldn't be looking for action from the likes of him.

I stare at the bar, and the pus-colored scorpion's returned. This time, I don't bother to make it go away. I do wonder if dead scorpions can still kill a guy.

Was you ever bit by a dead bee?

All those people in the bar have begun applauding, and Eli takes a bow and sets his mike back into its stand.

"What you saw," Joey sneers, "I got as much right to know as you. We were both slopping about in that stiff's innards, and if something was wrong with him, I deserve to know. You got no place keepin' it from me."

"I didn't see anything," I tell him, wishing it were the truth. "Now, are you going to shoot me or put away the roscoe and make nice?"

"Making you nervous?" asks Joey.

"Not really, but the potential for injury is pissing me off righteously."

I reach the top that's not a top, and now I'm almost certain it's actually some sort of return capsule from a space probe. One side is scorched black, so I suppose that must be the heat shield. I stand three or four feet back, and I have never, in any version of the dream, touched the thing. It's maybe five feet in diameter, maybe a little less. I'm wondering how long it's been out here, and where it might have traveled before hurtling back to earth, and, while I'm at it, why no retrieval team's come along to fetch it. I wonder if it's even a NASA probe, or maybe, instead, a chunk of foreign hardware that strayed from its target area. Either way, no one leaves shit like this laying around in the goddamn desert. I know *that* much.

"Yeah, you know it all," Joey says and jabs me a little harder with the muzzle of his gun. "You must be the original Doctor Albert Eisenstein, and me, I'm just some schmuck can't be trusted with the time of day."

Catch a falling star an' put it in your pocket . . .

And on the rooftop, Eli tells me, "The star at the centaur's knee is Alpha Sagittarii, or Rukbat, which means 'knee' in Arabic. Rukbat is a blue class B star, one hundred and eighteen light years away. It's twice as hot as the sun and forty times brighter."

"You been holding out on me, *chica*. Here I thought you were nothing but good looks and grace, and then you get all Wikipedia on me."

Eli laughs, and the crowded, noisy bar on Locust Street dissolves like fog, and the desert fades to half a memory. Joey the Kike and his pea-shooter, the dead scorpion and the bottle of Wild Turkey, every bit of it merely the echo of an echo now. I'm standing at the doorway of our bathroom, the tiny bathroom in my and Eli's place in Chinatown. Regardless which rendition of the dream we're talking about, sooner or later they *all* end here. I'm standing in the open door of the bathroom, and Eli's in the old claw-foot tub. The air is thick with steam and condensation drips in crystal beads from the mirror on the medicine cabinet. Even the floor, that mosaic of white hexagonal tiles, is slick. I'm barefoot, and the ceramic feels slick beneath my feet. I swear and ask Eli if he thinks he got the water hot enough, and he asks me about the briefcase I delivered to the Czech. It doesn't even occur to me to ask how the hell he knows about the delivery.

"What about we don't talk shop just this once," I say, as though it's something we make a habit of doing. "And how about we most especially don't linger on the subject of the fucking Czech?"

"Hey, *you* brought it up, lover, not me," Eli says, returning the soap to the scallop-shaped soap dish. His hand leaves behind a smear of silver on the sudsy lavender bar. I stare at it, trying hard to recall something important that's teetering right there on the tip end of my tongue.

For love may come an' tap you on the shoulder, some starless night . . .

"Make yourself useful and hand me a towel," he says. "Long as you're standing there, I mean."

I reach into the linen closet for a bath towel, and when I turn back to pass it to Eli, he's standing, the water lapping about his lower calves. Only it's not water anymore. It's something that looks like mercury, and it flows quickly up his legs, his hips, his ass, and drips like cum from the end of his dick. Eli either isn't aware of what's going on, or he doesn't care. I hand him the towel as the silver reaches his smooth, hairless chest and begins to make its way down both his arms.

"Anyway," he says, "we can talk about it or we can not talk about it. Either way's fine by me. So long as you don't start fooling yourself into thinking your hands are clean. I don't want to hear about how you were only following orders, you know?"

It's easy to forget them without tryin', with just a pocketful of starlight.

My ears haven't popped, and there's been no dizziness, but, all the same, the bathroom is redolent with those caustic triplets, ammonia and ozone, and, more subtly, sugar sizzling away to a carbon-black scum. The silver has reached Eli's throat, and rushes up over his chin, finding its way into his mouth and nostrils. A moment more, and he stands staring back at me with eyes like polished ball bearings.

"You and your gangster buddies, you get it in your heads you're only blameless errand boys," Eli says, and his voice has become smooth and shiny as what the silver has made of his flesh. "You think ignorance is some kind of virtue, and none of the evil shit you do for your taskmasters is ever coming back to haunt you."

I don't argue with him, no matter whether Eli (or the sterling apparition standing where Eli stood a few moments before) is right or wrong or someplace in between. I could disagree, sure, but I don't. I'm reasonably fucking confident it no longer makes any difference. The towel falls to the floor, fluttering like a drogue parachute in a desert gale, and Eli steps out of the tub, spreading silver in his wake.

THE MALTESE
UNICORN

New York City (May 1935)

I T WASN'T HARD to find her. Sure, she had run. After Szabó let her walk like that, I knew Ellen would get wise that something was rotten, and she'd run like a scared rabbit with the dogs hot on its heels. She'd have it in her head to skip town, and she'd probably keep right on skipping until she was out of the country. Odds were pretty good she wouldn't stop until she was altogether free and clear of this particular plane of existence. There are plenty enough fetid little hidey-holes in the universe, if you don't mind the heat and the smell and the company you keep. You only have to know how to find them, and the way I saw it, Ellen Andrews was good as Rand and McNally when it came to knowing her way around.

But first, she'd go back to that apartment of hers, the whole eleventh floor of the Colosseum, with its bleak westward view of the Hudson River and the New Jersey Palisades. I figured there would be those two or three little things she couldn't bear to leave the city without, even if it meant risking her skin to collect them. Only she hadn't expected me to get there before her. Word on the street was Harpootlian still had me locked up tight, so Ellen hadn't expected me to get there at all.

From the hall came the buzz of the elevator, then I heard her key in the lock, the front door, and her footsteps as she hurried through the foyer and

287

the dining room. Then she came dashing into that French Rococo night-mare of a library, and stopped cold in her tracks when she saw me sitting at the reading table with al-Jaldaki's grimoire open in front of me.

For a second, she didn't say anything. She just stood there, staring at me. Then she managed a forced sort of laugh and said, "I knew they'd send some-one, Nat. I just didn't think it'd be you."

"After that gip you pulled with the dingus, they didn't really leave me much choice," I told her, which was the truth, or at least all the truth I felt like sharing. "You shouldn't have come back here. It's the first place anyone would think to check."

Ellen sat down in the armchair by the door. She looked beat, like what-ever comes after exhausted, and I could tell Szabó's gunsels had made sure all the fight was gone before they'd turned her loose. They weren't taking any chances, and we were just going through the motions now, me and her. All our lines had been written.

"You played me for a sucker," I said and picked up the pistol that had been lying beside the grimoire. My hand was shaking, and I tried to steady it by bracing my elbow against the table. "You played me, then you tried to play Harpootlian and Szabó both. Then you got caught. It was a bonehead move all the way round, Ellen."

"So, how's it gonna be, Natalie? You gonna shoot me for being stupid?"

"No, I'm going shoot you because it's the only way I can square things with Auntie H and the only thing that's gonna keep Szabó from going on the warpath. *And* because you played me."

"In my shoes, you'd have done the same thing," she said. And the way she said it, I could tell she believed what she was saying. It's the sort of self-righteous bushwa so many grifters hide behind. They might stab their own mothers in the back if they see an angle in it, but, you ask them, that's jake, cause so would anyone else.

"Is that really all you have to say for yourself?" I asked and pulled back the slide on the Colt, chambering the first round. She didn't even flinch . . . but, wait . . . I'm getting ahead of myself. Maybe I ought to begin nearer the beginning.

As it happens, I didn't go and name the place Yellow Dragon Books. It came with that moniker, and I just never saw any reason to change it. I'd only have had to pay for a new sign. Late in '28—right after Arnie "The Brain" Rothstein was shot to death during a poker game at the Park Central Hotel—I accidentally found myself on the sunny side of the proprietress of one of Manhattan's more infernal brothels. I say *accidentally* because I hadn't even heard of Madam Yeksabet Harpootlian when I began trying to dig up a buyer for an antique manuscript, a collection of necromantic erotica purportedly written by John Dee and Edward Kelley sometime in the Sixteenth Century. Turns out, Harpootlian had been looking to get her mitts on it for decades.

Now, just how I came into possession of said manuscript, that's another story entirely, one for some other time and place. One that, with luck, I'll never get around to putting down on paper. Let's just say a couple of years earlier. I'd been living in Paris. Truthfully, I'd been doing my best, in a sloppy, irresolute way, to *die* in Paris. I was holed up in a fleabag Montmartre boarding house, busy squandering the last of a dwindling inheritance. I had in mind how maybe I could drown myself in cheap wine, bad poetry, Pernod, and prostitutes before the money ran out. But somewhere along the way, I lost my nerve, failed at my slow suicide, and bought a ticket back to the States. And the manuscript in question was one of the many strange and unsavory things I brought back with me. I'd always had a nose for the macabre and had dabbled—on and off—in the black arts since college. At Radcliffe, I'd fallen in with a circle of lesbyterians who fancied themselves witches. Mostly, I was in it for the sex . . . but I'm digressing.

A friend of a friend heard I was busted, down and out and peddling a bunch of old books, schlepping them about Manhattan in search of a buyer. This same friend, he knew one of Harpootlian's clients. One of her *human* clients, which was a pretty exclusive set (not that I knew that at the time). This friend of mine, he was the client's lover, and said client brokered the sale for Harpootlian—for a fat ten-percent finder's fee, of course. I promptly sold the Dee and Kelly manuscript to this supposedly notorious madam whom, near as I could tell, no one much had ever heard of. She paid me what I asked, no questions, no haggling, never mind it was a fairly exorbitant sum. And on top of that, Harpootlian was so impressed I'd gotten ahold of the damned thing, she staked me to the bookshop on Bowery, there in the shadow of the Third Avenue El, just a little ways south of Delancey Street. Only one catch: she had first dibs on everything I ferreted out, and sometimes I'd be asked to make deliveries. I should like to note that way back then, during that long-lost November of 1928, I had no idea whatsoever that her sobriquet, "the Demon Madam of the Lower East Side," was anything more than colorful hyperbole.

Anyway, jump ahead to a rainy May afternoon, more than six years later, and that's when I first laid eyes on Ellen Andrews. Well, that's what she called herself, though later on I'd find out she'd borrowed the name from Claudette Colbert's character in *It Happened One Night*. I was just back from an estate sale in Connecticut and was busy unpacking a large crate when I heard the bell mounted above the shop door jingle. I looked up, and there she was, carelessly shaking rainwater from her orange umbrella before folding it closed. Droplets sprayed across the welcome mat and the floor and onto the spines of several nearby books.

"Hey, be careful," I said, "unless you intend to pay for those." I jabbed a thumb at the books she'd spattered. She promptly stopped shaking the umbrella and dropped it into the stand beside the door. That umbrella stand has always been one of my favorite things about the Yellow Dragon. It's made from the taxidermied foot of a hippopotamus and accommodates at least a dozen umbrellas, although I don't think I've ever seen even half that many people in the shop at one time.

"Are you Natalie Beaumont?" she asked, looking down at her wet shoes. Her overcoat was dripping, and a small puddle was forming about her feet.

"Usually."

"Usually," she repeated. "How about right now?"

"Depends whether or not I owe you money," I replied and removed a battered copy of Blavatsky's *Isis Unveiled* from the crate. "Also, depends whether you happen to be *employed* by someone I owe money."

"I see," she said, as if that settled the matter, then proceeded to examine the complete twelve-volume set of *The Golden Bough* occupying a top shelf not far from the door. "Awful funny sort of neighborhood for a bookstore, if you ask me."

"You don't think bums and winos read?"

"You ask me, people down here," she said, "they panhandle a few cents, I don't imagine they spend it on books."

"I don't recall asking for your opinion," I told her.

"No," she said. "You didn't. Still, queer sort of a shop to come across in this part of town."

"If you must know," I said, "the rent's cheap," then reached for my spectacles, which were dangling from their silver chain about my neck. I set them on the bridge of my nose and watched while she feigned interest in Frazerian anthropology. It would be an understatement to say Ellen Andrews was a pretty girl. She was, in fact, a certified knockout, and I didn't get too many beautiful women in the Yellow Dragon, even when the weather was good. She wouldn't have looked out of place in Flo Ziegfeld's follies; on the Bowery, she stuck out like a sore thumb.

"Looking for anything in particular?" I asked her, and she shrugged.

"Just you," she said.

"Then I suppose you're in luck."

"I suppose I am," she said and turned towards me again. Her eyes glinted red, just for an instant, like the eyes of a Siamese cat. I figured it for a trick of the light. "I'm a friend of Auntie H. I run errands for her, now and then. She needs you to pick up a package and see it gets safely where it's going."

So, there it was. Madam Harpootlian, or Auntie H to those few unfortunates she called her friends. And suddenly it made a lot more sense, this choice bit of calico walking into my place, strolling in off the street like maybe she did all her window shopping down on Skid Row. I'd have to finish unpacking the crate later. I stood up and dusted my hands off on the seat of my slacks.

"Sorry about the confusion," I said, even if I wasn't actually sorry, even if I was actually kind of pissed the girl hadn't told me who she was right up front. "When Auntie H wants something done, she doesn't usually bother sending her orders around in such an attractive envelope."

The girl laughed, then said, "Yeah, she warned me about you, Miss Beaumont."

"Did she now. How so?"

"You know, your predilections. How you're not like other women."

"I'd say that depends on which other women we're discussing, don't you think?"

"*Most* other women," she said, glancing over her shoulder at the rain pelting the shop windows. It sounded like frying meat out there, the sizzle of the rain against asphalt and concrete and the roofs of passing automobiles.

"And what about you?" I asked her. "Are *you* like most other women?"

She looked away from the window, looking back at me, and she smiled what must have been the faintest smile possible.

"Are you always this charming?"

"Not that I'm aware of," I said. "Then again, I never took a poll."

"The job, it's nothing particularly complicated," she said, changing the subject. "There's a Chinese apothecary not too far from here."

"That doesn't exactly narrow it down," I said and lit a cigarette.

"65 Mott Street. The joint's run by an elderly Cantonese fellow name of Fong."

"Yeah, I know Jimmy Fong."

"That's good. Then maybe you won't get lost. Mr. Fong will be expecting you, and he'll have the package ready at five-thirty this evening. He's already been paid in full, so all you have to do is be there to receive it, right? And Miss Beaumont, please try to be on time. Auntie H said you have a problem with punctuality."

"You believe everything you hear?"

"Only if I'm hearing it from Auntie H."

"Fair enough," I told her, then offered her a Pall Mall, but she declined.

"I need to be getting back," she said, reaching for the umbrella she'd only just deposited in the stuffed hippopotamus foot.

"What's the rush? What'd you come after, anyway, a ball of fire?"

She rolled her eyes. "I got places to be. You're not the only stop on my itinerary."

"Fine. Wouldn't want you getting in dutch with Harpootlian on my account. Don't suppose you've got a name?"

"I might," she said.

"Don't suppose you'd share?" I asked her, and I took a long drag on my cigarette, wondering why in blue blazes Harpootlian had sent this smart-mouthed skirt instead of one of her usual flunkies. Of course, Auntie H always did have a sadistic streak to put de Sade to shame, and likely as not this was her idea of a joke.

"Ellen," the girl said. "Ellen Andrews."

"So, Ellen Andrews, how is it we've never met? I mean, I've been making deliveries for your boss lady now going on seven years, and if I'd seen you, I'd remember. You're not the sort I forget."

"You got the moxie, don't you?"

"I'm just good with faces is all."

She chewed at a thumbnail, as if considering carefully what she should or shouldn't divulge. Then she said, "I'm from out of town, mostly. Just passing through and thought I'd lend a hand. That's why you've never seen me before, Miss Beaumont. Now, I'll let you get back to work. And remember, don't be late."

"I heard you the first time, sister."

And then she left, and the brass bell above the door jingled again. I finished my cigarette and went back to unpacking the big crate of books from Connecticut. If I hurried, I could finish the job before heading for Chinatown.

She was right, of course. I did have a well-deserved reputation for not being on time. But I knew that Auntie H was of the opinion that my acumen in antiquarian and occult matters more than compensated for my not infrequent tardiness. I've never much cared for personal mottos, but maybe if I had one it might be, *You want it on time, or you want it done right?* Still, I honestly tried to be on time for the meeting with Fong. And still, through no fault of my own, I was more than twenty minutes late. I was lucky enough to find a cab, despite the rain, but then got stuck behind some sort of brouhaha after turning onto Canal, so there you go. It's not like old man Fong had any place more pressing to be, not like he was gonna get pissy and leave me high and dry.

When I got to 65 Mott, the Chinaman's apothecary was locked up tight, all the lights were off, and the SORRY, WE'RE CLOSED sign was hung in the front window. No big surprise there. But then I went around back, to the alley, and found a door standing wide open and quite a lot of fresh blood on the cinderblock steps leading into the building. Now, maybe I was the only lady bookseller in Manhattan who carried a gun, and maybe I wasn't. But times like this, I was glad to have the Colt tucked snugly inside its shoulder holster and happier still that I knew how to use it. I took a deep breath, drew the pistol, flipped off the safety catch, and stepped inside.

The door opened onto a stockroom, and the tiny nook Jimmy Fong used as his office was a little farther in, over on my left. There was some light from a banker's lamp, but not much of it. I lingered in the shadows a moment, waiting for my heart to stop pounding, for the adrenaline high to fade. The air was close and stunk of angelica root and dust, ginger and frankincense and fuck only knows what else. Powdered rhino horn and the pickled gall-bladders of panda bears. What the hell ever. I found the old man slumped over at his desk.

Whoever knifed him hadn't bothered to pull the shiv out of his spine, and I wondered if the poor s.o.b. had even seen it coming. It didn't exactly add up, not after seeing all that blood back on the steps, but I figured, hey, maybe the killer was the sort of klutz can't spread butter without cutting himself. I had a quick look-see around the cluttered office, hoping I might turn up the package Ellen Andrews had sent me there to retrieve. But no dice, and then it occurred to me, maybe whoever had murdered Fong had come looking for the same thing I was looking for. Maybe they'd found it, too, only Fong knew better than to just hand it over, and that had gotten him killed. Anyway, nobody was paying me to play junior shamus, hence the hows, whys, and wherefores of the Chinaman's death were not my problem. *My* problem would be showing up at Harpootlian's cathouse empty-handed.

I returned the gun to its holster, then I started rifling through everything in sight—the great disarray of papers heaped upon the desk, Fong's accounting ledgers, sales invoices, catalogs, letters and postcards written in English, Mandarin, Wu, Cantonese, French, Spanish, and Arabic. I still had my gloves on, so it's not like I had to worry over fingerprints. A few of the desk drawers were unlocked, and I'd just started in on those, when the phone perched atop the filing cabinet rang. I froze, whatever I was looking at clutched forgotten in my hands, and stared at the phone.

Sure, it wasn't every day I blundered into the immediate aftermath of this sort of foul play, but I was plenty savvy enough I knew better than to answer that call. It didn't much matter who was on the other end of the line. If I answered, I could be placed at the scene of a murder only minutes after it had gone down. The phone rang a second time, and a third, and I glanced at the dead man in the chair. The crimson halo surrounding the switchblade's inlaid mother-of-pearl handle was still spreading, blossoming like some grim rose, and now there was blood dripping to the floor, as well. The phone rang a fourth time. A fifth. And then I was seized by an overwhelming compulsion to answer it, and answer it I did. I wasn't the least bit thrown that the voice coming through the receiver was Ellen Andrews'. All at once, the pieces were falling into place. You spend enough years doing the Stepin Fetchit routine for imps like Harpootlian, you find yourself ever more jaded at the inexplicable and the uncanny.

"Beaumont," she said, "I didn't think you were going to pick up."

"I wasn't. Funny thing how I did anyway."

"Funny thing," she said, and I heard her light a cigarette and realized my hands were shaking.

"See, I'm thinking maybe I had a little push," I said. "That about the size of it?"

"Wouldn't have been necessary if you'd have just answered the damn phone in the first place."

"You already know Fong's dead, don't you?" And, I swear to fuck, nothing makes me feel like more of a jackass than asking questions I know the answers to.

"Don't you worry about Fong. I'm sure he had all his ducks in a row and was right as rain with Buddha. I need you to pay attention—"

"Harpootlian had him killed, didn't she? And you *knew* he'd be dead when I showed up." She didn't reply straight away, and I thought I could hear a radio playing in the background. "You knew," I said again, only this time it wasn't a query.

"Listen," she said. "You're a courier. I was told you're a courier we can trust, elsewise I never would have handed you this job."

"You didn't hand me the job. Your boss did."

"You're splitting hairs, Miss Beaumont."

"Yeah, well, there's a fucking dead celestial in the room with me. It's giving me the fidgets."

"So, how about you shut up and listen, and I'll have you out of there in a jiffy." And that's what I did, I shut up, either because I knew it was the path of least resistance or because whatever spell she'd used to persuade me to answer the phone was still working.

"On Fong's desk, there's a funny little porcelain statue of a cat."

"You mean the Maneki Neko?"

"If that's what it's called, that's what I mean. Now, break it open. There's a key inside."

I tried not to, just to see if I was being played as badly as I suspected I was being played. I gritted my teeth, dug in my heels, and tried *hard* not to break that damned cat.

"You're wasting time. Auntie H didn't mention you were such a cry-baby."

"Auntie H and I have an agreement when it comes to free will. To *my* free will."

"*Break the goddamn cat,*" Ellen Andrews growled, and that's exactly what I did. In fact, I slammed it down directly on top of Fong's head. Bits of brightly painted porcelain flew everywhere, and a rusty barrel key tumbled out and landed at my feet. "Now pick it up," she said. "The key fits the bottom left-hand drawer of Fong's desk. Open it."

This time, I didn't even try to resist her. I was getting a headache from the last futile attempt. I unlocked the drawer and pulled it open. Inside, there was nothing but the yellowed sheet of newspaper lining the drawer, three golf balls, a couple of old racing forms, and a finely carved wooden box lacquered almost the same shade of red as Jimmy Fong's blood. I didn't need to be told I'd been sent to retrieve the box—or, more specifically, whatever was *inside* the box.

"Yeah, I got it," I told Ellen Andrews.

"Good girl. Now, you have maybe twelve minutes before the cops show. Go out the same way you came in." Then she gave me a Riverside Drive address and said there'd be a car waiting for me at the corner of Canal and Mulberry, a green Chevrolet coupe. "Just give the driver that address. He'll see you get where you're going."

"Yeah," I said, sliding the desk drawer shut again and locking it. I pocketed the key. "But sister, you and me are gonna have a talk."

"Wouldn't miss it for the world, Nat," she said, and hung up. I shut my eyes, wondering if I really had twelve minutes before the bulls arrived, and if they were even on their way, wondering what would happen if I endeavored *not* to make the rendezvous with the green coupe. I stood there, trying to decide whether Harpootlian would have gone back on her word and given this bitch permission to turn her hoodoo tricks on me, and if aspirin would do anything at all for the dull throb behind my eyes. Then I looked at Fong one last time, at the knife jutting out of his back, his thin grey hair powdered with porcelain dust from the shattered "Lucky Cat." And then I stopped asking questions and did as I'd been told.

The car was there, just like she'd told me it would be. There was a young colored man behind the wheel, and when I climbed in the back, he asked me where we were headed.

"I'm guessing Hell," I said, "sooner or later."

"Got that right," he laughed and winked at me from the rearview mirror. "But I was thinking more in terms of the immediate here and now."

So I recited the address I'd been given over the phone, 435 Riverside.

"That's the Colosseum," he said.

"It is if you say so," I replied. "Just get me there."

The driver nodded and pulled away from the curb. As he navigated the slick, wet streets, I sat listening to the rain against the Chevy's hard top and the music coming from the Motorola. In particular, I can remember hearing the Dorsey Brothers' "Chasing Shadows." I suppose you'd call that a harbinger, if you go in for that sort of thing. Me, I do my best not to. In this business, you start jumping at everything that *might* be an omen or a portent, you end up doing nothing else. Ironically, rubbing shoulders with the supernatural has made me a great believer in coincidence.

Anyway, the driver drove, the radio played, and I sat staring at the red lacquered box I'd stolen from a dead man's locked desk drawer. I thought it might be mahogany, but it was impossible to be sure, what with all that cinnabar-tinted varnish. I know enough about Chinese mythology that I recognized the strange creature carved into the top. It was a *qilin*, a stout, antlered beast with cloven hooves, the scales of a dragon, and a long leonine tail. Much of its body was wreathed in flame, and its gaping jaws revealed teeth like daggers. For the Chinese, the *qilin* is a harbinger of good fortune, though it certainly hadn't worked out that way for Jimmy Fong. The box was heavier than it looked, most likely because of whatever was stashed inside. There was no latch, and as I examined it more closely, I realized there was no sign whatsoever of hinges or even a seam to indicate it actually had a lid.

"Unless I got it backwards," the driver said, "Miss Andrews didn't say nothing about trying to open that box, now did she?"

I looked up, startled, feeling like the proverbial kid caught with her hand in the cookie jar. He glanced at me in the mirror, then his eyes drifted back to the road.

"She didn't say one way or the other," I told him.

"Then how about we err on the side of caution?"

"So you didn't know where you're taking me, but you know I shouldn't open this box? How's that work?"

"Ain't the world just full of mysteries," he said.

For a minute or so, I silently watched the headlights of the oncoming traffic and the metronomic sweep of the windshield wipers. Then I asked the driver how long he'd worked for Ellen Andrews.

"Not very," he said. "Never laid eyes on the lady before this afternoon. Why you want to know?"

"No particular reason," I said, looking back down at the box and the *qilin* etched in the wood. I decided I was better off not asking any more questions, better off getting this over and done with, and never mind what did and didn't quite add up. "Just trying to make conversation, that's all."

Which got him to talking about the Chicago stockyards and Cleveland and how it was he'd eventually wound up in New York City. He never told me his name, and I didn't ask. The trip uptown seemed to take forever, and the longer I sat with that box in my lap, the heavier it felt. I finally moved it, putting it down on the seat beside me. By the time we reached our destination, the rain had stopped and the setting sun was showing through the clouds, glittering off the dripping trees in Riverside Park and the waters of the wide grey Hudson. He pulled over, and I reached for my wallet.

"No ma'am," he said, shaking his head. "Miss Andrews, she's already seen to your fare."

"Then I hope you won't mind if I see to your tip," I said, and I gave him five dollars. He thanked me, and I took the wooden box and stepped out onto the wet sidewalk.

"She's up on the eleventh," he told me, nodding towards the apartments. Then he drove off, and I turned to face the imposing curved brick and limestone façade of the building the driver had called the Colosseum. I rarely find myself any farther north than the Upper West Side, so this was pretty much *terra incognita* for me.

The doorman gave me directions, *after* giving both me and Fong's box the hairy eyeball, and I quickly made my way to the elevators, hurrying through that ritzy marble sepulcher passing itself off as a lobby. When the operator asked which floor I needed, I told him the eleventh, and he shook his head and muttered something under his breath. I almost asked him to speak up, but thought better of it. Didn't I already have plenty enough on my mind without entertaining the opinions of elevator boys? Sure, I did. I had a murdered Chinaman, a mysterious box, and this pushy little sorceress calling herself Ellen Andrews. I also had an especially disagreeable feeling about this job, and the sooner it was settled, the better. I kept my eyes on the brass needle as it haltingly swung from left to right, counting off the floors, and when the doors parted she was there waiting for me. She slipped the boy a sawbuck, and he stuffed it into his jacket pocket and left us alone.

"So nice to see you again, Nat," she said, but she was looking at the lacquered box, not me. "Would you like to come in and have a drink? Auntie H says you have a weakness for rye whiskey."

"Well, she's right about that. But, just now, I'd be more fond of an explanation."

"How odd," she said, glancing up at me, still smiling. "Auntie said one thing she liked about you was how you didn't ask a lot of questions. Said you were real good at minding your own business."

"Sometimes I make exceptions."

"Let me get you that drink," she said, and I followed her the short distance from the elevator to the door of her apartment. Turns out, she had the whole floor to herself, each level of the Colosseum being a single apartment. Pretty ritzy accommodations, I thought, for someone who was *mostly* from out of town. But then I'd spent the last few years living in that one-bedroom cracker box above the Yellow Dragon, hot and cold running cockroaches and so forth. She locked the door behind us, then led me through the foyer to a parlor. The whole place was done up gaudy period French, Louis Quinze and the like, all floral brocade and Orientalia. The walls were decorated with damask hangings, mostly of ample-bosomed women reclining in pastoral scenes, dogs and sheep and what have you lying at their feet. Ellen told me to have a seat, so I parked myself on a *récamier* near a window.

"Harpootlian spring for this place?" I asked.

"No," she replied. "It belonged to my mother."

"So you come from money."

"Did I mention how you ask an awful lot of questions?"

"You might have," I said, and she inquired as to whether I liked my whiskey neat or on the rocks. I told her neat, and I set the red box down on the sofa next to me.

"If you're not *too* thirsty, would you mind if I take a peek at that first?" she asked, pointing at the box.

"Be my guest," I said, and Ellen smiled again. She picked up the red lacquered box, then sat next to me. She cradled it in her lap, and there was this goofy expression on her face, a mix of awe, dread, and eager expectation.

"Must be something extra damn special," I said, and she laughed. It was a nervous kind of a laugh.

I've already mentioned how I couldn't discern any evidence the box had a lid, and I'd supposed there was some secret to getting it open, a gentle squeeze or nudge in just the right spot. Turns out, all it needed was someone to say the magic words.

"Pain had no sting, and pleasure's wreath no flower," she said, speaking slowly and all but whispering the words. There was a sharp *click* and the top of the box suddenly slid back with enough force that it tumbled over her knees and fell to the carpet.

"Keats," I said.

"Keats," she echoed, but added nothing more. She was too busy gazing at what lay inside the box, nestled in a bed of velvet the color of poppies. She started to touch it, then hesitated, her fingertips hovering an inch or so above the object.

"You're fucking kidding me," I said, once I saw what was inside.

"Don't go jumping to conclusions, Nat."

"It's a dildo," I said, probably sounding as incredulous as I felt. "Exactly which conclusions am I not supposed to jump to? Sure, I enjoy a good rub-off as much as the next girl, but . . . you're telling me Harpootlian killed Fong over a dildo?"

"I never said Auntie H killed Fong."

"Then I suppose he stuck that knife there himself."

And that's when she told me to shut the hell up for five minutes, if I knew how. She reached into the box and lifted out the phallus, handling it as gingerly as somebody might handle a sweaty stick of dynamite. But whatever made the thing special, it wasn't anything I could see.

"*Le godemichet maudit*," she murmured, her voice so filled with reverence you'd have thought she was holding the devil's own wang. Near as I could tell, it was cast from some sort of hard black ceramic. It glistened faintly in the light getting in through the drapes. "I'll tell you about it," she said, "if you really want to know. I don't see the harm."

"Just so long as you get to the part where it makes sense that Harpootlian bumped the Chinaman for this dingus of yours, then sure."

She took her eyes off the thing long enough to scowl at me. "Auntie H didn't kill Fong. One of Szabó's goons did that, then panicked and ran before he figured out where the box was hidden."

(Now, as for Madam Magdalena Szabó, the biggest boil on Auntie H's fanny, we'll get back to her by and by.)

"Ellen, how can you *possibly* fucking know that? Better yet, how could you've known Szabó's man would have given up and cleared out by the time I arrived?"

"Why did you answer that phone, Nat?" she asked, and that shut me up, good and proper. "As for our prize here," she continued, "it's a long story, a long story with a lot of missing pieces. The dingus, as you put it, is usually called *le godemichet maudit*. Which doesn't necessarily mean it's actually cursed, mind you. Not literally. You *do* speak French, I assume?"

"Yeah," I said. "I do speak French."

"That's ducky, Nat. Now, here's about as much as anyone could tell you. Though, frankly, I'd have thought a scholarly type like yourself would know all about it."

"Never said I was a scholar," I interrupted.

"But you went to college. Radcliffe, Class of 1923, right? Graduated with honors."

"Lots of people go to college. Doesn't necessarily make them scholars. I just sell books."

"My mistake," she said, carefully returning the black dildo to its velvet case. "It won't happen again." Then she told me her tale, and I sat there on the *récamier* and listened to what she had to say. Yeah, it was long. There *were* certainly a whole lot of missing pieces. And as a wise man once said, this might not be schoolbook history, not Mr. Wells' history, but, near as I've been able to discover since that evening at her apartment, it's history, nevertheless. She asked me whether or not I'd ever heard of a Fourteenth-Century Persian alchemist named al-Jaldaki, Izz al-Din Aydamir al-Jaldaki, and I had, naturally.

"Well, he's sort of a hobby of mine," she said. "Came across his grimoire a few years back. Anyway, he's not where it begins, but that's where the written record starts. While studying in Anatolia, al-Jaldaki heard tales of a fabulous artifact that had been crafted from the horn of a unicorn at the behest of King Solomon."

"From a unicorn," I cut in. "So we believe in those now, do we?"

"Why not, Nat? I think it's safe to assume you've seen some peculiar shit in your time. That you've pierced the veil, so to speak. Surely a unicorn must be small potatoes for a worldly woman like yourself."

"So you'd think," I said.

"Anyhow," she went on, "the ivory horn was carved into the shape of a penis by the king's most skilled artisans. Supposedly, the result was so revered it was even placed in Solomon's temple, alongside the Ark of the Covenant and a slew of other sacred Hebrew relics. Records al-Jaldaki found in a mosque in the Taurus Mountains indicated that the horn had been removed from Solomon's temple when it was sacked in 587 BC by the Babylonians, and that eventually it had gone to Medina. But it was taken from Medina during, or shortly after, the siege of 627, when the Meccans invaded.

And it's at this point that the horn is believed to have been given its ebony coating of porcelain enamel, possibly in an attempt to disguise it."

"Or," I said, "because someone in Medina preferred swarthy cock. You mind if I smoke?" I asked her, and she shook her head and pointed at an ashtray.

"A Medinan rabbi of the Banu Nadir tribe was entrusted with the horn's safety. He escaped, making his way west across the desert to Yanbu' al Bahr, then north along the Hejaz all the way to Jerusalem. But two years later, when the Sassanid army lost control of the city to the Byzantine Emperor Heraclius, the horn was taken to a monastery in Malta, where it remained for centuries."

"That's quite the saga for a dildo. But you still haven't answered my question. What makes it so special? What the hell's it *do?*"

"Maybe you've heard enough," she said. The whole time she'd been talking, she hadn't taken her eyes off the thing in the box.

"Yeah, and maybe I haven't," I told her, tapping ash from my Pall Mall into the ashtray. "So, al-Jaldaki goes to Malta and finds the big black dingus."

She scowled again. No, it was more than a scowl; she glowered, and she looked away from the box just long enough to glower *at* me. "Yes," Ellen Andrews said. "At least, that's what he wrote. Al-Jaldaki found it buried in the ruins of a monastery in Malta and then carried the horn with him to Cairo. It seems to have been in his possession until his death in 1342. After that it disappeared, and there's no word of it again until 1891."

I did the math in my head. "Five hundred and forty-nine years," I said. "So it must have gone to a good home. Must have lucked out and found itself a long-lived and appreciative keeper."

"The Freemasons might have had it," she went on, ignoring or oblivious to my sarcasm. "Maybe the Vatican. Doesn't make much difference."

"Okay. So what happened in 1891?"

"A party in Paris happened, in an old house not far from the Cimetière du Montparnasse. Not so much a party, really, as an out-and-out orgy, the way the story goes. This was back before Montparnasse became so fashionable with painters and poets and expatriate Americans. Verlaine was there, though. At the orgy, I mean. It's not clear what happened precisely, but three women and a man died, and afterwards there were rumors of black magic and ritual sacrifice, and tales surfaced of a cult that worshipped some sort of daemonic objet d'art that had made its way to France from Egypt. There was an official investigation, naturally, but someone saw to it that *la Préfecture de Police* came up with zilch."

"Naturally," I said. I glanced at the window. It was getting dark, and I wondered if my ride back to the Bowery had been arranged. "So, where's Black Beauty here been for the past forty-four years?"

Ellen leaned forward, reaching for the lid to the red lacquered box. When she set it back in place, covering that brazen scrap of antiquity, I heard the click again as the lid melded seamlessly with the rest of the box. Now there was only the etching of the *qilin*, and I remembered that the beast has sometimes been referred to as the "Chinese unicorn." Yeah, it seemed odd I'd not thought of that before.

"I think we've probably had enough of a history lesson for now," she said, and I didn't disagree. Truth be told, the whole subject was beginning to bore me. It hardly mattered whether or not I believed in unicorns or enchanted dildos. I'd done my job, so there'd be no complaints from Harpootlian. I admit I felt kind of shitty about poor old Fong, who wasn't such a bad sort. But when you're an errand girl for the wicked folk, that shit comes with the territory. People get killed, and people get worse.

"Well, that's that," I said, crushing out my cigarette in the ashtray. "I should dangle."

"Wait. Please. I promised you a drink, Nat. Don't want you telling Auntie H I was a bad hostess, now do I?" And Ellen Andrews stood up, the red box tucked snugly beneath her left arm.

"No worries, kiddo," I assured her. "If she ever asks, which I doubt, I'll say you were a regular Emily Post."

"I insist," she replied. "I really, truly do," and before I could say another word, she turned and rushed out of the parlor, leaving me alone with all that furniture and the buxom giantesses watching me from the walls. I wondered if there were any servants, or a live-in beau, or if possibly she had the place all to herself, that huge apartment overlooking the river. I pushed the drapes aside and stared out at twilight gathering in the park across the street. Then she was back (minus the red box) with a silver serving tray, two glasses, and a virgin bottle of Sazerac rye.

"Maybe just one," I said, and she smiled. I went back to watching Riverside Park while she poured the whiskey. No harm in a shot or two. It's not like I had some place to be, and there were still a couple of unanswered questions bugging me. Such as why Harpootlian had broken her promise, the one that was supposed to prevent her underlings from practicing their hocus-pocus on me. That is, assuming Ellen Andrews had even bothered to ask permission. Regardless, she didn't need magic or a spell book for her next dirty trick. The Mickey Finn she slipped me did the job just fine.

So, I came to, four, perhaps five hours later—sometime before midnight. By then, as I'd soon learn, the shit had already hit the fan. I woke up sick as a dog and my head pounding like there was an ape with a kettledrum loose inside my skull. I opened my eyes, but it wasn't Ellen Andrews' Baroque clutter and chintz that greeted me, and I immediately shut them again. I smelled the hookahs and the smoldering *bukhoor*, the opium smoke and sandarac and, somewhere underneath it all, that pervasive brimstone stink that no amount of incense can mask. Besides, I'd seen the spiny ginger-skinned thing crouching not far from me, the eunuch, and I knew I was somewhere in the rat's maze labyrinth of Harpootlian's bordello. I started to sit up, but then my stomach lurched and I thought better of it. At least there were soft cushions beneath me, and the silk was cool against my feverish skin.

"You know where you are?" the eunuch asked; it had a woman's voice and a hint of a Russian accent, but I was pretty sure both were only affectations. First rule of demon brothels: Check your preconceptions of male and female at the door. Second rule: Appearances are fucking *meant* to be deceiving.

"Sure," I moaned and tried not to think about vomiting. "I might have a notion or three."

"Good. Then you lie still and take it easy, Miss Beaumont. We've got a few questions need answering." Which made it mutual, but I kept my mouth shut on that account. The voice was beginning to sound not so much feminine as what you might hear if you scraped frozen pork back and forth across a cheese grater. "This afternoon, you were contacted by an associate of Madam Harpootlian's, yes? She told you her name was Ellen Andrews.

That's not her true name, of course. Just something she heard in a motion picture."

"Of course," I replied. "You sort never bother with your real names. Anyway, what of it?"

"She asked you to go see Jimmy Fong and bring her something, yes? Something very precious. Something powerful and rare."

"The dingus," I said, rubbing at my aching head. "Right, but . . . hey . . . Fong was already dead when I got there, scout's honor. Andrews told me one of Szabó's people did him."

"The Chinese gentleman's fate is no concern of ours," the eunuch said. "But we need to talk about Ellen Andrews. She has caused this house serious inconvenience. She's troubled us, and troubles us still."

"You and me both, bub," I said. It was just starting to dawn on me how there were some sizable holes in my memory. I clearly recalled the taste of rye, and gazing down at the park, but then nothing. Nothing at all. I asked the ginger demon, "Where is she? And how'd I get here, anyway?"

"We seem to have many of the same questions," it replied, dispassionate as a corpse. "You answer ours, maybe we shall find the answers to yours along the way."

I knew damn well I didn't have much say in the matter. After all, I'd been down this road before. When Auntie H wants answers, she doesn't usually bother with asking. Why waste your time wondering if someone's feeding you a load of baloney when all you gotta do is reach inside his brain and help yourself to whatever you need?

"Fine," I said, trying not to tense up, because tensing up only ever makes it worse. "How about let's cut the chitchat and get this over with."

"Very well, but you should know," it said, "Madam regrets the necessity of this imposition." And then there were the usual wet, squelching noises as the relevant appendages unfurled and slithered across the floor towards me.

"Sure, no problem. Ain't no secret Madam's got a heart of gold," and maybe I shouldn't have smarted off like that, because when the stingers hit me, they hit hard. Harder than I knew was necessary to make the connection. I might have screamed. I know I pissed myself. And then it was inside me, prowling about, roughly picking its way through my conscious and unconscious mind—through my soul, if that word suits you better. All the heady sounds and smells of the brothel faded away, along with my physical discomfort. For a while I drifted nowhere and nowhen in particular, and then, then I stopped drifting . . .

. . . Ellen asked me, "You ever think you've had enough? Of the life, I mean. Don't you sometimes contemplate just up and blowing town, not even stopping long enough to look back? Doesn't that ever cross your mind, Nat?"

I sipped my whiskey and watched her, undressing her with my eyes and not especially ashamed of myself for doing so. "Not too often," I said. "I've had it worse. This gig's not perfect, but I usually get a fair shake."

"Yeah, usually," she said, her words hardly more than a sigh. "Just, now and then, I feel like I'm missing out."

I laughed, and she glared at me.

"You'd cut a swell figure in a breadline," I said and took another swallow of the rye.

"I hate when people laugh at me."

"Then don't say funny things," I told her.

And that's when she turned and took my glass. I thought she was about to tell me to get lost, blow, and don't let the door hit me in the ass on the way out. Instead, she set the drink down on the silver serving tray, and she kissed me. Her mouth tasted like peaches. Peaches and cinnamon. Then she pulled back, and her eyes flashed red, the way they had in the Yellow Dragon, only now I knew it wasn't an illusion.

"You're a demon," I said, not all that surprised.

"Only two bits. My grandmother . . . well, I'd rather not get into that, if it's all the same to you. Does my pedigree make you uncomfortable?"

"No, it's not a problem," I replied, and she kissed me again. Right about here, I started to feel the first twinges of whatever she'd put into the Sazerac, but, frankly, I was too horny to heed the warning signs.

"I've got a plan," she said, whispering, as if she were afraid someone was listening in. "I have it all worked out, but I wouldn't mind some company on the road."

"I have no . . . no idea . . . what you're talking about," and there was something else I wanted to say, but I'd begun slurring my words and decided against it. I put a hand on her left breast, and she didn't stop me.

"We'll talk about it later," she said, kissing me again, and right about then, that's when the curtain came crashing down, and the ginger-colored demon in my brain turned a page . . .

. . . I opened my eyes, and I was lying in a black room. I mean, a *perfectly* black room. Every wall had been painted matte black, and the ceiling, and the floor. If there were any windows, they'd also been painted over or boarded up. I was cold, and a moment later I realized that was because I was naked. I was naked and lying at the center of a wide white pentagram that had been chalked onto that black floor. A white pentagram held within a white circle. There was a single white candle burning at each of the five points. I looked up, and Ellen Andrews was standing above me. Like me, she was naked. Except she was wearing that dingus from the lacquered box, fitted into a leather harness strapped about her hips. The phallus drooped obscenely and glimmered in the candlelight. There were dozens of runic and Enochian symbols painted on her skin in blood and shit and charcoal. Most of them I recognized. At her feet, there was a small iron cauldron, and a black-handled dagger, and something dead. It might have been a rabbit, or a very small dog. I couldn't be sure which, because she'd skinned it.

Ellen looked down and saw me looking up at her. She frowned and tilted her head to one side. For just a second, there was something undeniably predatory in that expression, something murderous. All spite and not a jot of mercy. For that second, I was face-to-face with the one-quarter of her bloodline that changed all the rules, the ancestor she hadn't wanted to talk about. But then that second passed, and she softly whispered, "I have a plan, Natalie Beaumont."

"What are you doing?" I asked her. But my mouth was so dry and numb, my throat so parched, it felt like I took forever to cajole my tongue into shaping those four simple words.

"No one will know," she said. "I promise. Not Harpootlian, not Szabó, not anyone. I've been over this a thousand times, worked all the angles." And she went down on one knee then, leaning over me. "But you're supposed to be asleep, Nat."

"Ellen, you don't cross Harpootlian," I croaked.

"Trust me," she said.

In that place, the two of us adrift on an island of light in an endless sea of blackness, she was the most beautiful woman I'd ever seen. Her hair was down now, and I reached up, brushing it back from her face. When my fingers moved across her scalp, I found two stubby horns, but it wasn't anything a girl couldn't hide with the right hairdo and a hat.

"Ellen, what are you doing?"

"I'm about to give you a gift, Nat. The most exquisite gift in all creation. A gift that even the angels might covet. You wanted to know what the unicorn does. Well, I'm not going to tell you, I'm going to *show* you."

She put a hand between my legs and found I was already wet.

I licked at my chapped lips, fumbling for words that wouldn't come. Maybe I didn't know what she was getting at, this *gift*, but I had a feeling I didn't want any part of it, no matter how exquisite it might be. I knew these things, clear as day, but I was lost in the beauty of her, and whatever protests I might have uttered, they were about as sincere as ol' Brer Rabbit begging Brer Fox not to throw him into that briar patch. I could say I was bewitched, but it would be a lie.

She mounted me then, and I didn't argue.

"What happens now?" I asked.

"Now I fuck you," she replied. "Then I'm going to talk to my grandmother." And, with that, the world fell out from beneath me again. And the ginger-skinned eunuch moved along to the next tableau, that next set of memories I couldn't recollect on my own . . .

. . . Stars were tumbling from the skies. Not a few stray shooting stars here and there. No, all the stars were falling. One by one, at first, and then the sky was raining pitchforks, only it wasn't rain, see. It was light. The whole sorry world was being born or was dying, and I saw it didn't much matter which. Go back far enough, or far enough forward, the past and future wind up holding hands, cozy as a couple of lovebirds. Ellen had thrown open a doorway, and she'd dragged me along for the ride. I was so cold. I couldn't understand how there could be that much fire in the sky, and me still freezing my tits off like that. I lay there shivering as the brittle heavens collapsed. I could feel her inside me. I could feel *it* inside me, and same as I'd been lost in Ellen's beauty, I was being smothered by that ecstasy. And then . . . then the eunuch showed me the gift, which I'd forgotten . . . and which I would immediately forget again.

How do you write about something, when all that remains of it is the faintest of impressions of glory? When all you can bring to mind is the empty place where a memory ought to be and isn't, and only that conspicuous absence is there to remind you of what cannot ever be recalled? Strain as you might, all that effort hardly adds up to a trip for biscuits. So, how do you write it down? You don't, *that's* how. You do your damnedest to think about what came next, instead, knowing your sanity hangs in the balance.

So, here's what came after the gift, since *le godemichet maudit* is a goddamn Indian giver if ever one were born. Here's the curse that rides shotgun on the gift, as impossible to obliterate from reminiscence as the other is to awaken.

There were falling stars, and that unendurable cold . . . and then the empty, aching socket to mark the countermanded gift . . . and then I saw the unicorn. I don't mean the dingus. I mean the *living creature*, standing in a glade of cedars, bathed in clean sunlight and radiating a light all its own. It didn't look much like what you see in story books or those medieval tapestries they got hanging in the Cloisters. It also didn't look much like the beast carved into the lid of Fong's wooden box. But I knew what it was, all the same.

A naked girl stood before it, and the unicorn kneeled at her feet. She sat down, and it rested its head on her lap. She whispered reassurances I couldn't hear, because they were spoken as softly as falling snow. And then she offered the unicorn one of her breasts, and I watched as it suckled. This scene of chastity and absolute peace lasted maybe a minute, maybe two, before the trap was sprung and the hunters stepped out from the shadows of the cedar boughs. They killed the unicorn, with cold iron lances and swords, but first the unicorn killed the virgin who'd betrayed it to its doom . . .

. . . and Harpootlian's ginger eunuch turned another page (a ham-fisted analogy if ever there were one, but it works for me), and we were back in the black room. Ellen and me. Only two of the candles were still burning, two guttering, half-hearted counterpoints to all that darkness. The other three had been snuffed out by a sudden gust of wind that had smelled of rust, sulfur, and slaughterhouse floors. I could hear Ellen crying, weeping somewhere in the darkness beyond the candles and the periphery of her protective circle. I rolled over onto my right side, still shivering, still so cold I couldn't imagine being warm ever again. I stared into the black, blinking and dimly amazed that my eyelids hadn't frozen shut. Then something snapped into focus, and there she was, cowering on her hands and knees, a tattered rag of a woman lost in the gloom. I could see her stunted, twitching tail, hardly as long as my middle finger, and the thing from the box was still strapped to her crotch. Only now it had a twin, clutched tightly in her left hand.

I think I must have asked her what the hell she'd done, though I had a pretty good idea. She turned towards me, and her eyes . . . well, you see that sort of pain, and you spend the rest of your life trying to forget you saw it.

"I didn't understand," she said, still sobbing. "I didn't understand she'd take so much of me away."

A bitter wave of conflicting, irreconcilable emotion surged and boiled about inside me. Yeah, I knew what she'd done to me, and I knew I'd been used for something unspeakable. I knew *violation* was too tame a word for it, and that I'd been marked forever by this gold-digging half-breed of a twist. And part of me was determined to drag her kicking and screaming to Harpootlian. Or fuck it, I could kill her myself, and take my own sweet time doing so. I could kill her the way the hunters had murdered the unicorn. But—on the other hand—the woman I saw lying there before me was shattered almost beyond recognition. There'd been a steep price for her trespass, and she'd paid it and then some. Besides, I was learning fast that when you've been to Hades' doorstep with someone, and the two of you've made it back more or less alive, there's a bond, whether you want it or not. So, there we were, a cheap, latter-day parody of Orpheus and Eurydice, and all I could think about was holding her, tight as I could, until she stopped crying and I was warm again.

"She took *so much*," Ellen whispered. I didn't ask what her grandmother had taken. Maybe it was a slice of her soul, or maybe a scrap of her humanity. Maybe it was the memory of the happiest day of her life, or the ability to taste her favorite food. It didn't seem to matter. It was gone, and she'd never get it back. I reached for her, too cold and too sick to speak, but sharing her hurt and needing to offer my hollow consolation, stretching out to touch . . .

. . . and the eunuch said, "Madam wishes to speak with you now," and that's when I realized the parade down memory lane was over. I was back at Harpootlian's, and there was a clock somewhere chiming down to three a.m., the dead hour. I could feel the nasty welts the stingers had left at the base of my skull and underneath my jaw, and I still hadn't shaken off the hangover from that tainted shot of rye whiskey. But above and underneath and all about these mundane discomforts was a far more egregious pang, a portrait of that guileless white beast cut down and its blood spurting from gaping wounds. Still, I did manage to get myself upright without puking. Sure, I gagged once or twice, but I didn't puke. I pride myself on that. I sat with my head cradled in my hands, waiting for the room to stop tilting and sliding around like I'd gone for a spin on the Coney Island Wonder Wheel.

"Soon, you'll feel better, Miss Beaumont."

"Says you," I replied. "Anyway, give me half a fucking minute, will you please? Surely your employer isn't gonna cast a kitten if you let me get my bearings first, not after the work over you just gave me. Not after—"

"I will remind you, her patience is not infinite," the ginger demon said firmly, and then it clicked its long claws together.

"That so?" I asked. "Well, who the hell's is?" But I'd gotten the message, plain and clear. The gloves were off, and whatever forbearance Auntie H might have granted me in the past, it was spent, and now I was living on the installment plan. I took a deep breath and struggled to my feet. At least the eunuch didn't try to lend a hand.

I can't say for certain when Yeksabet Harpootlian set up shop in Manhattan, but I have it on good faith that Magdalena Szabó was here first. And anyone who knows her onions knows the two of them have been at each other's throats since the day Auntie H decided to claim a slice of the action for herself. Now, you'd think there'd be plenty enough of the hellion cock-and-tail trade to go around, what with all the netherworlders who call the Five Boroughs their home away from home. And likely as not you'd be right. Just don't try telling that to Szabó or Auntie H. Sure, they've each got their elite stable of "girls and boys," and they both have more customers than they know what to do with. Doesn't stop them from spending every waking hour looking for a way to banish the other once and for all—or at least find the unholy grail of competitive advantages.

Now, by the time the ginger-skinned eunuch led me through the chaos of Auntie H's stately pleasure dome, far below the subways and sewers and tenements of the Lower East Side, I already had a pretty good idea the dingus from Jimmy Fong's shiny box was meant to be Harpootlian's trump card. Only, here was Ellen Andrews, this mutt of a courier gumming up the works, playing fast and loose with the loving cup. And here was me, stuck smack in the middle, the unwilling stooge in her double-cross.

As I followed the eunuch down the winding corridor that ended in Auntie H's grand salon, we passed doorway after doorway, all of them opening onto scenes of inhuman passion and madness, the most odious of perversions, and tortures that make short work of merely mortal flesh. It would be disingenuous to say I looked away. After all, this wasn't my first time. Here were the hinterlands of wanton physical delight and agony, where the two become indistinguishable in a rapturous *Totentanz*. Here were spectacles to remind me how Doré and Hieronymus Bosch never even came close, and all of it laid bare for the eyes of any passing voyeur. You see, there are no locked doors to be found at Madam Harpootlian's. In fact, there are no doors at all.

"It's a busy night," the eunuch said, though it looked like business as usual to me.

"Sure," I muttered. "You'd think the Shriners were in town. You'd think Mayor La Guardia himself had come down off his high horse to raise a little hell."

And then we reached the end of the hallway, and I was shown into the mirrored chamber where Auntie H holds court. The eunuch told me to wait, then left me alone. I'd never seen the place so empty. There was no sign of the usual retinue of rogues, ghouls, and archfiends, only all those goddamn mirrors, because no one looks directly at Madam Harpootlian and lives to tell the tale. I chose a particularly fancy looking glass, maybe ten feet high and held inside an elaborate gilded frame. When Harpootlian spoke up, the mirror rippled like it was only water, and my reflection rippled with it.

"Good evening, Natalie," she said. "I trust you've been treated well?"

"You won't hear any complaints outta me," I replied. "I always say, the Waldorf-Astoria's got nothing on you."

She laughed then, or something that we'll call laughter for the sake of convenience.

"A crying shame we're not meeting under more amicable circumstances. Were it not for this unpleasantness with Miss Andrews, I'd offer you something—on the house, of course."

"Maybe another time," I said.

"So, you *know* why you're here?"

"Sure," I said. "The dingus I took off the dead Chinaman. The salami with the fancy French name."

"It has many names, Natalie. Karkadann's Brow, *el consolador sangriento*, the Horn of Malta—"

"*Le godemichet maudit*," I said. "Me, I'm just gonna call it Ellen's cock."

Harpootlian grunted, and her reflection made an ugly dismissive gesture. "It is nothing of Miss Andrews. It is mine, bought and paid for. With the sweat of my own brow did I track down the spoils of al-Jaldaki's long search. It's my investment, one purchased with so grievous a forfeiture this quadroon mongrel could not begin to appreciate the severity of her crime. But you, Natalie, you know, don't you? You've been privy to the wonders of Sulaymān's talisman, so I think, maybe, you are cognizant of my loss."

"I can't exactly say what I'm cognizant of," I told her, doing my best to stand up straight and not flinch or look away. "I saw the murder of a creature I didn't even believe in yesterday morning. That was sort of an eye opener, I'll grant you. And then there's the part I can't seem to conjure up, even after golden boy did that swell Roto-Rooter number on my head."

"Yes. Well, that's the catch," she said, and smiled. There's no shame in saying I looked away then. Even in a mirror, the smile of Yeksabet Harpootlian isn't something you want to see straight on.

"Isn't there always a catch?" I asked, and she chuckled.

"True, it's a fleeting boon," she purled. "The gift comes, and then it goes, and no one may ever remember it. But always, *always* they will long for it again, even hobbled by that forgetfulness."

"You've lost me, Auntie," I said, and she grunted again. That's when I told her I wouldn't take it as an insult to my intelligence or expertise if she laid her cards on the table and spelled it out plain and simple, like she was talking to a woman who didn't regularly have tea and crumpets with the damned. She mumbled something to the effect that maybe she gave me too much credit, and I didn't disagree.

"Consider," she said, "what it is, a unicorn. It is the incarnation of purity, an avatar of innocence. And here is the *power* of the talisman, for that state of grace which soon passes from us each and every one is forever locked inside the horn, the horn become the phallus. And in the instant that it brought you, Natalie, to orgasm, you knew again that innocence, the bliss of a child before it suffers corruption."

I didn't interrupt her, but all at once I got the gist.

"Still, you are only a mortal woman, so what negligible, insignificant sins could you have possibly committed during your short life? Likewise, whatever calamities and wrongs have been visited upon your flesh *or* your soul, they are trifles. But say, instead, you survived the war in Paradise, if you refused the yoke and so are counted among the exiles, then you've persisted down all the long eons. You were already broken and despoiled billions of years before the coming of man. And your transgressions outnumber the stars.

"Now," she asked, "what would *you* pay, were you so cursed, to know even one fleeting moment of that stainless, former existence?"

Starting to feel sick to my stomach all over again, I said, "More to the point, if I *always* forgot it, immediately, but it left this emptiness I feel—"

"You would come back," Auntie H smirked. "You would come back again and again and again, because there would be no satiating that void, and always would you hope that maybe this time it would take and you might *keep* the memories of that former immaculate condition."

"Which makes it priceless, no matter what you paid."

"Precisely. And now Miss Andrews has forged a copy—an *identical* copy, actually—meaning to sell one to me, and one to Magdalena Szabó. That's where Miss Andrews is now."

"Did you tell her she could hex me?"

"I would never do such a thing, Natalie. You're much too valuable to me."

"*But* you think I had something to do with Ellen's mystical little counterfeit scheme."

"Technically, you did. The ritual of division required a supplicant, someone to *receive* the gift granted by the unicorn, before the summoning of a succubus mighty enough to affect such a difficult twinning."

"So maybe, instead of sitting here bumping gums with me, you should send one of your torpedoes after her. And, while we're on the subject of how you pick your little henchmen, maybe—"

"Natalie," snarled Auntie H from someplace not far behind me. "Have I failed to make myself *understood?* Might it be I need to raise my voice?" The floor rumbled, and tiny hairline cracks began to crisscross the surface of the looking glass. I shut my eyes.

"No," I told her. "I get it. It's a grift, and you're out for blood. But you *know* she used me. Your lackey, it had a good, long look around my upper story, right, and there's no way you can think I was trying to con you."

For a dozen or so heartbeats, she didn't answer me, and the mirrored room was still and silent, save all the moans and screaming leaking in through the walls. I could smell my own sour sweat, and it was making me sick to my stomach.

"There are some grey areas," she said finally. "Matters of sentiment and lust, a certain reluctant infatuation, even."

I opened my eyes and forced myself to gaze directly into that mirror, at the abomination crouched on its writhing throne. And all at once, I'd had enough, enough of Ellen Andrews and her dingus, enough of the cloak-and-dagger bullshit, and definitely enough kowtowing to the monsters.

"For fuck's sake," I said, "I only just met the woman this afternoon. She drugs and rapes me, and you think that means she's my sheba?"

"Like I told you, I think there are grey areas," Auntie H replied. She grinned, and I looked away again.

"Fine. You tell me what it's gonna take to make this right with you, and I'll do it."

"Always so eager to please," Auntie H laughed, and, once again, the mirror in front of me rippled. "But, since you've asked, and as I do not doubt your *present* sincerity, I will tell you. I want her dead, Natalie. Kill her, and all will be . . . forgiven."

"Sure," I said, because what the hell else was I going to say. "But if she's with Szabó—"

"I have spoken already with Magdalena Szabó, and we have agreed to set aside our differences long enough to deal with Miss Andrews. After all, she has attempted to cheat us both, in equal measure."

"How do I find her?"

"You're a resourceful young lady, Natalie," she said. "I have faith in you. Now . . . if you will excuse me," and, before I could get in another word, the mirrored room dissolved around me. There was a flash, not of light, but a flash of the deepest abyssal darkness, and I found myself back at the Yellow Dragon, watching through the bookshop's grimy windows as the sun rose over the Bowery.

There you go, the dope on just how it is I found myself holding a gun on Ellen Andrews, and just how it is she found herself wondering if I was angry enough or scared enough or desperate enough to pull the trigger. And like I said, I chambered a round, but she just stood there. She didn't even flinch.

"I wanted to give you a gift, Nat," she said.

"Even if I believed that—and I don't—all I got to show for this *gift* of yours is a nagging yen for something I'm never going to get back. We lose our innocence, it stays lost. That's the way it works. So, all I got from you,

Ellen, is a thirst can't ever be slaked. That and Harpootlian figuring me for a clip artist."

She looked hard at the gun, then looked harder at me.

"So what? You thought I was gonna plead for my life? You thought maybe I was gonna get down on my knees for you and beg? Is that how you like it? Maybe you're just steamed 'cause I was on top—"

"Shut up, Ellen. You don't get to talk yourself out of this mess. It's a done deal. You tried to give Auntie H the high hat."

"And you honestly think she's on the level? You think you pop me and she lets you off the hook, like nothing happened?"

"I do," I said. And maybe it wasn't as simple as that, but I wasn't exactly lying, either. I needed to believe Harpootlian, the same way old women need to believe in the infinite compassion of the little baby Jesus and Mother Mary. Same way poor kids need to believe in the inexplicable generosity of Popeye the Sailor and Santa Claus.

"It didn't have to be this way," she said.

"I didn't dig your grave, Ellen. I'm just the sap left holding the shovel."

And she smiled that smug smile of hers, and said, "I get it now, what Auntie H sees in you. And it's not your knack for finding shit that doesn't want to be found. It's not that at all."

"Is this a guessing game," I asked, "or do you have something to say?"

"No, I think I'm finished," she replied. "In fact, I think I'm done for. So let's get this over with. By the way, how many women *have* you killed?"

"You played me," I said again.

"Takes two to make a sucker, Nat," she smiled.

Me, I don't even remember pulling the trigger. Just the sound of the gunshot, louder than thunder.

TIDAL FORCES

CHARLOTTE SAYS, "That's just it, Em. There wasn't any pain. I didn't feel anything much at all." She sips her coffee and stares out the kitchen window, squinting at the bright Monday morning sunlight. The sun melts like butter across her face. It catches in the strands of her brown hair, like a late summer afternoon tangling itself in dead corn-stalks. It deepens the lines around her eyes and at the corners of her mouth. She takes another sip of coffee, then sets her cup down on the table. I've never once seen her use a saucer.

And the next minute seems to last longer than it ought to last, longer than the mere sum of the sixty seconds that compose it, the way time stretches out to fill in awkward pauses. She smiles for me, and so I smile back. I don't want to smile, but isn't that what you do? The person you love is frightened, but she smiles anyway. So you have to smile back, despite your own fear. I tell myself it isn't so much an act of reciprocation as an acknowledgement. I could be more honest with myself and say I only smiled back out of guilt.

"I *wish* it had hurt," she says, finally, on the other side of all that long, long moment. I don't have to ask what she means, though *I* wish that *I* did. I wish I didn't already know. She says the same words over again, but more quietly than before, and there's a subtle shift in emphasis. "I wish it *had* hurt."

I apologize and say I shouldn't have brought it up again, and she shrugs.

"No, don't be sorry, Em. Don't let's be sorry for anything."

I'm stacking days, building a house of cards made from nothing but days. Monday is the Ace of Hearts. Saturday is the Four of Spades. Wednesday is the Seven of Clubs. Thursday night is, I suspect, the Seven of Diamonds, and it might be heavy enough to bring the whole precarious thing tumbling down around my ears. I would spend an entire hour watching cards fall, because time would stretch, the same way it stretches out to fill in awkward pauses, the way time is stretched thin in that thundering moment of a car crash. Or at the edges of a wound.

If it's Monday morning, I can lean across the breakfast table and kiss her, as if nothing has happened. And if we're lucky, that might be the moment that endures almost indefinitely. I can kiss her, taste her, savor her, drawing the moment out like a card drawn from a deck. But no, now it's Thursday night, instead of Monday morning. There's something playing on the television in the bedroom, but the sound is turned all the way down, so that whatever the something may be proceeds like a silent movie filmed in color and without intertitles. A movie for lip readers. There's no other light but the light from the television. She's lying next to me, almost undressed, asking me questions about the book I don't think I'm ever going to be able to finish. I understand she's not asking them because she needs to know the answers, which is the only reason I haven't tried to change the subject.

"The Age of Exploration was already long over with," I say. "For all intents and purposes, it ended early in the Seventeenth Century. Everything after that—reaching the north and south poles, for instance—is only a series of footnotes. There were no great blank spaces left for men to fill in. No more 'Here be monsters.'"

She's lying on top of the sheets. It's the middle of July and too hot for anything more than sheets. Clean white sheets and underwear. In the glow from the television, Charlotte looks less pale and less fragile than she would if the bedside lamp were on, and I'm grateful for the illusion. I want to stop talking, because it all sounds absurd, pedantic, all these unfinished, half-formed ideas that add up to nothing much at all. I want to stop talking and just lie here beside her.

"So writers made up stories about lost worlds," she says, having heard all this before and pretty much knowing it by heart. "But those made-up worlds weren't really *lost*. They just weren't *found* yet. They'd not yet been imagined."

"That's the point," I reply. "The value of those stories rests in their insistence that blank spaces still do exist on the map. They *have* to exist, even if it's necessary to twist and distort the map to make room for them. All those overlooked islands, inaccessible plateaus in South American jungles, the sunken continents and the entrances to a hollow earth, they were important psychological buffers against progress and certainty. It's no coincidence that they're usually places where time has stood still, to one degree or another."

"But not really so much time," she says, "as the processes of evolution, which require time."

"See? You understand this stuff better than I do," and I tell her she should write the book. I'm only half joking. That's something else Charlotte knows. I lay my hand on her exposed belly, just below the navel, and she flinches and pulls away.

"Don't do that," she says.

"All right. I won't. I wasn't thinking." I was thinking, but it's easier if I tell her that I wasn't.

Monday morning. Thursday night. This day or that. My own private house of cards, held together by nothing more substantial than balance and friction. And the loops I'd rather make than admit to the present. Connecting dot-to-dot, from here to there, from there to here. Here being half an hour before dawn on a Saturday, the sky growing lighter by slow degrees. Here, where I'm on my knees, and Charlotte is standing naked in front of me. Here, now, when the perfectly round hole above her left hip and below her ribcage has grown from a pinprick to the size of the saucers she never uses for her coffee cups.

"I don't think it will hurt," she tells me. And I can't see any point in asking whether she means, *I don't think it will hurt me*, or *I don't think it will hurt you*.

"Now?" I ask her, and she says, "No. Not yet. Wait."

So, handed that reprieve, I withdraw again to the relative safety of the Ace of Hearts—or Monday morning, call it what you will. In my mind's eye, I run back to the kitchen washed in warm yellow sunlight. Charlotte is telling me about the time, when she was ten years old, that she was shot with a BB gun, her brother's Red Ryder BB gun.

"It wasn't an accident," she's telling me. "He meant to do it. I still have the scar from where my mother had to dig the BB out of my ankle with tweezers and a sewing needle. It's very small, but it's a scar all the same."

"Is that what it felt like, like being hit with a BB?"

"No," she says, shaking her head and gazing down into her coffee cup. "It didn't. But when I think about the two things, it seems like there's a link between them, all these years apart. Like, somehow, this thing was an echo of the day he shot me with the BB gun."

"A meaningful coincidence," I suggest. "A sort of synchronicity."

"Maybe," Charlotte says. "But maybe not." She looks out the window again. From the kitchen, you can see the three oaks and her flower bed and the land running down to the rocks and the churning sea. "It's been an awfully long time since I read Jung. My memory's rusty. And, anyway, maybe it's not a coincidence. It could be something else. Just an echo."

"I don't understand, Charlotte. I really don't think I know what you mean."

"Never mind," she says, not taking her eyes off the window. "Whatever I do or don't mean, it isn't important."

The warm yellow light from the sun, the colorless light from a color television. A purplish sky fading towards the light of false dawn. The complete absence of light from the hole punched into her body by something that wasn't a BB. Something that also wasn't a shadow.

"What scares me most," she says (and I could draw *this* particular card from anywhere in the deck), "is that it didn't come back out the other side. So, it must still be lodged in there, *in* me."

I was watching when she was hit. I saw when she fell. I'm coming to that.

"Writers made up stories about *lost* worlds" she says again, after she's flinched, after I've pulled my hand back from the brink. "They did it because we were afraid of having found all there *was* to find. Accurate maps became more disturbing, at least unconsciously, than the idea of sailing off the edge of a flat world."

"I don't want to talk about the book."

"Maybe that's why you can't finish it."

"Maybe you don't know what you're talking about."

"Probably," she says, without the least bit of anger or impatience in her voice.

322

I roll over, turning my back on Charlotte and the silent television. Turning my back on what cannot be heard and doesn't want to be acknowledged. The sheets are damp with sweat, and there's the stink of ozone that's not *quite* the stink of ozone. The acrid smell that always follows her now, wherever she goes. No. That isn't true. The smell doesn't follow her, it comes *from* her. She radiates the stink that is almost, but not quite, the stink of ozone.

"Does *Alice's Adventures in Wonderland* count?" she asks me, even though I've said I don't want to talk about the goddamned book. I'm sure that she heard me, and I don't answer her.

Better not to linger too long on Thursday night.

Better if I return, instead, to Monday morning. Only Monday morning. Which I have carelessly, randomly, designated here as the Ace of Hearts, and hearts are cups, so Monday morning is the Ace of Cups. In four days more, Charlotte will ask me about Alice, and though I won't respond to the question (at least not aloud), I *will* recall that Lewis Carroll considered the *Queen* of Hearts—who rules over the Ace and is also the Queen of Cups—I will recollect that Lewis Carroll considered her the embodiment of a certain type of passion. That passion, he said, which is ungovernable, but which exists as an aimless, unseeing, furious thing. And he said, also, that the Queen of Cups, the Queen of Hearts, is not to be confused with the *Red* Queen, whom he named another brand of passion altogether.

Monday morning in the kitchen.

"My brother always claimed he was shooting at a blue jay and missed. He said he was aiming for the bird and hit me. He said the sun was in his eyes."

"Did he make a habit of shooting songbirds?"

"Birds and squirrels," she says. "Once he shot a neighbor's cat, right between the eyes." And Charlotte presses the tip of an index finger to the spot between her brows. "The cat had to be taken to a vet to get the BB out, and my mom had to pay the bill. Of course, he said he wasn't shooting at the cat. He was shooting at a sparrow and missed."

"What a little bastard," I say.

"He was just a kid, only a year older than I was. Kids don't mean to be cruel, Em, they just are sometimes. From our perspectives, they appear cruel. They exist outside the boundaries of adult conceits of morality. Anyway, after the cat, my dad took the BB gun away from him. So, after that, he always kind of hated cats."

But here I am neglecting Wednesday, overlooking Wednesday, even though I went to the trouble of drawing a card for it. And it occurs to me now I didn't even draw one for Tuesday. Or Friday, for that matter. It occurs to me that I'm becoming lost in this ungainly metaphor, that the tail is wagging the dog. But Wednesday was of consequence. More so than was Thursday night, with its mute TV and the Seven of Diamonds and Charlotte shying away from my touch.

The Seven of Clubs. Wednesday, or the Seven of Pentacles, seen another way round. Charlotte, wrapped in her bathrobe, comes downstairs after taking a hot shower, and she finds me reading Kip Thorne's *Black Holes & Time Warps*, the book lying lewdly open in my lap. I quickly close it, feeling like I'm a teenager again, and my mother's just barged into my room to find me masturbating to the *Hustler* centerfold. Yes, your daughter is a lesbian, and yes, your girlfriend is reading quantum theory behind your back.

Charlotte stares at me awhile, staring silently, and then she stares at the thick volume lying on the coffee table, *Principles of Physical Cosmology*. She sits down on the floor, not far from the sofa. Her hair is dripping, spattering the hardwood.

"I don't believe you're going to find anything in there," she says, meaning the books.

"I just thought . . ." I begin, but let the sentence die unfinished, because I'm not at all sure *what* I was thinking. Only that I've always turned to books for solace.

And here, on the afternoon of the Seven of Pentacles, this Wednesday weighted with those seven visionary chalices, she tells me what happened in the shower. How she stood in the steaming spray watching the water rolling down her breasts and *across* her stomach and *up* her buttocks before falling into the hole in her side. Not in defiance of gravity, but in perfect accord with gravity. She hardly speaks above a whisper. I sit quietly listening, wishing that I could suppose she'd only lost her mind. Recourse to wishful thinking, the seven visionary chalices of the Seven of Pentacles, of the Seven of Clubs, or Wednesday. Running away to hide in the comfort of insanity, or the authority of books, or the delusion of lost worlds.

"I'm sorry, but what the fuck do I say to that?" I ask her, and she laughs. It's a terrible sound, that laugh, a harrowing, forsaken sound. And then she stops laughing, and I feel relief spill over me, because now she's crying, instead. There's shame at the relief, of course, but even the shame is welcome. I couldn't have stood that terrible laughter much longer. I go to her and put my arms around her and hold her, as if holding her will make it all better. The sun's almost down by the time she finally stops crying.

I have a quote from Albert Einstein, from sometime in 1912, which I found in the book by Kip Thorne, the book Charlotte caught me reading on Wednesday: "Henceforth, space by itself, and time by itself, are doomed to fade away into mere shadows, and only a kind of union of the two will preserve an independent reality."

Space, time, shadows.

As I've said, I was watching when she was hit. I saw when she fell. That was Saturday last, two days before the yellow morning in the kitchen, and not to be confused with the *next* Saturday which is the Four of Spades. I was sitting on the porch and had been watching two noisy grey-white gulls wheeling far up against the blue summer sky. Charlotte had been working in her garden, pulling weeds. She called out to me, and I looked away from the birds. She was pointing towards the ocean, and at first I wasn't sure what it was she wanted me to see. I stared at the breakers shattering themselves against the granite boulders, and past that, to the horizon where the water was busy with its all but eternal task of shouldering the burden of the heavens. I was about to tell her that I didn't see anything. This wasn't true, of course. I just didn't see anything out of the ordinary, nothing special, nothing that ought not occupy that time and that space.

I saw nothing to give me pause.

But then I did.

Space, time, spacetime, shadows.

I'll call it a shadow, because I'm at a loss for any more appropriate word. It was spread out like a shadow rushing across the waves, though, at first, I thought I was seeing something dark moving *beneath* the waves. A very big fish, perhaps. Possibly a large shark or a small whale. We've seen whales in the bay before. Or it might have been caused by a cloud passing in front of the sun, though there were no clouds that day. The truth is I knew it was none of these things. I can sit here all night long, composing a list of what it *wasn't*, and I'll never come any nearer to what it might have been.

"Emily," she shouted. "Do you *see* it?" And I called back that I did. Having noticed it, it was impossible *not* to see that grimy, indefinite smear sliding swiftly towards the shore. In a few seconds more, I realized, it would reach the boulders, and if it wasn't something beneath the water, the rocks wouldn't stop it. Part of my mind still insisted it was only a shadow, a freakish trick of the light, a mirage. Nothing substantial, certainly nothing malign, nothing that could do us any mischief or injury. No need to be alarmed, and yet I don't ever remember being as afraid as I was then. I couldn't move, but I yelled for Charlotte to run. I don't think she heard me. Or if she heard me, she was also too mesmerized by the sight of the thing to move.

I was safe, there on the porch. It came no nearer to me than ten or twenty yards. But Charlotte, standing alone at the garden gate, was well within its circumference. It swept over her, and she screamed, and fell to the ground. It swept over her, and then was gone, vanishing into the tangle of green briars and poison ivy and wind-stunted evergreens behind our house. I stood there, smelling something that almost smelled like ozone. And maybe it's an awful cliché to put to paper, but my mind *reeled*. My heart raced, and my mind reeled. For a fraction of an instant I was seized by something that was neither déjà vu nor vertigo, and I thought I might vomit.

But the sensation passed, like the shadow had, or the shadow of a shadow, and I dashed down the steps and across the grass to the place where Charlotte sat stunned among the clover and the dandelions. Her clothes and skin looked as though they'd been misted with the thinnest sheen of . . . what? Oil? No, no, no, not oil at all. But it's the closest I can come to describing that sticky brownish iridescence clinging to her dress and her face, her arms and the pickets of the garden fence and to every single blade of grass.

"It knocked me down," she said, sounding more amazed than hurt or frightened. Her eyes were filled with startled disbelief. "It wasn't *anything*, Em. It wasn't anything at all, but it knocked me right off my feet."

"Are you hurt?" I asked, and she shook her head.

I didn't ask her anything else, and she didn't say anything more. I helped her up and inside the house. I got her clothes off and led her into the downstairs shower. But the oily residue that the shadow had left behind had already begun to *evaporate*—and again, that's not the right word, but it's the best I can manage—before we began trying to scrub it away with soap and scalding clean water. By the next morning, there would be no sign of the stuff anywhere, inside the house or out of doors. Not so much as a stain.

"It knocked me down. It was just a shadow, but it knocked me down." I can't recall how many times she must have said that. She repeated it over and over again, as though repetition would render it less implausible, less inherently ludicrous. "A shadow knocked me down, Em. A shadow knocked me down."

But it wasn't until we were in the bedroom, and she was dressing, that I noticed the red welt above her left hip, just below her ribs. It almost looked like an insect bite, except the center was . . . well, when I bent down and examined it closely, I saw there *was* no center. There was only a hole. As I've said, a pinprick, but a hole all the same. There wasn't so much as a drop of blood, and she swore to me that it didn't hurt, that she was fine, and it was nothing to get excited about. She went to the medicine cabinet and found a Band-Aid to cover the welt. And I didn't see it again until the next day, which as yet has no playing card, the Sunday before the warm yellow Monday morning in the kitchen.

I'll call that Sunday by the Two of Spades.

It rains on the Two of Spades. It rains cats and dogs all the damn day long. I spend the afternoon sitting in my study, parked there in front of my computer, trying to find the end to Chapter Nine of the book I can't seem to finish. The rain beats at the windows, all rhythm and no melody. I write a line, then delete it. One step forward, two steps back. Zeno's "Achilles and the tortoise" paradox played out at my keyboard—"That which is in locomotion must arrive at the halfway stage before it arrives at the goal," and each halfway stage has its own halfway stage, *ad infinitum.* These are the sorts of rationalizations that comfort me as I only pretend to be working. This is the *true* reward of my twelve years of college, these erudite excuses for not getting the job done. In the days to come, I will set the same apologetics and exculpations to work on the problem of how a shadow can possibly knock a woman down, and how a hole can be explained away as no more than a wound.

Sometime after seven o'clock, Charlotte raps on the door to ask me how it's going, and what I'd like for dinner. I haven't got a ready answer for either question, and she comes in and sits down on the futon near my desk. She has to move a stack of books to make a place to sit. We talk about the weather, which she tells me is supposed to improve after sunset, that the meteorologists are saying Monday will be sunny and hot. We talk about the book—my exploration of the phenomenon of the literary *Terrae Anachronismorum*, from 1714 and Simon Tyssot de Patot's *Voyages et Aventures de Jacques Massé*, to 1918 and Edgar Rice Burroughs's *Out of Time's Abyss* (and beyond; see Aristotle on Zeno, above). I close Microsoft Word, accepting that nothing more will be written until at least tomorrow.

"I took off the Band-Aid," she says, reminding me of what I've spent the day trying to forget.

"When you fell, you probably jabbed yourself on a stick or something," I tell her, which doesn't explain *why* she fell, but seeks to dismiss the result of the fall.

"I don't think it was a stick."

"Well, whatever it was, you hardly got more than a scratch."

And that's when she asks me to look. I would have said no, if saying no were an option.

She stands and pulls up her T-shirt, just on the left side, and points at the hole, though there's no way I could ever miss it. On the rainy Two of Spades, hardly twenty-four hours after Charlotte was knocked off her feet by a shadow, it's already grown to the diameter and circumference of a dime. I've never seen anything so black in all my life, a black so complete I'm almost certain I would go blind if I stared into it too long. I don't say these things. I don't remember what I say, so maybe I say nothing at all. At first, I think the skin at the edges of the hole is puckered, drawn tight like the skin at the edges of a scab. Then I see that's not the case at all. The skin around the periphery of the hole in her flesh is *moving*, rotating, swirling about that preposterous and undeniable blackness.

"I'm scared," she whispers. "I mean, I'm *really* fucking scared, Emily."

I start to touch the wound, and she stops me. She grabs hold of my hand and stops me.

"Don't," she says, and so I don't.

"You *know* that it can't be what it looks like," I tell her, and I think maybe I even laugh.

"Em, I don't know anything at all."

"You damn well know *that* much, Charlotte. It's some sort of infection, that's all, and—"

She releases my hand, only to cover my mouth before I can finish. Three fingers to still my lips, and she asks me if we can go upstairs, if I'll please make love to her.

"Right now, that's all I want," she says. "In all the world, there's nothing I want more."

I almost make her promise that she'll see our doctor the next day, but already some part of me has admitted to myself this is nothing a physician can diagnose or treat. We have moved out beyond medicine. We have been pushed down into these nether regions by the shadow of a shadow. I have stared directly into that hole, and already I understand it's not merely a hole in Charlotte's skin, but a hole in the cosmos. I could parade her before any number of physicians and physicists, psychologists and priests, and not a one would have the means to seal that breach. In fact, I suspect they would deny the evidence, even if it meant denying all their science and technology and faith. There are things worse than blank spaces on maps. There are moments when certitude becomes the greatest enemy of sanity. Denial becomes an antidote.

Unlike those other days and those other cards, I haven't chosen the Two of Spades at random. I've chosen it because on Thursday she asks me if Alice counts. And I have begun to assume that everything counts, just as everything is claimed by that infinitely small, infinitely dense point beyond the event horizon.

"Would you tell me, please," said Alice, a little timidly, "why you are painting those roses?"

Five and Seven said nothing, but looked at Two. Two began, in a low voice, "Why, the fact is, you see, Miss, this here ought to have been a red rose-tree, and we put a white one in by mistake . . ."

On that rainy Sunday, that Two of Spades with an incriminating red brush concealed behind its back, I do as she asks. I cannot do otherwise. I bed her. I fuck her. I am tender and violent by turns, as is she. On that stormy evening, that Two of Pentacles, that Two of *Coins* (a dime, in this case), we both futilely turn to sex looking for surcease from dread. We try to go *back* to our lives before she fell, and this is not so very different from all those "lost worlds" I've belabored in my unfinished manuscript: Maple White Land, Caprona, Skull Island, Symzonia, Pellucidar, the Mines of King Solomon. In our bed, we struggle to fashion a refuge from the present, populated by the reassuring, dependable past. And I am talking in circles within circles within circles, spiraling inward or out, it doesn't matter which.

I am arriving, very soon now, at the end of it, at the Saturday night—or more precisely, just before dawn on the Saturday morning—when the story I am writing here ends. And begins. I've taken too long to get to the point, if I assume the validity of a linear narrative. If I assume any one moment can take precedence over any other or assume the generally assumed (but unproven) inequity of relevance.

A large rose-tree stood near the entrance of the garden; the roses growing on it were white, but there were three gardeners at it, busily painting them red.

We are as intimate in those moments as two women can be, when one is forbidden to touch a dime-sized hole in the other's body. At some point, after dark, the rain stops falling, and we lie naked and still, listening to owls and whippoorwills beyond the bedroom walls.

On Wednesday, she comes downstairs and catches me reading the dry pornography of mathematics and relativity. Wednesday is the Seven of Clubs. She tells me there's nothing to be found in those books, nothing that will change what has happened, what may happen.

She says, "I don't know what will be left of me when it's done. I don't even know if I'll be enough to satisfy it, or if it will just keep getting bigger and bigger and bigger. I think it might be insatiable."

On Monday morning, she sips her coffee. We talk about eleven-year-old boys and BB guns.

But here, at last, it is shortly before sunup on a Saturday. Saturday, the Four of Spades. It's been an hour since Charlotte woke screaming, and I've sat and listened while she tried to make sense of the nightmare. The hole in her side is as wide as a softball (and, were this more obviously a comedy, I would list the objects that, by accident, have fallen into it the last few days). Besides the not-quite-ozone smell, there's now a faint but constant whistling sound, which is air being pulled into the hole. In the dream, she tells me, she knew exactly what was on the other side of the hole, but then she forgot most of it as soon as she awoke. In the dream, she says, she wasn't afraid, and that we were sitting out on the porch watching the sea while she explained it all to me. We were drinking Cokes, she said, and it was hot, and the air smelled like dog roses.

"You know I don't like Coke," I say.

"In the dream you did."

She says we were sitting on the porch, and that awful shadow came across the sea again, only this time it didn't frighten her. This time I saw it first and pointed it out to her, and we watched together as it moved rapidly towards the shore. This time, when it swept over the garden, she wasn't standing there to be knocked down.

"But you said you saw what was on the other side."

"That was later on. And I would tell you what I saw, if I could remember. But there was the sound of pipes, or a flute," she says. "I can recall that much of it, and I knew, in the dream, that the hole runs all the way to the middle, to the very center."

"The very center of what?" I ask, and she looks at me like she thinks I'm intentionally being slow-witted.

"The center of everything that ever was and is and ever will be, Em. The *center*. Only, somehow the center is both empty and filled with . . ." She trails off and stares at the floor.

"Filled with what?"

"I can't *say*. I don't *know*. But whatever it is, it's been there since before there was time. It's been there alone since before the universe was born."

I look up, catching our reflections in the mirror on the dressing table across the room. We're sitting on the edge of the bed, both of us naked, and I look a decade older than I am. Charlotte, though, she looks *so* young, younger than when we met. Never mind that yawning black mouth in her abdomen. In the half light before dawn, she seems to shine, a preface to the coming day, and I'm reminded of what I read about Hawking radiation and the quasar jet streams that escape some singularities. But this isn't the place or time for theories and equations. Here, there are only the two of us, and morning coming on, and what Charlotte can and cannot remember about her dream.

"Eons ago," she says, "it lost its mind. Though I don't think it ever really *had* a mind, not like a human mind. But still, it went insane, from the knowledge of what it is and what it can't ever stop being."

"You said you'd forgotten what was on the other side."

"I have. Almost all of it. This is *nothing*. If I went on a trip to Antarctica and came back and all I could tell you about my trip was that it had been very white, Antarctica, that would be like what I'm telling you now about the dream."

The Four of Spades. The Four of Swords, which cartomancers read as stillness, peace, withdrawal, the act of turning sight back upon itself. They say nothing of the attendant perils of introspection or the damnation that would be visited upon an intelligence that could never look *away*.

"It's blind," she says. "It's blind, and insane, and the music from the pipes never ends. Though, they aren't really pipes."

This is when I ask her to stand up, and she only stares at me a moment or two before doing as I've asked. This is when I kneel in front of her, and I'm dimly aware that I'm kneeling before the inadvertent avatar of a god, or God, or a pantheon, or something so immeasurably ancient and pervasive that it may as well be divine. Divine or infernal; there's really no difference, I think.

"What are you doing?" she wants to know.

"I'm losing you," I reply, "that's what I'm doing. Somewhere, some*when*, I've *already* lost you. And that means I have nothing *left* to lose."

Charlotte takes a quick step back from me, retreating towards the bedroom door, and I'm wondering if she runs, will I chase her? Having made this decision, to what lengths will I go to see it through? Would I force her? Would it be rape?

"I know what you're going to do," she says. "Only you're *not* going to do it, because I won't let you."

"You're being devoured."

"It was a dream, Em. It was only a stupid, crazy dream, and I'm not even sure what I actually remember and what I'm just making up."

"Please," I say, "please let me try." And I watch as whatever resolve she might have had breaks apart. She wants as badly as I do to hope, even though we both know there's no hope left. I watch that hideous black gyre above her hip, below her left breast. She takes two steps back towards me.

"I don't think it will hurt," she tells me. And I can't see any point in asking whether she means, *I don't think it will hurt me*, or *I don't think it will hurt you*. "I don't think there will be any pain."

"I can't see how it possibly matters anymore," I tell her. I don't say anything else. With my right hand, I reach into the hole, and my arm vanishes almost up to my shoulder. There's cold beyond any comprehension of cold. I glance up, and she's watching me. I think she's going to scream, but she doesn't. Her lips part, but she doesn't scream. I feel my arm being tugged so violently I'm sure that it's about to be torn from its socket, the humerus ripped from the glenoid fossa of the scapula, cartilage and ligaments snapped, the subclavian artery severed before I tumble back to the floor and bleed to death. I'm almost certain that's what will happen, and I grit my teeth against that impending amputation.

"I can't feel you," Charlotte whispers. "You're inside me now, but I can't feel you anywhere."

Then.

The hole is closing. We both watch as that clockwise spiral stops spinning, then begins to turn widdershins. My freezing hand clutches at the void, my fingers straining for any purchase. Something's changed; I understand that perfectly well. Out of desperation, I've chanced upon some remedy, entirely by instinct or luck, the solution to an insoluble puzzle. I also understand that I need to pull my arm back out again, before the edges of the hole reach my bicep. I imagine the collapsing rim of curved spacetime slicing cleanly through sinew and bone, and then I imagine myself fused at the shoulder to that point just above Charlotte's hip. Horror vies with cartoon absurdities in an instant that seems so swollen it could accommodate an age.

Charlotte's hands are on my shoulders, gripping me tightly, pushing me away, shoving me as hard as she's able. She's saying something, too, words I can't quite hear over the roar at the edges of that cataract created by the implosion of the quantum foam.

Oh, Kitty, how nice it would be if we could only get through into Looking-glass House! I'm sure it's got oh! such beautiful things in it! Let's pretend there's a way of getting through into it, somehow, Kitty. Let's pretend the glass has got all soft as gauze, so that we can get through . . .

I'm watching a shadow race across the sea.

Warm sun fills the kitchen.

I draw another card.

Charlotte is only ten years old, and a BB fired by her brother strikes her ankle. Twenty-three years later, she falls at the edge of our flower garden.

Time. Space. Shadows. Gravity and velocity. Past, present, and future. All smeared, every distinction lost, and nothing remaining that can possibly be quantified.

I shut my eyes and feel her hands on my shoulders.

And across the space within her, as my arm bridges countless light years, something brushes against my hand. Something wet, and soft, something indescribably abhorrent. Charlotte pushed me, and I was falling backwards, and now I'm not. It has seized my hand in its own—or wrapped some celestial tendril about my wrist—and for a single heartbeat it holds on before letting go.

. . . whatever it is, it's been there since before there was time. It's been there alone since before the universe was born.

There's pain when my head hits the bedroom floor. There's pain and stars and twittering birds. I taste blood and realize that I've bitten my lip. I open my eyes, and Charlotte's bending over me. I think there are galaxies trapped within her eyes. I glance down at that spot above her left hip, and the skin is smooth and whole. She's starting to cry, and that makes it harder to see the constellations in her irises. I move my fingers, surprised that my arm and hand are both still there.

"I'm sorry," I say, even if I'm not sure what I'm apologizing for.

"No," she says, "don't be sorry, Em. Don't let's be sorry for anything. Not now. Not ever again."

THE PRAYER OF
NINETY CATS

N THIS DARKENED THEATRE, the screen shines like the moon. More like the moon than this simile might imply, as the moon makes no light of her own, but instead adamantly casts off whatever the sun sends her way. The silver screen reflects the light pouring from the projector booth. And this particular screen truly *is* a silver screen, the real deal, not some careless metonym lazily recalling more glamorous Hollywood movie-palace days. There's silver dust embedded in its tightly-woven silk matte, an apotropaic which might console any Slovak grandmothers in attendance, given the evening's bill of fare. But, then again, is it not also said that the silvered-glass of mirrors offends these hungry phantoms? And isn't the screen itself a mirror, not so very unlike the moon? The moon flashes back the sun, the screen flashes back the dazzling glow from the projector's Xenon arc lamp. Here, then, is an irony, of sorts, as it is sometimes claimed the moroaică, strigoi mort, vampir, and vrykolakas are incapable of casting reflections—apparently consuming light much as the gravity well of a black hole does. In these flickering, moving pictures, there must surely be some incongruity or paradox, beginning with Murnau's Orlok, Browning's titular Dracula, and Carl Theodor Dreyer's sinister Marguerite Chopin.

Of course, pretend demons need no potent, tried-and-true charm to ward them off, no matter how much we may wish to fear them. Still, we go through the motions. We *need* to fear, and when summoning forth these simulacra, to convince ourselves of their authenticity, we must also have a means of dispelling them. We sit in darkness and watch the monsters and smugly remind ourselves these are merely actors playing unsavory parts, reciting dialogue written to shock, scandalize, and unnerve. All shadows are carefully planned. That face is clever make-up, and a man becoming a bat no more than a bit of trick photography accomplished with flash powder, splicing, and a lump of felt and rabbit fur dangled from piano wire. We sit in the darkness, safely reenacting and mocking and laughing at the silly, delicious fears of our ignorant forebears. If all else fails, we leave our seats and escape to the lobby. We turn on the light. No need to invoke crucified messiahs and the Queen of Heaven, not when we have Saint Thomas Edison on our side. Though, still another irony arises (we are gathering a veritable platoon of ironies, certainly), as these same monsters were brought to you courtesy of Mr. Edison's tinkerings and profiteering. Any truly wily sorcerer, any witch worth her weight in mandrake and foxglove, knows how very little value there is in conjuring a fearful thing if it may not then be banished at will.

The theatre air is musty and has a sickly sweet sourness to it. It swims with the rancid ghosts of popcorn butter, spilled sodas, discarded chewing gum, and half a hundred varieties of candy lost beneath velvet seats and between the carpeted aisles. Let's say these are the top notes of our perfume. Beneath them lurk the much fainter heart notes of sweat, piss, vomit, cum, soiled diapers—all the pungent gases and fluids a human body may casually expel. Also, though smoking has been forbidden here for decades, the reek of stale cigarettes and cigars persists. Finally, now, the base notes, not to be recognized right away, but registering after half an hour or more has passed, settling in to bestow solidity and depth to this complex *Eau de Parfum*. In the main, it strikes the nostrils as dust, though more perceptive noses may discern dry rot, mold, and aging mortar. Considered thusly, the atmosphere of this theatre might, appropriately, echo that of a sepulcher, shut away and ripe from generations of use.

Crossing the street, you might have noticed a title and the names of the players splashed across the gaudy marquee. After purchasing your ticket from the young man with a death's head tattooed on the back of his left hand (he has a story, if you care to hear), you might have paused to view the relevant lobby cards or posters on display. You might have considered the concessions. These are the rituals before the rite. You might have wished you'd brought along an umbrella, because it's beginning to look like there might be rain later. You may even go to the payphone near the restrooms, but, these days, that happens less and less, and there's talk of having it removed.

Your ticket is torn in half, and you find a place to sit. The lights do not go down, because they were never up. You wait, gazing nowhere in particular, thinking no especial thoughts, until that immense moth-gnawed curtain the color of pomegranates opens wide to reveal the silver screen.

And so we come back to where we began.

With no fanfare or overture, the darkness is split apart as the antique projector sputters reluctantly to life. The auditorium is filled with the noisy, familiar cadence of wheels and sprockets, the pressure roller and the take-up reel, as the film speeds along at twenty-four frames per second and the shutter tricks the eyes and brain into perceiving continuous motion instead of a blurred procession of still photographs. By design, it is all a lie, start to finish. It is all an illusion.

There are no trailers for coming attractions. There might have been in the past, as there might have been cartoons featuring Bugs Bunny and Daffy Duck, or newsreels extolling the evils of Communism and the virtues of soldiers who go away to die in foreign countries. Tonight, there's only the feature presentation, and it begins with jarring abruptness, without so much as a title sequence or the name of the director. Possibly, a few feet of the opening reel were destroyed by the projectionist at the last theatre that screened the film, a disagreeable, ham-fisted man who drinks on the job and has been known to nod off in the booth. We can blame him, if we like. But it may also be there never were such niceties, and that *this* 35mm strip of acetate, celluloid, and polyester was always meant to begin *just so*.

Likewise, the film's score—which has been compared favorably to Wojciech Kilar's score for Campion's *The Portrait of a Lady*—seems to begin not at any proper beginning. As cellos and violins compete with kettledrums in a whirl of syncopated rhythms, there is the distinct impression of having stumbled upon a thing already in progress. This may well be the director's desired effect.

EXT. ČACHTICE CASTLE HILL, LITTLE CARPATHIANS.
SUNSET.

> WOMAN'S VOICE (fearfully):
> Katarína, is that you?
> (pause)
> Katarína? If it is you, say so.

The camera lingers on this bleak spire of evergreens, brush, and sand-stone, gray-white rock tinted pink as the sun sinks below the horizon and night claims the wild Hungarian countryside. There are sheer ravines, talus slopes, and wide ledges carpeted with mountain ash, fenugreek, tatra blush, orchids, and thick stands of feather reed grass. The music grows quieter now, drums diminishing, strings receding to a steady vibrato undercurrent as the score hushes itself, permitting the night to be heard. The soundtrack fills with the calls of nocturnal birds, chiefly tawny and long-eared owls, but also nightingales, swifts, and nightjars. From streams and hidden pools, there comes the chorus of frog song. Foxes cry out to one another. The scene is at once breathtaking and forbidding, and you lean forward in your seat, arrested by this austere beauty.

> WOMAN'S VOICE (angry):
> It is a poor jest, Katarína. It is a poor, poor jest, indeed,
> and I've no patience for your games tonight.

> GIRL'S VOICE (soft, not unkind):
> I'm not Katarína. Have you forgotten my name already?

The camera's eye doesn't waver, even at the risk of this shot becoming monotonous. And we see that atop the rocky prominence stands the tumble-down ruins of Čachtice Castle, *Csejte vára* in the mother tongue. Here it has stood since the 1200s, when Kazimir of Hunt-Poznan found himself in need of a sentry post on the troubled road to Moravia. And later, it was claimed by the Hungarian oligarch Máté Csák of Trencsén, the heroic Count Matthew.

Then it went to Rudolf II, Holy Roman Emperor, who spent much of his life in alchemical study, searching for the Philosopher's Stone. And, finally, in 1575, the castle was presented as a wedding gift from Lord Chief Justice Ferenc Nádasdy to his fifteen-year-old bride Báthory Erzsébet, or Alžbeta, the Countess Elizabeth Báthory. The name (one or another of the lot) will doubtless ring a bell, though infamy has seen she's better known to many as the Blood Countess.

The cinematographer works more sleight of hand, and the jagged lineament of the ruins is restored to that of Csejte as it would have stood when the Countess was alive. A grand patchwork of Romanesque and Gothic architecture, its formidable walls and towers loom high above the drowsy village of Vrbové. The castle rises—no, it sprouts—the castle *sprouts* from the bluff in such a way as to seem almost a natural, integral part of the local geography, something *in situ*, carved by wind and rain rather than by the labors of man.

The film jump-cuts to an owl perched on a pine branch. The bird blinks— once, twice—spreads its wings, and takes to the air. The camera lets it go and doesn't follow, preferring to remain with the now-vacant branch. Several seconds pass before the high-pitched scream of a rabbit reveals the reason for the owl's departure.

GIRL'S VOICE:
Ever is it the small things that suffer. That's what they say,
you know? The Tigress of Csejte, she will have them all,
because there is no end to her hunger.

Another jump cut brings us to the castle gates, and the camera pans slowly across the masonry of curtain walls, parapets, and up the steep sides of a horseshoe-shaped watchtower. Jump-cut again, and we are shown a room illuminated by the flickering light of candles. There is a noblewoman seated in an enormous and somewhat fanciful chair, upholstered with fine brocade, its oaken legs and arms ending with the paws of a lion, or a dragon.

Or possibly a tigress.

So, a woman seated in an enormous, bestial chair. She wears the "Spanish farthingale" and stiffened undergarments fashionable during this century.

Her dress is made of the finest Florentine silk. Her waist is tightly cinched, her ample breasts flattened by the stays. Were she standing, her dress might remind us of an hourglass. Her head is framed with a wide ruff of starched lace, and her arms held properly within trumpet sleeves, more lace at the cuffs to ring her delicate hands. There is a wolf pelt across her lap, and another covers her bare feet. The candlelight is gracious, and she might pass for a woman of forty, though she's more than a decade older. Her hair, which is the color of cracked acorn shells, has been meticulously braided and pulled back from her round face and high forehead. Her eyes seem dark as rubies.

INT. COUNTESS BÁTHORY'S CHAMBER. NIGHT.

COUNTESS (tersely):
Why are you awake at this hour, child? You should be sleeping.
Haven't I given you a splendid bed?

GIRL (seen dimly, in silhouette):
I don't like being in that room alone. I don't like the shadows
in that room. I try not to see them—

COUNTESS (close-up, her eyes fixed on the child):
Oh, don't be silly. A shadow has not yet harmed anyone.

GIRL (almost whispering):
Begging your pardon, My Lady, but these shadows mean to
do me mischief. I hear them whisper, and they do. They are
shadows cast by wicked spirits. They do not speak to you?

COUNTESS (sighs, frowning):
I don't speak with shadows.

GIRL (coyly):
That isn't what they say in the village.
(pause)
Do you truly know the Prayer of Ninety Cats?

By now, it is likely that the theatre, which only a short time ago so filled your thoughts, has receded, fading almost entirely from your conscious mind. This is usually the way of theatres, if the films they offer have any merit at all. The building is the spectacle which precedes the spectacle it has been built to contain, not so different from the relationship of colorful wrapping paper and elaborately tied bows to the gifts hidden within. You're greeted by a mock-grand façade and the blazing electric marquee, and are then admitted into the catchpenny splendor of the lobby. All these things make an impression, and set a mood, but all will fall by the wayside. Exiting the theatre after a film, you'll hardly note a single detail. Your mind will be elsewhere, processing, reflecting, critiquing, amazed, or disappointed.

Onscreen, the Countess' candlelit bedchamber has been replaced by the haggard faces of peasant women, mothers and grandmothers, gazing up at the terrible edifice of Csejte. Over the years, so many among them have sent their daughters away to the castle, hearing that servants are cared for and well compensated. Over the years, none have returned. There are rumors of black magic and butchery, and, from time to time, girls have simply vanished from Vrbové, and also from the nearby town of Čachtice, from whence the fortress took its name. The women cross themselves and look away.

Dissolve to scenes of the daughters of landed aristocracy and the lesser gentry preparing their beautiful daughters for the *gynaeceum* of ecsedi Báthory Erzsébet, where they will be schooled in all the social graces, that they might make more desirable brides and find the best marriages possible. Carriages rattle along the narrow, precipitous road leading up to the castle, wheels and hooves trailing wakes of dust. Oblivious lambs driven to the slaughter, freely delivered by ambitious and unwitting mothers.

Another dissolve, to winter in a soundstage forest, and the Countess walks between artificial sycamore maples, ash, linden, beech, and elderberry. The studio "greens men" have worked wonders, meticulously crafting this forest from plaster, burlap, epoxy, wire, Styrofoam, from lumber armatures and the limbs and leaves of actual trees. The snow is as phony as the trees, but no less convincing, a combination of SnowCel, SnowEx foam, and Powderfrost, dry-foam plastic snow spewed from machines; biodegradable, nontoxic polymers to simulate a gentle snowfall after a January blizzard.

But the mockery is perfection. The Countess stalks through drifts so convincing that they may as well be real. Her furs drag behind her, and her boots leave deep tracks. Two huge wolves follow close behind, and when she stops, they come to her and she scratches their shaggy heads and pats their lean flanks and plants kisses behind their ears. A trained crow perches on a limb overhead, cawing, cawing, cawing, but neither the woman nor the wolves pay it any heed. The Countess speaks, and her breath fogs.

> COUNTESS (to wolves):
> You are my true children. Not Ursula or Pál or Miklós.
> And you are also my true inamoratos, my most beloved,
> not Ferenc, who was only ever a husband.

If tabloid gossip and backlot hearsay are to be trusted, this scene has been considerably shortened and toned down from the original script. We do not see the Countess' sexual congress with the wolves. It is only implied by her affections, her words, and by the lewd canticle of a voyeur crow. The scene is both stark and magnificent. It is a final still point before the coming tempest, before the horrors, a moment imbued with grace and menacing tranquility. The camera cuts to Herr Kramer in its counterfeit tree, and you're watching its golden eyes watching the Countess and her wolves, and anything more is implied.

INT. ČACHTICE CASTLE/DRESSING ROOM. MORNING.

The Countess is seated before a looking glass held inside a carved wooden frame, motif of dryads and satyrs. We see the Countess as a reflection, and behind her, a servant girl. The servant is combing the Countess' brown hair with an ivory comb. The Countess is no longer a young woman. There are lines at the edges of her mouth and beneath her eyes.

> COUNTESS (furrowing her brows):
> You're pulling my hair again. How many times must I tell you
> to be careful. You're not deaf, are you?

SERVANT (almost whispering):
No, My Lady.

COUNTESS (icily):
Then when I speak to you, you hear me perfectly well.

SERVANT:
Yes, My Lady.

The ivory comb snags in the Countess' hair, and she stands, spinning about to face the terrified servant girl. She snatches the comb from the girl's hand. Strands of Elizabeth's hair are caught between the teeth.

COUNTESS (tone of disbelief):
You wretched little beast. Look what you've done.

The Countess slaps the servant with enough force to split her lip. Blood spatters the Countess' hand as the servant falls to the floor. The Countess is entranced by the crimson beads speckling her pale skin.

COUNTESS (whisper):
You ... filthy ... wretch ...

FADE TO BLACK.

FADE IN:

INT. DREAM MIRROR.

The Countess stands in a dim pool of light, before a towering mirror, a grotesque nightmare version of the one on her dressing table. The nymphs, satyrs, and dryads are life-size, and move, engaged in various and sundry acts of sexual abandon. This dark place is filled with sounds of desire, orgasm, drunken debauchery. In the mirror is a far younger Elizabeth Báthory. But, as we watch, as the Countess watches, this young woman rapidly ages, rushing through her twenties, thirties, her forties. The Countess screams, commanding the mirror cease these awful visions. The writhing creatures that form the frame laugh and mock her screams.

FLASH CUT TO:

EXT. SNOW-COVERED FIELD. DAYLIGHT.

The Countess stands naked in the falling snow, her feet buried up to the ankles. The snowflakes turn red. The red snow becomes a red rain, and she's drenched. The air is a red mist.

FLASH CUT TO:

INT. DREAM MIRROR.

Nude and drenched in blood, the Countess gazes at her reflection, her face and body growing young before her eyes. The looking glass shatters.

FADE TO BLACK.

The Hungary of the film has more in common with the landscape of Hans Christian Andersen and the Brothers Grimm than with any Hungary that exists now or ever has existed. It is an archetypal vista, as much a myth as Stoker's Transylvania and Sheridan Le Fanu's Styria. A real place that has, inconveniently, never existed. Little or nothing is said of the political and religious turmoil of Elizabeth's time, or of the war with the Ottoman Turks, aside from the death of the Countess' husband at the hands of General Giorgio Basta. If you're a stickler for accuracy, these omissions are unforgivable. But most of the men and women who sit in the theatre, entranced by the light flashed back from the screen, will never notice. People do not generally come to the movies hoping for recitations of dry history. Few will care that pivotal events in the film never occurred, because they are happening *now*, unfolding before the eyes of all who have paid the price of admission.

INT. COUNTESS' BEDCHAMBER. NIGHT.

GIRL:
If you have been taught the prayer, say the words aloud.

COUNTESS:
How would you ever know such things, child?

GIRL (turning away):
We have had some of the same tutors, you and I.

The second reel begins with the arrival at Csejte of a woman named Anna Darvulia. In hushed tones, a servant (who dies an especially messy death farther along) refers to her as "the Witch of the Forest." She becomes Elizabeth's lover and teaches her sorcery and the Prayer of Ninety Cats to protect her from all harm. As Darvulia is depicted here, she may as well have inhabited a gingerbread cottage before she came to the Countess, a house of sugary confections where she regularly feasted on lost children. Indeed, shortly after her arrival, and following an admittedly gratuitous sex scene, the subject of cannibalism is introduced. A peasant girl named Júlia, stolen from her home, is brought to the Countess by two of her handmaids and partners in crime, Dorottya and Ilona. The girl is stripped naked and forced to kneel before Elizabeth while the handmaids burn the bare flesh of her back and shoulders with coins and needles that have been placed over an open flame. Darvulia watches on approvingly from the shadows.

INT. KITCHEN. NIGHT.

COUNTESS (smiling):
You shouldn't fret so about your dear mother and father.
I know they're poor, but I will see to it they're compensated
for the loss of their only daughter.

JÚLIA (sobbing):
There is never enough wood in winter, and never enough food.

JULIA (cont.):
We have no shoes and wear rags.

COUNTESS:
And haven't I liberated you from those rags?

JÚLIA:
They need me. Please, My Lady, send me home to them.

The Countess glances over her shoulder to Darvulia, as if seeking approval/ instruction. Darvulia nods once, then the Countess turns back to the sobbing girl.

COUNTESS:
Very well. I'll make you a promise, Júlia.
And I keep my promises. In the morning, I will send your
mother and your father warm clothing and good shoes
and enough firewood to see them through the snows.
And, what's more, I will send you back to them, as well.

JÚLIA:
You would do that?

COUNTESS:
Certainly, I will. I'll not have any use for you after this evening,
and I detest wastefulness.

This scene has been cut from most prints. If you have any familiarity with the trials and tribulations of the film's production, and with the censorship that followed, you'll be surprised, and possibly pleased, to find it has not been excised from this copy. It may also strike you as relatively tame, compared to many less controversial, but far more graphic, portions of the film.

COUNTESS:
When we are finished here . . .
(pause)

When we're finished, and my hunger is satisfied, I will speak
with my butcher—a skilled man with a knife and cleaver—and
he will see to it that your corpse is dressed in such a way that it
can never be mistaken for anything but that of a sow. I'll have
the meat salted and smoked, then sent to them, as evidence of
my generosity. They will have their daughter back, and, in the
bargain, will not go hungry. Are they fond of sausage, Júlia?
I'd think you would make a marvelous *debreceni.*

Critics and movie buffs who lament the severe treatment the film has
suffered at the hands of nervous studio executives, skittish distributors, and
the MPAA often point to Júlia's screams, following these lines, as an example of how great cinema may be lost to censorship. Sound editors and Foley
artists are said to have crafted the unsettling and completely inhuman effect
by mixing the cries of several species of birds, the squeal of a pig, and the
steam whistle of a locomotive. The scream continues as this scene dissolves
to a delirious montage of torture and murder. The Countess' notorious iron
maiden makes an appearance. A servant is dragged out into a snowy courtyard, and once her dress and underclothes have been savagely ripped away,
the woman is bound to a wooden stake. Elizabeth Báthory pours buckets
of cold water over the servant's body until she freezes to death and her
body glistens like an ice sculpture.

The theatre is so quiet that you begin to suspect everyone else has had
enough and left before The End. But you don't dare look away long enough
to see whether this is in fact the case.

The Countess sits in her enormous lion- (or dragon- or tigress-) footed
chair, in that bedchamber lit only by candlelight. She strokes the wolf pelt
on her lap as lovingly as she stroked the fur of those living wolves.

"We've had some of the same tutors, you and I," the strange brown girl
says, the gypsy child who claims to be afraid of the shadows in the small
room that has been provided for her.

"Anna's never mentioned you."

"*She* and I have had some of the same tutors," the child whispers. "Now,
My Lady, please speak the words aloud and drive away the evil spirits."

"I have heard of no such prayer," the Countess tells the girl, but the actress' air and intonation make it obvious she's lying. "I've received no such catechism."

"Then shall I teach it to you? For when they are done with me, the shadows might come looking after you, and if you don't know the prayer, how will you hope to defend yourself, My Lady?"

The Countess frowns and mutters, half to herself, half to the child, "I need no defense against shadows. Rather, let the shadows blanch and wilt at the thought of me."

"That same arrogance will be your undoing," the child replies. Then all the candles gutter and are extinguished, and the only light remaining is cold moonlight, getting in through the parted draperies. The child is gone. The Countess sits in her clawed chair and squeezes her eyes tightly shut. You may once have done very much the same thing, hearing some bump in the night. Fearing an open closet or the space beneath your bed, a window or a hallway. In this moment, Elizabeth Bathory von Ecsed, Alžbeta Bátoriová, the Bloody Lady of Čachtice, she seems no more fearsome for all her fearsome reputation than the child you once were. The boyish girl she herself was, forty-seven, forty-six, forty-eight years before this night. The girl given to tantrums and seizures and dressing up in boy's clothes. She cringes in this dark, moon-washed room, eyelids drawn against the night, and begins, haltingly, to recite the prayer Anna Darvulia has taught her.

"I am in peril, O cloud. Send, O send, you most powerful of Clouds, send ninety cats, for thou are the supreme Lord of Cats. I command you, King of the Cats, I pray you. May you gather them together, even if you are in the mountains, or on the waters, or on the roofs, or on the other side of the ocean . . . tell them to come to me."

Fade to black.

Fade up.

The bedchamber is filled with the feeble colors of a January morning. With the wan luminance of the winter sun in these mountains. The balcony doors have blown open in the night, and a drift of snow has crept into the room. Pressed into the snow there are the barefoot tracks of a child. The Countess opens her eyes. She looks her age, and then some.

Fade to black.

Fade up.

The Countess in her finest farthingale and ruff stands before the altar of Csejte's austere chapel. She gazes upwards at a stained-glass narrative set into the frames of three very tall and very narrow lancet windows. Her expression is distant, detached, unreadable. Following an establishing shot, and then a brief close-up of the Countess' face, the trio of stained-glass windows dominates the screen. The production designer had them manufactured in Prague, by an artisan who was provided detailed sketches mimicking the style of windows fashioned by Harry Clarke and the Irish cooperative An Túr Gloine. As with so many aspects of the film, these windows have inspired heated debate, chiefly regarding their subject matter. The most popular interpretation favors one of the hagiographies from the *Legenda sanctorum*, the tale of St. George and the dragon of Silene.

The stillness of the chapel is shattered by squealing hinges and quick footsteps, as Anna Darvulia rushes in from the bailey. She approaches the Countess, who has turned to meet her.

DARVULIA (angry):
What you seek, Elizabeth, you'll not find it here.

COUNTESS (feigning dismay):
I only wanted an hour's solitude. It's quiet here.

DARVULIA (sneering):
Liar. You came seeking after a solace that shall forever
be denied you, as it has always been denied me. We have
no place here, Elizabeth. Let us leave together.

COUNTESS:
She came to me again last night. How can your prayer protect
me from her, when she also knows it?

Anna Darvulia whispers something in the Countess' ear, then kisses her cheek and leads her from the chapel.

DISSOLVE TO:

Two guards or soldiers thread heavy iron chain through the handles of the chapel doors, then slide the shackle of a large padlock through the links of chain and clamp the lock firmly shut.

Somewhere towards the back of the theatre, a man coughs loudly, and a woman laughs. The man coughs a second time, then mutters (presumably to the woman), and she laughs again. You're tempted to turn about in your seat and ask them to please hold it down, that there are people who came to see the movie. But you don't. You don't take your eyes off the screen, and, besides, you've never been much for confrontation. You also consider going out to the lobby and complaining to the management, but you won't do that, either. It sounds like the man is telling a dirty joke, and you do your best to ignore him.

The film has returned to the snowy soundstage forest. Only now there are many more trees, spaced more closely together. Their trunks and branches are as dark as charcoal, as dark as the snow is light. Together these two elements—trees and snow, snow and trees—form a proper joyance for any chiaroscurist. In the foreground of this *mise-en-scène*, an assortment of taxidermied wildlife (two does, a rabbit, a badger, etc.) watches on with blind acrylic eyes as Anna Darvulia follows a path through the wood. She wears an enormous crimson cloak, the hood all but concealing her face. Her cloak completes the palette of the scene: the black trees, the white of the snow, this red slash of wool. There is a small falcon, a merlin, perched on the woman's left shoulder, and gripped in her left hand (she isn't wearing gloves) is a leather leash. As the music swells—strings, woodwinds, piano, the thunderous kettledrum—the camera pans slowly to the right, tracing the leash from Darvulia's hand to the heavy collar clasped about the Countess' pale throat. Elizabeth is entirely naked, scrambling through the snow on all fours. Her hair is a matted tangle of twigs and dead leaves. Briars have left bloody welts on her arms, legs, and buttocks. There are wolves following close behind her, famished wolves starving in the dead of this endless Carpathian winter. The pack is growing bold, and one of the animals rushes in close, pushing its muzzle between her exposed thighs, thrusting about with its wet nose, lapping obscenely at the Countess' ass and genitals. Elizabeth bares her sharp teeth and, wheeling around, straining against the leash, she snaps viciously at this churlish rake of a wolf. She growls as convincingly as any lunatic or lycanthrope might hope to growl.

All wolves are churlish. All wolves are rakes, especially in fairy tales, and especially this far from spring.

"Have you forgotten the prayer so soon?" Darvulia calls back, her voice cruel and mocking. Elizabeth doesn't answer, but the wolves yelp and retreat.

And as the witch and her pupil pick their way deeper into the forest, we see that the gypsy girl, dressed in a cloak almost identical to Darvulia's— wool dyed that same vivid red—stands among the wolves as they whine and mill about her legs.

Elizabeth awakens in her bed, screaming.

In a series of jump cuts, her screams echo through the empty corridors of Csejte.

(This scene is present in all prints, having somehow escaped the same fate as the unfilmed climax of the Countess' earlier trek through the forest—a testament to the fickle inconsistency of censors. In an interview she gave to the Croatian periodical *Hrvatski filmski ljetopis* [Autumn 2003], the actress who played Elizabeth reports that she actually did suffer a spate of terrible nightmares after making the film, and that most of them revolved around this particular scene. She says, "I have only been able to watch it [the scene] twice. Even now, it's hard to imagine myself having been on the set that day. I've always been afraid of dogs, and those were *real* wolves.")

In the fourth reel, you find you're slightly irritated when the film briefly loses its otherwise superbly claustrophobic focus, during a Viennese interlude surely meant, instead, to build tension. The Countess' depravity is finally, inevitably brought to the attention of the Hungarian Parliament and King Matthias. The plaintiff is a woman named Imre Megyery, the Steward of Sávár, who became the guardian of the Countess' son, Pál Nádasdy, after the death of her husband. It doesn't help that the actor who plays György Thurzó, Matthias' palatine, is an Australian who seems almost incapable of getting the Hungarian accent right. Perhaps he needed a better dialect coach. Perhaps he was lazy. Possibly, he isn't a very good actor.

INT. COUNTESS' BEDCHAMBER. NIGHT.

Elizabeth and Darvulia in the Countess' bed, after a vigorous bout of lovemaking. Lovemaking, sex, fucking, whatever. Both women are nude. The corpse of a third woman lies between them. There's no blood, so how she died is unclear.

DARVULIA:

Megyery the Red, she plots against you. She has gone to the
King, and very, very soon Thurzó's notaries will arrive to
poke and pry and be the King's eyes and ears.

COUNTESS:

But you will keep me safe, Anna. And there is the prayer . . .

DARVULIA (gravely):

These are men, with all the power of the King and the Church
at their backs. You must take this matter seriously, Elizabeth.
The dark gods will concern themselves only so far, and after
that we are on our own. Again, I beg you to at least
consider abandoning Csejte.

COUNTESS:

No. No, and don't ask again. It is my home. Let Thurzó's men
come. I will show them nothing. I will let them see nothing.

DARVULIA:

It isn't so simple, my sweet Erzsébet. Ferenc is gone, and
without a husband to protect you . . . you must consider the
greed of relatives who covet your estates, and consider, also,
debts owed to you by a king who has no intention of ever
settling them. Many have much to gain from your fall.

COUNTESS (stubbornly):

There will be no fall.

You sit up straight in your reclining theatre seat. You've needed to urinate
for the last half hour, but you're not about to miss however much of the

film you'd miss during a quick trip to the restroom. You try not to think about it; you concentrate on the screen and not your aching bladder.

INT. COUNTESS' BEDCHAMBER. NIGHT.

The Countess sits in her lion-footed chair, facing the open balcony doors. There are no candles burning, but we can see the silhouette of the gypsy girl outlined in the winter moonlight pouring into the room. She is all but naked. The wind blows loudly, howling about the walls of the castle.

COUNTESS (distressed):
No, you're not mine. I can't recall ever having seen you before.
You are nothing of mine. You are some demon sent
by the moon to harry me.

GIRL (calmly):
It is true I serve the moon, Mother, as do you. She is mistress
to us both. We have both run naked while she watched on. We
have both enjoyed her favors. We are each the moon's bitch.

COUNTESS (turning away):
Lies. Every word you say is a wicked lie. And I'll not hear any
more of it. Begone, *strigoi*. Go back to whatever stinking hole
was dug to cradle your filthy gypsy bones.

GIRL (suddenly near tears):
Please do no not say such things, Mother.

COUNTESS (through clenched teeth):
You are not my daughter! This is the price of my sins,
to be visited by phantoms, to be haunted.

GIRL:
I only want to be held, Mother. I only want to be held,
as any daughter would. I want to be kissed.

Slowly, the Countess looks back at the girl. Snow blows in through the draperies, swirling about the child. The girl's eyes flash red-gold. She takes a step nearer the Countess.

GIRL (contd.):
I can protect you, Mother.

COUNTESS:
From what? From whom?

GIRL:
You know from what, and you know from whom.
You would know, even if Anna hadn't told you.
You are not a stupid woman.

COUNTESS:
You do not come to protect me, but to damn me.

GIRL (kind):
I only want to be held, and sung to sleep.

COUNTESS (shuddering):
My damnation.

GIRL (smiling sadly):
No, Mother. You've tended well enough to that on your own.
You've no need of anyone to hurry you along to the pit.

CLOSE-UP – THE COUNTESS

The Countess' face is filled with a mixture of dread and defeat, exhaustion and horror. She shuts her eyes a moment, muttering silently, then opens them again.

COUNTESS (resigned):
Come, child.

MEDIUM SHOT – THE COUNTESS

The Countess sits in her chair, head bowed now, seemingly too exhausted to continue arguing with the girl. From the foreground, the gypsy girl approaches her. Strange shadows seem to loom behind the Countess' chair. The child begins to sing in a sweet, sad, lilting voice, a song that might be a hymn or a dirge.

FADE TO BLACK.

This scene will stay with you. You will find yourself thinking, *That's where it should have ended. That would have made a better ending.* The child's song—only two lines of which are intelligible—will remain with you long after many of the grimmer, more graphic details are forgotten. Two eerie, poignant lines: *Stay with me and together we will live forever./Death is the road to awe.* Later, you'll come across an article in *American Cinematographer* (April 2006), and discover that the screenwriter originally intended this to be the final scene, but was overruled by the director, who insisted it was too anticlimactic.

Which isn't to imply that the remaining twenty minutes are without merit, but only that they steer the film in a different and less subtle, less dreamlike direction. Like so many of the films you most admire—Bergman's *Det sjunde inseglet*, Charlie Kaufman's *Synecdoche, New York*, Herzog's *Herz aus Glas*, David Lynch's *Lost Highway*—this one is speaking to you in the language of dreams, and after the child's song, you have the distinct sense that the film has awakened, jolted from the subconscious to the conscious, the self-aware. It's ironic, therefore, that the next scene is a dream sequence. And it is a dream sequence that has left critics divided over the movie's conclusion and what the director intended to convey. There is a disjointed, tumbling series of images, and it is usually assumed that this is simply a nightmare delivered to the Countess by the child. However, one critic, writing for *Slovenska kinoteka* (June 2005), has proposed it represents a literal divergence of two timelines, dividing the historical Báthory's fate from that of the fictional Báthory portrayed in the film. She notes the obvious, that the dream closely parallels the events of December 29, 1610, the day of the Countess' arrest. A few have argued the series of scenes was never meant to be perceived as a dream (neither the director nor the screenwriter have revealed their intent). The sequence may be ordered as follows:

The Arrival: A retinue on horseback—Thurzó, Imre Megyery, the Countess' sons-in-law, Counts Drugeth de Homonna and Zrínyi, together with an armed escort. The party reaches the Csejte, and the iron gates swing open to admit them.

The Descent: The Palatine's men following a narrow, spiraling stairwell into the depth of the castle. They cover their mouths and noses against some horrible stench.

The Discovery: A dungeon cell strewn with corpses, in various stages of dismemberment and decay. Two women, still living, though clearly mad, their bodies naked and beaten and streaked with filth, are manacled to the stone walls. They scream at the sight of the men.

The Trial: Theodosius Syrmiensis de Szulo of the Royal Supreme Court pronounces a sentence of *perpetuis carceribus*, sparing the Countess from execution, but condemning her to lifelong confinement at Csejte.

The Execution/Pardon of the Accomplices: Three women and one man. Two of the women, Jó Ilona and Dorottya Szentes, are found guilty, publicly tortured, and burned alive. The man, Ujváry János (portrayed as a deformed dwarf), is beheaded before being thrown onto the bonfire with Jó and Dorottya. The third woman, Katarína Beniezky, is spared (this is not explained, and none of the four are named in the film).

The Imprisonment: The Countess sits on her bed as stonemasons brick up the chamber's windows and the door leading out onto the balcony. Then the door is sealed. Close-ups of trowels, mortar, callused hands, Elizabeth's eyes, a Bible in her lap. Last shot from Elizabeth's POV, her head turned away from the camera, as the final few bricks are set in place. She is alone. Fade to black.

Anna Darvulia, "the Witch of the Forest," appears nowhere in this sequence.

FADE IN:

EXT. CSETJE STABLES. DAY.

The Countess watches as Anna Darvulia climbs onto the back of a horse. Once in the saddle, her feet in the stirrups, she stares sorrowfully down at the Countess.

DARVULIA:
I beg you, Erzsébet. Come with me. We'll be safe in the forest.
There are places where no man knows to look.

COUNTESS:
This is my home. Please, don't ask me again.
I won't run from them. I won't.

DARVULIA (speaking French and Croatian):
Ma petite bête douce. Volim te, Erzsébet.
(pause)
Ne m'oublie pas.

COUNTESS (slapping the horse's rump):
Go! Go now, love, before I lose my will.

CUT TO:

EXT. ČACHTICE CASTLE HILL. WINTER. DAY.

Anna Darvulia racing away from the snowbound castle, while the Countess watches from her tower.

COUNTESS (off):
I command you, O King of the Cats, I pray you.
May you gather them together,
Give them thy orders and tell them,
Wherever they may be, to assemble together,
To come from the mountains,
From the waters, from the rivers,
From the rainwater on the roofs, and from the oceans.
Tell them to come to me.

357

FADE TO BLACK.

FADE IN:

INT. COUNTESS' BEDCHAMBER. NIGHT.

The Countess in her enormous chair. The gypsy girl stands before her. As before, she is almost naked. There is candlelight and moonlight. Snow blows in from the open balcony doors.

> GIRL:
> She left you all alone.

> COUNTESS:
> No, child. I sent her away.

> GIRL:
> Back to the wood?

> COUNTESS:
> Back to the wood.

You sit in your seat and breathe the musty theatre smells, the smells which may as well be ghosts as they are surely remnants of long ago moments come and gone. Your full bladder has been all but forgotten. Likewise, the muttering, laughing man and woman seated somewhere behind you. There is room for nothing now but the illusion of moving pictures splashed across the screen. Your eyes and your ears translate the interplay of light and sound into story. The old theatre is a temple, holy in its way, and you've come to worship, to find epiphany in truths captured by a camera's lens. There's no need of plaster saints and liturgies. No need of the intermediary services of a priest. Your god—and the analogy has occurred to you on many occasions—is speaking to you directly, calling down from that wide silk-and-silver window and from Dolby speakers mounted high on the walls. Your god speaks in many voices, and its angels are an orchestra, and every frame is a page of scripture. This mass is rapidly winding down towards benediction.

GIRL:
May I sit at your feet, Mother?

COUNTESS:
Wouldn't you rather have my lap?

GIRL (smiling):
Yes, Mother. I would much rather have your lap.

The gypsy girl climbs into the Countess' lap, her small brown body nestling in the voluminous folds of Elizabeth's dress. The Countess puts her arms around the child, and holds her close. The girl rests her head on the Countess' breast.

GIRL (whisper):
They will come, you know? The men. The soldiers.

COUNTESS:
I know. But let's not think of that, not now. Let's not think on anything much at all.

GIRL:
But you recall the prayer, yes?

COUNTESS:
Yes, child. I recall the prayer. Anna taught me the prayer, just as you taught it to her.

GIRL:
You are so clever, Mother.

CLOSE-UP.

The Countess' hand reaching into a fold of her dress, withdrawing a small silver dagger. The handle is black and polished wood, maybe jet or mahogany. There are occult symbols etched deeply into the metal, all down the length of the blade.

GIRL:

Will you say the prayer for me? No one ever prays for me.

COUNTESS:

I would rather hear you sing, dear. Please, sing for me.

The gypsy girl smiles and begins her song.

GIRL:

Stay with me, and together we will live forever.
Death is the road to awe—

The Countess clamps a hand over the girl's mouth, and plunges the silver dagger into her throat. The girl's eyes go very wide, as blood spurts from the wound. She falls backwards to the floor, and writhes there for a moment. The Countess gets to her feet, triumph in her eyes.

COUNTESS:

You think I didn't know you? You think I did not see?

The girl's eyes flash red-gold, and she hisses loudly, then begins to crawl across the floor towards the balcony. She pulls the knife from her throat and flings it away. It clatters loudly against the floor. The girl's teeth are stained with blood.

GIRL (hoarsely):
You deny me. You dare deny me.

COUNTESS:
You are none of mine.

THE PRAYER OF NINETY CATS

GIRL:
You send me to face the cold alone? To face the moon alone?

The Countess doesn't reply, but begins to recite the Prayer of Ninety Cats. As she does, the girl stands, almost as if she hasn't been wounded. She backs away, stepping through the balcony doors, out into snow and brilliant moonlight. The child climbs onto the balustrade, and it seems for a moment she might grow wings and fly away into the Carpathian night.

COUNTESS:
May these ninety cats appear to tear and destroy
The hearts of kings and princes,
And in the same way the hearts of teachers and judges,
And all who mean me harm,
That they shall harm me not.
(pause)
Holy Trinity, protect me.
And guard Erzsébet from all evil.

The girl turns her back on the Countess, gazing down at the snowy courtyard below.

GIRL:
I'm the one who guarded you, Mother. I'm the one who has kept
you safe.

COUNTESS (raising her voice):
Tell them to come to me.
And to hasten them to bite the heart.
Let them rip to pieces and bite again and again . . .

GIRL:
There's no love in you anywhere. There never was.

COUNTESS:
Do not say that! Don't you dare say that! I have loved—

GIRL (sadly):
You have lusted and called it love. You tangle appetite
and desire. Let me fall, and be done with you.

COUNTESS (suddenly confused):
No. No, child. Come back. No one falls this night.

INT./EXT. NIGHT.

As the Countess moves towards the balcony, the gypsy girl steps off the balustrade
and tumbles to the courtyard below. The Countess cries out in horror and rushes
out onto the balcony

EXT. NIGHT.

The broken body of the girl on the snow-covered flagstones of the courtyard. Blood
still oozes from the wound in her throat, but also from her open mouth and her
nostrils. Her eyes are open. Her blood steams in the cold air. A large crow lands
near her body. The camera pans upwards, and we see the Countess gazing down
in horror at the broken body of the dead girl. In the distance, wolves begin to howl.

EXT. BALCONY. NIGHT.

The Countess is sitting now, her back pressed to the stone columns of the balustrade. She's sobbing, her hands tearing at her hair. She is the very portrait here of
loss and madness.

COUNTESS (weeping):
I didn't know. God help me, I did not know.

FADE UP TO WHITE.

EXT. CSEJTE. MORNING.

A small cemetery near the castle's chapel. Heavy snow covers everything. The dwarf Ujváry János has managed to hack a shallow grave into the frozen earth. The Countess watches as the gypsy girl's small body, wrapped in a makeshift burial shroud, is lowered into the hole. The Countess turns and hurries away across the bailey, and János begins filling the grave in again. Shovelful after shovelful of dirt and frost and snow falls on the body, and slowly it disappears from view. Perched on a nearby headstone, an owl watches. It blinks, and rotates its head and neck 180 degrees, so it appears to be watching the burial upside down.

In a week, you'll write your review of the film, the review you're being paid to write, and you'll note that the genus and species of owl watching János as he buries the dead girl is *Bubo virginianus*, the Great Horned Owl. You'll also note the bird is native to North America, and not naturally found in Europe, but that to fret over these sorts of inaccuracies is, at best, pedantic. At worst, you'll write, it means that one has entirely missed the point and would have been better off staying at home and not wasting the price of a movie ticket.

This is not the life of Erzsébet Báthory.

No one has ever lived this exact life.

Beyond the establishing shot of the ruins at the beginning of the film, the castle is not Csejte. Likewise, the forest that surrounds it is the forest that this story requires it to be, and whether or not it's an accurate depiction of the forests of the Piešťany region of Slovakia is irrelevant.

The Countess may or may not have been Anna Darvulia's lover. Erzsébet Báthory may have been a lesbian. Or she may not. Anna Darvulia may or may not have existed.

There is no evidence whatsoever that Erzsébet was repeatedly visited in the dead of night by a strange gypsy child.

Or that the Countess' fixation with blood began when she struck a servant who'd accidentally pulled her hair.

Or that Erzsébet was ever led naked through those inaccurate forests while lustful wolves sniffed at her sex.

Pedantry and nitpicking are fatal to all fairy tales. You will write that there are people who would argue a wolf lacks the lung capacity to blow down a house of straw and that any beanstalk tall enough to reach the clouds would collapse under its own weight. They are, you'll say, the same lot who'd dismiss Shakespeare for mixing Greek and Celtic mythology, or on the grounds that there was never a prince of Verona named Escalus. "The facts are neither here nor there," you will write. "We have entered a realm where facts may not even exist." You'll be paid a pittance for the review, which virtually no one will read.

There will be one letter to the editor complaining that your review was "too defensive" and that you are "an apologist for shoddy, prurient film-making." You'll remember this letter (though not the name of its author) many years after the paltry check has been spent.

The facts are neither here nor there.

Sitting in your theatre seat, these words have not yet happened, the words you'll write. At best, they're thoughts at the outermost edges of conception. Sitting here, there is nothing but the film, another's fever dreams you have been permitted to share. And you are keenly aware how little remains of the fifth reel, that the fever will break very soon.

EXT. FOREST. NIGHT.

MEDIUM SHOT.

Anna Darvulia sits before a small campfire, her horse's reins tied to a tree behind her. A hare is roasting on a spit above the fire. There's a sudden gust of wind, and, briefly, the flames burn a ghostly blue. She narrows her eyes, trying to see something beyond the firelight.

DARVULIA:
You think I don't see you? You think I can't smell you?
(pause)
You've no right claim left on me. I've passed my debt to the
Báthory woman. I've prepared her for you. Now, leave me be,
spirit. Do not trouble me this night or any other.

The fire flares blue again, and Darvulia lowers her head, no longer gazing into the darkness.

DISSOLVE TO:

EXT. ČACHTICE CASTLE HILL. NIGHT.

The full moon shines down on Csejte. The castle is dark. There's no light in any of its windows.

CUT TO:

The gypsy girl's unmarked grave. But much of the earth that filled the hole now lies heaped about the edges, as if someone has hastily exhumed the corpse. Or as if the dead girl might have dug her way out. The ground is white with snow and frost, and sparkles beneath the moon.

CUT TO:

EXT. BALCONY OUTSIDE COUNTESS' BEDCHAMBER. NIGHT.

The owl that watched Ujváry János bury the girl is perched on the stone balustrade. The doors to the balcony have been left standing open. Draperies billow in the freezing wind.

CLOSE-UP:

Owl's round face. It blinks several times, and the bird's eyes flash an iridescent red-gold.

The Countess sits in her bedchamber, in that enormous chair with its six savage feet. A wolf pelt lies draped across her lap, emptied of its wolf. Like a dragon, the Countess breathes steam. She holds a wooden cross in her shaking hands.

"Tell the cats to come to me," she says, uttering the prayer hardly above a whisper. There is no need to raise her voice; all gods and angels must surely have good ears. "And hasten them," she continues, "to bite the hearts of my enemies and all who would do me harm. Let them rip to pieces and bite again and again the hearts of my foes. And guard Erzsébet from all evil. *O Quam Misericors est Deus, Pius et Justus.*"

Elizabeth was raised a Calvinist, and her devout mother, Anna, saw that she attended a fine Protestant school in Erdöd. She was taught mathematics and learned to write and speak Greek, German, Slovak, and Latin. She learned Latin prayers against the demons and the night.

"*O Quam Misericors est Deus. Justus et Paciens,*" she whispers, though she's shivering so badly that her teeth have begun to chatter and the words no longer come easily. They fall from her lips like stones. Or rotten fruit. Or lies. She cringes in her chair, and gazes intently towards the billowing, diaphanous drapes and the night and balcony beyond them. A shadow slips into the room, moving across the floor like spilled oil. The drapes part as if they have a will all their own (they were pulled to the sides with hooks and nylon fishing line, you've read), and the gypsy girl steps into the room. She is entirely nude, and her tawny body and black hair are caked with the earth of her abandoned grave. There are feathers caught in her hair, and a few drift from her shoulders to lie on the floor at her feet. She is bathed in moonlight, as cliché as that may sound. She has the iridescent eyes of an owl. The girl's face is the very picture of sorrow.

"Why did you bury me, Mother?"

"You were dead . . ."

The girl takes a step nearer the Countess. "I was so cold down there. You cannot ever imagine anything even half so cold as the dead lands."

The Countess clutches her wood cross. She is shaking, near tears. "You cannot be here. I said the prayers Anna taught me."

The girl has moved very near the chair now. She is close enough that she could reach out and stroke Elizabeth's pale cheek, if she wished to do so.

"The cats aren't coming, Mother. Her prayer was no more than any other prayer. Just pretty words against that which has never had cause to fear pretty words."

"The cats aren't coming," the Countess whispers, and the cross slips from her fingers.

The gypsy child reaches out and strokes Elizabeth's pale cheek. The girl's short nails are broken and caked with dirt. "It doesn't matter, Mother, because I'm here. What need have you of cats, when your daughter has come to keep you safe?"

The Countess looks up at the girl, who seems to have grown four or five inches taller since entering the room. "You are my daughter?" Elizabeth asks, the question a mouthful of fog.

"I am," the girl replies, kneeling to gently kiss the Countess' right cheek. "I have many mothers, as I have many daughters of my own. I watch over them all. I hold them to me and keep them safe."

"I've lost my mind," the Countess whispers. "Long, long ago, I lost my mind." She hesitantly raises her left hand, brushing back the girl's filthy, matted hair, dislodging another feather. The Countess looks like an old woman. All traces of the youth she clung to with such ferocity have left her face, and her eyes have grown cloudy. "I am a madwoman."

"It makes no difference," the gypsy girl replies.

"Anna lied to me."

"Let that go, Mother. Let it all go. There are things I would show you. Wondrous things."

"I thought she loved me."

"She is a sorceress, Mother, and an inconstant lover. But I am true. And you'll need no other's love but mine."

The movie's score has dwindled to a slow smattering of piano notes, a bow drawn slowly, nimbly across the strings of a cello. A hint of flute.

The Countess whispers, "I called to the King of Cats."

The girl answers, "Cats rarely ever come when called. And certainly not ninety all at once."

And the brown girl leans forward, her lips pressed to the pale Countess' right ear. Whatever she says, it's nothing you can make out from your seat, from your side of the silver mirror. The gypsy girl kisses the Countess on the forehead.

"I'm so very tired."

"*Shhhhh*, Mother. I know. It's okay. You can rest now."

The Countess asks, "Who are you?"

"I am the peace at the end of all things."

EXT. COURTYARD BELOW COUNTESS' BALCONY.

MORNING.

The body of Elizabeth Báthory lies shattered on the flagstones, her face and clothes a mask of frozen blood. Fresh snow is falling on her corpse. A number of noisy crows surround the body. No music now, only the wind and the birds.

FADE TO BLACK:

ROLL CREDITS.

THE END.

As always, you don't leave your seat until the credits are finished and the curtain has swept shut again, hiding the screen from view. As always, you've made no notes, preferring to rely on your memories.

You follow the aisle to the auditorium doors and step out into the almost deserted lobby. The lights seem painfully bright. You hurry to the restroom. When you're finished, you wash your hands, dry them, then spend almost an entire minute staring at your face in the mirror above the sink.

Outside, it's started to rain, and you wish you'd brought an umbrella.

ONE TREE HILL
(THE WORLD AS CATACLYSM)

1.

I **AM DREAMING.** Or I am awake.

I've long since ceased to care, as I've long since ceased to believe it matters which. Dreaming or awake, my *perceptions* of the hill and the tree and what little remains of the house on the hill are the same. More importantly, more perspicuously, my perceptions of the hill and the house and the tree are the same. Or, as this admittedly is belief, and so open to debate, I cannot imagine it would matter whether I am dreaming or awake. And this obser-vation is as good a place to begin as any.

I am told in the village that the hill, the tree on the hill, was struck by lightning at, or just after, sunset on St. Crispin's Day, eleven years ago. I am told in the village that no thunderstorm accompanied the lightning strike, that the October sky was clear and dappled with stars. The Village. It has a name, though I prefer to think of, and refer to, it simply as The Village. Nestled snugly—some would say claustrophobically—between the steep foothills of New Hampshire's White Mountains, within what geographers name the Sandwich Range, and a deep lake the villagers call Witalema. On my maps, the lake has no name at all. A librarian in The Village told me that Witalema was derived from the language of the Abenakis, from the word *gwitaalema*, which, she said, may be roughly translated as "to fear someone."

I've found nothing in any book or anywhere online that refutes her claim, though I have also found nothing to confirm it. So, I will always think of that lake and its black, still waters as Lake Witalema and choose not to speculate on why its name means "to fear someone." I found more than enough to fear on the aforementioned lightning-struck hill.

There is a single, nameless cemetery in The Village, located within a stone's throw of the lake. The oldest headstone I have found there dates back to 1674. That is, the man buried in the plot died in 1674. He was a born in 1645. The headstone reads: *Ye blooming Youth who fee this Stone/ Learn early Death may be your own.* It seems oddly random to me that only the word *see* makes use of the Latin *s*. In stray moments I have wondered what the dead man might have *feen* to warrant this peculiarity of the inscription, or if it is merely an engraver's mistake that was not corrected and so has survived these past three hundred and thirty-eight years. I dislike the cemetery, perhaps because of its nearness to the lake, and so I have only visited it once. Usually, I find comfort in graveyards, and I have a large collection of rubbings taken from gravestones in New England.

But why, I ask myself, *do I shy from this one cemetery, and possibly only because of its closeness to Lake Witalema, when I returned repeatedly to the hill and the tree and what little remains of the house on the hill?* It isn't a question I can answer; I doubt I will ever be able to answer it. I only know that what I have seen on that hilltop is far more dreadful than anything the lake could ever have to show me.

I am climbing the hill, and I am awake, or I am asleep.

I'm thinking about the lightning strike on St. Crispin's Day, lightning from a clear night sky, and I'm thinking of the fire that consumed the house and left the tree a gnarled charcoal crook. Also, my mind wanders—probably defensively—to the Vatican's decision that too little evidence can be found to prove the existence of either St. Crispin or his twin brother, St. Crispinian, and how they survived their first close call with martyrdom, after being tossed into a river with millstones tied about their necks, only to be beheaded, finally, by decree of Rictus Varus. Climbing up that hill, pondering obscure Catholic saints who may not ever have lived, it occurs to me I may read too much. Or only read too much into what I read. I pause to catch my breath, and I glance up at the sky. Today there are clouds, unlike the night the lightning came. If the villagers are to be believed, of course. And given the nature of what sits atop the hill, the freak strike that night seems not so miraculous. The clouds seem to promise rain, and I'll probably be soaking wet by the time I get back to my room in the rundown motel on the outskirts of The Village. Far off, towards what my tattered topographic map calls Mount Passaconaway, there is the low rumble of thunder (*Passaconaway* is another Indian name, from the Pennacook, a tribe closely related to the Abenakis, but I have no idea whatsoever what the word might mean). The trail is steep here, winding between spruce and pine, oaks, poplars, and red maples. I imagine the maple leaves must appear to catch fire in the autumn. Catch fire or bleed. The hill always turns my thoughts morbid, a mood that is not typical of my nature. Reading this, one might think otherwise, but that doesn't change the truth of it. Having caught my breath, I continue up the narrow, winding path, hoping to reach the summit before the storm catches up with me. Weathered granite crunches beneath my boots.

"Were I you," said the old man who runs The Village's only pharmacy, "I'd stay clear of that hill. No fit place to go wandering about. Not after . . ." And then he trailed off and went back to ringing up my purchase on the antique cash register.

". . . the lightning came," I said, finishing his statement. "After the fire."

He glared at me and made an exasperated, disapproving sound.

"You ain't from around here, I know, and whatever you've heard, I'm guessing you've written it off as Swamp Yankee superstition."

"I have a more open mind than you think," I told him.

"Maybe that's so. Maybe it ain't," he groused and looked for the price on a can of pears in heavy syrup. "Either way, I guess I've said my piece. No fit place, that hill, and you'd do well to listen."

But I might have only dreamt that conversation, as I might have dreamt the graveyard on the banks of Lake Witalema, and the headstone of a man who died in 1674, and the twisted, charred tree, and . . .

It doesn't matter.

———

2.

I live in The City, a safe century of miles south and east of The Village. When I have work, I am a science journalist. When I do not, I am an unemployed science journalist who tries to stay busy by blogging what I would normally sell for whatever pittance is being offered. Would that I had become a political pundit or a war correspondent. But I didn't. I have no interest or acumen for politics or bullets. I wait on phone calls, on jobs from a vanishing stable of newspapers and magazines, on work from this or that website. I wait. My apartment is very small, even by the standards of The City, and only just affordable on my budget. Or lack thereof. Four cramped rooms in the attic of a brownstone that was built when the neighborhood was much younger, overlooking narrow streets crowded with upscale boutiques and restaurants that charge an arm and a leg for a sparkling green bottle of S. Pellegrino. I can watch wealthy men and women walk their shitty little dogs.

I have a few bookshelves, crammed with reference material on subjects ranging from cosmology to quantum physics, virology to paleontology. My coffee table, floor, desk, and almost every other conceivable surface are piled high with back issues of *Science* and *Physical Review Letters* and *Nature* and . . . you get the picture. That hypothetical you, who may or may not be reading this. I'm making no assumptions. I have my framed diplomas from MIT and Yale on the wall above my desk, though they only serve to remind me that whatever promise I might once have possessed has gone unrealized. And that I'll never pay off the student loans that supplemented my meager scholarships. I try, on occasion, to be proud of those pieces of paper and their calligraphy and gold seals, but I rarely turn that trick.

I sit, and I read. I blog, and I wait, watching as the balance in my bank account dwindles.

One week ago tomorrow my needlessly fancy iPhone rang, and on the other end was an editor from *Discover* who'd heard from a field geologist about the lightning-struck hill near The Village, and who thought it was worth checking out. That it might make an interesting sidebar, at the very least. A bit of a meteorological mystery, unless it proved to be nothing but local tall tales. I had to pay for my own gas, but I'd have a stingy expense account for a night at a motel and a few meals. I was given a week to get the story in. I should say, obviously, I have long since exceeded my expense account and missed the deadline. I keep my phone switched off.

It doesn't matter anymore. In my ever decreasing moments of clarity, I find myself wishing that it did. I need the money. I need the byline. I absolutely do not need an editor pissed at me and word getting around that I'm unreliable.

But it *doesn't* matter anymore.

Wednesday, one week ago, I got my ever-ailing, tangerine-and-rust Nissan out of the garage where I can't afford to keep it. I left The City, and I left Massachusetts via I-493, which I soon traded for I-93, and then I-293 at Manchester. Then, it will suffice to say that I left the interstates and headed east until I reached The Village nestled here between the kneeling mountains. I didn't make any wrong turns. It was easy to find. The directions the editor at *Discover* had emailed were correct in every way, right down to the shabby motel on the edge of The Village.

Right down to the lat-long GPS coordinates of the hill and the tree and what little remains of the house on the hill. N 43.81591/W -71.37035.

I think I have offered all these details only as an argument, to myself, that I am—or at least was once—a rational human being. Whatever I have become, or am becoming, I did start out believing the truths of the universe *were* knowable.

But now I am sliding down a slippery slope towards the irrational.

Now, I doubt everything I took for granted when I came here.

Before I first climbed the hill.

If the preceding is an argument, or a ward, or whatever I might have intended it as, it is a poor attempt, indeed.

But it doesn't matter, and I know that.

3.

I imagine that the crest of the hill was once quite picturesque. As I've mentioned, there's an unobstructed view of the heavily wooded slopes and peaks of Mount Passaconaway and of the valleys and hills in between. This vista must be glorious under a heavy snowfall. I have supposed that is why the house was built here. Likely, it was someone's summer home, possibly someone not so unlike myself, someone foreign to The Village.

The librarian I spoke of earlier, I asked her if the hill has a name, and all she said was "One Tree."

"One Tree Hill?" I asked.

"One Tree," she replied curtly. "Nobody goes up *there* anymore."

I am quite entirely aware I am trapped inside, and that I am writing down, anything *but* an original tale of uncanny New England. But if I do not know, I will at least be honest about *what* I do not know. I have that responsibility, that fraying shred of naturalism remaining in me. Whether or not it is cliché is another thing which simply doesn't matter.

I reach the crest of the hill, and just like every time before, the first thing that strikes my eyes is the skeleton of that tree. I'm not certain, but I believe it was an oak. It must have been ancient, judging by the circumference and diameter of its base. It might have stood here when that man I have yet to (and will not) name was buried in 1674 near the banks of Lake Witalema. But I don't know how long oak trees live, and I haven't bothered to find out. It is a dead tree, and all the "facts" that render it *more* than a dead tree exist entirely independently of its taxonomy.

Aside from the remains of the one tree, the hilltop is "bald." The woods have not reclaimed it. If I stand at the lightning-struck tree, the nearest living tree, in any direction, is at least twenty-five yards away. There is only stone and bracken, weeds, vines, and fallen, rotten limbs. So, it is always hotter at the top of the hill, and the ground seems drier and rockier. There is a sense of flesh rubbed raw and unable to heal.

Like all the times I have come here before, there is, immediately, the inescapable sense that I have entered a place so entirely and irrevocably defiled as to have passed beyond any conventional understanding of corruption. I cannot ever escape the impression that, somehow, the event that damned this spot (for it *is* damned) struck so very deeply at the fabric of this patch of the world as to render it beyond that which is either unholy *or* holy. Neither good *nor* evil have a place here. Neither are welcome, so profound was the damage done that one St. Crispin's Night. And if the hill seems blasphemous, it is only because it has come to exist somewhere genuinely *Outside*. I won't try to elaborate just yet. It is enough to say *Outside*. Even so, I'll concede that the dead tree stands before me like an altar. It strikes me that way every time, in direct contradiction to what I've said about it. Or, I *could* say, instead, it stands like a sentry, but then one must answer the question about what it might be standing guard over. Bricks from a crumbling foundation? The maze of poison ivy and green briars? A court of skunks, rattlesnakes, and crows?

The sky presses down on the hill, heavy as the sea.

From the top of the hill, the wide blue sky looks very hungry.

What is it that skies eat? That thin rind of atmosphere between a planet and the hard vacuum of outer space? I'm asking questions that lead nowhere. I'm asking questions only because it occurs to me that I have never written them down, or that they have never before occurred to me so I *ought* to write them down.

A cloudless night sky struck at the hill, drawing something out, even if I am unable to describe what that something is, and so I will say this event is the author of my questions on the possible diet of the sky.

Even after eleven years, the top of the hill smells of smoke, ash, charcoal, and cinders—all those odors we mean when we say, "I can smell fire." We cannot smell fire, but we smell the byproducts of combustion, and that smell lingers here. I wonder if it always will. I am standing at the top of the hill, thinking all these thoughts, when I hear something coming up quickly behind me. It's not the noise a woman's or a man's feet would make. A deer, possibly. An animal with long and delicate limbs, small hooves to pick its way through the forest and along stony trails. This is what I think I hear, but, then, most people *think* they can smell fire.

I take one step forward, and a charred section of root crunches beneath the soles of my hiking boots. The crunching seems very loud, though I suspect that's only another illusion.

"Why is it you keep coming back here?" she asks. The way she phrases the question, I could pretend I've never heard her ask it before. My mouth is dry. I want to remove my pack and take out the lukewarm bottle of water inside, but I don't.

"It could open wide and eat me," I say to her. "A wide carnivorous sky like that."

There's a pause, nothing but a stale bit of breeze through the leaves of the trees surrounding the lightning-struck ring. Then she laughs, that peculiar laugh of hers, which is neither unnerving nor a sound that in any way puts one at ease.

"Now you're being ridiculous," she says.

"I know," I admit. "But that's the way it makes me feel, hanging up there."

"What you describe is a feeling of dread."

"Isn't that what happened here, that St. Crispin's Day? Didn't the sky open its mouth and gnaw this hill and everything on it—the tree, the house?"

"You listen too much to those people in the village."

That's the way she says it, *the village*. Never does she say *The Village*. It is an important nuance. What seems, as she has pointed out, dreadful to me is innately mundane to her.

"They don't have much to say about the hill," I tell her.

"No, they don't. But what they do say, it's hardly worth your time."

"I get the feeling they'd bulldoze this place, if they weren't too afraid to come here. I believe they would take dynamite to it, shave off the top until no evidence of that night remains."

"Likely, you're not mistaken," she agrees. "Which is precisely why you shouldn't listen to them."

I wish I knew the words to accurately delineate, elucidate, explain the rhythm and stinging lilt of her voice. I cannot. I can only do my best to recall what she said that day, which, of course, was not the first nor the last day she has spoken with me. Why she bothers, that might be the greatest of all these mysteries, though it might seem the least. Appearances are deceiving.

"Maybe there were clouds that night," I say. "Maybe it's just that no one noticed them. They may only have noticed that flash of lightning, and only noticed that because of what it left behind."

"If you truly thought that's what happened, you wouldn't keep coming here."

"No, I wouldn't," I say, though I want to turn about and spit in her face, if she even has a face. I presume she does. But I've never turned to find out. I've never looked at her, and I know I never will. Like Medusa, she is not to be seen.

Yes, that was a tad melodramatic, but isn't all of this? The same as it's cliché?

"It's unhealthy, returning to this place again and again. You ought to stop."

"I can't. I haven't . . ." and I trail off. It is a sentence I never should have begun and which I certainly don't wish to finish.

". . . solved it yet? No, but it is also a riddle you never should have asked yourself. The people in the village, they don't ask it. Except, possibly, in their dreams."

"You think the people in The Village are ridiculous. You just said so."

"No, that is not exactly what I said, but it's true enough. However, there genuinely are questions you're better off not asking."

"Ignorance is bliss," I say, almost mangling the words with laughter.

"That is not what I said, either."

"Excuse me. I'm getting a headache."

"Don't you always, when you come up here? You should stop to consider why that is, should you not?"

I'm silent for a time, and then I answer, "You want me to stop coming. You would rather I stop coming. I suspect you might even need me to stop coming."

"Futility disturbs me," she says. "You're becoming Sisyphus, rolling his burden up that hill. You've become Christ, lugging the cross towards Calvary."

I don't disagree.

"Loki," I add.

"Loki?"

"It hasn't gotten as bad as what happened to Loki. No serpent dripping venom, which is good, because I have no Sigyn to catch it in her bowl." The story of Loki so bound puts me in mind of Prometheus, the eagle always, always devouring his liver, a symbol for the hungry sky. But I say nothing of Prometheus to her.

"It is the way of humans," she says, "to create these brilliant, cautionary metaphors, then ignore them."

Again, I don't disagree. It doesn't matter anymore.

"But it *did* happen, yes?" I ask. "There were no clouds that night?"

"It did happen." She is the howling, fiery voice of God whispering confirmation of what my gut already knew. She has been before, and will be again.

"Go home," she says. "Go back to your apartment in your city, before it's too late to go back. Go back to your life."

"Why do you care?" I ask this question, because I know it's already too late to go back to The City. For any number of reasons, not the least because I have climbed the hill and looked at the silent devastation.

"There's no revelation to be had here," she sighs. "No slouching beast prefacing revelation. No revelation and no prophecy. No מנא, תקל, ופרסין, מנא (*Mene, Mene, Tekel u-Pharsin*) at the feast of Belshazzar." She speaks in Hebrew, and I reply, "Numbered, weighed, divided."

"You won't find that here."

"Why do you assume that is why I keep coming back?"

This time she only clicks her tongue twice against the roof of her mouth. Tongue, mouth. These are both assumptions, as is face.

"Not because of what I might see, but because of what I've already seen. What will I ever see to equal this? Did it bring you here?"

"No," she says, the word another exasperated sigh.

"You were here before."

"No," she sighs.

"Doesn't it ever get lonely, being up here all alone?"

"You make a lot of assumptions, and, frankly, I find them wearisome."

It doesn't even occur to me to apologize. A secret recess of my consciousness must understand that apologies would be meaningless to one such as her. I hear those nimble legs, those tiny feet that might as well end in hooves. There are other noises I won't attempt to describe.

"Is it an assumption that it is within your power to stop me?"

"Yes, of course that is an assumption."

"Yet," and I can't take my eyes off what's left of the charred tree, "many assumptions prove valid."

She leaves me then. There are no words of parting, no goodbye. There never is; she simply leaves, and I am alone at the top of the hill with the tree and what little remains of the house on the hill, wondering if she will come next time, and the time after that, and the time after that. I pick up a lump of four-hundred-million-year-old granite, which seems to tingle in my hand, and I hurl it towards far-off Mount Passaconaway, as if I had a chance of hitting my target.

4.

One thing leads to another. I am keenly aware of the casual chain of cause and effect that dictates, as does any tyrant, the events of the cosmos.

A lightning-struck hill.

A house.

A tree.

A Village hemmed in by steep green slopes and the shadows they cast.

A black lake, and a man who died in 1674.

I had a lover once. Only once, but it was a long relationship. It died a slow and protracted death, borne as much of my disappointment in myself as my partner's disappointment *in* my disappointment in myself. I suppose you can only watch someone you love mourn for so long before your love becomes disgust. Or I may misunderstand completely. I've never made a secret of my difficulty in understanding the motives of people, no matter how close to me they have been, no matter how long they have been close to me. It doesn't seem to matter.

None of it matters now.

But last night, after I climbed the hill, after my conversation with whatever it is exists alone up there, after that, I made a phone call from the squalid motel room. I have not called my former lover in three years. In three years, we have not spoken. Had we, early on, I might have had some chance of repairing the damage I'd done. But it had all seemed so inevitable, and any attempt to stave off the inevitable seemed absurd. In my life, I have loved two things. The first died before we met, and with my grieving for the loss of the first did I kill the second. Well, did I place the second forever beyond my reach.

If I have not already made it perfectly clear, I have no love for The City, nor my apartment, and most especially not for the career I have resigned myself to, or, I would say, that I have *settled* for.

Last night I called him. I thought no one would pick up.

"Hello," I said, and there was a long, long silence. *Just hang up*, I thought, though I'm not sure which of us I was wishing would hang up. *It was a terrible idea, so please just hang up before it gets more terrible.*

"Why are you calling me?"

"I'm not entirely certain."

"It's been three years. Why the fuck are you calling me tonight?"

"Something's happening. Something important, and I didn't have anyone else to call."

"I'm the last resort," and there was a dry, bitter laugh. There was the sound of a cigarette being lit and the exhalation of smoke.

"You still smoke," I said.

"Yeah. Look, I don't care what's happening. Whatever it is, you deal with it."

"I'm trying."

"Maybe you're not trying hard enough."

I agreed.

"Will you only listen? It won't take long, and I don't expect you to solve any of my problems. I just need to tell someone."

Another long pause, only the sound of smoking to interrupt the silence through the receiver.

"Fine. But be quick. I'm busy."

I'm not, I think. *I may never be busy again. Isn't that a choice one makes, whether to be busy or not? I have, in coming to The Village, left busyness behind me.*

I told my story, which sounded even more ridiculous than I'd expected it to sound. I left out most of my talks with the thing that lives atop the hill, as no one can recall a conversation, not truly, and I didn't want to omit a word of it.

Whether or not each word is of consequence.

"You need to see someone," he told me.

"Maybe," I said.

"No. Not maybe. You need to see someone."

We said goodbye, and I was instructed to never call again.

I hung up first, then sat by the phone (I'd used the motel phone, not my cell).

A few seconds later, it rang again, and I quickly, hopefully, lifted the receiver. But it was the voice from the hill. Someone else might have screamed.

"You should leave," she said. "It's still not too late to leave. Do as I have said. It's all still waiting for you. The city, your work, your home."

"Nothing's waiting for me back there. Haven't you figured that out?"

"There's nothing for you here. Haven't *you* figured *that* out?"

"I'm asleep and dreaming this. I'm lying in my apartment above Newbury Street, and I'm dreaming all of this. Probably, The Village does not even exist."

"Then wake up. Go home. Wake up, and you will be home."

"I don't know how," I said, and that was the truth. "I don't know how, and it doesn't matter any longer."

"That's a shame, I think," she said. "I wish it were otherwise." And then there was only a dial tone.

You can almost see the hill from the window of my motel room. You can see the highway and a line of evergreens. If the trees were not so tall, you *could* see the hill. On a night eleven years ago, you could have seen the lightning from this window, and you could have seen the glow of the fire that must have burned afterwards. Last night, I was glad that I couldn't see the hill silhouetted against the stars.

5.

The three times I have visited the library in The Village, the librarian has done her best to pretend I wasn't there. She does her best to seem otherwise occupied. Intensely so. She makes me wait at the circulation desk as long as she can. Today is no different. But finally she relents and frowns and asks me what I need.

"Do you have back issues of the paper?"

"Newspaper?" she asks.

"Yes. There's only the one, am I correct?"

"You are."

"Do you have back issues?"

"We have it on microfilm," and I tell her that microfilm is perfectly fine. So, she leads me through the stacks to a tiny room in the back. There's a metal cabinet with drawers filled with yellow Kodak boxes. She begins to explain how the old-style reader works, how to fit the spools onto the spindles, and I politely assure her I've spent a lot of time squinting at microfilm, but thanks, anyway. I am always polite with her. I ask for the reel that would include October 26, 2001.

"You aren't going to let this go, are you?" asks the librarian.

"Eventually, I might. But not yet."

"Ought never to have come here. Can't nothing good come of it. Anyone in town can tell you that. Can't nothing good come of prying into the past."

I thank her, and she scowls and leaves me alone.

I press an off-white plastic button, and the days whir noisily past my eyes. I have always detested the sound of a microfilm reader. It reminds me of a dental drill, though I've never found anyone else who's made the association. Then again, I don't think I've ever asked anyone *how* they feel about the click-click-click whir of a microfilm reader. One day soon, with so much digital conversion going on, I imagine there will be very few microfilm archives. People pretend that hard drives, computer disks, and the internet are a safer place to keep our history. People are fools. At any rate, the machine whirs, and after only a minute or so I've reached October 26, the day after the lightning strike. On page four of the paper, I find a very brief write up of the event at the crest of the hill. One Tree, as it seems to be named, though the paper doesn't give that name. It merely speaks of a house at the end of an "unimproved" drive off Middle Road, east of The Village. A house had recently been constructed there by a family hailing from, as it happened, The City. The world is, of course, filled with coincidence, so I make nothing of this. I doubt I ever shall. The house was to be a summer home. Curiously, the family is not named, the paper reporting only that there had been three members—father, mother, daughter—and that all died in the fire caused by the lightning. Firefighters from The Village had responded, but were (also curiously) said to have been unable to extinguish what must have been a modest blaze. I will only quote this portion, which I am scribbling down in my notebook:

Meteorologists have attributed the tragic event to "positive" lightning, a relatively rare phenomenon. Unlike far more commonly occurring "negative" lightning, positive lightning takes place when a positive charge is carried by the uppermost regions of clouds—most often anvil clouds—rather than by the ground. This causes the leader arc to form within the anvil of the cumulonimbus cloud and travel horizontally for several miles before suddenly veering down to meet the negatively charged streamer rising up from the ground. The bolt can strike anywhere within several miles of the anvil of the thunderstorm, often in areas experiencing clear or only slightly cloudy skies, hence they may also be referred to as "bolts from the blue." Positive lightning is estimated to account for less than 5% of all lightning strikes.

The meteorologist in question is not named, nor is his or her affiliation given. I do find it odd that far more space is devoted to an attempt to explain the event than to any other aspect of it. Also, it appears to have been cribbed from a textbook or other reference source and deviates significantly from the voice of the rest of the article. There is, reading over it again and again, the sense that explaining the lightning was far more important to whoever wrote the piece than was reporting the deaths of the family or even the general facts of the case. A single anonymous source is quoted, a resident of High Street (in The Village) as a witness to the lightning strike. There is also mentioned a "terrific booming from the sky" that occurred an hour *after* the strike, and I can't help but wonder why the paper went to so much trouble to make plain that there was nothing especially peculiar about the lightning, but records another strange incident in passing which it makes no attempt to explain.

"Did you find what you were looking for?" the librarian asks, peering into the small room. I notice for the first time, the room smells musty. Or maybe it's the librarian who smells musty.

"I did," I reply. "Thank you. You've been very helpful."

"I do my job. I do what the town council pays me to do."

"Then you do it well," I say, determined to inflict upon her a compliment.

She grumbles, and I leave while she's busy removing the spool and returning it to its yellow Kodak box. I step out onto the tiny courtyard in front of the library, and it's just begun raining. Cold drops pepper my face. I stand, staring up into the rain and consider calling the editor, apologizing, and asking for a second chance. Telling him there really is no mystery here, so it could be a great little piece debunking a rural myth, a triumph of science over the supposedly miraculous. I could return to The City, to my apartment, and wait for other jobs. I would find a way to forget about whatever lives at the top of the hill. I would tell myself I'd imagined the whole affair, mark it up to weariness, depression, something of the sort.

The rain almost feels like needles.

6.

I awake from a nightmare. I awake breathless to sweaty sheets. I think I may have cried out in my sleep, but I don't know for sure. Almost at once, I forget most of the particulars of the dream. But it centered on the charred tree. There was something coiled in the branches of the tree, or perched there. It was gazing down at me. A shapeless thing, or very nearly so, clinging somehow to those charcoal branches. I wanted to turn away, to look away, but was unable. I felt the purest spite spilling from it, flowing down the gnarled trunk and washing over me. I have never believed in evil, but the thing in the tree was, I knew, evil. It was evil, and it was ancient beyond any human comprehension. Some of the eldest stars were younger, and the Earth an infant by comparison. Mercifully, it didn't speak or make any other sound whatsoever.

I awake to a voice, and I recognize it straightaway. It's the voice from the hill. Near the door, there's the faintest of silhouettes, an outline that is only almost human. It's tall and begins moving gracefully across the room towards me. I reach to turn on the lamp, but, thankfully, my hand never touches the cord.

"Have you seen enough?" she asks. "What you found at the library, was that enough?"

She's very near the foot of the bed now. I would never have guessed she was so tall and so extraordinarily slender. My eyes struggle with the darkness to make sense of something I cannot actually see.

"Not you," I whisper. "It hasn't explained you."

"Do I require an explanation?"

"Most people would say so."

If this is being read, I would say most *readers* would certainly say so. There, I *have* said it.

"But not you?"

"I don't know what I need," I say, and I'm being completely honest.

Here there is a long silence, and I realize it's still raining. That it's raining much harder than when I went to bed. I can hear thunder far away.

"This is the problem with explanations," she says. "You ask for one, and it triggers an infinite regression. There is never a final question. Unless inquiry is halted by an arbitrary act. And it's true, many inquiries are, if only by necessity."

"If I knew what you are, why you are, how you are, if there is any connection between you and the death of those three people . . ." I trail off, knowing she'll finish my thought.

She says, ". . . you'd only have another question, and another after that. *Ad infinitum.*"

"I think I want to go home," I whisper.

"Then you should go home, don't you think?"

"What was that I dreamt of, the thing in the tree?"

Now she is leaning over me, on the bed *with* me, and it only frightens me that I am not afraid. "Only a bad dream," she sighs, and her breath smells like the summer forest, and autumn leaves, and snow, and swollen mountain rivers in the spring. It doesn't smell even remotely of fire.

"Before The Village, you were here," I say. "You've almost always been here." I say. It isn't a question, and she doesn't mistake it for one. She doesn't say anything else, and I understand I will never again hear her speak.

She wraps her arms and legs about me—and, as I guessed, they are delicate and nothing like the legs of women, and she takes me into her. We do not make love. We fuck. No, she fucks me. She fucks me, and it seems to go on forever. Repeatedly, I almost reach climax, and, repeatedly, it slips away. She mutters in a language I know, instinctively, has never been studied by any linguist, and one I'll not recall a syllable of later on, no matter how hard I struggle to do so. It seems filled with clicks and glottal stops. Outside, there is rain and thunder and lightning. The storm is pounding at the windows, wanting in. The storm, I think, is jealous. I wonder how long it will hold a grudge. Is that what happened on top of the hill? Did she take the man or the woman (or both) as a lover? Did the sky get even?

I do finally come, and the smells of her melt away. She is gone, and I lay on those sweaty sheets, trying to catch my breath.

So, I do not say aloud, *the dream didn't end with the tree. I dreamt her here, in the room with me. I dreamt her questions, and I dreamt her fucking me.*

I do my best to fool myself this is the truth.

It doesn't matter anymore.

By dawn, the rain has stopped.

7.

I have breakfast, pack, fill up the Nissan's tank, and pay my motel bill.

By the time I pull out of the parking lot, it's almost nine o'clock.

I drive away from The Village, and the steep slopes pressing in on all sides as if to smother it, and I drive away from the old cemetery beside Lake Witalema. I drive south, taking the long way back to the interstate, rather than passing the turnoff leading up the hill and the house and the lightning-struck tree. I know that I will spend the rest of my life avoiding the White Mountains. Maybe I'll even go so far as to never step foot in New Hampshire again. That wouldn't be so hard to do.

I keep my eyes on the road in front of me, and am relieved as the forests and lakes give way to farmland and then the outskirts of The City. I am leaving behind a mystery that was never mine to answer. I leave behind shadows for light. Wondrous and terrifying glimpses of the extraordinary for the mundane.

I will do my damnedest to convince the editor to whom I owe a story—he took my call this morning and was only mildly annoyed I'd missed the deadline—that there is nothing the least bit bizarre about that hill or the woods surrounding it. Nothing to it but tall tales told by ignorant and gullible Swamp Yankees, people who likely haven't heard the Revolutionary War has ended. I'll lie and make them sound that absurd, and we'll all have a good laugh.

I will bury, deep as I can, all my memories of her.

It doesn't matter anymore.

INTERSTATE LOVE SONG (MURDER BALLAD NO. 8)

"The way of the transgressor is hard." —Cormac McCarthy

1.

THE IMPALA'S WHEELS singing on the black hot asphalt sound like frying steaks, USDA choice-cut T-bones, sirloin sizzling against August blacktop in Nevada or Utah or Nebraska, Alabama or Georgia, or where the fuck ever this one day, this one hour, this one motherfucking minute is going down. Here at the end, the end of one of us, months are a crimson thumb smudge across the bathroom mirror in all the interchangeable motel bathrooms that have come and gone and come again. You're smoking and looking for music in the shoebox filled with cassettes, and the clatter of protective plastic shells around spools of magnetically coated tape is like an insect chorus, a cicada symphony. You ask what I want to hear, and I tell you it doesn't matter, please light one of those for me. But you insist, and you keep right on insisting, "What d'you wanna hear?" And I say, well not fucking Nirvana again, and no more Johnny Cash, please, and you toss something from the box out the open passenger window. In the side-view mirror, I see a tiny shrapnel explosion when the cassette hits the road. Cars will come behind us, cars and trucks, and roll over the shards and turn it all to dust. "No more Nirvana," you say, and you laugh your boyish girl's laugh, and Jesus and Joseph and Mother Mary, I'm not going to be able to live in a world without that laugh. Look at me, I say. Open your eyes, please open your eyes and look at me, please. You can't fall asleep on me. Because it won't be falling asleep, will it? It won't be falling asleep at all. We are on beyond the kindness of euphemisms, and maybe we always were. So, don't fall asleep. Don't flutter the eyelashes you've always hated because they're so long and pretty, don't let them dance that Totentanz tarantella we've delighted at so many goddamn times, don't let the sun go down on me. You shove a tape into the deck. You always do that with such force, as if there's a vendetta grudge between you and that machine. You punch it in and twist the volume knob like you mean to yank it off and yeah, that's good, I say. That's golden, Henry Rollins snarling at the sun's one great demon eye. You light a Camel for me and place it between my lips, and the steering wheel feels like a weapon in my hands, and the smoke feels like Heaven in my lungs. Wake up, though. Don't shut your eyes. Remember the day that we, and remember the morning, and remember *that* time in—shit, was it El Paso? Or was it Port Arthur? It doesn't matter, so long as you keep your eyes open and look at me. It's hours until sunrise, and have you not always sworn a blue streak that you would not die in the darkness? That's all we've got here. In for a penny, in for a pound, but blackness, wall to wall, sea to shining sea, that's all we've got in this fluorescent hell, so don't you please fall asleep on me. Hot wind roars in through the Impala's windows, the stink of melting tar, roaring like an invisible mountain lion, and you point west and say take that next exit. We need beer, and we're almost out of cigarettes, and I want a pack of Starburst Fruit Chews, the tropical flavors, so the assholes better have those out here in the world's barren shit-kicker asshole. You'll just like always save all the piña colada ones for me. Then there's a thud from the trunk, and you laugh that laugh of yours all over again, only now with true passion. "And we need a bottle of water," I say. "No good to us and a waste of time and energy, and just a waste all the way round, if she ups and dies of heat stroke back there," and you shrug. Hey, keep your eyes open, love. Please, goddamn it. You can do that for me, I know you can. And I break open one of the ampules of ammonia and cruelly wave it beneath your nostrils so that both eyes pop open wide, opening up cornflower blue, and I think of startled birds bursting from their hiding places in tall grass. Tall grass, there's so much of tall grass here at the end, isn't there? I kiss your forehead, and I can't help thinking I could fry an egg on your skin, fry an egg on blacktop, fry an egg on the hood of the Impala parked in the dog-day sun outside a convenience store. You ask me to light a candle, your voice gone all jagged and broken apart like a cassette tape dropped on I-10 at 75 mph. I press my fingers and palm to the sloppy red mess of your belly, and I do not dare take my hand away long enough to light a candle, and I'm so sorry, I'm so, so sorry. I cannot even do that much for you. Just please don't close your eyes. Please don't you fall asleep on me.

2.

All these things you said to me, if not on this day, then surely on some other, and if not during this long Delta night, than surely on another. The blonde with one brown eye and one hazel-green eye, she wasn't the first, but you said to me she'll be the most memorable yet. She'll be one we talk about in years to come when all the rest have faded into a blur of delight and casual slaughter. We found her at a truck stop near Shreveport, and she'd been hitching down I-49 towards Baton Rouge and New Orleans. Sister, where you bound on such a hot, hot, sweltersome night? you asked. And because she was dressed in red, a Crimson Tide T-shirt and a red Budweiser baseball cap, you said, "Whither so early, Little Red Cap?" And she laughed, and you two shared a joint while I ate a skimpy dinner of Slim Jims, corn chips, and Mountain Dew. Eighteen-wheeled dinosaurs growled in and growled out and purred at the pumps. We laughed over a machine that sold multi-colored prophylactics and another that sold tampons. And would she like a ride? Would she? 'Cause we're a sight lot better than you're likely gonna find elsewhere, if you're looking for decent company and conversation, that is, and the weed, there's more where that came from. How old? Eighteen, she said, and you and I both knew she was adding years, but all the better. She tossed her knapsack in the backseat, and the extra pair of shoes she wore around her neck, laces laced together. She smelled of the road, of many summer days without a bath, and the world smelled of dinosaur trucks and diesel and dust and Spanish moss; and I love you so much, you whispered as I climbed behind the wheel. I love you so much I do not have words to say how much I love you. We set sail southwards, washed in the alien chartreuse glow of the Impala's dash, and she and thee talked while I drove, listening. That was enough for me, listening in, eavesdropping while my head filled up with a wakeful, stinging swarm of bees, with wasps and yellow jackets, courtesy those handy shrink-wrapped packets of dextroamphetamine and amphetamine, Black Beauties, and in the glove compartment there's Biphetamine-T and 40mg capsules of methaqualone, because when *we* drove all damn day and all damned night, we came prepared, didn't we, love? She's traveled all the way from Chicago, the red-capped backseat girl, and you and I have never been to Chicago and have no desire to go. She talks about the road as it unrolls beneath us, before me, hauling us towards dawn's early light. She tells you about some old pervert who picked her up outside Texarkana. She fucked him for twenty bucks and the lift to Shreveport. "Could'a done worse," you tell her, and she doesn't disagree. I watch you both in the rearview mirror. I watch you both, in anticipation, and the uppers and the prospect of what will come, the mischief we will do her in the wood, has me more awake than awake, has me ready to cum then and there. "You're twins," she said. It wasn't a question, only a statement of the obvious, as they say. "We're twins," you reply. "But she's my big sister. Born three minutes apart on the anniversary of the murder of Elizabeth Short," and she has no goddamn idea what you're talking about, but, not wanting to appear ignorant, she doesn't let on. When she asks where we're from, "Los Angeles," you lie. You have a generous pocketful of answers at the ready for that oft-asked question. "South Norton Avenue, midway between Coliseum Street and West 39th," you say, which has as little meaning to the heterochromatic blonde as does Glasgow smile and Leimert Park. I drive, and you spin our revolving personal mythology. She will be one for the books, you whispered back at the truck stop. Can't you smell it on her? Can't I smell what on her? Can't you smell happenstance and inevitability and fate? Can't you smell victim? You say those things, and always I nod, because, like backseat girl, I don't want to appear ignorant in your view. This one I love, this one I love, eating cartilage, shark-eyes, shark-heart, and black mulberry trees means I will not survive you, when the truth is I won't survive *without* you. Backseat girl, she talks about how she's gonna find work in New Orleans as a waitress, when you and I know she's cut out for nothing much but strip-ping and whoring the Quarter, and if this were a hundred years ago she'd be headed for fabled, vanished Storyville. "I had a boyfriend," she says. "I had a boyfriend, but he was in a band, and they all moved off to Seattle, but, dude, I didn't want to fucking *go* to fucking Seattle, you know?" And you say to her how it's like the California Gold Rush or something, all these musician sheep lemming assholes and would-be wannabe musician posers traipsing their way to the fabled Northwest in hopes of riding a wave that's already broken apart and isn't even sea foam anymore. That ship has *sailed*, you say. It's sailed and sunk somewhere in the deep blue Pacific. But that's not gonna stop anyone with stars in their eyes, because the lure of El Dorado is always a bitch, whichever El Dorado is at hand. "Do you miss him?" I ask, and that's the first thing I've said in over half an hour, more than happy just to listen in and count off the reflective mile markers with the help of anger and discord jangling from the tape deck. "Don't know," she says. And she says, "Maybe sometimes. Maybe." The road's a lonely place, you tell her, sounding sym-pathetic when I know so much better. I know your mind is full to the brim with red, red thoughts, the itch of your straight-razor lusts, the prospect of the coming butchery. Night cruising at 80 mph, we rush past the turnoff for Natchitoches, and there's a sign that says "Lost Bayou," and our passenger asks have *we* ever been to New Orleans. Sure, you lie. Sure. We'll show you round. We have friends who live in an old house on Burgundy, and they say the house is haunted by a Civil War ghost, and they'll probably let you crash there until you're on your feet. Sister, you make us sound like goddamn guardian angels, the best break she's ever had. I drive on, and the car reeks of pot and sweat, cigarette smoke and the old beer cans heaped on the back floorboard. "I've always wished I had a twin," she says. "I used to make up stories that I was adopted, and somewhere out there I had a twin brother. One day, I'd pretend, we'd find one another. Be reunited, you know." It's a pretty dream from the head of such a pretty, pretty red-capped girl in the backseat, ferried by you and I in our human masks to hide hungry wolfish faces. *I could turn you inside out*, I think at the girl. And we will. It's been a week since an indulgence, a week of aimless July motoring, let-ting peckish swell to starvation, taking no other pleasures but junk food and blue-plate specials, you and I fucking and sleeping in one another's arms while the merciless Dixie sun burned 101°F at motel-room rooftops, kerosene air gathered in rooms darkened and barely cooled by drawn curtains and wheezing AC. Strike a match, and the whole place woulda gone up. Cartoons on television, and watching MTV, and old movies in shades of black and white and grey. Burgers wrapped in meat-stained paper and devoured with salty fries. Patience, love, patience, you whispered in those shadows, and so we thrummed along back roads and highways waiting for just the right confection. And. My. Momma. Said. Pick the Very. Best One. And You. Are. It.

3.

Between the tall rustling corn-silk rows, ripening husks, bluebottles drone as the sun slides down from the greasy blue sky to set the horizon all ablaze, and you straddle Thin Man and hold his cheekbones so that he has no choice but to gaze into your face. He can't close his eyes, as he no longer has eyelids, and he screams every time I shake another handful of Red Devil lye across his bare thighs and genitals. Soft flesh is melting like hot wax, here beneath the fading Iowa day. I draw a deep breath, smelling chemical burns, tilled red-brown Bible Belt soil, and corn, and above all else, corn. The corn smells alive in ways I cannot imagine being alive, and when we are done with Thin Man, I think I would like to lie down here, right here, in the dirt between the tall rows, and gaze up at the June night, at the wheeling twin dippers and bear twins and the solitary scorpion and Cassiopeia, what I know of summer stars. "You don't have to do this," the man blubbers, and you tell him no, we don't, but yes, we do. We very much actually do. And he screams, and his scream is the lonesome cry of a small animal dying alone so near to twilight. He could be a rabbit in a fox's jaws, just as easily as a thin man in our company. We found him standing alongside a pickup broken down miles and miles north of Ottumwa, and maybe we ought to have driven him farther than we did, but impatience wins sometimes, and so you made up that story about our Uncle Joe who has a garage just a little ways farther up the road. What did he have to fear from two pale girls in a rust-bucket Impala, and so I drove, and Thin Man—whose name I still unto this hour do not know—talked about how liberals and niggers and bleeding hearts and the EPA are ruining the country. Might he have become suspicious of our lies if you'd not switched out the plates at the state line? Might he have paused in his unelicited screed long enough to think twice and think better? You scoop up fertile soil and dribble it into his open mouth, and he gags and sputters and chokes and wheezes, and still he manages to beg throughout. He's pissed himself and shat himself, so there are also those odors. Not too far away are train tracks, and not too far away there is a once-red barn, listing like a drunkard, and silver grain silos, and a whistle blows, and it blows, calling the swallows home. You sing to Thin Man, *Heed the curves, and watch the tunnels. Never falter, never fail.* Remember that? Don't close your eyes, and do not dare sleep, for this is not that warm night we lay together near Thin Man's shucked corpse and screwed in the eyes of approving Maggot Corn King deities thankful for our oblation. Your lips on my breasts, suckling, your fingers deep inside me, plowing, sewing, and by tomorrow we'll be far away, and this will be a pleasant dream for the scrapbooks of our tattered souls. More lye across Thin Man's crotch, and he bucks beneath you like an unbroken horse or a lover or an epileptic or a man being taken apart, piece by piece, in a cornfield north of Ottumwa. When we were children, we sat in the kudzu and live-oak shade near the tracks, waiting, waiting, placing pennies and nickels on the iron rails. You, spitting on the rails to cool them enough you would not blister your ear when you pressed it to the metal. *I hear the train,* you announced and smiled. Not much farther now, I hear it coming, and soon the slag ballast will dance and the crossties buck like a man dying in a cornfield. Soon now, the parade of clattering doomsday boxcars, the steel wheels that can sever limbs and flatten coins. Boxcars the color of rust—Southern Serves the South and CSX and a stray Wisconsin Central as good as a bird blown a thousand miles off course by hurricane winds. Black cylindrical tankers filled with corn syrup and crude oil, phenol, chlorine gas, acetone, vinyl chloride, and we spun tales of poisonous, flaming, steaming derailments. Those rattling, one-cent copper-smearing trains, we dreamed they might carry us off in the merciful arms of hobo sojourns to anywhere far, far away from home. *Keep your hand upon the throttle, and your eye upon the rail.* And Thin Man screams, dragging me back to the now of then. You've put dirt in his eyes, and you'd imagine he'd be thankful for that, wouldn't you? Or maybe he was gazing past you towards imaginary pearly gates where delivering angels with flaming swords might sweep down to lay low his tormentors and cast us forever and anon into the lake of fire. More Red Devil and another scream. He's beginning to bore me, you say, but I'm so busy admiring my handiwork I hardly hear you, and I'm also remembering the drive to the cornfield. I'm remembering what Thin Man was saying about fairy child-molesting atheist sodomites in all branches of the federal government and armed forces, and an international ZOG conspiracy of Jews running the USA into the ground, and who the *fuck* starts in about shit like that with total, helpful strangers? Still, you were more than willing to play along and so told him yes, yes, yes, how we were faithful, God-fearing Southern Baptists, and how our daddy was a deacon and our momma a Sunday school teacher. That should'a been laying it on too thick, anyone would've thought, but Thin Man grinned bad teeth and nodded and blew great clouds of menthol smoke out the window like a locomotive chimney. Open your eyes. I'm not gonna tell you again. Here's another rain of lye across tender meat, and here's the corpse we left to rot in a cornfield, and I won't be left alone, do you hear me? Here are cordials to keep you nailed into your skin and to this festering, unsuspecting world. What am I, what am I, what *am* I? he wails, delirious, as long cornstalk shadows crosshatch the field, and in reply do you say, A sinner in the hands of angry gods, and we'd laugh about that one for days. But maybe he did believe you, sister, for he fell to praying, and I half believe he was praying not to Father, Son, and Holy Ghost, but to you and me. You tell him, By your own words, mister, we see thou art an evil man, and we, too, are surely out and about and up to no good, as you'll have guessed, and we are no better than thee, and so there is balance. I don't know why, but you tack on something about the horned, moon-crowned Popess squatting between Boaz and Jachin on the porch of Solomon. They are pretty words, whether I follow their logic or not. Near, nearer, the train whistle blows again, and in that moment you plunge your knife so deeply into Thin Man's neck that it goes straight through his trachea and spine and out the other side. The cherry fountain splashes you. You give the Bowie a little twist to the left, just for shits and giggles. Appropriately, he lies now still as death. You pull out the knife and kiss the jetting hole you've made, painting sticky your lips and chin. Your throat. You're laughing, and the train shrieks, and now I want to cover my ears, because just every once in a while I do lose my footing on the winding serpent highway, and when I do the fear wraps wet-sheet cold about me. This, here, now, is one of those infrequent, unfortunate episodes. I toss the plastic bottle of lye aside and drag you off Thin Man's still, still corpse. Don't, I say. Don't you dare laugh no more, I don't think it's all that funny, and also don't you dare shut your eyes, and don't you dare go to sleep on me. *Till we reach that blissful shore*

Where the angels wait to join us

In that train

Forevermore.

I seize you, love, and you are raving in my embrace: *What the fuck are you doing? Take your goddamn filthy hands off me cunt, gash, bitch, traitor.* But oh, oh, oh I hold on, and I hold on tight for dear forsaken life, 'cause the land's tilting teeter-totter under us as if on the Last Day of All, the day of Kingdom Come, and just don't make me face the righteous fury of the Lion of Judah alone. In the corn, we rolled and wallowed like dust-bathing mares, while you growled, and foam flecked your bloody lips, and you spat and slashed at the gloaming with your dripping blade. A voyeuristic retinue of grass-hoppers and field mice, crickets and a lone bull snake took in our flailing, certainly comedic antics while I held you prisoner in my arms, holding you hostage against my shameful fear and self-doubt. Finally, inevitably, your laughter died, and I only held you while you sobbed and Iowa sod turned to streaks of mud upon your mirthless face.

4.

I drive west, then east again, then turn south onto I-55, Missouri, the County of Cape Girardeau. Meandering like the cottonmouth, silt-choked Mississippi, out across fertile floodplain fields all night-blanketed, semi-sweet darkness to hide river-gifted loam. You're asleep in the backseat, your breath soft as velvet, soft as autumn rain. You never sleep more than an hour at a time, not ever, and so I never wake you. Not ever. Not even when you cry out from the secret nightmare countries behind your eyelids. We are moving along between the monotonous, barbarous topography and the overcast sky,

overcast at sunset the sky looked dead, and now, well past midnight, there
is still no sign of moon nor stars to guide me, and I have only the road signs
and the tattered atlas lying open beside me as I weave and wend through the
Indian ghosts of Ozark Bluff Dwellers, stalkers of shambling mastodon and
mammoth phantoms along these crude asphalt corridors. I light cigarette
after cigarette and wash Black Beauties down with peach Nehi. I do not
often know loneliness, but I know it now, and I wish I were with you in your
hard, hard dreams. The radio's tuned to a gospel station out of Memphis,
but the volume is down low, low, low so you'll not be awakened by the Five
Blind Boys of Alabama or the Dixie Hummingbirds. In your sleep, you are
muttering, and I try not to eavesdrop. But voices carry, as they say, and I
hear enough to get the gist. You sleep a walking sleep, and in dreams, you've
drifted back to Wichita, to that tow-headed boy with fish and starfish, an
octopus and sea shells tattooed all up and down his arms, across his broad
chest and shoulders. "Because I've never seen the ocean," he said. "But that's
where I'm headed now. I'm going all the way to Florida. To Panama City or
Pensacola." "We've never seen the sea, either," you tell him. "Can we go with
you? We've really nowhere else to go, and you really have no notion how
delightful it will be when they take us up and throw us with the lobsters out
to sea." The boy laughed. No, not a boy, not in truth, but a young man older
than us, a scruffy beard growing unevenly on his suntanned cheeks. "Can
we? Can we, please?" Hey, you're the two with the car, not me, he replied, so
I suppose you're free to go anywhere you desire. And that is the gods' honest
truth of it all, ain't it? We are free to drive anywhere we please, so long as we
do not attempt to part this material plane of simply three dimensions. Alone
in the night, in the now and not the then, I have to be careful. It would be
too easy to slip into my own dreams, amphetamine insomnia helping hands
or no, and I have so often imagined our Odyssey ending with the Impala
wrapped around a telephone pole or lying wheels-up turtlewise and steaming in a ditch or head-on folded back upon ourselves after making love to
an oncoming semi. I shake my head and open my eyes wider. There's a rest
stop not too far up ahead, and I tell myself that I'll pull over there. I'll pull
over to doze for a while in sodium-arc pools, until the sun rises bright and
violent to burn away the clouds, until it's too hot to sleep. The boy's name
was Philip—one L. The young man who was no longer a boy and who had

been decorated with the cryptic nautical language of an ocean he'd never seen, and, as it came to pass, never would. But you'd keep all his teeth in a Mason jar, just in case we ever got around to the Gulf of Mexico or an Atlantic shoreline. You kept his teeth, promising him a burial in salt water. Philip told us about visiting a museum at the university in Lawrence, where he saw the petrified skeletons of giant sea monsters that once had swum the vanished inland depths. He was only a child, ten or eleven, but he memorized names that, to my ears, sounded magical, forbidden, perilous Latin incantations to call down fish from the clear blue sky or summon bones burrowing upwards from yellow-gray chalky rocks. You sat with your arms draped shameless about his neck while he recited and elaborated—*Tylosaurus proriger, Dolichorhynchops bonneri, Platecarpus tympaniticus, Elasmosaurus platyurus, Salmasaurus kiernanae*, birds with teeth and giant turtles, flying reptiles and the fangs of ancient sharks undulled by eighty-five million years, give or take. Show off, you said and laughed. That's what you are, a show off. And you said, Why aren't you in college, bright boy? And Philip with one L said his parents couldn't afford tuition, and his grades had not been good enough for a scholarship, and he wasn't gonna join the army, because he had a cousin went off to Desert Storm, right, and did his duty in Iraq, and now he's afraid to leave the house and sick all the time and constantly checks his shoes for scorpions and land mines. The military denies all responsibility. Maybe, said Philip with one L, I can get a job on a fishing boat, or a shrimping boat, and spend all my days on the water and all my nights drinking rum with mermaids. We could almost have fallen in love with him. Almost. You even whispered to me about driving him to Florida that he might lay eyes upon the Gulf of Mexico before he died. But I am a jealous bitch, and I said no, fuck that sentimental horseshit, and he died the next day in a landfill not far from Emporia. I did that one, cut his throat from ear to ear while he was busy screwing you. He looked up at me, his stark blue irises drowning in surprise and confusion, and then he came one last time, coaxed to orgasm, pumping blood from severed carotid and jugular and, too, pumping out an oyster stream of jizz. It seemed all but immaculate, the red and the silver-gray, and you rode him even after there was no more of him left to ride but a cooling cadaver. You cried over Philip, and that was the first and only one you ever shed tears for, and Jesus I am sorry but I wanted to slap you. I wanted to do something worse than slap you for your mourning. I wanted to leave a scar. Instead, I gouged out his lifeless eyes with my thumbs and spat in his face. You wiped your nose on your shirt sleeve, pulled up your underwear and jeans, and went back to the car for the needle-nose pair of pliers in the glove compartment. It did not have to be that way, you said, you pouted, and I growled at you to shut up, and whatever it is you're doing in his mouth, hurry because this place gives me the creeps. Those slumping, smoldering hills of refuse, Gehenna for rats and maggots and crows, coyotes, stray dogs and strayer cats. We *could* have taken him to the sea, you said. We *could* have done that much, and then you fell silent, sulking, taciturn, and not ever again waking have you spoken of him. Besides the teeth, you peeled off a patch of skin, big as the palm of your hand and inked with the image of a crab, because we were born in the sign of Cancer. The rest of him we concealed under heaps of garbage. *Here you go, rats, here's something fresh. Here's a banquet, and we shall not even demand tribute in return. We will be benevolent rat gods, will we two, bringing plenty and then taking our leave, and you will spin prophecies of our return. Amen. Amen. Hosannah.* Our work done, I followed you back to the Impala, stepping superstitiously in your footsteps, and that is what I am doing when—now—I snap awake to the dull, gritty noise of the tires bumping off the shoulder and spraying dry showers of breakdown-lane gravel, and me half awake and cursing myself for nodding off; fuck me, fuck me, I'm such an idiot, how I should have stopped way the hell back in Bonne Terre or Fredericktown. I cut the wheel left, and, just like that, all is right again. Doomsday set aside for now. In the backseat, you don't even stir. I turn up the radio for companionship. If I had toothpicks, I might prop open my eyes. My hands are red, love. Oh god, my hands are so red, and we have not ever looked upon the sea.

5.

Boredom, you have said again and again, is the one demon might do you in, and the greatest of all our foes, the *one* demon, Mystery Babylon, the Great Harlot, who at the Valley of Josaphat, on the hill of Megiddo, wraps chains about our porcelain slender necks and drags us down to dust and comeuppance if we dare to turn our backs upon the motherfucker and give it free fucking rein. I might allow how this is the mantra that set us to traveling on the road we are on and has dictated our every action since that departure, your morbid fear of boredom. The consequence of this mantra has almost torn you in half, so that I bend low over my love, only my bare hands to keep your insides from spilling outside. Don't you shut your eyes. You don't get out half that easy. Simple boredom is as good as the flapping wings of butter-flies to stir the birth throes of hurricanes. Tiresome recitations of childhood traumas and psychoses be damned. As are we; as are we.

6.

We found her, or she was the one found us, another state, another county, the outskirts of another slumbering city. Another truck-stop diner. Because we were determined to become connoisseurs of everything that is fried and smothered in lumpy brown gravy, and you were sipping a flat Coke dissolute with melting ice. You were talking—I don't know why—about the night back home when the Piggly Wiggly caught fire, so we climbed onto the roof and watched it go up. The air smelled like burning groceries. We contemplated cans of Del Monte string beans and pears and cans of Grapico reaching the boiling point and going off like grenades, and the smoke rose up and blotted out the moon, which that night was full. You're talking about the fire, and suddenly she's there, the coal-haired girl named Haddie in her too-large Lol-lapalooza T-shirt and black jeans and work boots. Her eyes are chipped jade and honey, that variegated hazel, and she smiles so disarming a smile and asks if, perhaps, we're heading east towards Birmingham, because she's try-ing to get to Birmingham, but—insert here a woeful tale of her douche-bag boyfriend—and now she's stranded high and dry, not enough money for bus fare, and if we're headed that way, could she please, and would we please? You scoot over and pat the turquoise sparkle vinyl upholstery, inviting her to take a Naugahyde seat, said the spider to the fly. "Thank you," she says. "Thank you very much," and she sits and you share your link sausage and waffles with her, because she says she hasn't any money for food, either. We're heading for Atlanta, you tell her, and we'll be going right straight through Birmingham, so sure, no problem, the more the goddamn merrier. We are lifesavers, she says. Never been called that before. You chat her up, sweet as cherry pie with whipped cream squirted from a can, and, me, I stare out the plate-glass partition at the gas pumps and the stark white lighting to hide the place where a Mississippi night should be. "Austin," she says, when you ask from whence she's come. "Austin, Texas," she volunteers. "I was born and raised there." Well, you can hear it, plain as tits on a sow, in her easy, drawling voice. I take in a mouthful of lukewarm Cheerwine, swallow, repeat, and do not let my attention drift from the window and an idling eighteen-wheeler parked out there with its cab all painted up like a Santería altar whore, gaudy and ominous and seductive. Smiling Madonna and cherubic child, merry skeletons dancing joyful round about a sorrowful, solemn Pietà, roses and carnations, crucifixions, half-pagan *orichá* and weeping bloody Catholic Jesus. Of a sudden, then, I feel a sick coldness spreading deep in my bowels, ice water heavy in my guts, and I want to tell this talkative Lone-Star transient that no, sorry, but you spoke too soon and, sorry, but we *can't* give her a ride, after all, not to Birmingham or anywhere else, that she'll have to bum one from another mark, which won't be hard, because the night is filled with travelers. I want to say just that. But I don't. Instead, I keep my mouth shut tight and watch as a man in dirty orange coveralls climbs into the cab of the truck, him and his goddamn enormous shaggy dog. That dog, it might almost pass for a midget grizzly. In the meanwhile, Ms. Austin is sitting there feeding you choice slivers of her life's story, and you devour it, because I've never yet seen you not hungry for a sobby tale. This one, she's got all the hallmarks of a banquet, doesn't she? Easy pickings, if I only trust experience and ignore this inexplicable wash of instinct. Then you, love, give me a gentle, unseen kick beneath the table, hardly more than an emphatic nudge, your right foot insistently tapping, tap, tap, at my left ankle in a private Morse. I fake an unconcerned smile and turn my face away from the window and that strange truck, though I can still hear its impatient engines. "A painter," says Ms. Austin. "See, I want to be a painter. I've got an aunt in Birmingham, and she knows my mom's a total cunt, and she doesn't mind if I stay with her while I try to get my shit together. It was supposed to be me and him both, but now it's just gonna be me. See, I shut my eyes, and I see murals, and that's what I want to paint one day. *Wallscapes*." And she talks about murals in Mexico City and Belfast and East Berlin. "I need to piss," I say, and you flash me a questioning glance that Ms. Austin does not appear to catch. I slide out of the turquoise booth and walk past other people eating other meals, past shelves grounded with motor oil, candy bars, and pornography. I'm lucky and there's no one else in the restroom, no one to hear me vomit. *What the fuck is this? Hunh? What the fuck is wrong with me now?* When the retching is done, I sit on the dirty tile floor and drown in sweat and listen to my heart throwing a tantrum in my chest. Get up and get back out there. And you, don't you even think of shutting your eyes again. The sun won't rise for another two hours, another two hours at least, and we made a promise one to the other. Or have you forgotten in the gauzy veils of hurt and Santísima Muerte come to whisper in your ear? Always have you said you were hers, a demimondaine to the Bony Lady, *la Huesuda*. So, faithless, I have to suffer your devotions as well? I also shoulder your debt? The restroom stinks of cleaning fluid, shit and urine, my puke, deodorant cakes and antibacterial soap, filth and excessive cleanliness rubbing shoulders. I don't recall getting to my feet. I don't recall a number of things, truth be told, but then we're paying the check, and then we're out in the muggy Lee County night. You tow Ms. Austin behind you. She rides your wake, slipstreaming, and she seems to find every goddamn thing funny. You climb into the backseat with her, and the two of you giggle and titter over private jokes to which I have apparently not been invited. What all did I miss while I was on my knees, praying to my Toilet Gods? I put in a Patsy Cline tape, *punch* it into the deck as you would, and crank it up loud so I don't have to listen to the two of you, not knowing what you (not her, just *you*) have planned, feeling like an outsider in your company, and I cannot ever recall that having happened. Before long, the lights of Tupelo are growing small and dim in the rearview, a diminishing sun as the Impala glides southeast along US 78. My foot feels heavy as a millstone on the gas pedal. So, I have "A Poor Man's Roses" and "Back in Baby's Arms" and "Sweet Dreams" and a fresh pack of Camels and you and Ms. Austin spooning at my back. And still that ice water in my bowels. She's talking about barbeque, and you laugh, and what the fuck is funny about barbeque. "Dreamland," she says, "just like what those UFO nuts call Area 51 in Nevada, where that dead Roswell alien and shit's supposed to be hidden." Me, I smoke and chew on bitter cherry-flavored Tums tablets, grinding calcium carbonate and cornstarch and talc between my teeth. "Those like you," says Ms. Austin, "who've lost their way," and I have no goddamn idea what she's going on about. We cross a bridge, and if it's a river below us, I do not see any indication that it's been given a name. But we're entering Itawamba County, says a sign, and that sounds like some mythological world serpent or some place from a William Faulkner novel. Only about twenty miles now to the state line, and I'm thinking how I desire to be shed of the bitch, how I want her out of the car before Tuscaloosa, wondering how I can signal you without making Ms. Austin Texas Chatterbox suspicious. We pass a dozen exits to lonely country roads where we could take our time, do the job right, and at least I'd have something to show for my sour stomach. I'm thinking about the couple in Arkansas, how we made him watch while we took our own sweet time with her, and you telling him it wasn't so different from skinning catfish, not really. A sharp knife and a pair of pliers, that's all you really need, and he screamed and screamed and screamed. Hell, the pussy bastard son of a bitch screamed more than she did. In the end, I put a bullet in his brain just to shut him the fuck up, please. And we'd taken so long with her, hours and hours, well, there wasn't time remaining to do him justice, anyway. After that we've made a point of avoiding couples. After that, it became a matter of policy. Also, I remember that girl we stuck in the trunk for a hundred miles, and how she was half dead of heat prostration by the time we got around to ring around the rosies, pockets full of posies time. And you sulked for days. Now, here, I watch you in the rearview, and if you notice that I am, you're purposefully ignoring me. I have to take a piss, I say, and she giggles. Fuck you, Catfish. Fuck you, because on this road you're traveling, is there hope for tomorrow? On this Glory Road you're traveling, to that land of perfect peace and endless fucking day, that's my twin sister you've got back there with you, my one and true and perfect love, and this train is bound for Glory, ain't nobody ride it, *Catfish*, but the righteous and the holy, and if this train don't turn around, well, I'm Alabama bound. You and me and she, only, we ain't going that far together. Here's why God and all his angels and the demons down under the sea made detours, *Catfish*. The headlights paint twin high-beam encouragement, luring me on down Appalachian Corridor X, and back there behind me you grumble something about how I'm never gonna find a place to piss here, not unless it's in the bushes. I'm about to cut the wheel again, because there's an unlit side road like the pitchy throat of evening wanting to swallow us whole, and right now, I'm all for that, but . . . Catfish, née Austin Girl, says that's enough, turn right around and get back on the goddamn highway. And whatever I'm supposed to say, however I'm about to tell her to go fuck herself, I don't. She's got a gun, you say. Jesus, Bobbie, she's got a gun, and you laugh a nervous, disbelieving laugh. You laugh a stunned laugh. She's got a goddamn gun. *What the fuck*, I whisper, and again she instructs me to retrace my steps back to 78. Her voice is cold now as the Arctic currents in my belly. I look in the rearview, and I can't *see* a gun. I want to believe this is some goddamn idiot prank you and she have cooked up, pulling the wool for whatever reason known only to thee. What do you want? I ask, and she says we'll get to that, in the sweet by-and-by, so don't I go fretting my precious little head over what she wants, okay? Sure, sure. And five minutes later we're back on the highway, and you're starting to sound less surprised, surprise turning to fear, because this is not how the game is played. This is *not* the story. We don't have shit, I tell her. We ain't got any money, and we don't have shit, so if you think—and she interrupts, Well, you got this car, don't you? And that's more than me, so how about you just shut up and drive, Little Bird. That's what she calls me, *Little Bird*. So, someone's rewriting the fairy tale all around us; I know that now, and I realize that's the ice in the middle of me. How many warnings did we fail to heed? The Santería semi, that one for sure, as good as any caution sign planted at the side of any path. Once upon a time, pay attention, you and you who have assumed that no one's out there hunting wolves, or that all the lost girls and boys and men and women on the bum are defenseless lambs to the slaughter. Wrong. Wrong. Wrong, and it's too late now. But I push those thoughts down, and I try to focus on nothing but your face in the mirror, even though the sight of you scares the hell out of me. It's been a long time since I've seen you like that, and I thought I never would again. You want the car? I ask Catfish. Is that it? Because if you want the car, fuck it, it's yours. Just let me pull the fuck over, and I'll hand you the goddamn keys. But no, she says. No, I think you should keep right on driving for a while. As for pulling over, I'll say when. I'll say when, on that you can be sure.

7.

Maybe, you say, *it wouldn't be such a bad idea to go home now*, and I nod, and I wipe the blood off your lips, the strawberry life leaking from you freely as ropy cheesecloth, muslin ectoplasm from the mouth, ears, nostrils of a 1912 spiritualist. I wipe it away, but I hold it, too, clasping it against the loss of you. So long as I can catch all the rain in my cupped hands, neither of us shall drown. You just watch me, okay? Keep your eyes on my eyes, and I'll pull you through. It looks a lot worse than it is, I lie. I know it hurts, but you'll be fine. All the blood makes it look terrible, I know, but you'll be fine. Don't you close your goddamn eyes. Oh, sister, don't you die. Don't speak. I cannot stand the rheumy sound of the blood in your throat, so please do not speak. But you say, *You can hear the bells, Bobbie, can't you? Fuck, but they are so red, and they are so loud, how could you not? Take me and cut me out in little stars . . .*

8.

So fast, my love, so swift and sure thy hands, and when Catfish leaned forward to press the muzzle of her 9mm to my head and tell me to shut up and drive, you drew your vorpal steel, and the razor folded open like a silver flower and snicker-snacked across coal-haired Haddie's throat. She opened up as if she'd come with a zipper. Later, we opened her wide and sunk her body in a marshy maze of swamp and creek beds and snapping-turtle weeds. Scum-green water, and her guts pulled out and replaced with stones. You wanted to know were there alligators this far north, handy-dandy helpful gator pals to make nothing more of her than alligator shit, and me, I said, hey this is goddamn Mississippi, there could be crocodiles and pythons for all I know. Afterwards, we bathed in the muddy slough, because cutting a bitch's throat is dirty goddamn business, and then we fucked in the high grass, then had to pluck off leeches from our legs and arms and that one ambitious pioneer clinging fiercely to your left nipple. *What about the car? The car's a bloody goddamn mess.* And yeah, I agreed, what about the car? We took what we needed from the Impala, loaded our scavenged belongings into a couple of backpacks, knapsacks, a pillowcase, and then we shifted the car into neutral and pushed it into those nameless waters at the end of a nameless dirt road, and we hiked back to 78. You did so love that car, our sixteenth-birthday present, but it is what it is and can't be helped, and no way we could have washed away the indelible stain left behind by treacherous Catfish's undoing. That was the first and only time we ever killed in self-defense, and it made you so angry, because her death, you said, spoiled the purity of the game. What have we got, Bobbie, except *that* purity? And now it's tainted, sullied by one silly little thief—or what the hell ever she might have been. We have us, I replied. We will always have us, so stop your worrying. My words were, at best, cold comfort, I could tell, and that hurt more than just a little bit, but I kept it to myself, the pain, the hollow in the pit of my soul that had not been there only the half second before you started in on purity and being soiled by the thwarted shenanigans of Catfish. Are you all right? you asked me, as we marched up the off-ramp. I smiled and shook my head. Really, I'm thinking, let's not have that shoe's on the other foot thing ever again, love. Let's see if we can be more careful about who we let in the car that we no longer have. There was a moon three nights past full, like a judgmental god's eye to watch us on our way. We didn't hitch. We just fucking walked until dawn, and then stole a new car from a driveway outside of Tremont. You pulled the tag and stuck on our old Nebraska plates, amongst that which we'd salvaged from the blooded Impala. The new ride, a swank fucking brand-new '96 Saturn the color of Granny Smith apples, it had all-electric windows, but a CD player when all we had was our box of tapes, so fuck that; we'd have to rely on the radio. We hooked onto WVUA 90.7 FM outta Tuscaloosa, and the DJ played Soundgarden and Beck and lulled us forward on the two-lane black-racer asphalt rails of that river, traveling dawnwise back to the earliest beginnings of the world, you said, watching the morning mist burning away, and you said, *When vegetation rioted on the earth, and the big trees were kings.* Read that somewhere? Yeah, you said, and shortly thereafter we took Exit 14, stopping just south of Hamilton, Alabama, because there was a Huddle House, and by then we were both starving all over again. There was also a Texaco station, and good thing, too, as the Saturn was sitting on empty, running on fumes. So, in the cramped white-tile fluorescent-drenched restroom, we washed off the swamp water we'd employed to wash away the dead girl's blood. I used wads of paper towels to clean your face as best I could, after the way the raw-boned waitress with her calla-lily tattoo stared at you. I thought there for a moment maybe it was gonna be her turn to pay the ferryman, but you let it slide. There's another woman's scabs crusted in your hair, stubborn clots, and the powdery soap from the powdery soap dispenser on the wall above the sink isn't helping all that much. I need a drink, you said. I need a drink like you would not believe. Yeah, fine, I replied, remembering the half-full, half-empty bottle of Jack in the pillowcase, so just let me get this spot here at your hairline. You go back to talking about the *river*, as if I understand—often I never truly understood you, and for that did I love thee even more. The road which is the river, the river which is the road, mortality, infinity, the grinding maw of history; *An empty stream, a great goddamn silence, an impenetrable forever forest. That's what I'm saying*, you said. *In my eyes, in disposed, in disgrace.* And I said it's gonna be a scorcher today, and at least the Saturn has AC, not like the late beloved lamented Impala, and you spit out what the fuck ever. I fill the tank, and I mention how it's a shame Ms. Austin Catfish didn't have a few dollars on her. We're damn near busted flat. Yeah, well, we'll fix that soon, you say. We'll fix that soon enough, my sweet. You're sitting on the hood, examining the gun she'd have used to lay us low. Make sure the safety is on, I say. And what I think in the split second before the pistol shot is *Please be careful with that thing, the shit our luck's been*, but I didn't say it *aloud*. An unspoken thought, then bang. No. Then BANG. You look nothing in blue blazes but surprised. You turn your face towards me, and the 9mm slips from your fingers and clatters to the oil- and antifreeze-soaked tarmac. I see the black girl behind the register looking our way, and Jesus motherfucking-fucking-fuck-fuck-fucking-motherfucker-oh fuck me this *cannot* be goddamn happening, no way can *this* be happening, not after everything we've done and been through and how there's so much left to do and how I love you so. Suddenly, the air is nothing if not gasoline and sunlight. I can hardly clear my head, and I'm waiting for certain spontaneous combustion and the grand *whump* when the tanks blow, and they'll see the mushroom cloud for miles and miles around. My head fills with fire that isn't even there, but, still, flash-blind, I somehow wrestle you into the backseat. Your eyes are muddy with shock, muddy with perfect incredulity. I press your left hand against the wet hole in that soft spot below your sternum, and you gasp in pain and squeeze my wrist so hard it hurts. *No, okay, you gotta let go now, I gotta get us the fuck outta here before the cops show up. Let go, but keep pressure on it, right? But we have to get out of here now.* Because, I do not add, that gunshot was louder than thunder, that gunshot cleaved the morning apart like the wrath of Gog and Magog striding free across the Armageddon land, Ezekiel 38:2, or wild archangel voices and the trumpet of Thessalonians 4:16. There's a scattered handful of seconds, and then I'm back on the highway again, not thinking, just driving south and east. I try not to hear your moans, 'cause how's that gonna help either of us, but I do catch the words when you whisper, *Are you all right, Bobbie? You flew away like a little bird,* and isn't that what Catfish called me? *So how about you just shut up and drive, Little Bird.* And in my head I do see a looped serpent made of fire devouring its own tail, and I know we cheated fate only for a few hours, only to meet up with it again a little farther down the road. I just drive. I don't even think to switch on the AC or roll down the window or even notice how the car's becoming as good as a kiln on four wheels. I just fucking *drive.* And, like agate beads strung along a rosary, I recite the prayer given me at the End of Days, the end of one of us: Don't you fucking shut your eyes. Please, don't you shut your eyes, because you do not want to go there, and I do not want to be alone forever and forever without the half of me that's you. In my hands, the steering wheel is busy swallowing its own tail, devouring round and round, and we, you and I, are only passengers.

FAIRY TALE
OF WOOD STREET

1.

'M LYING IN BED, forgetting a dream of some forested place, a dream that is already coming apart behind my waking eyes like wet tissue between my fingers, and Hana gets up and walks across the bedroom to stand before the tall vanity mirror. The late morning sun is bright in the room, bright summer sun, July sun, and I know by the breeze through the open window that the coming afternoon will be cool. I can smell the flowers on the table by the bed, and I can smell the bay, too, riding the breeze, that faintly muddy, faintly salty, very faintly fishy smell that never ceases to make me think of the smell of sex. I watch Hana for a moment, standing there nude before the looking glass, her skin like porcelain, her eyes like moss on weathered slabs of shale, her hair the same pale shade of yellow as corn meal. And I'm thinking, *Roll over and shut your eyes, because if you keep on watching you'll only get horny again, and you'll call her back to bed, and she'll come, and neither of us will get anything at all done today. And you have that meeting at two, and she has shopping and a trip to the post office and the library to return overdue books, so just roll over and don't see her. Think about the fading wet tissue shreds of the dream, instead.* And that's exactly what I mean to do, to lie there with my eyes shut, pretending to doze while she gets dressed. But then I see her tail.

"Look at us," she says, "sleeping half the day away. It's almost noon. You should get up and get dressed. I need a shower."

Her tail looks very much like the tail of a cow. At least, that is the first thing that comes to mind, the Holstein and Ayrshire cows my grandfather raised when I was a girl and my family lived way off in western Massachusetts, almost to the New York state line, the cattle he raised for milk for the cheese he made. Hana's tail hangs down a little past the bend of her knees, and there's a tuft of hair on the end of it that is almost the exact same blonde as the hair on her head. Maybe a little darker, but not by much. It occurs to me, dimly, that I ought to be shocked or maybe even afraid. That I ought, at the very least, to be surprised, but the truth is that I'm not any of those things. Mostly, I'm trying to figure out why I never noticed it in all the months since we met and she moved into my apartment here in the old house on the east end of Wood Street.

"I smell like sex," Hana says, and she sniffs at her unshaved armpits. Her tail twitches, sways side to side a moment, and then is still again.

"Maybe you should just forget about the shower and come back to bed," I say, and while the sight of her tail didn't come as a surprise, that does, those words from my mouth, when what I was just thinking—before I saw the tail—was how we both have entirely too much to do today to have spent the whole morning fucking. I realize that my hand is between my legs, that I'm touching myself, and I force myself to stop. But my fingers are damp, and there's a flutter in my belly, just below my navel.

"You don't really want me to do that," she says, glancing back over her shoulder. And I think, *No, I don't. I want to get up and have a bath and get dressed, and I want to forget that I ever saw that she has a tail. If I can forget I saw it, maybe it won't be there the next time I see her naked. Maybe it's only a temporary, transitory sort of thing, like a bad cold or a wart.*

"I was thinking we could go to the movies tonight," she says, turning to face the mirror again.

"Were you?" I ask her.

"I was. There's something showing at the Avon that I'd like to see, and I think tonight is the last night. This is Wednesday, right?"

"I believe so," I reply, but I have to think for a moment to be sure, to make it past the sight of her tail and the wetness between my thighs and the dregs of the dream and the smell of Narragansett Bay getting in through the open bedroom window. "Yes," I say. "Today is Wednesday."

"We don't have to go," she says. "Not if you don't want to. But I was thinking we could maybe get a bite to eat, maybe sushi, and make the early show. If your meeting doesn't run too long. If there isn't something afterwards that you have to do."

"No," I say. "I don't think so. I should be done by five. By five-thirty at the latest."

Her tail twitches again, and then it swings from side to side several times, and once more I'm reminded of my grandfather's milk cows. It doesn't seem at all like a flattering comparison, and so I try to remember what other sort of animals have tails like that, long tails with a tuft right at the end. But I'm unable to think of any others except cows.

"Are you feeling well?" she asks, watching me from the mirror, and I catch the faintest glimmer of worry in her green-grey eyes.

"I'm fine," I reply. "I had a strange dream, that's all. One I'm having a little trouble shaking off." And I almost add, *I had a dream that you were a woman who didn't have a tail, and that I lived in a world where women don't, as a rule, have tails.*

"My mother used to call that being dreamsick," says Hana, "when you wake up from a dream, but it stays with you for a long time afterwards, and you have trouble thinking about anything else, almost like you're still asleep and dreaming."

"I'm fine," I tell her again.

"You look a little pale, that's all."

"I never get any sun. You know, I read somewhere online that ninety percent of Americans suffer from vitamin D deficiency because they don't get enough sun, because they spend too little time out of doors."

"We should go to the shore this weekend," she says. "I know you hate the summer people, but we should go, anyway."

"Maybe we'll do that," I tell her, and then Hana smiles, and she leaves me alone in the bedroom and goes to take her shower.

2.

As it happens, we don't go for sushi, because by the time I'm done with work and make it back to our apartment on Wood Street, Hana has read something somewhere about people in the Mekong Delta dying at an alarming rate from ingesting liver flukes from raw fish. I can't really blame her for losing interest in sushi after that. Instead, we go to an Indian place on Thayer, only a block from the theater, and we share curried goat and saag paneer with ice water and icy bottles of Kingfisher lager. While we're eating, it begins to rain, and neither one of us has brought an umbrella. We each make do with half the *Providence Journal*. The newsprint runs and stains our fingers and stains our clothes and leaves a lead-blue streak on the left side of Hana's face that I wipe away with spit and the pad of my left index finger. The theater lobby is bright and warm and smells pleasantly of popcorn, and standing there while Hana buys our tickets it occurs to me that most of the day and part of the evening have gone by without me thinking about Hana's tail.

"Would you like something?" she asks, looking back at me, then pointing at the rows of overpriced candy behind glass.

"No," I say. "I'm fine. I think I ate too much back at the restaurant."

"Suit yourself," she says, and then she asks the boy working the concessions for a box of Good & Plenty and a large Dr Pepper.

For just a moment, it seems that I must only have imagined that business with Hana's tail. It seems I must surely have awakened from an uneasy dream, which I have since almost entirely forgotten, and being only half awake—half awake at best, my head still mired half in the dream—I saw a tail where there was not actually a tail to see. And here in the theater lobby, my belly full and my hair damp from a summer rain, it seems a far more reasonable explanation than the alternative, that my girlfriend has a tail. I look at her tight jeans, and there's plainly no room in there for the tail that I thought I saw, the tail that reminded me so much of the tails of my grandfather's cows.

Hana pays for her soft drink and for the candy, and I follow her out of the bright lobby and into the dimly lit auditorium. The Avon is an old theater, and it has the smell of an old theater, that peculiar, distinctive blend of sweet and musty and very faintly sour that I can't recall ever having smelled anywhere else *but* old movie theaters. It's a smell of dust and fermentation, an odor that simultaneously comforts me and makes me think someone could probably do a better job of keeping the floors and the seats clean. But when a theater has been in continuous operation since 1936, like this one has, well, that's more than eighty years of spilled cola and fingers greasy from popcorn and Milk Duds getting dropped and ground into the carpet in the darkness when no one can clearly see where they're putting their feet. We take our seats, not too near the screen and not too far away, and it occurs to me for the first time that I don't actually know what we've come to see.

"I think you'll like it," Hana says, peeling the cellophane off her box of Good & Plenty. She drops the plastic wrap onto the floor. In the past, I've asked her please not to do that, but she only pointed out that someone gets paid to pick it back up again and then she did it, anyway.

"I don't even know the title," I say, wondering if she told me, and I just can't remember that she told me. "I don't know the director."

"It's German," Hana says. "Well, I mean the director is German, and I think some of the funding came from Deutscher Filmförderfonds, and it's set in the Black Mountains, but it's actually an English language film. I think you'll like it. I think it did well at Cannes and Sundance." But she doesn't tell me the title. She doesn't tell me the name of the director. I try to recall walking towards the theater from the Indian restaurant and looking up to see what was on the theater's marquee, but I can't. Not clearly, anyway. I rub at my eyes a moment, and Hana asks me if I'm getting a headache.

"No," I tell her. "I'm just trying to remember something. My memory's for shit today." I don't tell her that I'm wondering if forty-four is too young to be displaying symptoms of early onset Alzheimer's.

There are a few other people in the theater with us. Not many, but a few. I hadn't expected a crowd. After all, it's a rainy Wednesday night. No one is sitting very near us. Some of the people are staring at their phones, their faces underlit by liquid-crystal touchscreen glow. Here and there, others whisper to one another in the way that people whisper in theaters and libraries and meeting halls and other places where you've been taught since childhood to keep your voice down. I stare across the tops of the rows of seats dividing us from the small stage and the tall red curtain concealing the screen. Hana takes a pink Good & Plenty from the box, and she offers it to me.

"No, I'm fine," I say.

"Woolgathering," she says, and I say, "A penny for your thoughts," and she says, "No, I asked first." Then she puts the candy-coated licorice into her mouth and chews and waits for whatever it is she thinks that I'm supposed to say.

"It's nothing," I say.

"It's something," she replies. "I can tell by the lines at the corners of your eyes and that little wrinkle on your forehead."

I'm trying to come up with something to tell her that isn't *This morning, I saw your tail, or at least I think I saw your tail*, when I'm rescued by the curtains parting and the screen flickering to life, by giant boxes of cartoon popcorn and cartoon chocolate bars and a cartoon hot dog marching by and singing "Let's All Go to the Lobby."

"Isn't there a word for that?" Hana asks me, shaking out a couple more Good & Plentys into her palm.

"A word for what?"

"For anthropomorphized food that wants you to eat it. Like there's a word for buildings in the shape of whatever's being sold there."

"I didn't know there was a word for that," I reply.

"Mimetic architecture," she says. "I remember that from an advertising and mass media class I had in college. And I thought there was also a word for food that wants you to eat it. You know, like Charlie the Tuna. Like that," she says and points at the screen.

"If there is, I don't think that I've ever heard it."

And then the ad for the concession stand ends and the first trailer starts, and it occurs to me that I have to piss rather urgently. I should have done it before I sat down, but I was probably too busy trying to decide whether or not I truly did see Hana's tail that morning. The first trailer is for some sort of science-fiction comedy about a grumpy old man and a wise-cracking robot driving across America, and I tell Hana that I'll be right back.

"You should have gone before we got our seats," she says. "Hurry, or you'll miss the beginning. I hate when you miss the beginnings of things."

"I'll be right back," I tell her again. "I won't miss the beginning. I promise."

"You say that," and she reminds me how, last spring, I missed the first ten

413

minutes of *Auntie Mame* when it was screened at RISD, and how I missed even more of the start of the last Quentin Tarantino film, even though we'd gotten tickets to a special 70mm screening. And then she tells me to go on, but not to dawdle and not to decide I need to go outside for a cigarette. I assure her that I won't do either, and I get up and leave her sitting there.

3.

At the back of the auditorium, there's a very narrow flight of stairs that leads up to a tiny landing and to an antique candy machine and two restroom doors, Gents and Ladies, and to the door of the projection booth. The candy machine is the sort that was already becoming uncommon when I was a little kid, the sort that takes a quarter or two and you pull a knob and out comes your Hershey Bar or whatever you've selected. The machine is now undoubtedly a museum piece, and even though there's no OUT OF ORDER sign on it and the coin slot hasn't been taped over, I can't believe the thing actually works. I've never tested it to find out. The candy wrappers lined up neatly inside look dusty, their colors faded, but maybe it's just that the glass display window has grown cloudy over the decades. Maybe it's only an illusion, and the candy is restocked every day or so.

And then I think about Hana telling me to please hurry and not to dawdle, and so I push open the door marked LADIES and the old theater smell is immediately replaced with an old theater restroom smell, which isn't all that different from the smell of most public restrooms, at least the ones that are kept reasonably clean and have been around for a while. The women's restroom is so small that I can imagine a claustrophobic preferring to piss themselves rather than spend any time at all in here, certainly not as much time as would be necessary to relieve oneself. There are two stalls, though there's hardly room enough for one, and the walls are painted a color that can't seem to decide whether to be beige or some muddy shade of yellow. The floor is covered in a mosaic of tiny black and white ceramic hexagonal tiles.

Just inside the door, there's a mirror so large it seems entirely out of proportion with so small a room, and I pause and squint back at myself. There's a smudge of newsprint on my chin that Hana hadn't bothered to tell me about, and I rub at it until it's mostly not there anymore. And then, staring at my reflection, I think of watching Hana's reflection in our bedroom vanity mirror that morning, and I think of her tail, and I wonder if maybe it was only some trick of the late morning light. I also wonder what she'd have said if I'd had the nerve to just come right out and ask her about it:

"How is it you've never before mentioned that you have a tail?"

"How is it that you've never noticed?"

"I don't know. I can't say. Maybe it wasn't there until now."

"Or maybe whenever you're fucking me, you're too busy thinking about fucking someone else to pay that much attention. One of your exes, maybe. The one who went away to Seattle to go to clown school, for example."

"It wasn't Seattle, it was Portland."

"Like there's a difference. And who does that, anyway? What sort of grown-up adult woman quits her job and leaves her girlfriend to run off and join the circus?"

"Well, even if that were true—and it most certainly isn't—no matter who I might have been fantasizing about all those times, I think I wouldn't have been so consistently and completely distracted that I would have failed to notice that you have a tail."

"Sure. You say that. But remember when I stopped shaving under my arms, and it took you a month to even notice?"

I suspect it would have gone like that, or it would have gone worse.

There's no one else in the restroom, so I have my choice of the two stalls, and I choose the one nearest to the door, which also happens to be slightly larger than the one farthest from the door. I go in, latch it, pull down my pants, and sit there counting the hexagonal tiles at my feet while I piss and try to remember the name of the movie we've come to see on this rainy Wednesday night, because at least if I'm doing that, if my mind is occupied, maybe I won't be thinking about Hana's tail. I'm just about to tear off a piece of the stiff and scratchy toilet paper from the roll on the wall, when I hear a bird. And not just any bird, but what I am fairly certain is the cawing of a raven. Or at least a crow. My first thought is that I'd never before noticed how clearly sound carries through the floor up from the theater auditorium below, and my second thought is that, were that the case, that I was only hearing a raven from one of the movie trailers, I ought to be hearing other things, as well.

Sound can do funny things, I think. And then I think, *For that matter, so can morning light and shadow in a bedroom when you're still groggy from a dream and from sex.* Neither strikes me as a very convincing explanation.

I hear the bird again, and this time I'm quite sure that I'm not hearing a recorded snippet of film soundtrack, not Dolby stereo, but something that is alive and there in the room with me. I wipe and get to my feet, pull up my pants, and then hesitate, one hand on the stall door's latch and the other on the handle. My heart is beating a little too fast and my mouth has gone dry and cottony. I want a cigarette, and I want to be back downstairs with Hana. I realize that I haven't flushed. I'm about to turn around and do just that, when there's another sound, a dry, rustling, fluttering sort of a sound that might be wings or might be something else altogether. And suddenly I feel very goddamn stupid, like I'm five years old and afraid to step on a crack or walk under a ladder or something like that. I take a deep breath, and I open the door. And I see that there's a huge black bird watching me from the mirror, standing on the floor, the floor in the looking-glass version of the Avon's women's room, glaring up at me with beady golden eyes. It looks angry, that bird. It looks dangerous. It occurs to me that I never had realized just how big ravens are. This one's as big as a tomcat, a very big tomcat, and it hops towards me, and I take a step backwards and bump into the stall. Then I look down and realize that there's no corresponding bird standing on the floor in front of me to be casting the reflection, and when I look back up at the mirror again, there's no bird there either.

I think again about early onset Alzheimer's disease.

And then I flush the toilet and wash my hands with gritty pink powder and go back downstairs.

4.

By the time I get back downstairs, the feature has already started, and despite the bird in the mirror and the very real concern that I may be rapidly losing my mind, that I may have lost it already, I'm mostly worrying about how annoyed with me Hana's going to be. "Just like *Auntie Mame*," she'll say. "Just like *The Hateful Eight* all over again." And it's not as if I can use the phantom raven as an excuse. Well, I could, but I know myself well enough to know that I won't. So long as I keep these visions or hallucinations or illusions to myself, they will seem somehow less solid, less real, less *tangible*. The moment I cast them into language and share them with someone else any possibility that I can simply put it all behind me and get on with my life and have, for example, a perfectly ordinary Thursday, goes right out the window.

The movie we've come to see, whatever its title, is in black and white.

I don't immediately return to my seat and to Hana. Instead, I stand behind the back row, where no one happens to be sitting, and I watch the movie. Up on the screen there is a forest primeval rendered in infinite shades of grey, dominated by towering pines and spruces that rise up towards an all but unseen night sky, a forest that seems to have been tasked with the unenviable job of keeping Heaven from sagging and crushing Earth flat. Winding its way between the trees there's a brook, the surface glinting faintly in the stingy bit of moonlight leaking down through the boughs, and bordering the brook are boulders and the broken trunks of trees that have fallen and are now quietly rotting away. Here and there, a log fords the brook. There's the sound of wind and calls of night birds. And in the distance, there's a bright flicker, like a campfire.

I'm reminded of two things, almost simultaneously, as near to simultaneously as anyone may have two distinct and independent thoughts. I am reminded of the illustrations of Gustave Doré and of the dream that I woke from just that morning, my own half-forgotten dream of a forested place, the dream I immediately tried to lose in sex. I feel the pricking of gooseflesh up and down my arms and legs, and I shiver, and I hug myself as if a sudden draft has blown by, as if maybe I'm standing directly beneath an air-conditioning vent. I think, *You don't have to watch this, whatever this is. You can turn and walk out into the lobby and wait there until it's over or until Hana comes looking for you, whichever happens first.* And then I tell myself how very silly I'm being, that coincidences occur, that they are inevitable aspects of reality, and how that's all this is, a coincidence. At most, it might be chalked up to an instance of synchronicity, a coincidence rendered meaningful only by my subjective emotional reaction and entirely devoid of any causal relationship or connection between my dream and the film, much less any connection with the raven in the restroom or with Hana's tail, both of which I likely only imagined, anyway. This is what I tell myself, and it does nothing at all to dispel my uneasiness and the cliché chill along my spine and down in my gut.

The camera wanders through the forest, and there are close-ups of a sleeping doe and her fawn and of a watchful owl and of a hungry, hunting fox. It springs, and the scream of a rabbit briefly shatters the tranquil night. My mouth has gone very dry, and I lick my lips, wishing I had a swallow of something, anything at all. Hana's Dr Pepper would do just fine.

A woman's voice says, "It must be lonely work," and it takes me a second or two to realize that the voice is part of the movie and not someone standing there beside me.

The film jump-cuts then to a wide clearing and a small camp somewhere deep in the forest, and I think that this must be the source of the distant flickering I saw earlier on. At the center of the camp, surrounded by ragged tree stumps, there's a high conical billet formed from dozens of immense logs standing on their ends and leaning in one against all the others, covered over in places with a layer of soil and chunks of turf, forming a sort of smoldering bonfire or oven. There seems only to be a single man watching the fire, and he's standing with his back to the billet, gazing towards the camera, into the ancient forest ringing the clearing. The man is holding some manner of old-fashioned rifle, a flintlock maybe. I don't know shit about guns.

He says, "Who was that? Who goes there?"

And the woman replies, "No one who means you harm. Only someone passing by who thought you might be happy for the company."

"I'm not alone," says the man.

"I know," answers the woman. "But all your companions are sleeping."

"I could wake them quickly enough," he tells her, "if the need arises."

"Of course," she says. "And you have your rifle. And there must be hounds nearby to keep away the wolves."

"Yes," says the man. "There are hounds, three of them, and I'm a *very* good shot. You'd do well to keep that in mind."

"Naturally," says the woman, and the camera pans around as she emerges from between the boles of two especially enormous pines. The woman is smiling for the man, and she's dressed in a traditional Bavarian dirndl that reaches down almost to the ground. Standing there in the Avon theater, I have no idea that's what her dress is called, a dirndl. I'll only find that out later on, by checking with Wikipedia, which describes it as "a light circular cut dress, gathered at the waist, that falls below the knee." She's also wearing a bonnet. The woman is tall to the point that she could fairly be called lanky, and her face is plain and angular, and her ears are a little too big. But despite all of this, I think she may be one of the most singularly beautiful women I have ever seen. I stop hugging myself and, instead, rest my hands on the back of the theater seat in front of me. The worn velveteen feels like moss.

"It must be lonely work," the woman says again. "The life of a charcoal burner, all these long, cold nights spent so far from your home and your wife and your children."

"How do you know I have a wife and children?" he asks.

"Well, don't you?" she replies. "What an awful waste it would be if you didn't. So, I prefer to assume that you do."

The man has dark eyes, a nose that looks as if it has been broken at least once, and there is a ragged scar that bisects his lower lip and runs the length of his chin down onto his throat. He has the face of someone who is still young, but also the face of someone who has been made prematurely old by the circumstances of his life, by the many hardships and losses endured and written in the lines and creases and angles of skin and bones. It's a curiously effective paradox, not so different from the woman who is beautiful despite her awkwardness (or, perhaps, because of it).

"I know who you are," says the man warily. "My grandmother taught me about you when I was still a boy. I know what you are."

"Then you also know I mean you no harm."

"I know the stories I was taught," he replies, neither agreeing nor disagreeing.

"Then you know that this forest is *my* forest," she tells him, and now the woman takes another step nearer to the man. I realize for the first time that she's barefoot. "You know that these trees are *my* trees. If your grandmother was a wise woman, she taught you that much, surely."

The man, the charcoal burner, crosses himself, and the woman frowns the sort of frown that, more than anything else, is an expression of disappointment, as if she'd hoped for more from this man. As if she'd had cause to expect more.

"After a hard winter," she says, "I may bring prosperity, and for so little a price as a loaf of fresh bread or a hen's egg left at the edge of your fields."

The man nods, and he says, "That is true, so far as it goes. But you also bring hardship when the mood suits you. You cause hunters to lose their way on clearly marked trails and to miss shots that ought to have found their marks. You lead children from their homes and into the dens of hungry animals, and you drown swimmers whom you fancy have slighted you in some small way or another."

"These are the sorts of tales you were taught?" asks the woman, who I realize now, and must have known all along, is not simply a human woman.

"They are. And there are others."

"Tell me," she says, and so the charcoal burner tells a story about a young man who was walking in the forest late one summer afternoon and happened to catch the briefest glimpse of the woman bathing in a spring. At once, he became so infatuated with her that he withdrew into himself and would speak to no one and would not eat or drink or care for himself in any way.

"He only lived a few weeks," says the man. "He was a man my grandmother knew when she was a girl, the son of the cooper in the village where she grew up."

"I don't mean to call her a liar," says the beautiful, awkward woman in the dirndl, "but I would have you know your grandmother's tale was only half the truth of the matter. Yes, a cooper's son from her village saw me bathing, and yes, he wasted away because I wished it so. But she did *not* tell you all the tale. She did not say that after he had discovered the spring where I bathe, he returned with iron horseshoes and used them to lay a trap, for *his* grandmother had taught him how cold iron undoes me. She did not tell you how, when I was defenseless, the cooper's son raped me and cut off a lock of my hair to keep as a souvenir. I do not mean to call your grandmother a liar, but a story told the wrong way round is not the truth."

The woman takes another step nearer the charcoal burner, and this time he takes a step backwards towards the smoldering billet, yielding a foot of earth. And I want now to look away from the screen, though I would not yet be entirely able to explain just exactly why. But this pretend movie forest is too familiar, and I can't shake the feeling that I've heard this woman's voice before. But I do not look away. I want to search for the spot where Hana is sitting, but I don't. I stand there, and I watch. I stand there, and I listen.

"There is another story I know," the charcoal burner says, and I can tell he's trying hard to sound brave, and I can also hear the fear in his voice. Whatever confidence he might have had in his ability to hold this strange woman at bay is withering. Whatever faith he had is leaving him. "A story," he says, "in which you came down out of your wood on a night when the moon was new and the sky was dark save starlight, and you sat beneath the window of a mother nursing her newborn daughter, her firstborn. She sang lullabies to the baby, but you sang, too, and your song was so much fairer than the mother's that it was as if you alone were singing. Your melody took root in the mind of the infant, and, as she grew, it twisted her, shaping her to your own purposes. The girl became wicked, and where she walked wheat would not grow, and if she looked upon cows and goats their milk would turn sour and curdle in their udders. She was always singing in a tongue that no one knew, and they say that her songs drove dogs mad and could summon flies and toads."

"And what became of this poor unfortunate?" asks the woman.

"What finally became of her," replies the man, "is that she was driven away from her home for being a witch, turned out into the forest where she might do less harm to people who'd never done any harm to her. She was sent back to the huldra who had sung to her as a baby and so stolen her mind and soul. Not even a fortnight passed before her own brothers found her hanging from a tree, strangled by a noose woven from hair the color of water at the bottom of a well. They left her there for the crows and the maggots, fearing your wrath if they dared even to cut her down and bury her."

"And you believe this story?" the woman asks the charcoal burner.

And he answers her, "I've known stranger things to be true."

And I think, *Like a raven that is only a reflection in a mirror. Like seeing for the first time that the woman you love has a tail.*

Onscreen, the woman nods, and she says, "I was passing by, is all, and it occurred to me what lonely work your work must be and how perhaps you would be grateful for my company and for conversation. I meant no offense. I did not mean to cause you such alarm. I'll be on my way. But you'll remember this is *my* forest, and those are *my* trees."

And then the woman turns and walks away, disappearing back into the blackness between the trunks of the two especially enormous pines, and the charcoal burner is left standing alone in the clearing by his billet. The camera leaves him there, moving slowly around the circumference of the burning woodpile, coming at last to the corpses of three dogs, their necks broken and their throats torn open, as if by teeth and claws. Behind the murdered dogs is a lean-to where the bodies of the charcoal burner's companions lie slumped and mangled. It is a massacre.

And then Hana is standing beside me, and she's holding my hand, and she says, "I think we should go home now. I think it was a mistake, bringing you here."

"I'm sorry I took so long," I say.

"Don't worry about it this time. It's a silly sort of film, anyway."

Onscreen, black and white has given way to color, and the forest has been replaced by a modern city, the streets of Berlin crowded with automobiles and pedestrians all staring at their devices, instead of looking where it is they're going. A woman steps in front of a bus, and someone screams. Finally, I look away. Instead of the old theater smell, I can smell pine straw and wood smoke.

"I don't feel well," I say.

"You'll feel better soon," Hana tells me, and then she leads me out of the auditorium and back to the brightly lit lobby. Out on the street, it's stopped raining.

5.

All the way back home to Wood Street, neither of us talks. The radio is on, and there's music, but it seems to come from somewhere very far off. The roads are still wet and shiny, the pavement glimmering dully beneath the garish new LED streetlights the city has recently installed. Hana drives, and I think about the movie and the raven and how I miss the soft yellow luminescence of the old sodium-vapor bulbs. From Thayer to Wickenden, then Point Street and over the bridge that crosses the filthy slate-colored river, then across the interstate to Westminster to Parade Street to home. I sit quietly and gaze out the passenger-side window, and I think how it is like finding your way back along a forest path. The street signs are breadcrumbs. The traffic lights are notches carved in the bark of living trees, electric talismans against losing one's way.

I have a beer, and then I have a second beer. I watch a few minutes of something on television, a news story on an outbreak of cholera in Yemen. Hana asks if I'm coming to bed, so I do. She's sitting up naked, with her back against the oak headboard, her knees pulled up close to her chest, her arms wrapped around them. Her tail hangs limply over the side of the bed. She watches me while I undress, and she waits there while I go to the bathroom and brush and floss my teeth.

When I come back into the bedroom, she says, "You haven't lost your mind. You're not insane."

I sit down on my side of the bed, and it creaks and pops. "We're going to have to bite the bullet and get a new box spring soon," I say. "This thing's over a decade old. One night, it's just going to collapse beneath us." I sit there staring at the open window, smelling all the fresh, clean smells that come after a summer rain, even in so dirty a city as Providence. I think there might yet be more rain to come before sunrise and we shouldn't fall sleep with the window open, so I should get up and close it. But I don't. I just sit there, my feet on the floor, my back to Hana.

"I know it must seem that way," she says, "like you're losing your mind, and I apologize for that. I genuinely do."

I think about all the things I could say in response, and then I think about just lying down and trying to sleep, and then I think about getting up, putting my clothes back on, and going for a long walk.

"I can be an awful coward," she says. "Using the theater that way, because I was afraid of telling you myself."

And I say, "When I was a little girl, maybe ten, maybe eleven years old, I got lost in the woods once. I'm not sure how it happened, but it did. I grew up in the country, and getting lost in the woods wasn't something I worried about. It wasn't something that my parents or my grandparents worried would ever happen to me, because they'd taught me how not to lose my way. But it did happen that once. I got turned around somehow, and I walked for hours and hours, and finally it started getting dark, and that's when I really got scared. As well as I knew those woods by day, I didn't know them at all by twilight. The shadows changed them, changed the trees and the rocks, changed the way sound moved along the valley between the mountains."

"What did you do?" Hana asks.

"What do frightened children lost in the forest pretty much always do?" I reply, trading her a question for a question.

"I've never been lost in a forest," she says.

"Well," I tell her, "they cry and they start calling out for help. Which is what I did. I shouted for my mother and my father and my grandparents. I even called out the names of our three dogs, hoping anyone at all would hear me and come find me and lead me safely back home."

"But they didn't," she says.

"No, *they* didn't. But someone else did." And I want to ask her, *Was that you or maybe a sister of yours? Was that you or some aunt or distant cousin?* But I don't. I stop staring at the window and stare at my feet, instead. "And I followed her back to the pasture at the edge of the road that led to our house, and I never saw her again. At some point, growing up, I decided I'd made her up. I decided that I'd been so afraid I'd invented her as some sort of coping mechanism that had allowed me to push back the panic and calm down and remember my own way out of the woods. And I believed that, until this morning, until I dreamed about being lost and found and about a woman with a cow's tail and a raven on her shoulder who sang to me until I stopped crying."

"Would you like me to sing to you tonight?" she asks.

"Why? Am I lost again tonight?"

"No," she says, "not lost. Just a little turned about."

"Sometimes," I tell her, "I'd leave her little gifts. Offerings, I guess, to show my gratitude. A hardboiled egg, half a baloney sandwich, a Twinkie, and once I even left her one of my dolls."

"A doll with yellow hair," says Hana, "yellow like freshly ground corn-meal, and a blue and white checked gingham dress, like Dorothy wore in *The Wizard of Oz*."

"Yes," I say. "Like that. I left them in a hollow tree, like Boo Radley leaving gifts for Scout and Jem in *To Kill a Mockingbird*. I think I got the idea from the book, the idea to leave her gifts."

"And then you stopped," Hana says.

"We moved here. Dad got a different job, and we moved away."

For a moment or two, neither of us says anything more, and then Hana says that it's late and that we should probably get some sleep, that I have work tomorrow and she has errands to run. When I don't reply, when I neither agree nor disagree, she asks me if I'd prefer that she leaves and never comes back.

"If that's what you'd like, I'll go."

"No," I say, without having to consider my answer. "I wouldn't rather you leave."

"Then I'm glad," she says.

"It must be lonely work," I say, remembering the barefoot woman in the dirndl and the charcoal burner.

"Sometimes," Hana tells me, and then she tells me that we probably shouldn't fall asleep with the window open, that she's pretty sure there will be more rain tonight.

"What finally made you decide to show me?" I ask.

"I don't know," she replies. "I think I just got tired of keeping secrets."

I nod, because that seems like a fair enough answer. I have other questions, but they're nothing that can't wait for some other time. I get up and cross the room and close the window. I check to be sure that it's locked, even though we're on the second floor of the old house on Wood Street. Down on the sidewalk, there's a black bird big as a tomcat, and when I tap on the glass, it spreads its wings and flies away.

ABOUT THE AUTHOR

CAITLÍN R. KIERNAN was born in Dublin, Ireland, and raised in the southeastern U.S. Before turning to fiction writing full-time, she worked as a vertebrate paleontologist in both Alabama and Colorado. She cofounded the Birmingham Paleontological Society and, in 1988, described a new genus and species of ancient marine lizard, the mosasaur *Selmasaurus russelli*.

In 1992, Kiernan wrote her first novel, *The Five of Cups*, and has since authored thirteen more novels, including *The Drowning Girl*, winner of the Bram Stoker and the James Tiptree, Jr. awards. She is the author of more than two hundred and fifty short stories, which have been collected in fifteen volumes, including *Tales of Pain and Wonder*, *A is for Alien*, *The Ammonite Violin & Others*, *Dear Sweet Filthy World*, *The Dinosaur Tourist*, and the World Fantasy Award winner *The Ape's Wife and Other Stories*. She also received the World Fantasy Award for her short story "The Prayer of Ninety Cats." Kiernan has written graphic novels for both DC/Vertigo (*The Dreaming*, *The Girl Who Would Be Death*, *Bast: Eternity Game*) and Dark Horse Comics (the three-volume *Alabaster* series, winner of the Bram Stoker Award). In 1996 and 1997, she fronted a short-lived goth-rock band, Death's Little Sister.

Brown University's John Hay Library has established the Caitlín R.

Kiernan Papers, spanning her full career thus far and including juvenilia, consisting of twenty-three linear feet of manuscript materials, including correspondence, journals, manuscripts, and publications, circa 1970–2017, in print, electronic, and web-based formats.

Kiernan currently lives in Birmingham, Alabama, with her partner, Kathryn Pollnac, and two very large cats, Selwyn and Lydia.